Their
Last
Breath

OTHER TITLES BY SIBEL HODGE

Fiction

Duplicity (Detective Warren Carter Book 1)
Into the Darkness (Detective Warren Carter Book 2)
The Disappeared (Detective Becky Harris)
Beneath the Surface
Untouchable
Where the Memories Lie
Look Behind You
Butterfly
Trafficked: The Diary of a Sex Slave
Fashion, Lies, and Murder (Amber Fox Mystery No 1)
Money, Lies, and Murder (Amber Fox Mystery No 2)
Voodoo, Lies, and Murder (Amber Fox Mystery No 3)
Chocolate, Lies, and Murder (Amber Fox Mystery No 4)
Santa Claus, Lies, and Murder (Amber Fox Mystery No 4.5)
Vegas, Lies, and Murder (Amber Fox Mystery No 5)
Murder and Mai Tais (Danger Cove Cocktail Mystery No 1)
Killer Colada (Danger Cove Cocktail Mystery No 2)
The See-Through Leopard
Fourteen Days Later
My Perfect Wedding
The Baby Trap
It's a Catastrophe

Non-Fiction

Deliciously Vegan Soup Kitchen
Healing Meditations for Surviving Grief and Loss

Their Last Breath

SIBEL HODGE

THOMAS & MERCER

Published by Thomas & Mercer, Seattle

www.apub.com

Amazon, the Amazon logo, and Thomas & Mercer are trademarks of Amazon.com, Inc., or its affiliates.

ISBN-13: 9781542014083
ISBN-10: 1542014085

Cover design by @blacksheep-uk.com

Printed in the United States of America

'I'm for truth, no matter who tells it. I'm for justice, no matter who it is for or against. I'm a human being, first and foremost, and as such I'm for whoever and whatever benefits humanity as a whole.'

– Malcolm X

GILLIAN

Chapter 1

Sometimes being in the wrong place at the wrong time meant the difference between life and death. But Gillian Lane didn't know that yet.

She parked the Mini on her driveway, took her suitcase and handbag from the boot, and approached her front door. As she stood on the doorstep, she heard the first noise that alerted her to the fact something wasn't quite right.

A light was on in the upstairs landing, glowing softly through the hallway window, but she and her husband Neal always left it on when they were asleep because Neal thought it would deter any potential burglars. So it wasn't the light she was worried about. It was the low moan, almost like a hoarse cry, that came from inside. And it sounded distinctly male.

Keys in hand, she strained her ears to listen, but she heard nothing further.

She shook her head and told herself not to be so stupid. It was just jet lag from the flight causing her mind to work overtime. She'd almost fallen asleep at the wheel on the way back from the airport. And now she was hearing things.

She fumbled with the keys, found the one for the front door jumbled in between the big bunch, slid it in the lock, pushed the door open. It creaked loudly. She'd been on at Neal to put some WD40 on it for ages, but it always took him months to get round to doing house-related things, and she knew she'd end up doing it herself.

She took her keys from the door and stuffed them in the pocket of her coat, as was her usual habit. It always wound Neal up when he couldn't find the car keys because they were in one of her pockets or jackets instead of the kitchen drawer where they were supposed to be kept.

She pulled her suitcase inside, put her handbag on top of it, and paused in the hallway, the dim light from the upstairs landing filtering down the stairs. Everything looked OK. The door to the kitchen opposite her along the corridor was closed, and the only sound she could hear was the fridge humming away.

She turned to close the front door.

Then she heard the creak of a floorboard coming from behind the kitchen door.

'Neal?' She stepped along the hallway, expecting her husband to come out of the kitchen, his grey hair mussed up from sleep, wearing his favourite, faded old T-shirt and boxers, telling her she was home early and what a great surprise this was.

But it wasn't Neal who opened the door.

For a few seconds she froze, staring at the bulky person in front of her, dressed all in black, wearing a balaclava that covered his face.

She didn't know how long it took for her brain to translate what she was seeing into a message to *Run!* But as she hurtled through the front door, she didn't know if it was going to be enough time to save her.

She ran out of the drive. Her house was at the end of a quiet lane. She knew her immediate neighbours, an old-age pensioner who was housebound and had someone call on him with Meals on Wheels, and a middle-aged couple with young children. But she couldn't go to either of them. By the time she'd knocked on their doors and they'd opened up, the man would have caught up to her. If she turned right, it would take her to a small wood and fields behind. Left led her to the main road. If her brain had been thinking straight maybe she would've run into the woods and been able to hide from him behind a tree in the darkness, but her brain was just a screaming jumble of noises, and instinctively, she turned left.

She ran down the middle of the street in the darkness with no idea where she was heading, just that she needed to get away.

His shoes slapped on the tarmac behind her. He was gaining on her.

She screamed. Or tried to. Fear closed her throat so that the word *HELP!* she was trying to say came out more like a strangled *Eellllip.*

Panic squeezed her chest. She pumped her legs as hard as they would go, her fists clenched tight. Where could she hide? At the end of her lane was a T-junction where it turned into a main road. There was nowhere she could go without him seeing. She had no choice but to keep running until her legs gave out.

She was almost at the junction when she heard his breath. Any minute now she knew his fingers would reach out, clutching and grabbing at her.

She shrieked and launched her torso forwards, buying herself a little more time. He was going to get her. And do what? What the hell had he done to Neal?

As she ran into the main road, she was only thinking about what was behind her, so she didn't even register the car hurtling along from her right until it slammed into her and sent her flying into the air.

Brakes screeched. She bounced onto the tarmac, hit her head. Footsteps. A car door opened. And then she tumbled into blackness.

DETECTIVE WARREN CARTER

Chapter 2

03.33
03.34
03.35

I had hoped that retirement would mean more leisurely lie-ins but no, that wasn't happening. I watched the luminous red numbers changing on my bedside clock and closed my eyes. I'd been awake since 02.24. The insomnia had started when my wife Denise had been dying of breast cancer. I'd been afraid to fall asleep in case she needed something, and I didn't hear her. Then I was afraid in case she left me in the middle of the night, and I wasn't there to say goodbye. I'd wanted my face to be the last thing she ever saw.

After her death, it was the dreams – of her suffering and in pain – that kept me awake. Every time I closed my eyes, I had nightmares tormenting me. It had been fifteen months since she'd gone and my whole world caved in on me. I'd walked a tightrope of anger, sadness, and depression that I couldn't get off for a long time. Gradually, the grief of losing Denise was becoming more like a mild squeezing around my throat rather than a full-on claw-like grip. But now I had another thing keeping me awake. Whenever I closed my eyes I kept seeing over and over again what had happened at the place the media were calling Bloodbath Farm. I kept thinking about what I'd done there and when I was going to get caught out.

I opened my eyes. 03.56.

I groaned. It was a paradox. I didn't want to get up because I couldn't face the thought of another endless day sprawling out in front of me with a choice of monotonous daytime TV reruns like *Homes Under the Hammer* and *Escape to the Sun*. I'd toyed with the idea of a fresh start, selling the house and moving to Spain or Portugal, but I knew I'd never do either of those things so what was the point in watching the programmes? I couldn't seem to concentrate on reading. I could only walk so far in a day. It was too cold for gardening at this time of year. And yet, I couldn't seem to sleep the day away, either.

I got up at the lovely even time of 04.00. I showered, made a coffee, and stared into the gloomy darkness of my garden. I'd left the police force behind, and I should've been living it up. Going on holiday, learning to play golf, finding a hobby. Doing *something*. Except I couldn't. I'd been a copper for over thirty years, and I didn't know what to do with myself now. I was bored out of my nut.

When my mobile phone rang on the kitchen counter, I sprang towards it, an instinctive reaction after all my years of being on call. I answered it before I even remembered I wasn't a copper any more and could wonder who would possibly be calling at this hour.

'DS Carter,' I said automatically before correcting myself. 'I mean, Warren speaking.'

'Morning, Warren. It's Chief Superintendent Barker. I'm sorry for waking you up.'

'Chance would be a fine thing, ma'am,' I said. 'I've been awake for hours.' I tried to make my tone light, but I was immediately on high alert. I'd had many conversations and interviews with Chief Superintendent Caroline Barker over the last two months about what had happened at Bloodbath Farm. After uncovering high-level police corruption and a major crime, I'd gone to her Professional Standards Department's Anti-Corruption Unit and passed on what I knew with the evidence I'd found. But there could be only one reason that she was ringing me so early: they'd discovered my role in what had happened that night.

I gripped the phone tight and waited for her to request my presence at their office to explain the reasons my DNA had been found on a murder weapon at the scene. What had we missed that night that could lead back to me or the others who'd got away?

I was so busy anticipating my impending arrest that her next words threw me completely.

'I need your help, Warren.'

'My help?' I frowned. Whatever help I could give her at just gone five in the morning would surely be the kind that only incriminated myself. Otherwise she would've called at a more reasonable time.

'I don't want to talk about it over the phone. Can you come into the office?'

I ran a hand through my hair. *Shit! Shit, fuck, shit!* 'Um . . . yes. What, now?'

'As soon as you can get here would be expedient.'

'Right. Well . . . um . . . yes, of course.'

'Thank you. I'll see you soon. Ring me when you're outside and I'll come and let you in.'

She hung up, and I stared at the phone, panic rising from my stomach up to my chest.

I grabbed my car keys and looked around the kitchen, wondering if I was about to be arrested. If this was the last time I'd see the home I'd shared with my wife for most of our married life. I paused in front of a photograph of Denise on the hallway table. Touched my fingertips to my lips and then pressed them to the picture.

As I drove down the roads, which were still quiet at that ungodly hour, I rehearsed my story in my head. The trick to lying was to make sure it came out naturally, sticking as close to the truth as possible. Saying the same thing over and over again until you talked your brain into believing a new truth and it slid off the tongue with ease. At least, I hoped so.

The Hertfordshire Constabulary's Professional Standards Department, or PSD, was housed in a separate building in the grounds of Police Headquarters with strictly controlled access. The coppers who investigated coppers wanted to be away from the prying eyes of any police officer able to wander into their offices willy-nilly.

I no longer had a warrant card to swipe across the HQ car park's entrance to let me in, and it was too early for anyone to be manning reception, so I pulled up to the barrier and called Chief Superintendent Barker back, trying to keep my breathing steady.

She appeared a minute or so later from the doors to the main reception. She strode over to the barrier, swiped her own warrant card on it so I could gain access and waited for me to park.

Despite the early start she was turned out in a neatly pressed uniform, her jaw-length hair in an immaculate shiny bob.

'Thank you for coming in.' She gave me a tight smile and held out her hand.

I shook it, worrying about the sweat on my palms giving me away.

'We'll go to my office,' she said over her shoulder as I followed behind, wiping my hands on my trousers. She probably wanted to do the same but was too poised to make it obvious.

We headed along the side of the main building, around to the back where the brick-built PSD unit was housed. She entered a code on a numbered keypad on the front door, shielding it with her back. Once inside we walked past the empty reception desk and through a set of double doors that led to a corridor. I was trying to work out why we weren't going to the interview room that I knew was along the opposite corridor.

As we walked, I glanced sideways at her face, but she wasn't giving anything away. We were both silent. Well, she was. My heart was anything but, hammering away so loudly I thought she'd be able to hear it, too.

We entered a large open-plan office with workstations that were far more modern than in most of the police stations I'd been to in the county during my long career. At the end was her office with glass partition walls. I followed her in.

'Have a seat, please, Warren.' She indicated the padded armchair opposite her desk.

I sat and gave her what I thought was a suitably questioning look, as opposed to an *I'm guilty* look. I didn't ask her what was going on. A tactic I'd learned from my years of interviewing criminals was that in this situation, I shouldn't give anything away unless asked a direct question. Silence made criminals uncomfortable and they tended to babble away and fill it, hopefully incriminating themselves in the process. I had no intention of incriminating myself.

'Do you want something to drink?' She sat down, and I half-expected her to lace her fingers together on the desk in a posture I'd seen many of the brass adopt over the years. One I suspected they were taught on management courses. But instead she leaned back and looked at me with a pinched frown on her face.

I waved the offer away and tried for being casual Carter. 'I've had two coffees this morning already. At my age I'll be going to the loo all day if I have another one.'

She gave me another tight smile, which didn't seem like a good sign.

'Right. Well, I'll get straight to it then.'

A bead of sweat trickled down my back beneath my shirt.

'In the early hours of this morning there was an emergency call to the fire brigade. They attended the scene of an old hospital building located just off a country lane between the villages of Hall's Green and Warren's Green.'

'Right.' I frowned, wondering how the hell this related to what had happened at Bloodbath Farm and feeling my stress levels crank down a notch when I realised it couldn't possibly be connected to anything I'd done.

'When the fire officers went inside, they found six women in the building. All of them were inside rooms on a lower floor and held captive by chains securing them to the walls.'

'Jesus,' I said. 'Did they get to them in time?'

She shook her head sadly. 'Only one is still alive but she's in a critical condition. She's in the hospital, fighting for her life.' She paused. 'One of the deceased women's bodies was found partly burned, and discovered near her person was an item that was partially melted.'

'Ma'am, this is terrible, but why are you telling me?'

'I'll get to that.' She picked up a Samsung tablet and passed it over to me. 'Take a look at these first photos from the scene.'

The screen was filled with an image of a dead woman lying on her stomach on the floor, her left cheek resting against the ground. On her right cheek and the surrounding areas of her face, her skin was burned and melted, as was her long dark hair. Her mouth was open in what could've been a gasp for air or a final scream. A metal cuff attached to a long chain was attached around one slim wrist. I swiped across to the next photo and saw a close-up of a metal bracket on the wall that the other end of the chain was connected to.

I'd seen burned remains many times before, but this touched something in my heart. 'Poor woman.'

'Keep going and you'll see why I got called out to the scene.'

I swiped across to a wider shot of the room that showed a single bed behind her. The next photo was of the floor and the woman's right hand. About four inches away from it was an item that looked like it had once been a plastic electronic card key or credit card with a brown magnetic strip running along its centre. Part of it had melted in the fire and was now just molten plastic around the edges. In the next photo there was a close-up of the other side of the card, placed next to a numbered evidence marker. Although parts of it had melted to nothing, there was no mistaking what it was.

'A warrant card,' I said.

'Yes.'

The Hertfordshire Constabulary logo was still intact, as was the edging of where a photograph had once been, although the actual photo had been obliterated. Similarly, the name of who it had been issued to and their rank had melted so it was also unreadable.

'And I want to know how the hell one of our warrant cards ended up in the room of a dead woman chained to a bed.'

DETECTIVE WARREN CARTER

Chapter 3

'PSD will be taking over this investigation and that's why I need you,' Chief Superintendent Barker said.

I opened my mouth to speak – to say no, I couldn't. I'd retired so I could get away from the awfulness of the world. I'd had enough of people hurting each other in the worst possible ways.

She held her hand up to cut off any protest and carried on. 'Look, I know you've retired but just hear me out, please. My teams are already overwhelmed with the investigation into the Bloodbath Farm case. You can imagine how much work is going into that to get a conviction.'

I could. I was the one who'd brought all the evidence of police corruption to her and knew how much of a trail they were going to have to unravel. Due to the nature of the murders and police involvement, it was a high-profile case, and the Constabulary was being crucified in the press because of it, so I knew how much pressure both her department and the Chief Constable would be under.

'And now this has happened.' She flicked her gaze down to the tablet. 'As if that wasn't bad enough, we're already down one member of staff on maternity leave and one on long-term sick.' She paused and gave me a smile that managed to portray both friendliness and sadness. 'You've already proved you've got the integrity to work for Anti-Corruption by what you exposed. Plus, taking on a major inquiry like this needs someone with experience in murder investigations, and I don't have enough spare resources who are adequately trained to deal with it. I want you. I *need* you.'

'Well . . .' I was about to mask my relief that this wasn't about any impending arrest with my usual sarcasm by saying *It's been a long time since a woman said that to me.* But I didn't know her well enough for that to be appropriate at that moment.

She smiled properly for the first time. 'If you were to rejoin the force and work with me, you'd be looking at an Acting Detective Inspector role. The Chief Constable has already OK'd it.'

'Blimey.' I sat back, surprised.

She looked me pointedly in the eye. 'I know all about your reputation for unorthodox investigating. For not following the rank and file's orders. For not being the politically correct clone the force wants churned out these days. In a lot of cases there's no room for that in a team environment, but with you I'd make an exception. You're a bloody good investigator. You've dealt with some complex cases where it was only your dogged tenacity that secured a conviction. And I need someone pig-headed, stubborn, and tenacious, who thinks outside the box.'

Never once in all my career had anyone thought those traits of mine were a good thing. Quite the opposite, in fact.

'The kidnapped victims held in locked cells in that hospital are an echo of what happened at Bloodbath Farm.' She pointed to the tablet. 'Either the same people are involved in all this, too, or someone else is. But the bottom line is, it looks like a member of our staff is most likely somehow a party to chaining these women up and keeping them prisoner in that place.' She paused. 'I understand this has come out of the blue and you might need some time to think about it. If you don't want to make a permanent decision now, you could rejoin to deal with this case and then make a final decision afterwards. I've only come back from the scene to try to get you on board as soon as possible.'

I stared down at the tablet still in front of me, rubbed a hand across my forehead and took a breath. Did I really want to get immersed in the vileness of humanity again? I'd given it up because I was disillusioned with, and had little respect for, a legal process that often failed victims, with offenders either getting away with their crimes or being given insanely light sentences. I was fed up to my back teeth of the police force's bullshit bureaucracy that inhibited us actually doing our jobs, of the brass fiddling their statistics, of the budget cuts. Policing in the twenty-first century was just about politics, not right and wrong. I'd had enough of not making a difference any more and wanted a life that no longer included murders, abused children, rape victims, knife crimes, and the other endless supply of cruelty humans were capable of inflicting on each other. It was hard enough working my arse off to put criminals away, but when those criminals had turned out to be a copper, it had well and truly obliterated my faith in humanity.

But what had happened to those poor women was gruesome. Whoever had done that to them needed to be stopped. Could I really live with myself for not getting justice for these victims? I knew the answer was no. Because the same reasons for retiring were exactly the same reasons why I couldn't walk away from this. The only thing that had ever mattered to me was getting the bad guys off the streets and protecting the innocent. And, anyway, the alternative was dying of boredom.

I glanced at her. 'I'll do it.'

She stood up and grinned. 'Great to have you with us, DI Carter. Your team will be here in a couple of hours. In the meantime, let me take you to the scene.'

DETECTIVE BECKY HARRIS
Chapter 4

Detective Sergeant Becky Harris didn't hear her mobile phone ringing at first. Still dark outside, it felt as if she'd only just gone to bed. It was her husband's elbow digging into her ribs that roused her from sleep.

'Answer the bloody phone,' Ian grumbled with an exaggerated huff.

She blinked her eyes open and grabbed her job phone. 'DS Harris.'

'Becky, it's DI Thornton. Sorry to wake you up, but I'm at a double-murder scene and I need you to come in early.'

'Right.' She rubbed the sleep out of her eyes.

Her boss gave her the address and hung up.

She took a deep breath and glanced over at her husband, who glared at her. Ever since she'd been promoted to Detective Sergeant he'd had the big fat hump with her, complaining that he never saw her. Which, to be fair, had been true lately. She was proud of herself and she loved her job, but Ian was getting increasingly pissed off with her. Now he wanted them to start a family. It wasn't that she didn't want kids. She did. Or at least, she'd always thought she did. Some day. Just not now, when her career was taking off, when she finally had the responsibility of a DS and was proving herself.

She touched his shoulder, a peace offering after the row they'd had last night. One of many rows lately. 'I've got to go in early.'

'What a surprise.' He turned over and treated her to his rigid back.

'Look, let's talk later.'

'I don't really know what there is to talk about. You said you don't want kids, and I do. You're always at work and don't have time for us any more.'

'I said I didn't want kids *yet*.'

He rolled over onto his stomach and pulled the pillow over his head.

She sighed and got up, leaving him to stew in his own anger.

As she dressed, downed a glass of water, and brushed her teeth, she kept wondering if there was any way back for them. Wondered if she should just give in and try for a baby to keep him happy. But she'd seen plenty of people have kids to fix their broken relationships and it never worked in the long run. She'd expected support from him in her new job. Not resentment.

She drove to the scene with the window open to wake herself up, the chilly December air an icy slap across the face. Frost covered the ground and she'd had to de-ice the windows before leaving. It was three weeks until Christmas and they were predicting a white one. But didn't they say that every year?

She drove up Chancellors Road and as she rounded a bend, just before the T-junction that led to Oak Drive, she found two traffic police cars on scene and bollards cordoning off a section of the road. A Scene Of Crime Officers' van was also there, along with a marked patrol car and DI Thornton's car. Some of the traffic officers were measuring a set of skid marks. Photos were being taken. She pulled up behind the cordon and flashed her warrant card. 'DS Harris. Is this to do with the murders?' She frowned. DI Thornton hadn't mentioned a hit-and-run.

'Looks like it,' the traffic sergeant said. 'Your DI's in the house. Down there. Number one.' He pointed into Oak Drive, a lane leading off the main road to the left. 'He'll explain what's happened.'

She nodded and left her car behind the SOCO van since she couldn't get it through the cordon where they were still gathering evidence. After retrieving a white crime-scene suit and shoe coveralls from the boot of her car, she walked down the turning into the quiet, leafy street. It was a short, straight road with about twenty houses on it, and the one she wanted was right at the end, just before the entrance to some woods.

A female PC stood at the front door with a clipboard in hand, stamping her feet, trying to keep warm, her breath coming out in thick plumes of vapour.

Becky slipped on the forensic suit, looking at the house. It was a quaint, detached property of red brick with a bay window and a cottagey feel. Wisteria grew around the front door and trailed up to the first floor. It would look lovely in bloom. Now it just looked dead. An ominous sign of what was inside. The driveway housed two vehicles, a red Mini and an older black Volkswagen Polo.

She gave her name to the PC, who recorded it on her scene log, and stepped inside. 'Guv?' she called out for her boss. When DI Thornton had first been transferred to her CID department a few months before, she'd thought he was a twat. A career copper who dismissed her theories and wasn't open to alternative possibilities. Her opinions hadn't changed since. It was only *her* dogged determination in the end that had solved a recent very high-profile case, and she'd earned a commendation from the Chief Constable for her diligent work. It had also earned DI Thornton a promotion, although, unfortunately for him (and also Becky), there were no openings at any other police stations for DCIs at the moment – a subject he'd complained about incessantly – so she was stuck with him for the time being. Still, she was the golden girl at the moment. Despite how useless Ian thought she was as a wife.

'In here,' Thornton called out from a room at the back of the house directly down the hallway.

She looked around. There was a suitcase near the front door with a handbag on top of it, but apart from that the hallway was tidy. No shoes kicked off haphazardly like at her house. No coats hanging on the banister.

She glanced up the beige-carpeted staircase briefly and walked forwards along the hallway, peeked into the lounge where two wine glasses and an empty bottle of wine sat on a coffee table, then entered a large kitchen-diner. Her gaze swept around the horrific scene, noting the salient points quickly in her head. At one side of the room were the usual kitchen units. An unopened bottle of wine and corkscrew sat on the worktop. The dining-room side housed a walnut-coloured wooden table with six matching chairs around it in front of a single-paned glass door leading out to the garden. Two victims were tied to two of the chairs, heads lolling sideways. The female looked about mid-thirties, long dark hair, tanned skin, slim. Impossible to tell the colour of her eyes as they were closed. She wore jeans and a white sweatshirt, Vans shoes. Her wrists were secured to the chair's armrests with plastic cable ties. Her ankles restrained in the same way around the chair legs. A piece of duct tape was over her mouth. Becky stepped closer and crouched down beside her, looking at the deep mark embedded in her neck that had been left from some kind of cord or material. She had stab wounds on her arms and legs where blood had seeped through the slashed material of her clothes.

The male looked older. His short grey hair was matted with blood at the back of his head with a visible, nasty head injury. He had a few days' worth of grey stubble on his cheeks, and wore jeans and a faded maroon sweatshirt. He was also restrained in the same manner and had the same multiple stab wounds on his arms and legs. An identical mark was embedded in his neck and he also had duct tape over his mouth.

On the side wall, behind where DI Thornton stood, were written the words *DIE PIGGY DIE*. Thick capital letters in what looked like black marker pen.

A member of the SOCO team, decked out in the same forensic garb, took photos of the scene, the intense flashes of light coupled with the whirring of her camera echoing in Becky's ear. The SOCO looked over and Becky saw it was Emma Bolton, a senior forensic officer who she'd worked with many times.

'Grim, eh?' Emma said to her.

'Very.' Becky pointed at the words on the wall. 'Those words ring a bell.'

Thornton nodded. 'Last year, a couple were killed in their home in the village of Willian with a similar MO. It wasn't my patch, but I heard about some of the details. Both were tied to chairs in the kitchen, both stabbed multiple times before being strangled, and the same words were written on the wall.'

'A serial killer?' Becky's eyes widened. Hertfordshire Constabulary had only ever had one that she knew of – Graham Young, a poisoner who was sent to Broadmoor in the sixties.

'I need to speak with the Senior Investigating Officer on that case to get more info, but it seems like it,' Thornton said, looking excited at the prospect of another high-profile case.

Emma leaned over the bodies and took more photos. 'Home Office pathologist is en route. From what I've seen so far, it looks like the stab wounds to their arms and legs wouldn't have been fatal.' She peered at the neck wound on the female. 'There are distinct ligature marks on both victims. Looks like they were both strangled with something thin and smooth, possibly with electrical cord or similar.'

'The male is Neal Lane,' Thornton said. 'His photo matches a driving licence in his wallet found in the lounge, but this woman isn't the victim's wife.'

Becky glanced up from where she'd been staring at the bodies.

'We don't know much yet,' Thornton said. 'But it looks like the wife came home, entered the house and disturbed the killer. She ran out, down the lane, and got hit by a car on the main road.'

'Poor woman. How is she?'

'She was unconscious when the paramedics picked her up. That's all we know so far.'

'So who's this then?' Becky glanced down at the female victim.

'Don't know. There's no ID on her. I've had a quick look around and can't find a handbag anywhere. Emma's taken fingerprints to see if we can ID her from those.'

Becky's gaze darted around, settling on a silver-framed photo on one wall. It was of a couple with beaming smiles, standing in front of a lighthouse. The woman had her head on the man's shoulders, her long dark hair flying up in the wind. The male had his arm around her. She glanced from the photo to the male victim. Definitely the same guy. The female wasn't.

'She looks similar to the woman in the photo, doesn't she?' Becky indicated the victim. 'Maybe she's the wife's sister?'

'Maybe. But what was she doing here at this time in the morning while the wife was away? Was Mr Lane playing around?' Thornton quirked an eyebrow up. 'His wife is Gillian Lane. She's currently in Lister Hospital. The driver of the taxi that hit her said she came from nowhere and ran out in front of him. The control room received a call from a neighbour who lives across the road. He said he heard a car pull up outside and looked out of the window. Saw Gillian parking Neal's Mini on the drive. Then a little while later he heard a scream, looked outside again and saw her running with someone chasing her. I want you to speak to the neighbour who made the call. Do some house-to-house in the street and then head to the hospital and see if you can get anything out of her.'

'I'm on it.' She stepped to the doorway, then took one last glance over her shoulder at the words written on the wall.

DIE PIGGY DIE.

She couldn't deny the ripple of excitement that fizzed inside. If this was a serial killer, it would be a huge case with untold exposure that she desperately wanted to be involved in. But she wasn't thinking of it as a step up the career ladder, like she knew Thornton would be. Whether it was a serial killer or not, the offender had to be stopped.

DETECTIVE WARREN CARTER
Chapter 5

'It used to be a mental asylum when it was first built,' Caroline said as we arrived at a property surrounded by an eight-foot-high brick wall and a set of iron gates. A sign on the gates said *Private Property Keep Out*. A guy wearing a thick parka stood guard outside.

'That's DC Potter from B Team in PSD. I didn't want a uniform here to guard the scene. The less anyone else knows about this from outside our department the better.'

DC Potter said hello to Caroline, who in turn introduced me. He recorded us on the scene log before letting us through.

'Over the years it's been used as a hospital in the war, a children's hospital, then a convalescent home,' she carried on. 'But apparently, the NHS couldn't afford the upkeep any more and they sold it off to a private company who ran it as a drug-rehab centre for five years before they sold it. It's been left standing empty for about nine months.'

Set in several acres of surrounding woodland, the driveway that led up to Brampton Hospital was long and imposing and lined with beech trees. At the end was a large brick manor house with creepy Victorian gothic architecture. Two fire engines, a fire van, two SOCO vans, and a uniformed car were parked up.

The first thing I noticed as I got out was the smell of smoke permeating the frigid air.

'Do we know who owns the building now?' I asked Caroline.

'Not yet.' She got out and grabbed a forensic overall from the boot of her car, passed me one, then pointed to two sets of wellington boots. 'You're a size nine, right?'

I nodded. She *had* been thorough. I dreaded to think what else she knew about me.

When we were suited and booted, a tall man dressed in identical coveralls stepped out of the building and strode towards us, followed by a shorter, chunkier guy in a padded firefighter's uniform.

Caroline introduced the tall guy as Chief Superintendent Rowles. The other man was a senior officer from the Hertfordshire Fire and Rescue Service's Investigation Team and gave his name to us as something unpronounceable that sounded Polish or Russian and I didn't catch.

When the intros were done, Rowles said he was handing over the scene to Caroline and then left.

I asked Chunky if it was safe inside the building.

'Yes. My team's in there, along with your SOCO. But watch your step. Some of the debris is still very hot in places. And you'll need a hard hat.' He pointed to some safety hats resting on the edge of one of the fire engines.

'Can you tell how the fire started yet?' I asked as I grabbed hats for Caroline and myself.

'Not definitively. Although at this stage it looks like it was an electrical fire that started in one of the downstairs rooms. Do you want me to show you?'

'Yes, please,' Caroline said.

We followed Chunky in through the front doors, which had once most likely been impressive heavy, carved wood, but were now fire-damaged and half hanging off their hinges where the fire service had obviously forced entry into the building.

The large stone hallway we entered was a blackened shell of its former self. The walls were charred and sooty, and in certain areas chunks of plaster had fallen to reveal old-fashioned brickwork behind it. Puddles of dark, murky water were thick under foot. The cloying smell of smoke made me cough behind my mask. In front of me stood an impressive staircase that had survived the fire due to it being made of stone or marble. It was impossible to tell which because it was covered in more blackened, sooty water. What remained of the wooden banisters, now blistered and black stubby pieces of wood, littered the floor below.

Dead ahead was a charred wooden desk that might've been a reception or greeting point at one time. Two chairs nearby were just melted skeletons of their former selves. I started sweating beneath my suit from the heat.

Several doorways led off the entrance hall to my left and in front. A long corridor led off to the right.

Chunky marched briskly through to one of the rooms on the left, our footsteps making a loud slapping noise in the puddles.

It was a large space that housed a stainless-steel worktop along the back wall. To the left of it was what looked like some kind of small industrial chest freezer unit, lying on its side, the front door blown off, some of the plastic innards melted. The outside of it was blackened with soot. To the right were stainless-steel trays with remnants of melted plastic on them, covered in more soot and water. A melted piece of machinery, about the size of a thick box file, sat on the worktop. It had six individual compartments with lids that hung off. Part of the ceiling had collapsed, exposing charred wooden beams. There were bottles of what looked like liquid gas and spray canisters dotted around the room. We crunched over the debris on the floor, and I spotted several needles in among it.

Next to the freezer unit was a metal electric wall socket that the unit had been plugged into. Chunky pointed to it. 'We're still taking samples to analyse but I don't think it was arson. It looks like this socket was the point of origin. You see this V-shaped pattern of fire spreading up the wall? The wiring in here must've been a nightmare. It's an old building and has had bits added on here and there over the years. Looks like they weren't adhering to fire regs, either. Or it could've been some kind of electrical malfunction caused by this chest freezer.'

I looked at the outside of the freezer unit, searching for a manufacturer's name or serial number, but it was damaged too much to find one. The bench-top machine was in much the same condition. Inside the individual compartments was just more melted, warped plastic.

I turned and looked at the large sash window. The glass had exploded, and the curtains were burned to a crisp.

Chunky pointed to the gas bottles. 'They contain a mixture of carbon dioxide and oxygen. It's usually stable under normal conditions but it can react explosively when heated.' He picked up one of the small aerosol canisters on the floor that was still intact. Some of the others had exploded. He turned it around so the label that had been partially burned off could be read. *Hospital Surface Disinfectant. Effective against MRSA, HIV-1*, and the rest was unreadable. 'These are flammable. So the presence of about ten cans of these added to the explosion and fed the fire.'

I surveyed the room as Chunky talked about oxygen and heat and liquid gas accelerant.

Caroline turned to me. 'You go and do what you're good at.'

She didn't need to say any more. I was itching to look around.

I stepped out of the room and went into the one next to it. What once was a wooden doorway had suffered the same fate as the front doors. Blistered, blackened, half hanging off its hinges. The walls were a mess of water spray, soot, damaged plaster, bubbled paintwork. A partially melted examination couch sat next to a movable privacy screen, just fragments of charred material clinging on to the remaining metal framework. A stainless-steel trolley lay on its side with more melted plastic equipment around it. A fire-damaged wooden desk in the corner. A partially melted plastic chair.

Back out in the entrance hall, I looked down the corridor on the opposite side. A female decked out in the same clothes as mine walked over, camera hanging around her neck.

'I take it you're SOCO?' I said.

'Yep. Senior SOCO. I'm Lyndsey Downs. There's a bunch of my team all over the place.'

'I'm DI Carter from PSD.'

She nodded grimly. 'They said you were coming.'

'I'm sure Chief Superintendent Barker has already briefed you all, but I don't want anyone to mention the warrant card outside of this building.'

'Of course, sir. That's already been made clear. It was me that found it. As soon as I did I called Chief Superintendent Rowles out and then he called PSD. There's been no mention of it over the radio.'

'Good. Can you give me a quick update yet?'

'Upstairs are just empty rooms.' She turned and pointed along the corridor. 'But down there we've got the bodies of five women. The sixth woman is at the hospital. The victim in the nearest room to where we're standing suffered partial burns. She's the one who had the warrant card near to her body. The other victims in rooms adjacent were burn-free so most likely suffered from smoke inhalation. Home Office pathologist is in the first room. All victims have been photographed and fingerprinted. The scene's been videoed. We're now collecting evidence but it's going to be a huge job. The place is massive, and it's been severely compromised by the fire and the fire service.'

'Anything else?'

'Yeah. I hope you catch the bastard that put those women in there.'

'So do I.'

She headed towards the back of the hospital, and I trudged across the hallway, through a stone archway to the corridor opposite, and paused outside the first room. The wooden door had caught fire and fallen inwards. Flames had licked at the walls. The linoleum floor was scorched. This room had been closer to the source of the fire and so was more damaged. The Home Office pathologist was in there, crouched over the deceased body of the female victim I'd previously seen the photos of. I took a breath and tried to ignore the feeling of intense anger and sadness twisting my guts so I could do my job. No matter how often I'd witnessed violence and death it never got any easier to bear, but I was no good to anyone if I didn't take those feelings and make them work for me.

I carried on walking, passing eight more rooms, but the fire's effects weren't as extensive up there. In four of the rooms there were more dead female victims. One in a foetal position, partially huddled under a soggy blanket. One halfway under the bed. One slumped next to a boarded-up window. One curled up on a bed. The other was now at the hospital, fighting for her life.

I swallowed down the lump clogging my throat and retraced my steps back along the corridor to enter the first room.

I looked down at the bedroom door that was now on the floor. On the outside of it, next to the handle and where a lock would be, was what looked like a melted box, the type used for an electronic key-card entry system, commonly used in hotels. There was no bolt on the outside but whoever had kept these women imprisoned didn't need one if they'd been chained to the walls.

'I'm Acting DI Carter,' I said to the pathologist examining the body as I stepped further into the room.

She chuckled from behind her mask and looked up. 'I thought you'd retired.'

I recognised the voice. Professor Elizabeth Hanley, one of the HO pathologists I'd worked with for years. 'So did I.'

'How long have you been back?'

'About an hour.'

'Welcome to the madhouse,' she said grimly.

I stood beside her and looked down at the victim, the smell of charred flesh invading my nostrils. She looked to be late teens, early twenties. The chain around her wrist and connected to the wall was still in situ. It appeared long enough for her to move around the room, to enter the en suite bathroom in the corner where a sliding door stood open. Thick plywood had been screwed into the wall in front of where a window should've been.

In the photo I'd seen on Caroline's tablet the female had been lying on her stomach. Professor Hanley had obviously turned her body and she was now on her back. The right side of her face was partially burned and blistered. A thin layer of ash covered her clothing. Her eyelashes were singed. Dark brown eyes had been opened. I hated to think of the last thing she'd seen.

'She has moderate burns on her head, face, and arms. Not enough to kill her.'

'Smoke inhalation?'

'She's got soot in her mouth and throat, in her nasal cavities. She was alive and breathing when the fire started.'

I winced. 'Poor woman.'

'I'll have to wait until I've done the PM to be certain but it's very likely they all died from smoke inhalation.'

I felt sick, a mixture of the smell of charred flesh and the incensed anger that had intensified. Sick at the thought of how she'd ended up like that. At what must've happened to her. The horror she must've felt, gasping for her last breath, suffocating with scalding smoke, the terror of knowing the fire was spreading and not being able to escape.

'I've got five victims here, they're going to take some time to PM, but I'll start with this one.'

I stared up at the blackened ceiling and blinked rapidly.

'It's normal for the residual smoke to make your eyes dry. Your tear ducts are working overtime to protect them,' Professor Hanley said softly.

I looked down at her and nodded, although we both knew that wasn't why my eyes were wet.

'When I turned her over, I found this.' Professor Hanley pointed to something beneath where the victim's body had lain.

I crouched down, my knees giving a loud crack. A single word scratched into the lino.

Hayat.

HAYAT

Chapter 6

'My name is Hayat Hasani.'

'How old are you?' she asks.

'I am twenty-four. It is my birthday today.'

She smiles. 'Happy birthday!'

I shake my head. If only it was happy.

'How long have you been here?' she asks.

She is nice. A reporter. She gave me some sweets that taste of peppermint and a colourful scarf that can be worn as a hijab, although I don't wear the headscarf myself. She has a warm smile. No one has smiled at me like that in a long time. There are few smiles in this place.

We are sitting at a plastic table outside one of the women's blocks. It is too hot. The oppressive heat of summer that leaves you in a constant sweat. Here I have no air-conditioning unit, no fans to keep me cool. The dust is always around – on my skin, in my throat, my eyes. I do not know which season is worse now. People think the desert is warm, but winter is so brutal that I can barely feel my toes in my thin socks and there is never enough warmth in the Portakabin I share with five other women. I think about before. About my mother and father. About the house we lived in. Thick stone walls built to keep the cold winter out but that stayed cool in the summer. Orange and lemon trees in the garden, bulging with fruit. My eyes well up as I glance down at the table and run my fingertip along a scratch embedded in the plastic.

'I have been here five years. I cannot be here another five.'

'What about your family? Are they here?'

I shake my head. A vision swims behind my eyes. 'They are dead. Our home . . .' I stare off into the distance, to the tents and Portakabins as far as the eye can see. There are people everywhere. Thousands and thousands of them in this place. 'It was bombed. I was at work. I was a student, studying English literature, but I worked in my spare time in one of the nice hotels in the city. I was a chambermaid but I was going to be promoted to the reception desk. I speak good English, you see. My father, he was a teacher. From a very early age he taught me.' I picture myself aged seven, curled up on my father's lap, reading a book out loud to him. His familiar warmth and smell. The smells here are of desperation, gas canisters from the people cooking, dirty sewers, unwashed bodies. 'They said it was not safe to go back to the house, but I went anyway. And they . . .' I wipe at a tear dribbling down my cheek. 'They were buried under the rubble. All the houses and apartments on that block. Gone. Poof! Dead.' I look up at her.

She reaches out and takes my hand. 'I'm so sorry, Hayat.'

I nod. 'I am not so different to everyone here. We all have the same stories to tell. Homes lost, loved ones dead. Nothing left. Nothing but the clothes on our backs.'

She gives me a sympathetic smile. 'Do you mind if I take your photo?'

I nod, unsure what to do. Does she want me to smile? I can't.

'Just be natural,' she says, lifting the complicated-looking camera off her chest, where it hangs on a strap.

I do not bother to wipe more tears. Let people see me as I am – forgotten, inconsequential, drowning in blackness. 'Can you help me get out of here?'

She smiles again but this time it is sad. 'Oh, Hayat, I wish I could. But I hope in some way my story will help to improve things.'

I shake my head. 'Do you know the average time a refugee is stuck in a camp for?'

She looks back at me, swallows, looks guilty but it is not her fault. 'A long time.'

'Seventeen years,' I say. 'Seventeen years! I cannot stay here another twelve years. Another ten. Another five. I have *nothing*.' My voice rises, cracking. 'I have dreams. I have hopes. But I am in a prison. I have no place to call my own. No future. Reliant on someone else for my food. My life was shattered and it is *still* shattered in here. Sometimes I think it is better not to have survived.' I look towards the chain-link fencing surrounding the camp with barbed wire on top. Some people leave. Escape. But to what? And where? How do I fend for myself in a country where I have no papers? No passport. No ID. I am no one and nothing. I cannot travel legally. I cannot get work. The country that is now my home has its own troubles with high unemployment and limited resources so how do I get a job that can support me? I am scared.

'Tell me about your hopes and dreams,' she says softly.

There is a tape recorder on the table, listening to everything we say. I watch it whirring away for a moment. 'I want freedom. I want a life. I want to work. Have a family. Be happy. I want the same as everyone else.'

'Tell me about your daily life here,' she asks.

I stand up. 'It is better if I show you.'

DETECTIVE BECKY HARRIS

Chapter 7

DS Becky Harris walked outside and stood in the middle of Oak Drive, looking up and down. It was a quiet street, becoming a dead end past the Lanes' house where it led to some woods and fields beyond, so only residents and their guests would be using it. There were several cars parked on the driveways of the houses and none parked in the street. The sun was a smudgy hint of light on the skyline but two people wouldn't be around to see another day.

She strode across to the house of the neighbour opposite – Harold Barnes, who'd dialled 999 to report someone chasing Gillian Lane.

He opened the door, looking hastily dressed in a grey cardigan pulled over tartan pyjamas. He was probably in his early eighties, stooped over at the shoulders, his eyes magnified behind thick-lens glasses. He had a Zimmer frame in front of him.

Becky introduced herself and he moved slowly back with the frame to let her in, a worried expression on his wrinkled face.

'Are they all right? I've seen a lot of police but no ambulance yet.'

'I'm afraid not,' Becky said as she followed his snail's pace shuffle along the hallway to the rear of the house.

'They're not . . . dead, are they?' He slumped into a chair beside a Formica table at one end of a large kitchen that looked like it hadn't seen any improvements since the seventies.

Becky took a seat in front of him. 'A male we believe to be Neal Lane was found deceased in the house, along with an unknown female victim. Gillian Lane is at the hospital. I don't know any more at this stage, but I need to get some details from you.'

'Oh dear. Oh dear, oh dear.' Tears sprang to his eyes. He lifted his glasses and wiped them away with the cuff of his cardigan, his hands trembling. 'They're lovely people, the Lanes. Will Gill be OK?'

'I hope so.'

He pressed his hands to his face with a horrified expression. 'Lord. How awful.'

'How long have you known them?' Becky pulled out her notebook and pen.

'Probably about fifteen years. That's when they moved in. I bought this house with my wife forty years ago. I've lived here the longest out of everyone.'

'Do they have children?'

'No.' He leaned forward. 'They lost a little girl. She was about eight. She drowned in a swimming pool when they were on holiday. It was terribly tragic. And now this.'

'Does Gillian have a sister?'

'No. She has no family left now.'

'Can you tell me exactly what you saw over there?'

'Well, I don't sleep that well any more. I heard a car outside and looked out of the window. You can't be too careful these days, can you? When I first moved here there was no crime. Nowadays you hear about all sorts. I live on my own, so I'd be a pretty good target for a burglar.' He paused to take a ragged breath. 'I saw Neal's car pull up on the drive – the Mini. And I knew Gillian had been driving it, so I waited at the window to make sure she got inside OK. She had a suitcase with her. She'd been out to one of those exotic places again looking for furniture.'

'Furniture?'

'She's got her own company that sells lovely-looking things. She goes away a lot. Actually, Neal often works away, too.'

'OK. So, then what happened? After she went inside.'

'Um . . . I was about to get back into bed. But then I heard a scream, and I opened the curtain again and she was running down the street. And there was a man chasing her.'

'Can you describe him?'

He frowned and looked down at the table, his hands in his lap. He looked back up at Becky. 'No. The street lights aren't on these days. Council cutbacks, you know. They only seem to light up the main roads now. So it was quite dark, and my eyesight's not what it was. I just saw a dark figure chasing her.'

'Why did you think it was a man and not a woman?'

'Um . . . well, he was taller than Gill. He looked quite big. Bulky.'

'Any idea what this person was wearing?'

'Dark trousers, a dark top. I think he had something over his head. It was just a dark shadow really, though.'

'And then what happened?'

'I called 999 as soon as I realised what I was seeing. And I heard the screech of brakes from up by the main road.'

'Did you see the man come back again?'

'No, but I was on the phone for a few minutes, which is over there, so I wouldn't have seen anything.' He pointed to an old-fashioned corded phone on a small coffee table in the corner of the room.

'Did you see or hear any other vehicles arrive or leave? Or any other people? Any other suspicious noises?'

'Um . . . no.'

'Which window did you see this from?'

'I'll show you.' He got slowly to his feet and shuffled back towards the front door, taking the left-hand door just before it.

Inside was what would've once been a living room but was now decked out as a bedroom. In the centre, a bed with rumpled sheets, and a small Formica unit beside it with a glass of water on top.

'I sleep down here now. Can't get upstairs any more.'

Becky went to the window. From here there was a clear view of the front of the Lanes' house.

'Did you see a woman with long dark hair go into their house recently?'

'That would be Gill.'

'No. Another woman.' She turned to him.

He shook his head. 'No.'

'What about any other visitors to the house? Any friends or family? Or anyone suspicious hanging around?'

'I don't . . . I don't really know. I don't make a habit of watching the neighbours.'

She smiled at him with disappointment. At the time when she really needed a nosy neighbour she was out of luck.

'I only use this room for sleeping. I'm usually in the kitchen at the back of the house – it's smaller and easier to heat in the winter – so I don't notice that much of what goes on in the street. But Neal's got a brother who lives a few miles away. He often came to visit. Both Gill's and Neal's parents are dead now.' He sat on the edge of the bed.

'OK, thank you. You've been a big help. Will you be all right? You've had quite a shock. Do you want me to call someone to come over?'

'I'll be OK, dear.' He gave Becky a resigned smile. 'There's no one left these days. My son died, too.' He glanced at the floor. 'I'm outliving everybody.'

'What about eating and cleaning? Do you have a carer?'

'Meals on Wheels come in. And I have a carer come three times a week. Used to be every day, but the cutbacks, you know.'

Sadness swelled in her gut as she left, thinking about poor Harold stuck in that house alone.

The property next to Harold's had the curtains open, despite it being the early hours of the morning. A woman with blonde hair stood at the window, watching Becky's colleagues coming and going. Hopefully this *was* a nosy neighbour. She was so intent on staring at the macabre scene unfolding that she jumped when she noticed Becky heading towards her.

Becky knocked on the door and the woman opened it. She was early forties and obviously took pride in her appearance. Even at this time in the morning she had lipstick on and was dressed in tight skinny jeans and a trendy top. For a moment Becky felt slightly envious. If she paid more attention to her appearance instead of making do with raking her fingers through her hair and tying it up in a bun and splashing water on her face in the mornings, would Ian be happier with her? Then she thought sod it. She was never going to be one of those polished women who always looked immaculate. She was more of a tomboy. And he'd known who she was when they'd met each other and got married. Why should she have to change to please someone?

Becky introduced herself to Mrs Immaculate and explained why she was there. 'And what's your name?'

'Lisa Carroll. I live here with my husband and two kids. They're dead, aren't they?' she said with a hint of too much excitement for Becky's liking.

'I can confirm there's been a double murder at the house.'

She gasped. 'Omigod! What happened?'

'I'm afraid I can't go into details. Did you see or hear anything in the early hours of this morning?'

'Yes. Don't you all talk to each other? I phoned 999. They said someone was already coming out.'

Becky bit her tongue at the woman's rude tone. If multiple calls were received that related to the same incident they were recorded in the control room and then added to one active log. 'Well, thank you for calling us but I need to know exactly what you saw.'

'I heard a scream. It woke me up. By the time I looked out of the window I saw someone running up the lane, and I thought it was my neighbour, Gill. Someone else looked like they were chasing her.' Her eyes widened. 'I called out to my husband, who was fast asleep, *as usual.* He doesn't wake up for anything. It was just the same when the kids were young. *I* was always the one who had to—'

'And then what happened?' Becky butted in.

'Well, I called the police! I just said so. I heard a bang. And a screech of brakes. Or was the bang after the brakes? I don't know. It all happened so quick.'

'Were you still looking out of the window when you were on the phone? Did you see the man come back at all after you heard the noise and the brakes?'

'No, I got scared then. I was worried whoever was out there would see me looking and come after me. You hear about it all the time, don't you? People who intervene in muggings and things get stabbed and killed. I wasn't going out there, and I wouldn't let my husband go, either. I didn't dare have a look because my kids are in the house.'

'Right. Can you describe who was chasing Gill?'

'No. It happened too quick. They were big, I know that. I couldn't see a face or anything. It was too dark.'

'Did you see or hear anything else?'

'No. Just the sirens. Eventually.'

'What about before that? Did you see a woman with long dark hair go into the house?'

She pursed her lips and thought about that. 'No. But we were out all day. Didn't get back until about 10 p.m. because we'd taken the kids to a Christmas panto.'

'How about any other visitors to the house recently?'

She shrugged. 'Just some Ocado delivery people now and then. And an older man who looks a bit like Neal who might be his brother. But I don't know them that well. We only moved in four months ago.'

'Have you ever seen anyone suspicious hanging around?'

'No.'

'Right. Well, if you think of anything, please contact me.' Becky handed over her card and went to the next house along, frustrated she hadn't got a clear description of the offender yet, and wondering exactly who the brunette was in the Lanes' house.

DETECTIVE WARREN CARTER
Chapter 8

It was just gone 9 a.m. when Caroline and I left Brampton Hospital and headed back to the PSD office, discussing pertinent points on the way. I was used to the brass hindering me and mocking my theories, but Caroline and I seemed to be on the same wavelength. She was encouraging and incredibly pleased to have me on board. It was refreshing, but now the shock of the sudden job offer in the middle of the night was wearing off, the nerves kicked in hard. Could I really do this all again?

I pictured the women in that hospital and knew I had no choice. They were someone's daughter, maybe someone's wife, girlfriend, sister. Kidnapped from somewhere, imprisoned, and left to die a horrendous death. A hot flame of anger reignited inside me, knocking the nerves away.

'Come on, I'll introduce you to the team and we'll do a briefing.' Caroline pressed an entry code on the doorway to our office.

In our absence the workstations had been taken up by people on the phone, typing, perusing documents. Part of the room was home to Team A in the Anti-Corruption Unit – the team investigating Bloodbath Farm. At the near end was Team B – my team. 'Morning everyone,' Caroline addressed Team B. 'I need you in the briefing room right now, please.'

Briefing room? It was all mod cons here, I thought, as I followed Caroline into a separate room just off the open-plan area. Whiteboards were set up along the side walls, a TV screen on the wall at the back. Several rows of chairs. In my old, cramped CID unit we were lucky to find a spare paper clip, let alone a whole room specifically for briefing. Or a tablet.

I stood next to Caroline at the front of the room while she paired her tablet to the smart TV behind me.

Four pairs of eyes looked back expectantly at me from their seats. The nerves kicked in again. I swallowed and gave them all my best confident smile.

'Right. This is Warren Carter,' Caroline began. 'As of now, he's your new Acting DI. Some of you may have seen him around here recently in relation to the Bloodbath Farm case.'

There were a few nods.

'So let me introduce your team,' Caroline said to me. 'This is DS Jack Evans.' Caroline swept her hand towards a stocky guy with cauliflower ears and a nose that had been broken a few times. He looked as if he'd be more at home on a rugby pitch than in an office wearing a suit and tie.

Jack smiled and held up his hand in a wave. 'Morning, guv.'

'DC Katrina Lowrie.' Caroline nodded towards her. 'She's a HOLMES-trained officer we're lucky to have on our team.'

HOLMES was the Home Office Large Major Enquiry System. Software designed to help police with their investigations but which often spouted out numerous pointless enquiries that hindered our job when we were frequently suffering from limited resources. Still, never let it be said the police couldn't do acronyms well.

'Welcome, sir,' Katrina said. She was slim and short with long blonde hair.

'DC Koray Kemal.' Caroline indicated a dark-haired man with dark brown eyes and olive skin who looked more like a Mediterranean male model than a copper.

'Sir.' Koray nodded back, running a hand through his thick, wavy curls, front to back.

'And Liz here is our civvie investigator.' Caroline nodded at a woman in her mid-forties with her hair cut into a no-nonsense crop.

'Welcome, sir.' Liz smiled.

'You can take it from here.' Caroline handed me the tablet, sat down next to Koray, crossed her legs.

'Right. Thanks for the nice welcome, everyone. You're probably as surprised to see me here as I am this morning.' I glanced briefly at Caroline. 'I'll spare you the boring introduction speech. As Chief Superintendent Barker just said, most of you probably know who I am. So . . . at 01.43 this morning, the fire brigade received a call from a woman reporting a fire at Brampton Hospital.' I called up the first pictures from the tablet onto the TV screen. 'At present, they suspect it was caused by an electrical fault from a freezer unit in one of the downstairs rooms, or dodgy wiring.' I swiped the tablet to the next photo of the large room we'd visited with the medical equipment inside. 'There was a lot of wood in the building so no wonder it took off quickly.' More swiping, to the waterlogged, charred entrance hallway. 'Inside the property, the fire brigade discovered six women in the eastern corridor. They were held captive in individual rooms. Five of the doors were locked when the brigade arrived, causing them to force entry. The sixth door had suffered enough fire damage that it fell off on its own. As well as being locked in, these women were chained to the walls.'

'Bloody hell,' Jack said as I kept swiping through scenes of the fire damage.

I nodded. 'By the time the fire was under control, it was sadly too late for all but one. One survivor was taken to hospital, unconscious, suspected of severe smoke inhalation. We don't know if she's going to make it.'

I brought up the pictures showing the bodies we'd found in situ.

There were looks of disgust and despair all round. Liz put her hand to her mouth. Jack's jaw clamped tight.

'Awful,' Katrina said sadly.

'What a horrendous way to go,' Koray said.

'Yeah, it's horrific.' I brought up photos of the last woman who'd had the warrant card next to her body, picturing her terror and fear, knowing there was no way out. 'The windows in these rooms were boarded up from the inside and we found evidence of the kind of electronic locks on the doors you find in hotel rooms that need a key-card to open.'

'Why is this coming to PSD?' Jack asked.

Caroline held up the warrant card found at the scene, now encased in a plastic evidence bag. 'You all know what this is.' She showed them the half-melted remains.

'Shit.' Recognition dawned on Jack's face.

'Exactly,' Caroline replied as I brought the close-up photo of where the warrant card had been positioned next to the victim's body onto the TV screen. The next shot was of the word scratched on the floorboards beneath where she'd been lying.

'Hayat,' I said, surveying my new team. 'It seems she scored this in the lino floor with the edge of the warrant card. Anyone know what it means?'

There were looks of confusion all round. Except for Koray.

'It's a Turkish word. The English translation means "life". But it can also be a person's name.'

'You're of Turkish origin?' I asked.

'My mum's Turkish Cypriot. Dad's English.'

'So she could be Turkish?'

'Possibly, but a lot of neighbouring countries share common words or part of the language – Kurdistan, Turkmenistan, Albania, Syria,

Cyprus, Azerbaijan, plus a lot more. There are a lot of Arabic words used in Turkish, too.'

I nodded. 'OK. But this could be her name?'

'It could,' Koray agreed.

I stared at the word. 'It would make sense that she tried to leave a clue as to her name rather than the word "life" so let's call this victim Hayat for now.' I turned back to them. 'We need to know who these women are. They're all dark-haired, with dark eyes and Mediterranean complexions. If her name *is* Hayat there's a strong Turkish or Middle Eastern connection. I need missing persons records checked for our force, nationally, and then if that throws nothing up let's check Interpol. DNA and fingerprint databases are being checked, too.'

'I can do that,' Koray said.

'Thanks.'

'How about checking dental records?' Jack asked.

I glanced at Caroline.

'We'll see what state their teeth are in at the PM,' she said. 'Without anyone to narrow a potential search to, I don't think that line of inquiry has any merit right now.' She lifted up the warrant card again and pointed to the magnetic swipe strip at the back, which held information similar to how a debit card or magnetic key-card worked. The card would've gained the holder access to official police areas, as well as being used as their identification. 'I'm going to find out if there's any salvageable information still held on the data strip on this card. And if not, then we need to know *who* is missing a warrant card.'

'We also need to know who owns that property, so Land Registry needs to be checked,' I said.

'I'll take that,' Jack said.

'Thanks. I want utility companies checked also.' I looked at them. 'There was obviously electric there, along with water. I want to know who was paying the bills.'

'Yep, I can do that,' Liz said.

'Good. There's no CCTV at the property. It's set in very private grounds and accessed by a quiet country lane that won't get a lot of use. The nearest village is a couple of miles away. So we're probably clutching at straws here, but we need to check for any council or private cameras anywhere nearby. Katrina, can you do that until the HOLMES inputting gets under way?'

'Absolutely.'

I nodded my thanks.

'DC Potter from A team will be stationed at the front gates for the foreseeable future in case their captor returns to the hospital,' Caroline said. 'There were remnants of food and drink there. Someone had been feeding those women so they must be making regular trips. I'm going to try and keep this out of the press for as long as possible so we can try to catch whoever goes back there.'

'We also need to speak to the woman who called the fire brigade,' I said. 'She gave her name as Melanie Dwyer and the fire brigade have the number she was calling from. She said she was driving down the lane past the hospital on her way back from a friend's house.'

'Leave that with me,' Jack said.

'OK, great. Now, SOCO will be busy for days up there, trying to recover any forensics, but with the fire and water damage, it's likely we're going to get bugger all.' I sighed. 'The other thing is this . . .' I brought up the photos of what looked like a treatment room that hadn't fared well in the fire.

Jack leaned forward in his seat. 'Is that a massage couch?'

'It looks like the kind of couch used for medical examinations and massage work, yes. There were also detachable leg rests that were found nearby.' I looked around the room.

'Maybe the women were trafficked as sex slaves,' Katrina said. 'The couch could be where they were forced to give people *massages*.' She did quote marks in the air, all of us knowing full well that the seedy massage parlours around the UK were anything but.

'Yes, that's a strong possibility, but there was also other medical equipment in this room.' I swiped through the photos to the ones I wanted. 'Professor Hanley has said that the freezer unit we believe started the fire was some kind of cryogenic chest freezer.' I pointed to shots of the freezer and then the desktop machine I'd seen. 'And this molten piece of plastic used to be an incubator, which is used for cell or bacterial culturing. There were also needles found in that room, along with other bits of melted plastic medical equipment. I want to know if this stuff was left by the previous owners of the property when it was sold, and if not, what the hell was it being used for now with those women in the house?'

'Apparently the hospital was last used as a private residential drug-rehabilitation clinic but was sold some time ago,' Caroline told them. 'The needles I can understand being left in situ, but an incubator and cryogenic freezer doesn't fit some kind of sex-trafficking ring. The first PMs are being done this morning and I'll be attending, so hopefully Professor Hanley will be able to tell us more afterwards.'

'The freezer unit and incubator were too damaged to find a serial number or make on them,' I added. 'Without that it will probably be impossible to trace who brought them there, but I want medical suppliers checked just in case we get lucky. And who put in those electronic door locks? Was it the rehab place or our kidnappers? They had to get those supplies from somewhere.'

'I can do that,' Liz said.

I turned around and studied the picture of the scene behind me on the TV, thinking about everything I'd witnessed. I wasn't sure yet why these women had been taken or for what purpose. It was heinous enough for anyone to be involved in, but if a police officer had crossed that thin blue line into something black and murky then I was going to do all I could to get them.

DETECTIVE BECKY HARRIS
Chapter 9

Becky entered the hospital ward and glanced around. The nurses' station stood empty and the place had a neglected feel, like the whole of the NHS these days. She spotted an Asian nurse in one of the side rooms, looking flushed and harassed as she pulled the curtain around a patient.

'Bloody cutbacks,' Becky muttered to herself as she waited. No one was immune these days. Her team in CID had been dwindling for years yet the work just piled up. For a brief moment she wondered if she *should* give it all up now and get pregnant. Be a stay-at-home mum. Leave the force on a high from her last case. Then she shook her head. Nah. No way was that going to happen. The excitement, the buzz, the knowledge that she could make a difference was too much to leave behind.

'Can I help you?' a voice said from behind her.

She turned and saw a male nurse carrying a bed pan covered with a paper towel. 'Hi. I'm DS Harris.' She flashed her warrant card. 'I'm here to see Gillian Lane.'

'Ah, yes. One of your colleagues is already here.'

A uniformed officer had been placed outside of Gillian's room for her protection as a precaution. It wasn't clear yet whether she was a witness or a suspect.

He jerked his head towards a corridor. 'This way.'

'How is she?'

'Incredibly lucky, actually. She's got a fractured radius and ulna, a sprained ankle, a big bump on the head, and a lot of bruising. But it could've been a lot worse.'

'Is she awake?'

'She is now, but she's dosed up on strong pain meds so don't take it personally if she falls asleep on you. She's got mild concussion so she might be a bit confused.'

Becky followed along beside him, trying to ignore the smell of vomit and shit that hung in the air, until she spotted a male police officer further up the corridor, sitting in a plastic chair outside a private side room, tapping on his phone. She thanked the nurse as he disappeared. The PC was so engrossed in what he was doing he didn't look up.

Becky coughed loudly.

The PC finally jerked his head up, tucked the phone into his pocket, and blushed at being caught.

'You're supposed to be guarding this woman. Anyone could've got in or out while you played Candy Crush.'

'Sorry, sarge. Won't happen again.' At least he looked embarrassed, but it wasn't good enough. If Gillian Lane was a witness, they had no idea whether the killer would try to target her again.

'It had better not,' she said. 'Have SOCO been to see her yet?'

'Yes, they finished taking her clothing and examining her for trace evidence about fifteen minutes ago.'

'Good.' She pushed open the door to the room.

Gillian lay on the bed, her eyes closed, her right arm encased in plaster in a foam sling against her chest. Bruising covered her forehead and she had a black eye.

'Mrs Lane?' Becky approached the bed.

Gillian's eyes fluttered open and took a minute to focus.

'I'm Detective Sergeant Harris.' She pulled a plastic visitor's chair closer to the bed and sat down. 'I know you've had a horrendous time but it's vital that I get some information from you as soon as possible. Are you up to talking?'

Gillian tried to sit upright but struggled with one arm so Becky helped her into a comfortable position.

'How's Neal?' An edge of desperation crept into her voice that sounded groggy from the pain meds. 'They wouldn't tell me anything when I woke up. Please let me know if he's OK.'

Becky took a deep breath, knowing there was no way to prepare Gillian for the worst news she'd ever hear. 'I'm very sorry to have to tell you that we found your husband deceased inside your house. We believe he was murdered,' she said, feeling like a complete shit. It never got any easier telling relatives their loved ones had died.

Gillian's eyes welled up with tears. She sank back onto the pillows and blinked rapidly. 'No. He can't be. He *can't*.' She shook her head, refusing to believe it.

Gillian didn't bother wiping away the tears trickling down her cheeks as she sobbed uncontrollably, her whole body wracked with shudders. Becky passed her a box of tissues and tried to console her as Gillian repeated over and over again that Neal couldn't be dead.

Eventually, Gillian cried herself out. She blew her nose, wiped the tears away from her puffy eyes with a shaky hand and took a few minutes to compose herself.

Becky poured a glass of water from a jug on the tray beside her bed, handed it to her. Gillian took a small sip and then put it back on the tray.

'Are you OK to talk? I know this is really difficult. But I do need to ask you some questions. Are you up to that? It's very important. I'll make it as quick as I can.' Becky reached out and touched Gillian's good hand gently. 'I'm afraid I can't go into more details at the moment, but can you tell me what happened at the house? I appreciate this is a shock, and you've been injured, but in order to catch the person that did this we need your help.'

Gillian nodded vacantly.

'Can you tell me what happened when you arrived home?'

'I . . . shouldn't have run. I should've tried to fight him. Maybe then . . . maybe he'd still be alive.' Her face crumpled again. She wiped away a fresh batch of tears with a soggy tissue.

'It's not your fault,' Becky said, wanting to believe she was a victim in this and not responsible. For all she knew Gillian could've been a jealous wife, aware her husband had been having an affair, and who'd staged his murder. It wouldn't be the first time she'd dealt with a case where everything was the opposite of what it seemed. 'One of your neighbours saw you arrive home in your car with a suitcase. He said you'd been away,' Becky prompted her.

'Yes. I was . . . um . . . on a buying trip. To Bali. I have my own business. An online furniture company. I source exotic and ethnic pieces so I'm away quite often.'

Becky pulled her notebook out and scribbled that down.

'I . . . um . . . caught an earlier flight. I was due to come back next week but I cut the trip short because I'd managed to get everything I needed.'

'Was your husband aware you were coming back early?'

'No. I wanted to surprise him. Oh, God!' Gillian pressed her good hand to her face, eyes squeezed shut.

Becky paused for a moment, letting Gillian compose herself again, wondering if things had been different, if the murderer hadn't been in the house, would Gillian have had another surprise of finding a woman in bed with her husband instead. 'OK. So what happened when you got to the house?'

Gillian looked up again. 'I . . . well, I parked the car on the drive and went to open the front door. And I thought I heard something from inside. Like a moan or cry. But I just put it down to being tired. Or the wind.'

'Then what happened?'

'I was trying to be quiet. It was about half two in the morning, and I didn't want to wake Neal up like that, all crumpled and sweaty from the flight. I wanted to freshen up first and then surprise him by sliding into bed next to him. So I put the suitcase down at the bottom of the stairs. And then—' Her left hand flew to her mouth, her breathing growing fast. She blinked back more tears. 'Was it Neal who groaned?' Her eyes widened. 'Was he still alive when I stood at the front door?'

'We don't know yet, Gillian. We're still trying to find out what happened.' Becky gave her a sympathetic smile. 'Can you go on?'

It took a moment for Gillian's breathing to slow a little more so she was able to speak. 'Um . . . then someone opened the door to the kitchen. There was a nightlight plugged in the hallway upstairs. We always leave it on. And it was filtering downstairs, so I could see it definitely wasn't Neal. He was taller, wider. And he was dressed in black with a balaclava over his head.'

Becky's gaze snapped up to meet Gillian's. She was thinking about another case she'd worked with her old boss DS Warren Carter, involving a couple called Max and Alissa Burbeck, back when she was a DC. There were some similarities. A murdered husband. A black-clad intruder wearing a balaclava and wielding a knife. A wife running for her life. But the offender had been caught and the case was over. She jerked back to the present again. Wrote down *Why did he chase her?*

Gillian spoke again. 'I just ran instinctively. I was almost at the main road and thought I could feel him grab hold of my hair. I just tried . . . I tried to run harder, and I was concentrating on getting away. I didn't even see the car.'

'So you didn't get a good look at the person?'

'No.'

'But you think it was a man?'

'Yes. His build. Height. I'm sure it was a man.'

'Does anyone else live at your house?'

A flash of confusion danced across her distressed face. 'No. Why?'

And now for the other horrible bit that Becky didn't relish telling her. Becky pulled out her mobile phone. Found the image she'd taken of the dead woman in the kitchen. Zoomed in on her uninjured face so Gillian couldn't see the extent of the damage to her neck. 'I'll warn you in advance that I need you to look at a picture of someone who is deceased. But it's very important to see if you recognise her.' Becky held the phone out closer to Gillian.

Gillian's forehead creased as she studied the image. 'No. But . . . she looks a bit familiar.'

She looks a lot like you, Becky thought.

'Why are you showing me this? What—' And she stopped abruptly. She was obviously an intelligent woman and the penny dropped instantly. 'She was in my house? With Neal?'

There was no way to sugar-coat the truth so Becky just said yes.

She gasped. 'In bed together?'

'No. They were both fully clothed and found in the kitchen.' And it looked as if they'd been drinking wine together in the lounge earlier, but Becky didn't tell her that.

Gillian dropped her chin to her chest and stared down at the sheet, squeezing it with her good fist. Her voice was just a whisper as she said, 'Are you telling me he was having an affair?'

Becky had learned from Warren Carter that nothing should ever be assumed. Occam's Razor wasn't always right. And instead she said, 'Was he acting strangely? Were you suspicious he could've been having an affair?'

'God, I'm such an idiot.' Gillian squeezed the sheet so hard her knuckles turned white. 'I thought it was just stress or something.' She shook her head, her mouth falling open.

'What was?'

'Well . . . he'd been acting really weird lately. But the project he was working on had suddenly had the funding cut so he'd been let go. I thought it was because of that. Because he didn't have any work lined up and was worried about money. But I told him he didn't need to be. My business is doing well. We would've been fine.'

'Where did he work?'

'He was a freelance project manager. His last job was for World Food Corps.'

'And what did that entail?'

'Well . . . World Food Corps are an international NGO. They provide food aid for refugee camps, but they also run their own refugee camp in Jordan for people fleeing Syria. Neal was managing a pilot project out in Jordan that meant refugees could regain legal identities they'd lost after they left their homes. It was a bit over my head, to be honest. Neal's expertise is in software and technology. It was something to do with collecting their biometric data for an identity system. Apart from that, I don't know too much. But . . .' She took a deep breath, blinked eyelids wet with more unshed tears. 'He'd been out in Jordan for the last six months, working on the project so he'd been away a lot recently, only coming back once a month for a week at a time. Then all of a sudden, two weeks ago, he said that World Food Corps had had their funding cut and the project would have to be put on hold for the indeterminate future.'

'And that's when he started acting differently?'

'Yes. He seemed depressed. Distant. He was being secretive about things. Whispered phone calls in the bathroom. Going for walks at strange times of the night. You can imagine some of the things he saw out there on a daily basis. I thought it was possibly the start of PTSD and urged him to speak to someone professional about it. I was worried about him but . . . it didn't click he was having an affair.'

'We don't know for sure that he was.'

'So what was he doing with this woman in the house while I was away? At that time in the morning?' she snapped, the shock and stress and grief now manifesting as anger.

Becky didn't have an answer for that. Yet.

'If it was innocent he would've told me, wouldn't he?'

Becky changed the subject slightly. 'Was Neal in the habit of leaving the back door unlocked if he was in the house?' The unlocked back door was how they suspected the killer had gained entry. And the rear garden was accessible from the fields and woods at the back of the house that would've provided good cover.

'Yes. He often went outside for a smoke and didn't bother to lock it.'

'When was the last time you spoke to your husband?'

'Five days ago. When I got to Bali. I called him to say I'd landed and . . .' She broke off, took a shuddering breath. 'We ended up in an argument. I'd had to take his Mini to the airport because my Polo wouldn't start. Neal couldn't take me because he was in London for a job interview – he'd taken the train. So I just took his car. I didn't think there'd be a problem. All he had to do was call the garage out. It was probably just the battery. But he was really annoyed about it. I ended up putting the phone down on him. That's why I didn't tell him I was coming home early and wanted to surprise him. I was hoping to make up for the stupid row. You see . . . this is the kind of weird behaviour I was talking about. He was bad-tempered lately, snapping at me. Irrational. But it wasn't stress, was it? It was because he wasn't in love with me any more. Because he was having an affair!'

Becky repeated again gently that they had no proof of that yet, but Gillian shook her head as if she'd already made her mind up.

'Have you or Neal received any threats recently? Had any problems with someone? Seen anyone hanging around the house?'

'No.'

'Do you know a couple called Donna and Jim Wilson?'

She started to shake her head and then winced in pain. 'I don't think so . . . but the names ring a bell.'

Becky wasn't surprised Gillian had heard of them. They were the names of the other couple who'd been murdered in a similar situation that DI Thornton had mentioned and had been splashed all over the papers the previous year.

'Is that . . . *her* name?' She pointed to Becky's phone. 'The woman . . . in the photo.'

'No.' Becky paused, noting the slowed speech, the tiredness etched on Gillian's face. She looked as if she was about to pass out.

Becky thought about the words written on the wall at Gillian's house. 'This might seem like a strange question, but did you or Neal have any kind of connection to pigs?'

Gillian shook her head. 'No, why?'

'I can't say at the moment. Do you perhaps sell any items on your website that are pig-related? Ornaments or anything like that? Or did you or Neal have an interest in them?'

'No. I have absolutely no idea what you're talking about.'

'OK. Can you give me a list of your friends and family we can speak to?'

'Yes, but why?'

Becky didn't want to tell her that both Neal's and her life would be micro-analysed now. That if this was a serial killer, then there could be some connection between the Lanes and the Wilsons that had made the murderer target them. But for now, they were keeping the possibility of a serial killer under wraps. No one wanted the press getting hold of it and starting a full-scale panic yet. 'It's just routine, Gillian. We need to know how and why your husband and this woman were targeted.'

Gillian blinked back more tears and said, 'I don't have any family left. We're close to Neal's brother, Dean.' She told Becky some of their friends' names. 'But . . . what with me being busy with work, and Neal having been out in Jordan a lot, we haven't really seen anyone regularly recently.' She wiped her cheek with her trembling left hand. 'I can't . . . I can't believe . . . Neal must've been sleeping with her if she was in our house. If it was something innocent, I'd know who she was, wouldn't I?' She turned to look at Becky, her bloodshot watery eyes wide open.

'How long have you been married?'

'Twenty-five years,' she said bitterly. 'We've been through some really rough times. We lost our daughter. I thought if we could survive that, we'd survive anything.' She flopped her head back on the pillow and closed her eyes. 'Obviously not.'

Becky wanted to comfort her again but there wasn't time for that. She had a job to do. 'There's something else we need to do. We need to get a formal ID of Neal's body. If you're not up to it, I can call Dean to do it for you.'

She blinked rapidly. Sniffed a few times. 'Where is he?'

'In the morgue, downstairs.'

'Um . . . OK. I'll . . . I'll do it.'

'All right. I'll arrange for a wheelchair to take you down there. When we've done the ID someone will take a formal statement from you. And we'll be assigning a Family Liaison Officer to you. They'll be your point of contact in the investigation and can stay with you and give you some support.'

'Stay with me?' She gulped in some air. 'I don't want anyone staying with me. I don't even know if I can go back to that house now. Not after what's happened.' The tears fell again, the anger being replaced by grief once more.

'That's absolutely your choice, Gillian. Try not to worry about that just yet. Just concentrate on getting better.' Becky stood up to organise Gillian's wheelchair. 'Do you want me to speak to Dean for you and tell him you're here?'

She nodded. 'Yes. Yes, please.'

'OK. I'll be back soon.' She closed the door behind her and gave a meaningful *Do not look at your bloody phone* glare to the PC before heading to the nurses' station.

Twenty minutes later, after Gillian had tearfully ID'd her husband's body, Becky took her back to the ward and then left.

She shared the lift down to the main entrance with a pregnant woman, snatching sideways glances at her bulging stomach, thinking about the kind of world she was living in. Did she really want to bring a child into a place where beatings, rapes, murders, and knife crime were on the increase? It could only get worse. Knowing and seeing everything she had on the job, was it even fair to a child? Becky would probably be one of those overprotective parents who never wanted to let their kid out of their sight.

Her phone rang as she stepped out of the lift. It was DI Thornton.

'All right, guv?' she said, walking towards the main entrance. 'I'm leaving the hospital now.' She gave him a quick rundown of what Gillian and the witnesses had told her.

'I'm just leaving the scene. I'll see you back at the nick for a briefing. Can you swing by a coffee place and pick up some drinks on your way in? That stuff in the machine's gross.'

'Yeah. What's the ord—'

'One big latte and a big Americano. Oh, and a peppermint tea for Ronnie,' he scoffed.

Becky bristled, feeling overprotective of DC Ronnie Pickering. He was quirkily different but a great guy without a bad bone in his body.

'Bloody press is all over it now at the house,' Thornton carried on. 'Knew it wouldn't be long till they showed up.'

Becky fought back the urge to say *Well, you didn't mind the press being involved in the last case, did you?* But in that instance Thornton had used it to his advantage to gain as much publicity as he could to further his career.

'I don't want any of our lot talking to the press about this. The specific words written on the wall were never included in the incident log, and I don't want anyone finding out about them from us.'

'As if I would,' Becky bristled, miffed at the implication that she didn't know how to do her job.

She hung up and pulled a face at the phone in her hand. 'Knobhead,' she muttered.

DETECTIVE WARREN CARTER
Chapter 10

'If the wind changes you'll stay like that,' I said to Becky as she curled her top lip at her mobile.

She jerked her head up and grinned. 'Bloody hell. Warren!' She gave me a hug. 'What are you doing here? You're all right, aren't you?' She pulled back, a frown of concern forming.

'Yeah, why?'

She rolled her eyes. 'Well, we *are* in a hospital. You're not ill, are you?'

'No.' I grinned back.

'Are you visiting someone?'

'Yes.'

'Who?'

'Nosy.' I raised an eyebrow. 'You're never going to believe what happened to me today.'

'You won the lottery?'

'I wish. In the space of . . .' – I glanced at my watch – 'nearly five hours, I've accepted a job offer, attended a crime scene, and given my first briefing as new Acting DI.'

Becky's mouth fell open. 'What? Explain. Right now. Very, very quickly as I've got my own briefing to get to.'

'What's the briefing for?'

'You tell me yours first.' She made ushering motions with her hands.

I chuckled. I'd missed her. Missed our banter. 'PSD.'

'Complaints?'

'Anti-Corruption Unit.'

'What? I knew it. I *knew* you couldn't retire. What's the case?'

More eyebrow-raising from me. 'I could tell you but . . .'

'Yeah. You'd have to kill me, blah, blah, blah.' She grinned.

'What are you doing here?'

'Double murder.' She explained what she knew so far.

'Reminds me of the Burbeck case,' I said.

'Yeah, that thought crossed my mind, too.'

I touched her forearm. 'I'd love to catch up properly, but I need to go.'

'Me too. Promise me we'll go for a drink or something? Anyone would think you'd been avoiding me.'

'Promise,' I said.

She rushed off towards the car park, and I headed to the Intensive Care Unit, thinking Becky was right. I had been avoiding her. She'd been my ally in CID, and a great detective. We were mates but we only had one thing in common. The job. And if I wasn't in the job what would I even talk about? It had been my life for so long, and as I'd found out in the last two months of retirement, I had nothing left without it.

I pressed the buzzer to gain entry to the ward and waited.

A female nurse let me in. I introduced myself but I had no official ID to show her yet, so I handed her Caroline's business card. She'd already called ahead and let them know I'd be arriving.

'Yes, they said you were coming.' She took the card and studied it carefully before saying, 'She's down this way.' She took off at a brisk walk, the soles of her shoes squeaking on the lino floor. 'There's been no change, I'm afraid. She's still unconscious and hooked up to breathing apparatus. She's sustained severe burns to her respiratory system.' She led me to a private room.

I stood in the doorway for a moment, watching the young woman who was connected to several machines with regular beeps emitting from them, her dark skin a stark contrast among the white sheets. Numbers flashed up on a screen. An automatic blood-pressure cuff was wrapped around her arm. A pulse monitor connected to her fingertip. She had an IV drip. 'Do you think she'll survive?' I asked quietly.

The nurse gave me a solemn smile. 'It's too early to say. Smoke inhalation can be a tricky one. The delayed effects can be profound and a patient can go downhill rapidly into respiratory failure.'

She patted my arm and said, 'I'll leave you to it.' Her footsteps squeaked back up the corridor.

I stepped inside the room, pulled up a chair and sat down next to her. I smelled the smoke again from Brampton Hospital clinging to her hair, her skin, as it was to me. I took hold of the hand without the pulse monitor. Her fingertips were cold, but the room was stifling.

'What's your name?' I asked her, even though I knew she wouldn't answer me. I shook my head to myself. 'I'm so sorry you ended up like this. I'm going to get them. I'm going to find them and throw the book at them. Trust me.'

I sat there with her, the beeps echoing around the room, the cuff of the blood-pressure machine pumping itself up every now and then, and I spoke to her, telling her she was brave. She was strong. She could make it. She'd get through this.

And then the steady beeping changed rapidly, going into overdrive. Numbers on the machine started dropping. An alarm sounded. Nurses ran into the room.

I stepped out into the corridor to let them work on her as she was surrounded by a hive of activity. Two doctors rushed in. A defibrillator arrived. Someone shouted *clear!*

I watched them work on her from the doorway, a huddle of bodies trying so desperately to save her life, my anxiety levels growing every second, hoping she'd make it. This victim was the only person left alive who could've told us what happened. She was still young. Still had a life ahead of her, even though it would be filled with memories of God only knew what. But she could survive it, if she was given the chance.

Except she couldn't.

The frenzy of activity stopped. A horrible stillness filled the air. The doctor called time of death.

It was all over.

HAYAT

Chapter 11

We walk side by side through the busy, dusty paths that wind their way through the huge refugee camp. She takes photos as we go. We pass a big storage depot made from corrugated metal. There are metal gates at the front, but we can see through the bars as we stop outside.

'This is where you get your equipment when you arrive. You must register first. Give your name and date of birth and some other details. You are given some pieces of paper. Cards that you must show in exchange for personal items and food, bedding, blankets. We get cooking items, pots, small gas stoves, storage bottles to collect water with, that kind of thing. If you are alone, you live in one of the same-sex Portakabins. Families get tents.'

We walk past a shower and toilet block and water pumps that the tankers supply every day.

I point through the wire fencing to the distance. 'Syria is seven miles that way. We are so close, but a universe away.'

She snaps off more photos. Then I walk with her towards a horde of people, queuing, jostling. There are so many that you cannot see beyond the swarm.

I point at them. 'Every day you must queue and show your food card. They give you one piece of bread, some rice, a few vegetables. The basics.'

'And is it enough? Do you go hungry?'

'It is not enough to be healthy. But there is a market here. We have ten dollars per month to buy extra things.'

'A market?' she asks, surprised.

'Not really like the market we knew before. It is this way.' We walk past lines of tents. Some families sit outside, cross-legged on the ground. A woman rocks a swaddled baby. They all watch us as we go by. Some of them are cooking big pots of rice or vegetables on top of portable gas stoves. Women hang washing on lines strung up between tents. Children play in the dusty ground, running in their tattered clothes, kicking a football around. And I see myself then, aged eleven, out in the street near home with my friends, playing. Carefree. Happy. Loved. Something squeezes my throat, a hard lump that stops me breathing.

She takes more photos as we walk.

'They are trying a new system now,' I say. 'I hear that you can get some identification. I spoke to the man. His name is Mr Neal. He is making this computer program and it takes your photograph and fingerprints and DNA and eye . . . photograph. Then you can prove who you are. You can buy things at the market. One day in the future it means you can travel with no papers because it is all on computer.'

'Yes. I've spoken to him about it. He's very excited about how it could help refugees.'

'I tried to get on the beta testing but he says he already has enough people.' I blink back more tears. 'I thought it would help me get out of here.'

'I'm sorry.' She glances over at me, and I can tell she really is sorry.

We come to the market. Rows and rows of little shacks selling wares.

She takes a lot of photos as we wander past them.

'There are about three thousand stalls,' I tell her. 'You can buy anything from food to second-hand clothes, furniture. There is even a barber and wedding-dress stall.'

'I've never seen such a thriving street market in a refugee camp before,' she says.

'This is informal business. It is not legally allowed but the camp tolerates it. The refugees partner with Jordanians who bring things to sell. Syrians are very resourceful people. Some of them make things to earn a living as well.'

'An opportunity out of crisis,' she says.

I raise my eyebrows. 'For *some*. This place is as big as a city so it is the same as any other city. There is black market here, too. There are gangs – many thugs who control the market from the inside. Rob people in their tents, they . . .'

'What?'

I look at her. 'My friend was raped by one gang leader.'

Her eyes are wide, full of anguish and sympathy. 'Did she report it? What happened?'

I snort. Laughter that is not laughter because I do not know how it feels to laugh any more. 'Why do you think anyone cares? And even if they did, how do they stop it?'

I think I hear her swear under her breath, but I am not sure.

DETECTIVE BECKY HARRIS
Chapter 12

The queue in Costa moved slowly. Becky had missed breakfast due to the early call-out and her stomach was protesting loudly. She was a grazer and needed to snack every couple of hours. She was deciding whether to get a mince pie or a mini Christmas cake or both when a text came through. She opened the message from DI Thornton.

Thornton: Get a hot chocolate too while you're at Costa. Special guest just arrived for the briefing.

Becky: Special guest? Who is it? Tom Hardy?

No answer. Thornton wasn't the same as Warren Carter, who she'd always had a great laugh with. You needed to in this job or you'd go mad. Thornton had had a sense of humour bypass. Probably at birth.

The queue shuffled along. Why couldn't he just tell her instead of being so secretive?

Eventually, Becky pushed her way into the office laden with drinks. She'd eaten two cakes on the way back.

'Morning all,' she said to DC Ronnie Pickering and DC Colin Etheridge who were at their desks. Colin had been seconded to their office from Letchworth CID after Warren Carter's retirement and her promotion to even up the numbers of their dwindling staff. There was also another man perched on the edge of Colin's desk, chatting with him.

'Did they have peppermint?' Ronnie asked like an eager child anticipating a Christmas present. Thornton would probably describe Ronnie as 'on the spectrum', but Ronnie's quirks just meant his strengths lay in areas that the rest of the team didn't have. His Rain Man-like obsession with numbers meant he could go through financial and telephone accounts, finding paper trails and links to crimes that would take everyone else weeks.

'Peppermint, as requested.' She lifted the paper cup from its carrier and deposited it on his desk then gave Colin his Americano.

Although Colin had only been on their team for a couple of months, Becky liked him already. He was HOLMES-trained and eager to learn all he could without moaning about the boring bits that made up a lot of detective work.

'Thanks, sarge,' Colin said. 'This is DC Jamal Faris. He's been seconded to this investigation.'

'Oh. Right. Seconded from where?' Becky asked as she did a quick appraisal of Faris. Olive skin, swarthy, shirt covered with crumbs and straining at the stomach area, scruffy hair.

Jamal stood up and adjusted his wonky tie. 'Morning, sarge. I'm from Letchworth CID, too. Colin and I were involved in the investigation into the Wilson murders so we've been brought onto this one because of our prior knowledge and the similarities between them.'

'We?' She tilted her head.

'DCI Munroe. She's in there.' Jamal pointed to the glass wall of Thornton's office where a woman with long dark hair sat in Thornton's chair behind his desk, while Thornton sat in the spot normally reserved for his subordinates.

'Oh, great.' Becky had never met Munroe, but she knew her by reputation. In fact, Becky had kind of a fangirl crush on her. Munroe had been the youngest DCI on the force. Not only was that a huge achievement, but for a woman to have done it first inspired Becky no end. She had a reputation for being a ball-breaker, which Becky dismissed as the usual sexist, jealous bollocks. Despite it being the twentieth century, some people still couldn't handle a woman getting on in the job. If she was a man they wouldn't go round calling her that. One day Becky would be where Munroe was sitting. At least, that was her long-term goal, the ambition Becky had nurtured ever since she'd joined as a probationary patrol officer. She'd dealt with all the years of crap jobs and she finally felt like she was getting somewhere. Becky looked forward to learning a lot from Munroe.

'Is the hot chocolate for you?' she asked Jamal.

'No. For the DCI.'

She dumped her own coffee on her desk and entered Thornton's office.

Thornton was talking about the highly publicised case he and Becky had just been involved in, bigging up his own role in solving it and conveniently forgetting that if it hadn't been for her, the case would still be unsolved. DCI Munroe listened with a smile that Thornton probably mistook for patient indulgence, but Becky thought looked more like she was bored out of her brains.

'Coffee delivery!' Becky smiled at them.

'Thanks.' Thornton took his usual latte. 'Hot chocolate for DCI Munroe.'

'Ma'am.' Becky held out the tray for Munroe to take her drink and noticed she looked relieved by the interruption.

'This is DS Becky Harris.' Thornton swung an arm in Becky's direction by way of introduction.

'I know. I saw you in the *Police Gazette*,' Munroe said in an upper-class accent. 'Congratulations on the Palmer case and your commendation.' She smiled at Becky with genuine warmth and pride. A smile from one high-ranking female officer to an aspiring one. A smile that showed Becky she knew how hard it was to get anywhere in what was still a male-orientated profession.

'Thanks, ma'am. I'm really happy to have you on board with this case. I think—'

'Yes, well, as I was just saying,' Thornton interrupted. '*We* were instrumental in solving the Palmer case. You should've seen it when we went to . . .' Thornton droned on again. Unfortunately, he'd never get bored of his own voice, but luckily Munroe stood up and cut him off by saying, 'Everyone's here so let's start the briefing,' and pointing through the window to the CID office.

By the time Becky was back at her desk, Thornton and Munroe stood at the head of the room.

'Right.' Thornton clapped his hands together. 'The big news is that DCI Munroe will be seconded to investigate this case as SIO because of her previous work on the similar murders of Jim and Donna Wilson last year. And *I* will be seconded to her unit in Letchworth as Temporary DCI.' He grinned at everyone.

Becky secretly thought that the big news was a double murder they had to investigate, not Thornton's obvious glee at the promotion slot he'd been waiting for. Full of his own self-importance, as usual. She watched Munroe looking at Thornton and thought the DCI was trying really hard not to roll her eyes. Becky's gaze drifted back to Thornton as he went on to explain to the team the double-murder scene at the Lanes' house.

DCI Munroe cut Thornton off after he'd taken the floor for long enough. 'As Colin and Jamal already know, this is identical to a murder we worked on in the village of Willian last year. Donna and Jim Wilson were killed in their kitchen. Both stabbed multiple times, resulting in superficial wounds on their arms and legs. The same words were written on the wall in black marker pen. They were strangled using some kind of ligature that was narrow and smooth, most likely electrical wire. We believe the killer entered the back door of the property, which they were in the habit of leaving unlocked when they were in the house. We believe he surprised Jim and hit him on the head with a blunt instrument, which incapacitated him enough so he was unable to fight back while the killer secured him to a chair in the kitchen. We believe Donna Wilson was upstairs at that time washing her hair and didn't hear anything at first. We think the killer secured her to a chair next to her husband, forcing her to comply at knifepoint. No useful forensics were found at that scene. Following an intensive investigation, there were no viable suspects, and the case has remained unsolved. The words on the wall were never released to the press.' She paused to take a sip of hot chocolate. 'This new murder scene is identical. No defensive wounds were found on either of the victims, therefore I believe Neal Lane was incapacitated, most likely as he entered the kitchen to refill the wine, because a full bottle and corkscrew were found on the worktop near to where a few small blood speckles were discovered, which must've come from his head injury. He was then tied to the chair. The female victim maybe heard something and entered the kitchen or the offender entered the lounge where she had been drinking. She probably would've been threatened at knifepoint to comply.' She paused and looked around the team, letting that sink in.

Ronnie stuck his hand in the air to ask a question, another little foible of his. If Munroe thought it was odd that a twenty-eight-year-old man looked like a kid trying to get his teacher's attention, she didn't make it obvious.

'Yes, DC Pickering.' Munroe nodded at him.

'So, we've got a serial killer?' Ronnie had awe written all over his face.

'I think so, yes,' Munroe said.

'So the wife, Gillian, isn't a suspect?' Ronnie asked.

'Let's hear from DS Harris,' Munroe said. 'You've spoken to her and some witnesses.'

'Thank you, ma'am.' Becky flicked through a few pages in her notebook and briefed the team on what the witnesses had seen. 'Gillian had arrived home earlier than expected after a business trip and obviously disturbed the killer. She was in the house for a few minutes only so there wouldn't have been enough time for her to carry out the attacks, and my gut tells me she's not involved. I think she's genuinely distraught. But, of course, we can't rule out the possibility that Gillian could be a jealous wife who knew her husband was having an affair and arranged for them to be killed.'

'I think the similarities between the two cases are too stark to ignore, but I still want it checked out that Gillian was on that flight,' Munroe said. 'Colin, can you oblige?'

'Yes, ma'am.'

She gave him a brief nod then turned back to Becky. 'You said she arrived unexpectedly. The husband wasn't aware of her arrival?'

'No. She wanted to surprise him.'

'But she ended up with the worst surprise of her life,' Colin said.

'The victim looked very similar to the wife,' Becky added. 'It's possible the killer mistook her for Gillian Lane, which meant he could've been watching them. Although the neighbours I spoke to hadn't seen anyone suspicious hanging around the property recently.'

'So who is this woman?' Munroe said, taking another sip of hot chocolate and placing the cup on the edge of Colin's desk. 'We found no ID for her and no handbag belonging to her at the scene. Her fingerprints are currently being run. DNA will take a while. But we need to find that out as soon as possible.'

'Gillian said she didn't recognise her. And none of the neighbours seemed to, either,' Becky said.

'OK, find out who she was,' Munroe said. 'Was Neal having an affair with her? I'm going to get uniforms from Letchworth to revisit the Wilsons' friends and family and see if they knew Neal Lane and this unknown victim.'

'Maybe the husband or boyfriend of the unknown woman put a hit on them,' Ronnie said.

'Die Piggy Die,' Munroe repeated the words and crossed her arms. 'Let's not get sidetracked on other lines of inquiry. No one knew about those words apart from the killer of Donna and Jim Wilson and the investigating team. The writing on the walls in both crime scenes is identical in every way. This is a serial killer, and for some reason he's killing couples.'

'I can just imagine the name the press are going to give this guy when they find out about this link,' Becky said.

'Yes, and when they do we're going to be under a tremendous amount of pressure not only to catch the bastard, but it will spark wide-scale panic and we'll be inundated with useless information that's only going to bog us down. Needless to say, those words stay in this room. I want to delay the press getting hold of this connection for as long as we can and creating bloody mayhem.'

'I asked Gillian if she or Neal had any kind of connection to pigs. She didn't have a clue what I was talking about.'

'You didn't actually tell her what was written on the wall, did you?' Thornton piped up.

'Of course not,' Becky said. 'Did Donna and Jim Wilson have any kind of connection to pigs?'

'No. We couldn't find anything that related to it at all,' Munroe said.

'I'd have thought that was obvious,' Jamal said. 'He's taking the "die" part literally.'

'Yes, but what about the piggy bit?' Ronnie asked. 'Maybe he's saying the victims are pigs, unworthy of living.'

'The killer's obviously a psychopath.' Thornton put his forefinger to his temple and wound it in a circle. 'Who knows what goes on in their heads?'

'It might be a she,' Becky said. 'And psychopaths still have a reason for doing something, even if it doesn't make sense to us.'

'The neighbouring witnesses believed the killer was male, and statistically it's more likely to be a male offender, so let's refer to the killer as a he for now,' Munroe said.

'Did you consider the possibility the words were a reference to us? The police?' Becky asked. 'We get called pigs a lot.'

Munroe grinned and pointed at Becky. 'Full marks for raising that angle. Of course, we considered that with the previous investigation. I think it is indeed a dig at us. He's taunting us. Telling us he can get away with it and calling us pigs in the meantime.'

Ronnie's hand shot in the air again. 'So are we going to be bringing in an offender profiler to help us? Those words, or their interpretation to the killer, might be really important in narrowing down suspects.'

'No. Our budget's just been slashed again so that's a non-starter.' Munroe paused for a beat. 'So. Was the killer watching the victims or do they have some link to the previous victims? How is our offender choosing them? We need to work on that. And I want the usual phone and financial records checked.'

Ronnie's hand shot in the air. 'I volunteer for that.'

'Good.' Munroe took a hurried sip of her drink. 'We've had some footage sent to us from the Road Policing Unit who were called out to the collision with Gillian Lane. It was a taxi that hit her and luckily for us, because of insurance reasons, it was fitted with a dashcam. Let me show you.' She retrieved her laptop from a leather bag in Thornton's office and placed it on a desk in front of them before starting the footage.

It showed Chancellors Road, where the cab was travelling down. No other vehicles coming in the other direction. All eyes watched a few seconds of empty road, street lamps whizzing by, and then, there, suddenly, Gillian ran out of the turning from Oak Drive, in front of the taxi, which had no time to stop and sent her flying up in the air.

Everyone collectively jumped at the point of impact.

'Ouch.' Ronnie grimaced.

'Quite,' Munroe said. 'Luckily the taxi driver was sticking to the thirty-mile-an-hour limit or it could've been much worse. He wasn't significantly injured. Just shaken and bruised from the air bag. What injuries did Gillian Lane sustain?' she asked Becky, who told the team.

'Can you play that again, ma'am?' Colin asked.

She replayed it, slowing down the footage. Just after Gillian appeared another figure was visible at the edge of the frame. She pressed pause and pointed to the shadowy person dressed all in black, wearing the balaclava Gillian had mentioned, with a black rucksack strapped onto his back.

'This is our killer but it's impossible to identify them. Height and build here also suggest this is a male,' Munroe said. 'I want CCTV checked in the surrounding areas. After the RTA, the taxi driver's car stopped and was blocking the main road, so the killer didn't get away from Oak Drive by car and must've been on foot, at least initially. The logical explanation is that after he chased Gillian and saw the accident, he came back down Oak Drive and slipped away into the woods to make his escape. Did he arrive on foot, too? Or was a vehicle stashed somewhere else? We've got a couple of uniforms extending house-to-house enquiries in the surrounding area.' She closed the laptop. 'Now, in the Wilson inquiry, Donna and Jim's house was in a similar location to this one – at the end of a small lane that led to some woods that provided easy access to cover his movements. Unfortunately, the surrounding area wasn't monitored by CCTV so we didn't manage to trace anyone of significance arriving or leaving the area around the time of their murders. We need to do better this time.'

'That's bugging me, ma'am,' Becky said. '*Why* did he chase her down the road? Why not just flee the scene into the woods straight away or get to his vehicle and drive away? He took a big risk of someone witnessing him and possibly tackling him.'

Thornton shrugged. 'Maybe he wanted to add another one to his list of kills.'

But that didn't cut it for Becky. Something about that wasn't right. 'Surely, when he was disturbed, his first thought would be to get away, not go after another victim.'

Munroe perched on the edge of a desk, looking at Becky with a thoughtful expression. 'Maybe he just panicked and went after her. Or, if Neal was having an affair with this woman and the killer mistook her for Gillian, he wanted to make sure he finished off the wife, too, which was most likely his intention in the beginning when he went to their house.'

'Perhaps he just didn't want to leave any witnesses,' Jamal said.

'But she couldn't ID him if he had a balaclava on anyway,' Becky said.

'That's something we'll put to him when we find him,' Munroe said. 'Killing couples is obviously his thing, and if he realised at that point that he'd made a mistake, that he hadn't got his intended target, maybe whatever urge or mental rationality that makes him do this wouldn't let her get away.'

'Do you think Gillian Lane is in danger?' Becky asked. 'If he went after her once, he might try again. Should we think about protective custody for her?'

Munroe thought about that for a moment. 'I don't think we can justify the expense of that. As you said, she couldn't identify him, which I'll make completely clear in the press conference in a couple of hours when I appeal for information. I can't see any reason why he'd try again now, not after he's fled the scene. If anything, it might make him pick another couple, so we have to find him before he strikes again. Now, I won't be divulging the link between the two cases publicly at this stage. It'll take a while for the hard copies of the case files from the Wilson murders to be sent over but, since Colin, Jamal, and I worked on them, if you have any particular questions in the meantime, then just ask one of us. Or you can access the computerised copies under this case number.' She read out a number that the team scribbled down.

'Is there anything particularly significant that we should know now from the previous case?' Becky asked, knowing there wouldn't be enough hours in the days to wade through the previous multitude of statements and forms when they needed to follow the trail for the most recent murders as a matter of urgency.

Munroe pursed her lips together. 'I think I've summarised the most important points for now.' That was her final word on the briefing. The jobs were divvied up and Munroe left the office.

DETECTIVE WARREN CARTER
Chapter 13

I strode towards my car in the hospital parking area, fists clenched, teeth grinding. I yanked open the door, got inside, slammed it. Hit the steering wheel a few times with the flat of my hand until it hurt. One more life lost at the hands of a brutal kidnapper who'd left them all to die.

My phone rang. I looked at DS Jack Evans's name flashing up on screen. I waited a few moments, trying to get it together.

'Jack, I was about to call you. The last victim just died.'

'Poor bloody woman.'

'Yeah.' I rubbed at my forehead. 'And most likely she was the only witness who might've been able to tell us who did that to them.'

'Well, I've got a quick update for you.'

'Go ahead.'

'So . . . first off, Melanie Dwyer's call to the fire brigade. She checks out. She's a retired teacher and there's absolutely nothing suspicious about her at all. She'd been to a friend's house, was driving down the lane in front of Brampton Hospital and spotted flames in the distance so she called it in. She didn't see anyone around the area and can't give us any more information. Also, Koray's had no luck so far with the

Hertfordshire Constabulary's misper database. A notice has been sent to all forces, and he's still working through the national database.'

And no doubt he'd be working on it for a long time, I thought. There were over 300,000 people reported missing to the police in the UK every year.

'We've found out that Brampton Hospital was sold nine months ago to a company called Odesa Investments. The Land Registry website only shows the company name with no address, and I can't find any trace of them being registered in the UK so it's got to be an offshore company. There are no hits for Odesa Investments that pop up on the internet. The utilities are also registered in the same company name.'

'Either an offshore company or some kind of front, then.' I sighed. That was all we needed. Even when a crime had been committed, getting information on offshore companies was often a nightmare. Depending on the jurisdiction and the manner in which it was set up, it could be virtually impossible to find out details of the beneficial owner.

'Most likely. Enquiries are still ongoing to trace a bank trail of exactly where the utility payments are coming from.'

'OK.'

'I spoke to William Johnson, director of the Harwey Trust, who were the previous owners of the hospital when it was a drug-rehab place. He told me that when he sold the property he dealt exclusively with someone called Powell Acton from Acton Associates, a company that specialises in corporate law and was purchasing it for a client. And the Harwey Trust didn't leave any equipment in the place when they left, so whatever was in there was brought afterwards. They did, however, install the key-card electronic locks on the doors.'

I thought about the incubator, cryogenic freezer, and needles, and wondered if those women were being subjected to some kind of bizarre medical experiments. I glanced at my watch. The first post-mortem would be going on right about now, and I didn't envy Caroline attending to watch. 'Right. Good work. I'll go and pay a visit to Mr Acton later.

See what he's got to say about his client. What about the warrant-card angle?'

'Five have been reported lost in the last year. They were all deactivated once they were reported. Out of that five, two were found and handed back shortly after the officers received new cards so we can rule those out.'

'Who are the three left?'

'DI John Beckett from the Dog Unit at Police Headquarters. PC Helen Davies, a patrol officer at St Albans. And DC Colin Etheridge who's—'

'I know where he is. He was seconded to my old CID unit from Letchworth CID after I retired. OK. I'll pay a visit to Colin and DI Beckett. I want you to visit PC Davies.'

'Sure thing.'

'Anything else for me?'

'Katrina's been looking for CCTV cameras in the immediate area but since the hospital is accessed by country lanes with no cameras, we probably won't get anything useful. She'll keep looking and contact private owners of houses in the nearest villages. Liz is on to the manufacturers of medical equipment. And there's some bad news from DC Potter. A woman was driving past Brampton Hospital and stopped to ask him questions about what was going on. Said she was a reporter for the local radio station, Heart Hertfordshire. He told her to get lost in the nicest possible terms and wouldn't answer any of her questions. He spoke to Chief Superintendent Barker about it and she's trying to get hold of someone from Heart right now to enforce a press blackout.'

'Bugger! That's all we need.'

I hung up and switched the radio on to Heart Hertfordshire. The news was just starting . . .

'Four fire crews were called out earlier this morning to a fire in a disused building located between the hamlets of Hall's Green and Warren's Green. Hertfordshire Constabulary were also at the scene.'

Shit! We were too late to stop it.

I turned up the volume.

'It has not been revealed how the fire started or how badly the building has been damaged. Our local reporter, Tina Coles, who lives nearby, was driving past the scene on the way to work and was the first to report the incident to Heart Hertfordshire. She had this to say . . .'

A soundbite followed. 'I couldn't see much from outside the property, but it was obvious there had been some major incident due to the amount of emergency vehicles on scene. So far the police and fire brigade aren't making any kind of statement.'

'Yeah, and we're not going to, either,' I muttered, cursing our bad luck that a reporter, of all people, happened to be driving by at the worst possible time. And although they hadn't named the hospital, nor found out what had been discovered inside, whoever had been keeping those women there would most likely know from the location given that it was Brampton Hospital. Which meant they wouldn't return to the scene because they'd know we'd found the victims inside. Our best chance of finding whoever had been responsible for regularly feeding those women had just vanished.

I let out a snarl of frustration as the news moved on to a report of a celebrity's new Brazilian bum lift, which a) wasn't bloody news, and b) was the most ridiculous thing I'd ever heard in my life. What the hell was a bum lift, for God's sake?

I flicked off the radio in disgust as I drove to Stevenage nick, trying to remember what Becky had told me about Colin Etheridge when we'd popped out for the one and only drink I'd had with her shortly after I'd retired. He'd been transferred to take over her DC role when she'd been promoted. He seemed reliable, eager to learn and to please. But was he involved in the kidnapping of six women? Only one way to find out.

I called Becky on the hands-free to see if she could give me any more background info on him.

'Uh-oh. That's twice in a few hours I've spoken to you when I haven't seen you for ages,' she said. 'Are you after my scintillating conversation or has someone put in a complaint about me?' Her voice was laced with amusement.

'Scintillating conversation aside, are you at the nick? I'm heading over there.'

'I'm just about to leave but I can hang around for a bit if it's urgent. Why?'

'I haven't got a new warrant card yet so I can't access the car park or building, and I want someone to sneak me in. Don't want to advertise the fact PSD is in the station and who I'm talking to. I'll be there in five.'

By the time I pulled up outside the electric gates Becky was already there, waiting just inside them. She released the gate entry system, and I found an empty spot and parked up.

'What's going on?' she asked as I got out.

I glanced around. I trusted her 100 per cent. She was as honest as they came. Damn good at her job. And she'd stuck her neck out for me on more than one occasion, especially when I'd been suspended and needed access to case information. I wanted to tell her, but I couldn't. 'You know I'd tell you if I could.'

'Fair enough.'

A couple of patrol officers headed our way. They glanced over, said hello, and walked towards a marked car. I waited until they were driving towards the gates before saying, 'What can you tell me about Colin Etheridge?'

Her eyebrows shot upwards. 'Colin?'

I nodded.

'Probably just what I told you that time before in the pub. Um . . . he seems to be conscientious. He's not a sleaze. He doesn't get pissed off with doing the routine crap stuff. Smells nice. What do you want to know?'

'There's no hint of anything dodgy about him?'

'You think he's bent?'

I held my hand up. 'I don't think anything yet. But a bit of background would be good.'

She studied my face for a moment. 'I've never seen anything that's made me suspicious of him, put it that way.'

'What's his personal situation?'

'Um . . . he's single. Lives in a two-bedroomed flat. He drinks Americanos. Oh, and he likes tartan socks.' She leaned in closer. 'Which is definitely dodgy.'

I snorted. 'OK, thanks. Did you know he'd lost a warrant card in November?'

'Yeah, he asked if I'd found it anywhere. Is that why you're here? To give him a bollocking for it?'

I did a mouth-zipping action and grinned.

'All right. Don't tell me, then.' She stuck her tongue out, glanced at her watch. 'I need to go. We've got a bloody serial killer on the loose.'

'What?' It was my turn for raised eyebrows.

'DCI Munroe and a DC are over from Letchworth. Their team was on the last investigation into a double murder of a couple. Looks like our killer is the same person.'

'Wait till the press get hold of that.'

We walked towards the rear doors of the building. 'Munroe, eh? You'll be in better hands than with DI Thornton.'

'Too right.' Becky swiped me in with her warrant card.

'Thanks, mate,' I said.

'No worries. Call if you need me for anything.' She paused. Smiled. 'It's really good to see you.'

She hurried off. I took the stairs two at a time and walked along the corridor towards the CID office where I'd worked for the last fifteen years.

I stood in the doorway, watching Ronnie bent over some paperwork, an orange marker pen in hand. Two other guys sat at their desks, one on the phone scribbling down notes, the other tapping on his keyboard.

'Morning,' I said.

The guy typing looked up. He was about the right age to be Colin. Blond hair bordering on ginger. Pale skin with plenty of freckles. The guy on the phone glanced briefly at me. Badly-fitting suit, olive skin, bad-hair day.

'Can I help?' the Typer asked.

'Warren!' Ronnie finally looked up.

I grinned back. I liked Ronnie. He was straight as a die. Sometimes too straight. Preferring to follow procedures to the letter and take the brass's opinions as gospel. But he was a good lad. And despite him being different, he had a quick brain and an amazing way with numbers.

'Good to see you, Ronnie.' I reached my hand out to shake his.

He stared down at it with a grimace. He didn't like shaking hands, but eventually he took it, shook, and I didn't take it personally when he tried to surreptitiously wipe his hand on his trousers afterwards. OCD at its finest. 'How are you, then?'

'Um . . . well, my dicky tummy is playing up again. But I think I've found out what the problem is. Sugar. If I eat too much it ferments in my—'

I held my hand up. 'You're not going to tell me about your irritable bowel again, are you? As much as I've missed you going on about it.' That was the other thing with Ronnie. For some reason he thought his colleagues loved hearing about his various intestinally challenged ailments.

Ronnie's permanently ruddy cheeks blushed even more.

I grinned fondly at him, then my gaze caught a glass of green gloopy stuff on the corner of his desk. 'I see the coffee machine's still spouting out crap.'

'Oh, that's not out of the coffee machine.'

'Bloody looks like it.'

'It's spirulina. Algae. Really good for your intestinal flora.'

'Sounds lovely.' I pulled a face at it. 'Anyway, unfortunately this isn't a social visit. I need to speak to DC Etheridge.' I turned to the two other guys in the room.

'That would be me.'

Ah, the Typer.

'I can help if you need something,' Ronnie said. I'd actually missed his eager-beaver routine.

'It's an official inquiry, Ronnie. Something only Colin can assist me with.'

'Official?' Ronnie asked. 'You're retired, though.'

'I'm back.'

'Are you coming back here?' Ronnie asked, eyebrows raised pleadingly. 'Please say you are.'

'Unfortunately not. New Acting DI in PSD.'

'Complaints?' Colin asked. The Professional Standards Department had changed their name many times over the years according to the new buzzword of the moment but would probably always be referred to by the majority as the Complaints. A frown pinched Colin's forehead. 'Has there been a complaint about me?'

Bad-hair Guy on the phone looked at me with narrow-eyed interest.

I didn't want to correct him by saying Anti-Corruption in front of an audience. 'I just need a quick chat.'

The office in the corner of the room was empty. I pointed towards it. 'Is that free for a while?'

'Yes. DCI Munroe's out,' Colin said. 'But don't you need to serve me with a regulation notice before you speak to me? And should I get a Federation Rep?'

'It's just a quick chat,' I reiterated, studying his body language – his cheeks flushing a brighter shade than Ronnie's had. Whether it was with worry or embarrassment, I couldn't tell yet. 'And I'm sure you don't want to do it out here.'

Colin stood up and walked towards the office. Bad-hair Guy, who must've been the other Letchworth DC, watched us carefully while pretending not to. Nosy lot, police officers. Nosiest buggers on the planet.

I closed the door behind us and sat down at what was usually the DI's desk but was now being taken over by DCI Munroe. I'd met her on a training course at headquarters years ago, back when we were both DCs. She'd been a graduate entry-level, and even then I could tell she was going to be fast-tracked up the promotion ladder, unlike naughty old me. All credit to her, she had a reputation for being a very good detective, even if they called her Ball-breaker behind her back, which was just sexist shite as far as I was concerned, and completely unoriginal to boot. She was ambitious, extremely professional, and ferociously tough. But then she'd had to be to get where she was. The pervasive sexism that used to be rife in the force had never completely been stamped out.

'Have a seat, Colin.' I nodded at the chair opposite.

Colin sat. 'So has there? Been a complaint, I mean?'

There was something in his expression. A flash of fear or anxiety. But it was gone almost as quickly as it arrived, and I wondered exactly what he had to be worried about.

'No.' I watched him carefully. 'This is about your warrant card.'

His eyes narrowed with confusion.

'On the fifteenth of November you reported your warrant card as lost.'

He blew out a breath. 'Oh! Yes. Look, sir, I know it can be a disciplinary matter, but it was just an accident. I wasn't negligent.'

'You're quite right. If it was due to negligence, it could well be grounds for a disciplinary, but I'm not interested in that.' I sat back in the chair. 'What were the circumstances surrounding the loss?'

'Well . . . I didn't notice it until I was leaving for work in the morning and I couldn't find it.'

'When was the last time you saw it?'

'The day before I reported it missing. Um . . .' He glanced upwards, thinking. 'I definitely had it that day because I let myself into the police bar here with it at about 6 p.m. I'd arranged to meet my CID team from Letchworth in there for a drink and a catch-up.'

'Right. So you swiped yourself into the bar area with your warrant card, then what?'

'I stayed until about ten and then went home. The next day, when I went to wear my suit jacket again, I patted the pocket to make sure my warrant card was inside before I left home, which is where I always keep it, and I discovered it had gone.'

'So are you saying it fell out of your pocket sometime between 6 p.m. and the time you got back home?'

'Yes. I have no idea how.'

'Were you wearing your jacket in the bar?'

'Yes. At first. But it was hot in there so I took it off. We were sitting in one of the booths. I slung it on the bench seat behind me while we were in there. It's possible it fell out then.'

'Did you speak to the bar staff to see if they'd found it?'

'Yes. The next morning. I spoke to Jen Summers, who was working in the bar. She also works in the canteen. She's PC Steve Summers's wife. It wasn't handed in and she didn't see it when she was closing up.'

'Who else was there that night?' I asked.

'Jamal. DC Jamal Faris.' He pointed through the glass to Bad-hair Guy, who was looking over with all the excitement of an office gossip. 'And DCI Munroe as well. DS Diane Flynn and DC Paul Hopton were supposed to be coming but they got a call-out at the last minute and couldn't make it in the end.'

'Did anyone else come in the bar that night?'

'Um . . . no, not that I remember. It was a quiet night.'

'Did you ask DC Faris or DCI Munroe if they'd found it?'

'Yes. I asked Jamal the next day, but he hadn't seen it. The DCI was off on annual leave for a few days, and I didn't want to bother her at home, so I asked when she got back. She hadn't spotted it, either.' He squirmed a little in his chair. 'But losing it was a genuine accident.'

'Did you all leave the bar at the same time?'

'I left first.'

'And then what? You picked up your jacket from the seat and went to your car?'

'Pretty much. I picked my jacket up and put it back on. I was parked in the car park here, and I got into my car. The next day I looked in my car but couldn't find it there, either.'

'So it could've fallen out in the car park or bar?'

'Most likely the bar. I can't see how it could've fallen out of my pocket while I was wearing it down to the car park. But it was never handed in. I checked with the front desk.'

I stood up. 'OK, we're done here.'

Colin shot up with a look of relief. 'So you're not going to discipline me?'

I studied him. My first impressions were that I couldn't see him as a cold-blooded kidnapper, but it was too early to tell anything yet. 'Not unless anything else comes to light. Can you send Jamal in, please?'

'Uh, yeah.' Colin edged out of the door.

I watched the brief exchange between Colin and Jamal before Jamal headed inside the office and shut the door after him.

'Morning, Jamal. I'm ADI Carter from PSD. Have a seat.'

Jamal sat. 'Colin just said you asked him about his missing warrant card.' He fiddled with his hair, patting down a tuft that stuck up.

'That's right. You didn't happen to see it on the seat in the booth you were all sitting at in the police bar on the fifteenth of November, did you?'

'No,' he said instantly, which I thought was strange, as if he'd had time to prepare the response.

'No one else who was there made a comment that they'd found it?'

'No.' He looked straight back at me and there was something in his expression I didn't like. Something cocky and arrogant.

I waited for him to say something else. He didn't. 'Do you remember who was the first to leave?'

This time he did think about it. 'Colin. Then I headed to the toilet and the DCI went up to the bar to get a bottle of water before she left.'

'And did you leave together?'

'No. She told me to go while she was still waiting for her drink.'

'Was there anyone else in the bar while you were there?'

He tilted his head for a moment, thinking. 'I don't think so.'

'Did you see Colin put his jacket on before he left the bar?'

He shrugged. 'I don't remember.'

'OK, that's all. Thanks.'

He stood up slowly and sauntered out of the office.

I followed him and asked Ronnie to ring DCI Munroe and see if she was free for a quick word.

DCI Munroe swept into the office about ten minutes later, oozing an air of professionalism, dressed in a tailored, expensive-looking trouser suit, white blouse, and heels.

'Warren Carter.' She treated me to a warm smile as she held out her hand. 'Haven't seen you for a long time.'

I stood and shook it, returning the smile. 'Ma'am. How are you?'

'Busy.' She looked me up and down briefly. 'I thought you'd retired.'

'So did I. But as of today I'm Acting DI in PSD.'

I thought I saw something in her eyes, a flicker of animosity, which wasn't that uncommon. A lot of officers hated PSD. I'd done my fair share of moaning about them when I'd been suspended previously. Coppers investigating coppers didn't go down too well.

'Right. Well, I don't have a lot of time so what can I do for you?' She glanced at her watch. 'I've got a press conference in ten minutes to appeal for witnesses on our double murder. Maybe you should schedule an appointment.'

'I'll be quick.'

She glanced pointedly at her watch again. 'I can give you five minutes.' She looked at the DI's chair I'd been sitting in, a clear hint that she wanted to sit there.

I walked around to the opposite side of the desk, while she sat and casually crossed one leg over the other and waited for me to tell her why I was there.

I jumped right in. 'On the fifteenth of November you went for a drink in the bar here with some members of your CID team.'

'Yes, that's right. We weren't on duty and we all paid for the drinks so there's absolutely no question of any of us being bribed with a gin and tonic by the bar staff.'

'I'm not suggesting that at all.' I smiled even though she didn't. 'But did you happen to see Colin's warrant card lying around after he'd left?'

'No. If I had I would've picked it up and given it back to him, wouldn't I?' She blew out an impatient breath, glancing at her watch again.

'Did you notice anyone else in the bar that night?'

She shrugged. 'I don't remember. Is there a suggestion of negligence here?'

'No.'

'No. Exactly. So there's no reason to discipline him, is there? Surely this is just a waste of an Acting Detective Inspector's time.' She stood up, put her hands on the desk and leaned over towards me. 'And I'm far too busy trying to catch paedos and rapists and murderers to sit around and chat about lost warrant cards. Or have you forgotten what that's like already?' Defensive now. And I was betting it was a sentiment PSD officers had heard hundreds of times before.

I stood up, too. 'OK, thanks for your time. I'll leave you to it.'

I asked Ronnie if I could borrow his warrant card for a few minutes to gain access to the bar. He handed it over and I slipped out of the office, feeling Munroe's eyes on me through the glass wall.

I headed up the stairs towards the police bar at the top of the building near to the canteen. It only served drinks in the evenings and was only accessible to members of the public for special functions. When I was stationed here, I'd been there many times for a cheap after-work drink to unwind with colleagues or for parties. I swiped myself inside using Ronnie's card and had a look around the booths, under chairs, and behind the bar to see if, by some miracle, Colin's warrant card was still lying around somewhere. It wasn't, so I went to the canteen and spotted Jen Summers. She was dishing up beans on toast for a uniformed patrol officer who I had a quick chat with. When she'd handed him the plate she turned to me.

'Blimey, I thought you'd retired.' She smiled.

'I'm back.' I returned the smile.

'Do you want the usual poached egg on toast?'

'No, thanks. I actually need a quick word with you.'

'With me?' She raised her eyebrows.

I nodded and pointed towards the corner of the room.

'Oh, OK.' She called out to her colleague in the kitchen, letting her know what was happening and that she'd be back in a moment, then rounded the counter.

I sat opposite her at a table for four and said, 'On the fifteenth of November were you working in the bar here?'

'Um . . . what day was it?'

'A Thursday.'

'Then, yes. I would've been here. I do all the weeknights in the bar.'

'Do you know if anyone left any property there that night? A warrant card specifically.'

'No. One of the new detectives in CID asked me about it before, but the only thing left in there in the last couple of months was an umbrella and a packet of fags.'

'You're sure?'

'I clean the tables and booths after people leave. I also sweep and mop up after I close so I would've seen something if it was left behind. And if I'd found a warrant card I would've given it to the duty inspector or front desk to pass back on. It definitely wasn't left in there.'

'Do you remember if anyone else was in the bar that night?'

She scrunched up her face, thinking. 'Now you've got me. Um . . . I really can't remember. Sorry.'

I dropped Ronnie's card back off, then went to the station's front desk to check whether Colin's card had been logged in and forgotten about but it hadn't, so next up was a visit to DI John Beckett from the Dog Unit.

I found him in the canteen at Police Headquarters, stuffing down a bacon butty. I'd left home before I'd had the chance to have breakfast, and my stomach took this opportune moment to remind me of the fact with a loud grumble. But as I stood next to his table, looking at the gristly fat poking out the side of his roll, I decided to give it a miss. I asked him if he wanted a coffee, then went and joined the queue, passing a congealed lasagne with a crusty, dry edge and weird-coloured sauce that looked like wallpaper paste. Its accompanying wrinkled peas and chips seemed as if they'd been dunked in fat and left there solidifying for a week. While my stomach shrieked in fear at the far-from-fetching display, the only spot of good news was that they'd installed a proper coffee machine since the last time I'd been there. Now I had a choice of a latte, a cappuccino, a mochaccino, or an espresso. I chose a double espresso to wake me up and then joined the DI. I took one sip of coffee, swirled it around in my mouth and raised my eyebrows with surprise. It was pretty good. Much better than the crap in the coffee machines that should've been banned as a public-health hazard years ago.

'Yeah. The coffee's not bad now. Don't try the tea, though. Unless you want the roof of your mouth stripped off.' DI Beckett chuckled. 'Anyway, what can I do for PSD?' He shoved the last of his roll in his mouth and chewed quickly.

I looked him in the eye as he wiped his hands on a paper napkin. 'You reported your warrant card as lost on the sixth of July.'

He rolled his eyes at me, but it was with disbelief rather than annoyance. 'Don't tell me PSD haven't got better things to be doing than investigating lost warrants cards.'

'I need to ask you some questions about it.'

He leaned back, an equal mixture of suspicion and amusement showing on his face. 'Why?'

'I can't divulge that, I'm afraid.'

He quirked up an eyebrow. 'Because it's part of an ongoing investigation into something.'

I didn't say anything. I thought my poker face was pretty good.

'Is this about the restricted log earlier?' He meant the incident log. All emergency calls to us were added as an incident log on our computer systems. What happened at the scene, who attended, and all manner of actions were recorded on the log. But there were thousands of people in the force who had access to look at them. Something we didn't want when there was the possibility of police involvement, hence viewing it had now been restricted to a need-to-know basis. Although that was far from foolproof to stop people finding out. If you knew someone in the control room who'd dealt with the log, there was nothing stopping them from gossiping about it. The same was true about anyone who'd attended the scene.

I didn't confirm or deny it.

He glanced around the room, then back to me. 'OK.' He shrugged. 'It was Samson.'

'Excuse me?'

'Samson. My police dog.'

'Your dog ran off with your warrant card?'

'No. He *ate* it. Chewed it in half.'

An adult version of the dog ate my homework. 'It was recorded as being lost not eaten.'

He shrugged again as if he didn't have anything to hide. 'That's an admin error. I even handed the pieces back in when I reported it.'

That was easy to verify, and I could see no point in him lying about it. 'OK. Well, thanks for that.'

'That's it?'

I nodded.

He opened his mouth to ask me something, most likely trying to wheedle information about the log again, but thought better of it as he stood up and wandered off.

HAYAT

Chapter 14

'There is another way to get out of here,' I tell the reporter as we stand and drink sweet tea she bought from a man in the market. You cannot see the fencing surrounding the camp from this crowded street, but it is there, always, closing in.

'What do you mean?' She blows on her hot tea.

'I know some people who have gone.' I start walking again, away from the crowds. I do not want others to hear. 'There are brokers here. They arrange it. Another black market.'

She gives me a worried look. 'Are you talking about people-trafficking?'

I shrug. 'People-*smuggling*.'

'What do they have to pay the brokers to get them away from here?'

'They will have to sell a kidney to pay for the fare. There are ways out of the camp not through the gates. They cannot patrol the area, it is too big. And besides, security does not want to. No one really wants us here. They do not care if someone goes missing. And someone else can use their food card when they are gone.'

She stops, puts a hand on my shoulder. 'Have you seen this happening?'

'Yes. There are few gangs who arrange it. Or there is a new way I heard about recently. A . . .' I shake my head and carry on walking. 'They will go to England or Germany or another country. Anywhere is better than this prison. They will get a job. They can be happy again.'

'Or they could be killed on the way, dying in over-cramped vehicles, washed up on beaches. Dying from complications of surgery to remove organs. Or they could be trafficked into the sex industry and never be free. Or end up in other refugee camps in another country because the governments won't help. I went to Calais recently, in France. There are thousands of refugees clustered together in makeshift camps. It's very dangerous for them. They're not allowed to enter the country legally. It's not safe for you to even consider it.'

'Safe?' I spit out. 'I haven't been safe for years! And I may be living but I am not alive. I am a living dead girl here. I am just waiting to die so I can escape my life!' I pour my tea into the dusty ground, watching it turn a deep red colour. The colour of blood. Like a wound that never heals. I imagine my insides splitting open, spilling out, seeping into the earth.

'OK, let's say you do get to Britain safely. What then? Anyone can take advantage of you in terrible ways. Asylum seekers can't get a job. They must rely on government handouts – the same as here. Even if you apply for asylum the government might not grant it. You'll be stuck in a detention centre, sometimes for years. With the possibility of having your application denied and you being deported back to Syria.' She reaches out and holds my forearm. 'There are so many things against you. Have you really thought this through?'

Tears of anger and frustration well up in my eyes. 'I have thought of nothing else!'

'Hayat, there are various resettlement schemes you could take advantage of instead. The United Nations High Commission for Refugees might be able to help you. If you seek protection from them and they agree, they can resettle you to another state. That means you apply now, from Salama Camp. And if they approve your application you'd be given permanent residence status in the UK before you leave Jordan. If you did it that way, you'd have access to civil, political, economic, social, and cultural rights similar to those of British people. You'd also have the opportunity to become a naturalised citizen. Why don't you look into applying for that instead of taking such a risk?'

'*If! If!* How many people are doing the same thing? They can't grant this for all of them. So what if they refuse me? Then I have no hope. And how long would it take?'

She looks uncomfortable. I know what the answer must be. Years. And I cannot, I *cannot* stay here for that long.

I turn and run away from her. What does she know?

DETECTIVE BECKY HARRIS

Chapter 15

From: EmmaBolton@HertfordshireConstabulary.co.uk
To: SusanMunroe@HertfordshireConstabulary.co.uk
CC: BeckyHarris@HertfordshireConstabulary.co.uk

Subject: Update on Neal Lane and unknown female victim – Case 463475/18

There was no forensic evidence found on Gillian Lane's person or clothing that indicates she was in contact with either victim.

No mobile phones or computer equipment belonging to either victim were discovered at the scene. The only laptop and mobile phone recovered belonged to Gillian Lane and were found in her handbag. These have gone to Technical Services for analysis.

Fingerprints and DNA samples taken from the unknown female victim at 1 Oak Drive are still being searched through the national database.

Updates will follow as and when we receive further information from the lab.

Becky finished reading the email. Ever since the Bloodbath Farm case had been plunged into the headlines and Hertfordshire Constabulary had been crucified in the press because of police corruption, new measurements had been put in place where all forensic evidence had to be emailed to the SIO, plus at least one other member of the investigation team, to counteract any cover-up of evidence and show a paper trail.

She frowned, disappointed they were no closer to finding out who the woman was yet. But the thing standing out so far was that no phones or computer equipment from the victims had been found. According to Gillian Lane's information, her husband was experienced in technology, so Becky found it hard to believe he didn't own either item. And what about the unknown woman? These days everyone had a mobile phone. Becky was still pondering that as she arrived at the house of Neal's brother, Dean. It was a town house on a new estate about five miles from Neal and Gillian's house and had a tiny front garden that had been laid with shingle.

She knocked on the door and it was opened by someone who looked very much like Neal, which didn't exactly test her detective skills. For the second time that day she had the much-hated job of telling a relative their loved one had died a brutal death. 'Morning, Mr Lane. I'm Detective Harris. Can I come in, sir?'

'Why?' It wasn't aggressive. Just surprised.

'I'm afraid it's about your brother and sister-in-law.'

He took a faltering step back. The inbuilt knowledge that a police officer turning up out of the blue with a grave expression and asking to talk to them would never be good news. 'What's happened?'

'It's probably best if we go inside, sir.'

He carried on staring at her for a few seconds, forehead bunched up, eyes wide. Then said, 'Yes. Come through.'

She followed him up the stairs, past the open door to a bedroom on her right, and into a spacious lounge that ran the length of the house. He stood by a window that overlooked a box garden, the light behind him creating a halo effect around his head.

She took a deep breath and broke the news as gently as she could.

His hand flew to his mouth. 'What? No!' He carried on staring at her, denial in his eyes. 'No. He can't be.'

'I know this is a very difficult time, but I'm afraid I need to ask you some questions.'

'What happened?' He slumped onto the arm of a fabric sofa, turning pale.

'I can't go into specific details at this stage, I'm afraid.' Becky went on to tell him about Gillian fleeing the scene and being in hospital.

'Oh, my God!' He put his head in his hands. Then looked up, his hand once again pressed to his mouth in horror. 'Is Gillian . . . is she all right?'

'She suffered a broken arm and a sprained ankle. She's very bruised and battered, but she's alive. She was very lucky.'

He shook his head as if in a trance.

'She wanted me to tell you where she was so you can go and see her.'

'Of course. I must . . . I must go and see if . . .' He trailed off, staring into space as he tried to absorb the news.

'I do need to show you a photo of the female victim to see if you can identify her.' She pulled out her phone and showed him the same photo she'd shown Gillian. Handing it over, she said, 'Do you recognise her?'

He studied it for a moment, his features registering surprise. 'That's Hannah Ryan.' He glanced up at Becky, confused. 'I mean, I don't *know* her. But I know who she is. I've seen some articles she's written.'

Becky scribbled down her name in her notebook. 'She's a journalist?'

'Yes. Neal told me they'd met in Jordan. At the Salama Camp, where he was managing a project. She went out there to do a story about the camp and the refugees.'

'And did he say anything else?'

'Like what?'

'Well, were they friends? Or was there more to it than that?'

His eyes widened. 'Are you asking if he was having an affair?'

'Was he?'

His eyes widened a fraction more. 'No! Definitely not. He wouldn't do that. He's been married to Gill for twenty-five years. They've had their ups and downs, of course. But they got through their daughter's death and that brought them closer together. They're a loving couple. I can't imagine him doing anything like that. Definitely not. He *loved* Gill. He only mentioned Hannah's name in passing.'

'So, he didn't tell you he'd seen Hannah outside of the Salama Camp?'

He took a steadying breath, thinking. 'No, he just said he'd met her in Jordan and she'd been interested in learning more about his project and how it could help the refugees. He didn't say he was in regular contact with her or anything like that.'

So why hadn't Neal told Gillian about Hannah, Becky wondered. 'Gillian said Neal was a project manager for World Food Corps.'

'That's right. He was working on some kind of biometric ID system. The technicalities went over my head, but Neal was an expert in that stuff. He's worked for many companies as a freelance project manager.'

Becky scribbled that down. 'When the project was pulled and Neal came back home, did you notice anything strange about his behaviour? Gillian thought he'd been acting odd.'

'Yes. He seemed a bit depressed, to be honest. Gill and I thought he had PTSD. From what he'd seen out there in the camp. I know Gill was trying to get him to speak to someone about it, but he refused.'

'Did he mention if anyone was hanging around or following him?'

'No.'

'Do you know if he'd received any threats or had any altercations with anyone?'

He shook his head slowly. 'He never said anything like that.'

'Did he know a couple called Donna and Jim Wilson?'

He pursed his lips together. 'Um . . . no, I don't think so. We're pretty close so I know all his friends. He certainly hasn't mentioned those names to me, but of course he might've worked with them.'

Which Becky doubted. Donna Wilson had been a lollipop lady and Jim a bus driver. Absolutely nothing to do with technical computer projects.

'Do you have a wife or partner who might know anything that might help?'

Dean shook his head. 'I'm divorced. Two years now.'

'Well, thank you for your time, and again, I'm sorry to be the bearer of such bad news.'

Neal's face was a blank mask of shock as he showed her out.

She dialled Ronnie's number as she walked to her car. 'I know who the female victim is. Hannah Ryan. She's a journalist.'

'Oh, that's spooky. I just this minute did a database check on her vehicle for one of the uniforms doing house-to-house. They spotted her white Volvo parked in Boswell Gardens, which is the next street along Chancellor's Road, and thought it might be of interest.'

'Right. So it's possible she parked in the next street, out of the way, to avoid the neighbours hearing or seeing a car arriving at Neal Lane's house while his wife was away.'

'They *must've* been having an affair,' Ronnie said. 'That's what DCI Munroe thinks, and I agree with her. Why try to hide her vehicle otherwise?'

'Maybe. Can you do a check on Hannah Ryan's address?'

'Already done. It's an apartment in Bromley. Voters' register shows she's the only one listed there.'

'Great stuff, Ronnie,' she said after she'd scribbled it down. 'Can you try and trace any next of kin, please?'

'Okey-doke. Just a quick update for you while you're on the line. Jamal has been doing phone enquiries with the list of friends Gillian gave us and cross-checking any connection to the Wilsons. So far, nothing useful. None of them had seen the Lanes for a few months and they never heard Gillian or Neal mention Donna or Jim Wilson. Also, Gillian Lane *was* on that flight. And Colin's searching for any CCTV footage around the area to see if we can spot the offender.'

'Right. We should check Gillian's customers from her furniture website, too. See if anyone who purchased something from her had anything to do with the Wilsons.'

'All right. Also, I've only just got the phone records from both Gillian and Neal Lane but I'll put in another request for Hannah Ryan's now. Oh, and the DCI has just finished a press conference and she's going to the morgue for the post-mortems.'

'OK. Let her know about Hannah Ryan. I'm going to head to Hannah's house now. Might take me a while to get there.'

'Approximately one hour and nineteen minutes.'

'Huh?'

'Well, calculating the distance, and allowing for an average speed, and depending on traffic, of course. I just worked it out in my head.'

'This is why I love you, Ronnie.'

He made a noise on the other end of the line that sounded like a shriek of surprise. 'I . . . um . . . like you too, but . . . well, you're married.'

She chuckled fondly. Ronnie took things very literally. 'Not like that!'

'Yes, I . . . um, knew that.'

She laughed again and hung up then googled the journalist's name. Hannah Ryan's website was the first hit, followed by a number of articles she'd written.

Becky clicked on the website. A photo of Hannah came up. A head shot of her in black and white. It was the same woman she'd seen at Neal Lane's house and was now lying in the morgue, waiting to be sliced open. Becky scrolled down the home page, reading. Hannah was a freelance investigative journalist who'd tackled some high-profile social and geopolitical issues. Her CV was long and colourful, and she'd won many awards. On one page were links to some recent articles and exposés. There was nothing about the refugee camp in Jordan. Becky tapped her phone against her lips. Was Hannah at the Lanes' house gathering information from Neal about refugees? Or was Neal sleeping with her? And if this was the work of a serial killer, did it really matter either way? The most important thing, Becky thought, was to find out how the killer had chosen and met their victims. Find that out and they might just find the killer.

She went through the crime scene in her head. No handbag had been found so far belonging to Hannah Ryan, but she'd met very few women who didn't carry a bag or purse. So where was it? Had the killer taken it as some kind of souvenir? And if so, had he also taken their mobile phones and a laptop belonging to Neal?

She called Emma Bolton, the senior SOCO on scene, to ask how things were going.

'Slowly. Did you get the email update?'

'Yes, thanks for that. We've just found out who the victim is. Hannah Ryan. Her vehicle's parked up in the next street, Boswell Gardens. A white Volvo. Can you do a check on her car while you're there?'

'Yes. Sure.'

'When I had a look around earlier I found Neal Lane's wallet on the coffee table but no handbag belonging to Hannah Ryan. Can you see if it's in the car? Or if you can find any car keys for her Volvo anywhere? Also, the email you sent said there were no mobile phones or computer equipment found belonging to either of them, so I think the killer might've taken them.'

'Will do. I've been working in the bedroom but Scott's processing downstairs so I'll nip down and ask him if there are any keys. There's definitely no handbag for Hannah Ryan here. I'll call you back in a minute.'

Becky delved in her handbag, found a half-eaten packet of cola bottles at the bottom and munched while she waited, picturing the rucksack the killer had been wearing on the dashcam footage. He could easily have stashed Neal's laptop and the phones in them. He could—

Her mobile interrupted her thoughts. It was Ian. She thought about not answering but didn't really want to fan the flames any more.

'What time are you going to be back tonight?' he asked, his voice like a taut elastic band.

'Um . . . actually, I'm going to be late back tonight.' She winced, waiting for the angry backlash.

There was a pause. Becky could almost feel his anger oozing through the line as she bit her lip. She rubbed at her forehead, really not in the mood for another sodding row.

'I don't know why you even bother coming home at all,' he snapped.

'Look, I'm sorry. We've got a double murder to deal with. It's—' Her phone beeped in her ear, letting her know someone else was ringing. 'Oh, bugger. Sorry. I've got to go, another call's coming in.'

'When are you going to put *us* before your fucking job?'

'I—' But she stopped when she realised he'd hung up. Maybe it was for the best. Because what could she say? It was times like this she didn't even know if she loved him any more. She connected to the call, which was from Emma. 'Hi,' Becky said wearily, leaning back against the headrest.

'The only car keys we can find are for a Volkswagen Polo on the drive registered to Gillian Lane. Plus what looks like a spare set for the Mini registered to Neal.'

'Right. Thanks,' she said, sure that Hannah Ryan's handbag and her Volvo keys had been taken, too. Hannah's car didn't drive there by itself.

'There's something else you might want to know. We're still collecting evidence, but we've found some distinctive glove prints at the house. On the outer handle of the rear kitchen door that led from the garden and on the chair Neal Lane was tied to.'

Becky sat upright. 'Will you be able to match the print to something?'

'I think so, if you can find the gloves. Leather gloves have a tendency to wrinkle or crack over time and can pick up grease or grime and then deposit them as a latent print on surfaces. I'll be sending an email update out as soon as I get a sec.'

'Great, thanks for that.' Becky hung up.

As she drove towards Hannah's address she called Jamal. DCI Munroe had said there were no useful forensics found at the previous Wilsons' murder scene, but she wanted to double-check.

'No,' Jamal said. 'We never found any glove prints at the Wilsons' house. In fact, there was a distinct lack of forensics to help us.'

'Was anything missing from the Wilsons' house?'

'Um . . . Yes. Jim Wilson's wallet was missing.'

'Really?'

'We don't know how much cash he had in it. It's likely his Barclaycard was inside as that was never recovered but it was never used after their murder.'

'Anything else taken? Car keys? Handbag? Mobiles? Laptop or other computer equipment?'

'No. Both Jim's and Donna's laptops and mobiles were found at the scene. Donna's handbag was found in situ, too, with cash and cards in it. Nothing else appeared to have been taken apart from Jim's wallet.'

She thanked him and hung up, thinking about everything as she drove to Hannah's house. Why had the killer been sloppier this time? Leaving glove prints where he hadn't before? Taking more items belonging to the victims with him? Were they trophies? And if the offender had taken the Volvo keys, why didn't he take the actual Volvo? Was it because he couldn't find it due to it being parked in the next street? Why had he taken Jim Wilson's wallet but not Neal Lane's, which had been in plain sight? She wondered why DCI Munroe had failed to mention a missing wallet from the Wilsons' murder scene when it was very pertinent information. Maybe she'd forgotten after all this time, but Becky doubted it. Munroe hadn't got to where she was today without being thorough.

DETECTIVE WARREN CARTER
Chapter 16

I stifled a yawn as I got back to the PSD office and helped myself to a mug of filter coffee that, according to the packet, was Premium Jamaican Blue Mountain Coffee. Very nice it was, too. There was even a box of fresh pastries to ease the hunger pangs I'd been trying to ignore. I took a big bite of a cinnamon swirl, my stomach doing an appreciative gurgle. At this rate there would be nothing to complain about any more, which was unheard of in the police force. I felt like I'd died and gone to police-officer heaven.

I swallowed everything down as quickly as I could without burning my mouth or choking, then told my team to meet me in the briefing room in five.

'I've got your new warrant card.' Jack handed me a brown envelope.

I almost felt important then. The force could move exceptionally fast when it wanted to. On the flip side, it was bogged down in paperwork and regulations and hitting target numbers and meetings about bugger-all. Just before I'd retired I'd had to fill in a form in triplicate just to get a bloody light bulb in the office changed.

I tipped the contents of the envelope onto the empty desk next to him that I would commandeer, pulled out the card, a wallet-style holder, a lanyard holder, and a clip holder designed to be attached to clothing. I slid the warrant card into the wallet and put it in my pocket before heading into the briefing room.

I stared for a moment at the whiteboards that had been filled with photos of the six victims, along with a satellite map of Brampton Hospital and scribbled notes of salient points. Under the first woman's photo was written what we assumed was her name, *Hayat*, and underlined. I felt the familiar rage return. So intense my hands shook. Tears pricked at my eyes. 'Who are you?' I whispered. 'How did you get there? Who did this to you?'

I took a deep breath, clenched and unclenched my fists, dragged my gaze away and turned to Koray, Jack, Katrina, and Liz filing in and sitting down. 'I know you're up to your necks so I'll keep this brief.' I told them what I'd discovered about the lost warrant cards. 'Jack, did you manage to speak to the other officer?'

'Yes. First off, Technical Services say there's no useable data info on the fire-damaged warrant card. I spoke to PC Helen Davies like you asked me to. She lost hers on a course at Police Headquarters in February. The last time she remembers using it was to gain entrance into the canteen.'

I relayed the story Colin had told me about his card, and DI Beckett's hungry dog. 'Doesn't take us any further forward then,' I said. 'Those cards have been lost in environments where there are hundreds of other police officers or civilian staff around. Anyone could've got hold of them. Let's put that on the back burner for now.'

'OK.' Jack nodded. 'DC Potter, who's still on the gates at Brampton Hospital, just called in. He spotted a car slowing down along the lane outside, but unfortunately one of the fire engines was leaving at the time and blocked his view. By the time he could get a good look the vehicle had sped off. All he can say is it was some kind of dark grey sports car.'

'Bugger. If it was someone involved, then they won't come back now they've seen the police presence, and if it wasn't anyone important then by now whoever is involved has probably already heard about it on the news so they're not likely to return. OK, we'll leave him in place until 5 p.m., but if no one's come back by then I don't think they're going to. Katrina, any luck with CCTV?'

'No, guv. There's no council-run CCTV anywhere in the surrounding area that's going to help us. No houses in the nearest village with private CCTV. Plus, there are numerous country lanes that they could take to get to Brampton Hospital that have no cameras.'

'I've been trying to look at medical equipment suppliers,' Liz said. 'But there are thousands of companies who supply that type of equipment all over the world. Without a make or serial number we're not going to get anywhere. And they could, of course, have visited a supplier and paid in cash.'

'OK.' I sighed and looked at Koray. 'Anything from mispers yet?'

'No local missing persons with our criteria. Still no trace on the national database for our girls,' Koray said. 'And definitely no one with the name Hayat. I'm still checking, though.'

'Six girls and none of them so far reported missing.' My gaze drifted back to the photographs on the board. 'A Middle Eastern or Turkish connection. I'm thinking these girls might've been trafficked from somewhere else.'

'Which means we might never find out who they are,' Koray said.

My phone pinged with an email alert then:

From: AmyTolley@HertfordshireConstabulary.co.uk
To: CarolineBarker@HertfordshireConstabulary.co.uk
CC: WarrenCarter@HertfordshireConstabulary.co.uk

Subject: Update on unknown female victims – Case 463481 /18

Six sets of fingerprints taken from the female deceased victims at Brampton Hospital have been run through the national database. Unfortunately, there are no matches.

DNA test samples taken from the victims are currently being run through the DNA database.

I read out the message to my team.

'Are you thinking sex slaves, boss?' Koray asked.

'I hope to God not. But then any scenario is bloody horrifying.' I felt the rage returning. 'And what was that medical equipment doing there when the Harwey Trust emptied the place before it was sold? We'll know more when Chief Superintendent Barker gets back from the PMs.' I paused. 'All right. I'm going to see the lawyer, Powell Acton. See what I can find out about the owner of the building, Odesa Investments. We'll reconvene for another briefing later.'

I left them to it, set up the satnav in my vehicle, and headed off to Marlow in Buckinghamshire, images of those poor women invading my head space. I'd dealt with trafficking several times in many different formats – organ-trafficking, sex-trafficking, child-trafficking. My ex-boss DI Ellie Nash had even gone on to set up a Wildlife Unit to combat the trafficking of endangered species. So I knew it was rife, and the situation was getting worse. People and animals were the new valuable commodity to rival guns and drugs because there were endless supplies of them – the gift that kept on giving. I wondered exactly where those girls had come from. Had they gone willingly, thinking they were starting a new life with employment and hope? Or had they been kidnapped or coerced? Only to end up dying a terrible death. And were one or more of our own involved in it? My blood had reached boiling point by the time I arrived.

I'd never been to Marlow before, but it was situated on the Thames, about thirty miles from central London. The offices of Acton Associates were a quaint converted Victorian house right on the riverbank. The receptionist was young and immaculately turned out in a grey skirt suit.

I introduced myself and asked to speak to Powell Acton. I knew I shouldn't make judgements about people, but coppers did every single day. Sometimes it was the only thing that saved your life in a dodgy situation. I had a preconceived idea of what kind of guy he was by looking around the reception area, and he didn't defy the pretentious stereotype. The man who sat behind the desk in the large office I was ushered into was early forties. He wore a suit that must've cost a packet. Not a hair out of place. Smooth complexion, as if he'd been at it with the Botox. Cufflinks. Shoes that had been buffed so shiny he probably had shares in Kiwi polish. Maybe he'd even had a bum lift.

He stood up and rounded his desk, a welcoming half-smile on his face, although the Botox might not have allowed a full version. He held out a soft, manicured hand for me to shake.

'How can I help you, Detective Constable?' He frowned questioningly, but there was a split second before he injected just the right amount of surprise that made me think he'd been waiting for me, or someone like me, to arrive.

I smiled back. 'Actually, it's Acting Detective Inspector.'

'Oh.' He raised his eyebrows. 'Well, what can I do for you?' He sat back down behind his mammoth desk that was neatly covered in files. He shut the lid of his laptop in case I had X-ray eyes and could see through the back of the screen. Leaning back in his chair, he interlaced his hands and gave me his full attention.

'I'm investigating a fire at a property I believe is owned by one of your clients – Odesa Investments.'

The frown crinkled a little further. 'That doesn't ring a bell.'

'Really? Well, apparently you acted for them when they purchased Brampton Hospital in Hertfordshire nine months ago.'

'Hmmm . . .' He made a big show of pretending to think about that. 'Yes, I remember now.'

'Who owns the company?'

'That's confidential, I'm afraid.'

'This is a multiple-murder inquiry,' I said as calmly as I could. 'I can come back with a warrant and confiscate all your records if you want me to.'

He blew out a breath. Leaned his elbows on his desk. 'I've acted for a number of offshore clients, advising them on purchasing properties in the UK, so I can't remember off the top of my head something that happened nine months ago.'

I waited for him to elaborate. He didn't. And I thought it was interesting he didn't probe me further on such a serious incident that could cost his client a packet in money for repairs, if nothing else. Most people would've done. Was that because he already knew the details?

'So shall I go and get a warrant and come back?' I suggested, making a move to stand up.

'Ah. Well, I'm afraid that won't do you any good. You see, there was an incident here a few months back – a flood in our basement. A lot of our paper records were destroyed in the water damage. Those records would've been lost.'

'Really?' How convenient. 'Did you report that to your insurance company?'

He smiled. 'Yes, we did.'

'Are you saying you don't keep computerised copies?'

'No, we don't. A lot of our clients are influential international corporations who require discretion. You must know how easy it is for hackers to get information these days, so we don't keep computerised back-up copies of anything.'

'Right.' I forced myself to take a breath. 'Well, you must remember something about them.'

He tilted his head as if thinking. 'If I remember rightly, Odesa Investments are a Ukrainian company who've been buying up investment opportunities all over the world. They want to get their money out of Ukraine, and overseas property is a good way to do it.'

Or because they're laundering money.

'It's all perfectly legal and above board. Many offshore companies are doing the same, the Chinese in particular.'

'And what was your role in the purchase?'

'I gave them legal advice on how, as an offshore company, they could purchase property in the UK. They transferred the funds into our client account, and it was duly paid on to the previous owner's solicitors. We filed the relevant documents at Land Registry on their behalf and that was it.'

'Who is the director or beneficial owner of the company?'

'I'm afraid I can't remember the name.'

I quirked up an eyebrow. 'You can't remember the name of your client?'

He smiled. 'You already know the client's name – Odesa Investments.'

This time I fought hard not to smack him. Six women were dead, and he definitely knew way more than he was saying. I gripped the arms of the chair to stop me from grabbing him by the scruff of his expensive shirt and throwing him up against the wall. 'You must've received emails or spoken to a representative on the phone.'

'Yes, but I really can't remember a name. It was Ukrainian, and I'm afraid those Eastern European names all sound very much alike to me. That's all I can tell you.'

'Uh-huh. How did you correspond?'

'By email.'

'Do you have copies of these emails you received from them?'

'No. Like I said, we don't keep data online after it's been processed.' His half-smile didn't slip.

Frustration built beneath my skin. 'What else can you tell me?'

He gave an arrogant little shrug. 'Nothing.'

'Well, I don't think that's quite good enough, Mr Acton. When the fire brigade attended they discovered six women held captive and chained in some of the rooms. Six women who were *killed*.' I watched and waited to see what other little tells he'd give me.

'Oh.' He raised his eyebrows, in what I was sure he hoped was a genuine surprised look, but the expression in his eyes didn't change. Very few people, even practised liars, could tell a lie without their body showing some kind of reaction.

Oh? Seriously? That was all he had? I took a breath to try and stay calm. 'Have you got any idea how they came to be there?'

'Absolutely none. As I said, I don't know what else I can tell you. I have no responsibility for what clients do with their properties. And I can assure you I have no knowledge of anyone being inside.'

I changed tactics slightly. 'What exactly does a corporate lawyer do?'

'How long have you got?' He quirked an arrogant eyebrow. 'The short answer is we handle a wide range of legal matters for businesses, from mergers and acquisitions and divestitures and trusts to advising on a myriad of business and employment issues that might include intellectual property, contracts, liability issues. Basically, anything from large, complex, cross-jurisdictional transactions to advising businesses about the everyday running of their company and their legal responsibilities.'

'And advise them on property purchasing?'

'If that's their line of business, or if they want to acquire another asset for investment or development, yes, of course.'

'How was Odesa Investments aware that the hospital was for sale?'

He tapped a finger on his desk for a moment. 'I have no idea.'

'Did *you* ever visit Brampton Hospital?'

'No,' he said, but his cheeks flushed slightly.

In reality, any number of people could've known that property was empty, but I'd wanted to rattle him. Judging from the colour of his face, it had worked.

He stood up and smoothed down his tie. 'Now, I really think that's all I can tell you.'

As I got back into my car I called Jack and told him I wanted a full check carried out on Powell Acton and Acton Associates. Financials, phone records, anything. He definitely knew much more than he was telling me.

DETECTIVE BECKY HARRIS

Chapter 17

When Becky arrived at Hannah Ryan's apartment building, she received an email update stating that Hannah had been officially ID'd from her fingerprints. She'd been arrested fifteen years ago for breach of the peace following a demonstration at an anti-war rally in London. Her next of kin given at that time was her parents who'd lived in Saudi. The phone number listed for them on Hannah's custody record was no longer in use.

The small block was an expensive new development called Wells Heights on the outskirts of Bromley. Becky parked between a bottle-green Jaguar and a Mercedes 4x4, lowering the prestigious tone with the CID's dirty Ford Mondeo. There was an intercom system at the communal front door. She pressed Hannah's buzzer, hoping she had a partner living there who could let her in but at the same time hoping there wasn't. She couldn't stand the thought of breaking such horrible news for a third time that day. There was no reply so she tried one of the neighbours and a well-spoken voice answered.

Becky introduced herself. 'I'm trying to find out if there's anyone else living in Hannah Ryan's apartment with her.'

'Erm . . . no. There isn't. Why?'

'I can't say at the moment, I'm afraid.' Becky didn't want to tell anyone before she'd broken the news to Hannah's parents. 'Do you know how I can reach her parents or any other family?'

'Has something happened? Only I saw Hannah last night as she was leaving.'

'What time was that?'

'About sixish.'

'Can I come up and see you rather than talking on the doorstep?'

'Yes, certainly. I'm on the top floor. C4.'

The buzzer sounded. Becky let herself into the immaculate lobby, ignored the lift, and took the three flights of stairs to the top floor, where there were two apartments. C4, and C5, which was Hannah's.

Becky knocked on the door. It was answered by a woman in her fifties who'd gone grey gracefully. A cloud of perfume snuck out of the room as she pulled the door open and invited Becky in after seeing her warrant card.

'Can you tell me exactly what you saw, please?' Becky pulled out her notebook and pen from her bag.

'I was just leaving for my bridge group, and I saw Hannah coming out of her apartment so we walked down the stairs together. She's OK, isn't she?'

Becky ignored the question and asked one of her own. 'Did she have anything with her? A handbag perhaps?'

She thought about that for a moment. 'Yes, she had one of those laptop bags over her shoulder.'

'Do you know her well?'

'Fairly well. I take in her post if a package gets delivered when she's away, and we have drinks sometimes. That kind of thing. She's away a lot. She's a journalist. Goes to all these dangerous places. She writes some really good pieces. I think she even won a—'

'Do you know any of her friends or family?'

'Her parents are in Saudi somewhere. Her dad's in the oil industry. But I don't have a contact for them. Their names are Phillip and Joan Ryan.'

Becky wrote that down. She didn't know which was worse, breaking the sad news face to face or with an impersonal telephone call to them.

'Hannah has a friend over quite a lot. Her first name's Katherine, but I can't remember her surname. She's an editor at one of those magazines. Um . . . which one is it?' She scrunched up her face, thinking. '*Life Style*, that's it.'

'Have you seen anyone else go into her flat recently? Or anyone suspicious hanging around?'

'No.'

'Does anyone have a key to the property?'

'Yes. I've got a key. She's got one of mine, too. Just in case of emergencies.'

'Can you let me have it? I need to have a look inside.'

'Is that necessary?'

'Unfortunately, yes. I'm involved in a serious investigation.'

'But you can't tell me what?'

'No. I'm afraid not.'

She looked disappointed but disappeared into another room to collect the key. When she returned she said, 'Shall I come with you?'

'I need to check it alone.'

Becky left her there and entered Hannah's front door, which opened up into a light and airy entrance hallway. There was a large print on the wall of a famous photo she was familiar with that had come from a *National Geographic* issue sometime in the eighties – a haunting portrait of a young girl with green eyes and wearing a red headscarf, looking intensely into the camera. From what Becky could remember, she was of Afghan origin and living in a refugee camp when the picture was taken.

She walked into an open-plan living space with a lounge area that overlooked the car park. A copy of *Life Style* was on the coffee

115

table. Becky opened it up, found the name of the editor and contact information and scribbled it in her notebook. There was a broadsheet folded up next to it. A pair of slippers discarded in front of the sofa.

Along the far wall was a kitchen. Next to that an area at the back that overlooked a communal garden had been marked out as an office space. There was a desk, a scanner/printer/copier combi on top, the lead for a laptop plugged into the wall and trailing on the floor. In the desk were stationery supplies, a thesaurus, a dictionary. An A4 folder, inside which were photocopies of printed articles Hannah had written that included stunning depictions of photojournalism. Becky flipped through them – death and destruction of both humans and buildings in war-torn Iraq, two men in Yemen who were so thin they looked like skeletons sitting on the dusty ground, a father carrying his dead son to shore after taking a gruelling journey from Syria to Greece to flee the fighting, the anguish on his face heartbreaking, a ghetto in Africa somewhere, the opiate-addicted from Nigeria, UK street drug dealers and gangs. She skim-read some of them. Hannah was an eloquent writer. Obviously a journalist with a conscience, not a sleazy hack. Some of the stories brought tears to Becky's eyes.

She put them in an evidence bag and then opened the bottom drawer and reached for another folder bursting at the seams. She put it on the desk, flicking through. Bills and receipts for household items and expenses. Becky bagged that, too.

There was nothing else of interest in the desk, so she turned her attention to the kitchen but didn't find anything important. She headed along the hallway just as the landline rang, echoing in the stillness of the house.

Becky picked up the cordless phone from its base and answered.

'Oh, hello? I think I've dialled the wrong number,' a woman's voice said.

'You were trying to reach Hannah Ryan?' Becky asked.

'Yes. Where is she? I'm her mother.'

Becky closed her eyes for a moment. 'I'm really sorry to tell you this over the phone, but I have some bad news and understand you're not in the country?'

'What's . . . what's happened?' Her voice dropped a notch, fear audible in it.

Becky briefly explained the circumstances of Hannah's murder then said, 'I'm very sorry for your loss.'

Silence on the line for a moment was replaced by sniffing. 'I don't . . . I can't . . .'

'I know this is a huge shock, but we're going to do everything we can to find out who did this. Can I ask you some questions while you're on the line? The quicker we can gather as much background information, the more it will help us track down your daughter's killer.'

She blew her nose. And then gave a very quiet, 'Yes. Yes, I understand. I'll do anything I can to help.'

Becky started with the basics. 'When did you last speak to your daughter?'

'Two days ago.'

'And how was she?'

Another sniff. 'She was fine.'

'She didn't mention anyone following her? Or acting suspiciously? Anyone who'd been hanging around, threatening her?'

'No. And she'd have noticed if anyone was. She was a journalist and photographer. She's covered some very dangerous stories and been to some very unsafe places so she was always observant of people.'

'Did she mention the name Neal Lane?'

'Yes. Yes, she did. She said he was helping with a story. She'd met him in Jordan, at the refugee camp there. He was working on some kind of identity project.'

'So their relationship was purely professional?'

'Yes. As far as I know, anyway. Did he have something to do with her death?'

'No, he didn't.' Becky made her way along the corridor as she spoke and nosed around the bathroom, picking up toiletries on a glass unit, looking in a medicine cabinet. 'Do you know if Hannah knew a couple called Donna and Jim Wilson? They lived in Willian, in Hertfordshire.'

'I never heard her mention them. But she meets all sorts of people through her work.'

Becky entered what looked like a guest room with an unmade double bed, an empty wrought-iron and glass bedside table and some built-in cupboards. She opened the cupboard doors and found a couple of coats on hangers. She tucked the phone under her ear and rifled through the pockets. 'Did she work for any particular newspapers or magazines on a regular basis?'

'She was freelance. She wrote the story and then used her contacts to see if anyone was interested in it.'

Finding nothing in the pockets, Becky went up the hallway to the master bedroom. The bed was neatly made with scatter cushions. She sat down on it and rifled through a bedside drawer. 'Do you know who she was writing the refugee story for?'

'Um, I think it was *Life Style*.'

'Did she use a camera for her articles?'

'Yes. She mixed photojournalism with the written word in her articles. She'd just got a new camera recently, actually. Some kind of digital SLR thing. She told me about it but it went a little over my head, I'm afraid. I think it was a Canon.'

'And she must've had a laptop for her work.'

'Yes.'

So where are they? Becky thought. Where's her laptop bag and laptop? And surely she must've had notebooks? Photos? 'Do you know if she stored her documents or work anywhere? On a cloud or hard drive or something like that?'

'She always backed up her work on flashdrives.'

Which, again, seemed nowhere to be found.

'I saw Hannah had an email address listed on her website. Do you know what her password was, by any chance?'

'I'm afraid not.'

'Did she have a boyfriend?'

'No. She hasn't been involved with anyone for a long time. I think she was enjoying being single actually.'

'Can you give me a list of her friends or anyone she saw or spoke to regularly?'

'Um, yes, of course.'

Becky pulled her notebook out of her jacket pocket along with a pen and started writing. When she finished she had the names of four friends. She passed on her condolences again, thanked Hannah's mum, hung up, and let out a sad sigh as she turned her attention to the rest of the room.

Clothes and shoes in the wardrobe, along with a box of non-fiction books, mostly about social issues, not much else.

Becky's mobile rang as she exited the bedroom some time later, having discovered nothing helpful. It was DCI Munroe asking where she was.

'I'm still at Hannah Ryan's house.' Becky gave her a quick rundown. 'It would be good to get a forensic team in here. A neighbour saw Hannah leaving last night with a laptop bag, which wasn't recovered from the Lanes' house. Her mobile phone, camera, and flashdrives she stored her work on are also nowhere to be found. Her car keys were also missing from the murder scene, along with Neal's laptop and his mobile. I think the killer took them all, which seems suspicious to me, especially when the only thing taken from the Wilsons' house was Jim Wilson's wallet.'

'Ah, yes, the wallet. I forgot to mention that in my briefing earlier. Sorry. My mind was on the next thing on my to-do list. As you can imagine, my hands are pretty full at the moment.'

'Of course, ma'am. But I think it's possible the killer also returned here using Hannah's keys to conduct a search and take items.'

There was a pause on the other end of the line as Munroe digested the new information. 'Is there any evidence of a search?'

'No.' She glanced around. 'It's just a feeling. It's unlikely Hannah could've fitted a large, professional camera in a laptop bag with a laptop in it.'

'If there's no evidence of a break-in I don't think a forensic team's going to serve any purpose when it's not the murder scene, not to mention the expense. Hannah Ryan may have had the camera someplace else or in her car, which is being searched.'

'But why take the laptops and mobiles, back-up flashdrives, and the rest of the missing things, if this was a serial killer?'

'A trophy of some kind. Maybe he wants something to remember his victims by. He's probably going to get off on going through their stuff.'

'Yes, maybe, but why didn't the offender take those kinds of things before, when he murdered the Wilsons? Jamal told me they were found intact at the scene.'

'Jim Wilson's wallet *was* taken.'

'But Neal Lane's wasn't, and it was in plain sight in the lounge. If that's his MO, why not do the same as before?'

'They could just be escalating things. Or defining their MO in the evolution of offending. Many serial killers take trophies, some of them things we would think are completely bizarre. Ivan Milat took his victim's camping supplies. Jerome Brudos took shoes. Anatoly Onoprienko took underwear. Who knows what kinds of things make psychopaths tick?'

'Yes, but there could be more to—'

'The post-mortem results are in,' Munroe butted in. 'Time of death is given as between 1.30 a.m. and 2.30 a.m. It's likely they were killed just before Gillian Lane arrived home. Both Hannah Ryan and Neal

Lane died from cerebral hypoxia. The oxygen to the brain was cut off due to their airways being blocked. It's just as we'd been expecting. From the angle and depth of the ligature marks they were strangled from behind.'

'Any idea what they used as a ligature?'

'Professor Hanley suspects an electrical cord. Exactly the same as was used with Donna and Jim Wilson.'

'And what about the knife wounds? Do they match the same type of weapon as the Wilsons?'

'Without something to match it to they can't say if it's definitely the same weapon, but measurements of the width, thickness, and depth confirm they were from a very sharp, straight-edge blade, causing wounds that were two centimetres wide. Exactly the same as in the Wilsons' murders. It's the same killer all right.'

'What do you think is the significance of the knife wounds?' Becky asked.

'It was either some kind of ritual or the killer was worked up to a frenzy and wanted to terrorise their victims before they killed them. And we've got lucky. Apart from the glove print at the scene, the killer also left some DNA in a small sample of saliva recovered from Hannah's forehead, most likely left when he was tying her to the chair or talking in close proximity, possibly from dribble or spit. It's going to take time for the lab results to come back but it's a good break.'

Not if he isn't in the system, Becky thought.

'We still haven't found anything connecting the Wilsons to Neal Lane and Hannah Ryan. How did he target these particular people? That's what we need to find out.'

'Maybe he emailed them and that's why the laptops and phones are missing,' Becky said.

'We went through the Wilsons' communications thoroughly at the time and there was no digital communication that couldn't be accounted for so I very much doubt that. As I said, I think he took those things as trophies.'

'But we should still check emails, ma'am.'

'That's in hand. Technical Services have established by going through Gillian's laptop that she sent Neal emails to a Gmail account. We've found nothing untoward in her communications, but make enquiries with Gillian to see if she knows Neal's password, because if we have to request records direct from Gmail they'll take a while.'

'Will do. We have Hannah's email address, which was listed on her website, although she might've had a personal one, too. Has a request been put in to her email provider yet?'

'Yes, but like I said, we're not expecting anything back soon. They never do anything in a hurry. We're searching through their mobile phone records at the moment. In the meantime, I want you to speak to Hannah's friends and see if you can establish a link to the Wilsons that will lead us to the killer.'

'Yes, will do. We should also talk to Neal's boss at World Food Corps and see if he can shed any light on anything. Neal and Hannah may have come into contact with the killer through their work.' Becky hung up and took one more glance around the apartment.

The anomaly of the wallet was bugging her. And why was the killer careless enough to leave his DNA and a glove print at the second murder scene but clever enough not to leave any forensics at the first? Organised enough to choose their victims, presumably watch and stalk them with meticulous planning so they were never seen, but then stab them in what appeared to be a disorganised frenzy of anger before strangling them. Were they looking at a highly organised person or someone completely chaotic? Either way, she had the first niggling feeling worming its way under her skin that something about this wasn't quite adding up.

HAYAT

Chapter 18

I curl up on my hard bed. The mattress is so thin I can feel the metal slats poking through. I pull the blanket over my head, even though the heat is stifling, but it is the only privacy I have here. I can never get away from anyone.

A baby screams in the next tent. One poor old lady I share the Portakabin with wails. She is always wailing. Wailing for her dead son and her dead husband. She is a body who has lost her soul. I try to comfort her whenever I can, but sometimes it is too much to bear and I want to scream at her. Yell. Tell her to be quiet. That we have all lost someone. We are all lost.

And then the booming starts again. Artillery and mortar fire that pounds inside my head and reverberates through my bones from seven miles away in my homeland. The ground trembles. When will it stop? Nothing will ever stop now. Unless I make it.

I put my hands over my ears but can't block out the sound. Anger and grief unfurl inside me, like smoke, coiling through every cell.

I know I am slowly going mad. I cannot take this any more. There has to be something better outside of the camp. There *has* to be. One of the men who organises a new smuggling ring, he told a friend who told a friend that the women can get jobs. In England. In Germany. In Greece. Plenty of places. I could be a chambermaid again. Maybe one day work in a nice hotel. Get promoted. I speak English and Arabic. I could be a translator. I could be alive again.

I will go and speak to him. His name is Mr Gavin and he is friends with the big boss man, Mr David, who comes here sometimes. I *will* get away. Mr Gavin said to my friend that he can arrange it so no officials stop the World Food Corps vehicles on their journeys. They are humanitarian aid. They are protected. He guarantees you will be OK.

I sweat under the blanket and think about the price I am willing to pay. A kidney? I only need one. My body? I am not as naive as the reporter thinks. I can have sex with someone in exchange for my life. It is a chance I have to take. Better to give my virginity for my survival than have someone take it from me with force.

I am still thinking about this when I hear the reporter's voice beside my bed.

'Hayat, I'm sorry if I upset you.'

'You don't understand.' My voice is muffled beneath the blanket.

'I want to. I want to tell your story so people out there know.'

'It is too late for that. Five years I have been here, and no one helps us except World Food Corps.'

'Talk to me. Let me help.'

'You cannot help.' I twist around under the blanket so my back is to her. I chew on my lip until I hear her footsteps walk away.

Eventually I fall asleep. It is not blissful – no nice dreams – it is a release, an escape. A short one. Too short. Because I always wake up and it is always the same.

The dormitory is full of my Portakabin neighbours now. Women talking, playing cards, cooking. More noise and wailing and people crying. It is too hot in here from all the bodies. It smells of sewage and sweat and fetid breath. I cannot breathe.

I push the blanket away and sit up, rubbing my eyes.

Outside, the dim lights show the path to the shower block. I splash my face with water that is never cold in summer and icy in winter and look at myself in the chipped mirror.

I look dead already. I have nothing to lose now. I have finally given up hope that someone will come and rescue me. That I can go back to my country, my home. That I will ever be free.

So I must take my own chances. Make my own luck.

I run my fingers through my hair. It is long and dark. My eyes are wide. Wild.

I will do what it takes.

I inhale a deep breath and walk out into the night, towards one of the administration Portakabins. If I stop to think about what I am going to do I will talk myself out of it.

A light glows from within but I cannot see inside through the frosted-glass windows.

I walk up the steps. Knock on the door. Take another steadying breath.

The door opens. The man stands there. The one who told the friend of a friend. Mr Gavin. He has brown hair and blue eyes, bad skin.

Cool air from a small air-conditioning unit inside seeps out, wrapping itself around me as he frowns questioningly.

'I want to get out of here,' I say. 'I heard you can help me.'

He stares down at me. Then glances behind me, around the camp. Back to me. 'Come inside.'

DETECTIVE WARREN CARTER
Chapter 19

I needed a strong caffeine hit. It was going on for 5 p.m. when I got back to the office, and I'd been up thirteen hours, working solidly for most of that. But my day wouldn't end soon.

Jack had his phone pressed to his ear, talking quietly. While waiting for him to finish, I poured a mug of strong coffee and walked into the briefing room. I stared at the whiteboards again, letting the faces of those women sear into my brain so I knew each of them by heart. I was convinced these girls had been trafficked from somewhere, which meant no one would've reported them as missing. They wouldn't be found in a database somewhere. But I made a promise to myself that they wouldn't be left unknown and forgotten. I *would* find out who they were.

I left the room and sat down at the desk next to Jack as he ended his call. He wheeled his chair closer to mine.

'Right. The utility companies have told us that payments made on behalf of Odesa Investments came from Privatnyy Bank in Ukraine.'

I rolled my eyes and muttered a swear word under my breath. 'A sodding offshore bank to accompany a sodding offshore company.' It was a nightmare trying to prise information out of offshore banks, whose main role was to provide secrecy for their clients, which often included very rich and influential people. Although offshore banks were obliged to cough up details when there was a criminal investigation going on, often they still didn't comply. And from what I'd heard, a lot of the banks and government infrastructure in Ukraine were run by the mafia, so I seriously doubted we'd get anything out of them. But I said to Jack, 'Get on to the bank and Ukrainian authorities. I want details of who this bloody company is.'

'I'll do my best, but I'm not holding out much hope.'

'Neither am I.'

'I've also got an update on Powell Acton. Studied Law at Oxford Uni. Divorced. No kids. So far I've requested personal telephone records from his home address and mobile phone provider, but if he's involved in this he's clever enough not to be using them.'

'I agree. But he's shifty and overconfident. He knows more than he's telling us.'

'I checked out the alleged flooding at his premises and he did report it to his insurance company a month ago to make a claim.'

'How convenient.'

'His personal financial stuff has been requested. You definitely want business financial records, too? If he's dodgy and he was getting rid of evidence with a fake flood, he's not going to have anything lying around.'

'We still need to try.'

'That's going to be a mammoth task.'

'I know. Divvy it up between Koray, Katrina, and Liz.'

Koray heard his name and looked up over the partition wall between his desk and Jack's. 'Boss, I've exhausted enquiries on misper reports for those women. I've even checked UK-based Turkish community groups and found nothing.'

I blew out a breath. 'Thought not.'

'Shall I try Interpol?'

'Yes. But maybe they're not Turkish or Middle Eastern. Maybe they're coming from the Ukraine if a Ukrainian company is involved.' I steepled my fingers and rested my fingertips beneath my chin, swivelling the chair to the right and left in some kind of rhythm as I wondered where the hell to go next while we waited for paperwork to come in. I didn't have to wait long. Caroline entered the office a few minutes later, briefcase in hand. She'd been on duty longer than me and she didn't even look rumpled. Her hair was still immaculate, uniform unwrinkled, no black circles under her eyes. I'd seen my reflection in the rear-view mirror as I was driving back and my eyes were bloodshot. I caught myself studying her a bit too long and then wondered what the hell I was doing.

'Briefing room in five minutes, please, everyone,' she said as she breezed past before heading into her office.

I followed her in and knocked on the open door. 'Do you want a coffee, ma'am?'

'Oh, God, yes please, you lifesaver. Can you bring it into the briefing with you?' She opened her briefcase and pulled out a folder before flicking through it, distracted.

Everyone filed into the room and took their seats. I deposited Caroline's coffee on a table at the front of the room and sat down next to Jack.

We all shared our discoveries, then I said, 'We know now that those women could only have been put there sometime since March, after the sale of the hospital to Odesa Investments, so going back to the warrant cards . . . it's likely we can narrow down the timeline and exclude the officer who lost it prior to that date, which was PC Helen Davies in February.'

'I'm not sure we can narrow it down,' Jack said. 'Hayat could've got hold of it outside of Brampton Hospital, either if they were being held somewhere else or during transportation there.'

'It could've happened. But I think it's unlikely. Those women were wearing simple clothing with no pockets. There was barely anything in the rooms they were kept in, apart from bedding, a table, the bathroom, and a few books and changes of clothes. Yes, they could secrete a card inside their underwear or under the mattress, but I don't think it would be there for long without being noticed.'

Caroline interjected, agreeing it was unlikely but not impossible.

'In light of the fact we've got no witnesses and nothing to go on, let's just go with that timeline for now,' I said.

'OK.' Caroline nodded.

'Which leaves two cards. DI Jim Beckett and DC Colin Etheridge. Beckett claims his was eaten by the dog and handed back and there was an admin error in the recording of the circumstances it was lost in. Have we checked that out?'

Jack said he had. 'It was just as DI Beckett said. An admin error. It really was eaten by the dog.'

'One card left then,' I said.

'I made more enquiries on that, too,' Jack said. 'And the last time Colin Etheridge's card was registered in the system as being used was to access the bar at Stevenage police station.'

'So if it was lost as DC Colin Etheridge told me, then DC Jamal Faris and DCI Susan Munroe could've picked it up that night in the police bar after he left,' I said. 'It was never found by the lady working in the bar or given in as lost property. On the other hand, that could well be a story concocted by Colin to cover up the fact he left it in Brampton Hospital. I want to dig further into their backgrounds.'

'If Colin's telling the truth, and Faris or Munroe found it that night, surely they would've just told Colin and handed it back,' Liz said. 'It's more likely Colin's lying about where he lost it.'

I ran that through my head. 'Unless one of them picked it up after Colin left, thinking they'd give it back to him, then *they* lost it at

Brampton Hospital before they got the chance. Either way, it has to be his card we found with Hayat, and it didn't get there on its own.'

Caroline chewed on her lip for a moment then nodded at me. 'It could've been lost in the car park or picked up by a member of staff who was in the bar after they all left, but if that was the case I can't see why it wasn't handed into the front desk straight away if an officer or civilian employee found it there, so I think the circumstances warrant digging into all three of them.'

'Good,' I said, then told them about my visit to Powell Acton. 'It's too convenient that his paper records with details of Odesa Investments were destroyed in a flood, and I don't believe him.'

'What makes you suspicious that Powell Acton's got some knowledge of what happened at Brampton Hospital?' Caroline asked.

'Because he's arrogant and trying so hard to be cool and smooth that he's playing it overconfidently. And I don't like him.'

She snorted, a half-laugh. 'We're going to need more than that to start searching around in his business records.'

I paused. 'I think he's hiding something. I got the strong impression he was prepared for my visit, which meant he already knew what had happened with the fire and the discovery of the bodies. He would also have known the place was empty. My gut tells me he knows something or is involved in something he doesn't want us to find out about.'

She studied me for a moment, lips pursed together. They were nice lips. Full. Her top lip slightly bigger than the bottom one. And why was I even noticing her lips, for God's sake? A picture of Denise flashed into my head. Throughout the twenty-two years we'd been married, I didn't think I'd ever noticed someone else's lips. I felt my face flushing under Caroline's scrutiny. I was obviously overtired.

I cleared my throat. 'We need to get a warrant to look at Acton Associates' records. At the very least, I suspect he's likely to be laundering money for his offshore clients. There's been an influx of offshore companies from all over the place buying up UK properties recently to get their money out of their own countries and clean it up.'

Caroline stood, hand on hip, thinking. 'I'll give authorisation for the usual business records – phone data and financial transactions. But we don't have enough to seize any of his files. There's going to be massive data-protection issues covering his clients and we have nothing concrete to suggest he's involved, other than organising the purchase of the property.'

'Well, he says there aren't any files left anyway.' I raised sarcastic eyebrows.

'He could well be laundering money for his clients,' Caroline said. 'But it's perfectly legal for offshore companies to buy UK properties, and he'll argue that whatever his client did with the property afterwards was nothing to do with him.'

'What about emails? He said he was in contact with someone from Odesa Investments via email but conveniently can't remember the name. Even if he deleted everything, like he told me, there should still be records with his email provider.'

'Yes. Get Technical Services to check into his email servers and see what they can give us and then we can review things. But if it's one of the major email companies, then we'll be lucky to get anything back from them until *next* bloody Christmas. Have you contacted Interpol to find out if they're aware of Odesa Investments?'

'Already put in an enquiry,' Liz said. 'They're going to get back to me.'

'And I'll be dealing with Privatnyy Bank in Ukraine,' Jack said.

'Oh, for Christ's sake.' Caroline threw a hand in the air. 'Ukraine banks will be even harder to get info out of than the bloody Cayman Islands or South American ones!' She stared at the ground for a moment. Then snapped back to herself. 'Maybe these girls are being trafficked from Ukraine,' Caroline said. 'Maybe Hayat wasn't writing her name. Or maybe she's an Arabic Ukrainian?'

'Exactly what I was thinking,' I said.

'Let's wait to see if Interpol come up with anything on Odesa Investments.' She took a sip of coffee and said, 'Right. Moving on. The Fire Investigation Team have confirmed that this was *definitely* an electrical fire caused by the faulty cryogenic freezer unit. And I do have an update from the post-mortems.' She shook her head slightly and pinched the bridge of her nose. 'Three have been done so far, on Hayat, victim two, and victim three. The others will be carried out tomorrow.' She looked up at us all in turn. 'And they tell us something I've never seen before in all my years on the job.'

DETECTIVE BECKY HARRIS
Chapter 20

Becky had telephoned the offices of World Food Corps before leaving Hannah Ryan's house to make sure the CEO, David Bennington, would be around. She'd been informed that he was working from home, so she called Bennington himself and arranged to meet him at his house in Aylesford, Kent. He'd tried to press her on what was going on, but she didn't want to break the news of his employee's death over the phone.

Cursing another long drive, this time through rush-hour traffic, she arrived at the small village of sixty or so houses and found Bennington's old thatched cottage, situated on the banks of the River Medway.

Bennington opened the door with a mug of coffee in hand. He was tall and dynamic-looking. He had a golden tan, dirty-blond hair, and a nose too big for his face to call him attractive. 'You're the detective?'

'DS Harris, yes.'

'Come in.' He stepped back to let her in and strode into a lounge with low ceilings and lots of wooden beams.

She followed him in. A half-filled suitcase sat on the floor. He put the mug on a coffee table that looked like it had once been used as an old plough but renovated with a glass top.

'I can't imagine what this is about.' He turned to her. 'But you're lucky you caught me, actually. I just got back from Jordan this morning.'

'I'm very sorry to tell you this but one of your ex-employees was found murdered in his home earlier today.'

He stood very still, staring at her. 'That's awful. Who?'

'Neal Lane. I believe he was a project m—'

'Yes, yes. He was working on the ID Blockchain Project. Well. I'm . . .' He stared at the ground. Shook his head. 'I'm shocked. What happened?'

'I'm afraid I can't go into details at the moment, but I need to ask you some questions.'

'Of course.' He sat down on the edge of a Chesterfield sofa and indicated Becky should sit. 'Anything I can do to help.'

She perched on the edge of an identical sofa opposite. 'Can you tell me a bit more about the project he was working on?'

He scratched the back of his neck and looked surprised. 'Surely you can't think that's somehow relevant to his death?'

'I don't know at this stage what's relevant and what's not.'

He shrugged. 'Well, it was basically a project that would use blockchain technology for humanitarian aid. Eventually, there's going to be a United Nations database of refugees so that they can use the system for ID and as a payment mechanism. If it succeeded, it would eventually speed up the adoption of blockchain technology for sister UN agencies and beyond. Currently World Food Corps helps to feed forty million people around the globe, but the emphasis of this has changed from delivering food to transferring money to people who *need* food. This system would allow us to feed more people and work with local and regional banks, and actually save us money by creating a 98 per cent reduction in outside monetary fees.

'It also addresses the problems of refugees with no identity documents or bank accounts, without which it would be very difficult to get jobs or become independent and productive members of society.

Without ID you can't get a bank account. Without a bank account you'd be hard-pressed to get a legal job or find somewhere to live. It's a vicious circle.' He paused for a moment, then said, 'My dream for the project was that one day refugees could walk out of Salama Camp with their digital wallet, government ID, and access to financial accounts that would all be linked by the blockchain ID system. That means they can re-enter the world economy. They'd have a place where employers could deposit wages. Banks could check their credit history from purchases carried out in Salama. And border controls and immigration agencies could check their identities. They could move to anywhere in the world and easily prove their credentials or history.'

Becky scribbled down brief notes. 'How well did you know Neal?'

He shrugged. 'Um . . . only in a professional capacity, really. World Food Corps was given funding for the project from the UN. The position was advertised. Neal's expertise was working with similar blockchain technology so we employed him. He was running it from the Salama refugee camp, doing beta testing and collecting data. Then, as often happens, the funding was pulled. We couldn't afford to run the programme off our own backs so we had to cancel it two weeks ago and let Neal go.'

'Did you spend quite a bit of time together while he was working on the project in Jordan?'

'A little, I suppose, but mainly discussing the logistics of things and updates. We didn't socialise outside of work, if that's what you mean. There's not much socialising in Salama, as you can imagine. I'm the CEO so I'm often stuck at our UK head office, delegating matters for all our enterprises, and time with individual employees is limited.'

'What can you tell me about him?'

He tilted his head, staring at his coffee mug. 'He was a good guy. Solid. Reliable. Enthusiastic. Incredibly knowledgeable in his field. I was sad when we had to let him go.'

'Did he mention his home life at all? Talk about friends, family, anything that was bothering him?'

'I knew he was married and he'd lost his daughter some time ago.'

'Did he mention anyone called Jim or Donna Wilson?'

He pursed his lips. 'Um . . . not that I recall. We didn't really talk about personal things that much. He was there to do a job and he got on with it. I don't really think I can be of much help.'

'Did he seem close to any other staff members at World Food Corps?'

'I'm not sure. Like I said, I'm here, there, and everywhere. As far as I knew he had a good working relationship with everyone. He never went to our head office here in the UK. He was interviewed via a video link, offered the job, then he went out to Jordan to start working on it a month later. But I can give you a list of names and contact numbers for other members of staff in Jordan if you like?'

'Great. If you could do that before I leave that would be helpful.'

'Oh, sorry. Where are my manners? Can I get you something to drink?'

'No, I'm fine, thanks. Do you know a journalist called Hannah Ryan?'

'Yes. I met Hannah in Jordan. She was writing a story about the refugees. Why are you asking about her?'

'She was also murdered at the Lanes' house.'

'Oh.' His eyes widened. 'That's terrible.'

'We believe she'd visited Neal last night in connection with this story she was working on.'

'I guess that's possible. She was very passionate about raising awareness of the conditions the refugees were living in and about the long-term solutions to their displacement and how to go about rebuilding their lives. Neal would've been out there at the same time as her, so they could've met there. He might've been telling her about the project. I spoke to her myself on many occasions, giving her background information for the piece, as I know a lot of other World Food Corps employees did.'

'When was the last time you had contact with Neal?'

'Unfortunately, it was when I had to break the news to him about the funding problem. Two weeks ago.'

'But you were on good terms when he left?'

'Yes. He understood. We're an NGO so we have to rely on grants and donations. As much as we would've loved to see the project progress, we have to assess where our funds are going to be best spent for the welfare of the refugees.'

'Had he received any threats of any kind? I would imagine the subject of Syria and refugees is a highly emotive one.'

'If he had, he didn't tell me about them. As far as I was aware, everyone on the ground in Jordan liked him. He was easy to get along with, knew his stuff inside and out, and was resourceful.'

'When did you last speak to Hannah or see her at Salama?'

'Um . . .' He scratched his head, thinking. 'Probably about a month ago.'

'OK, thank you.' She stood up to leave.

He stood, too, and stared into the suitcase, looking distracted, which wasn't too unusual given the news he'd just received. What was unusual, Becky thought, was that he knew Neal had been married but he hadn't once asked about Gillian. Nor had he asked any questions about the circumstances surrounding Hannah's death or seemed surprised that Neal and Hannah had been found together.

DETECTIVE WARREN CARTER
Chapter 21

Caroline read from a sheet of paper, giving us the preliminary PM reports on the first three victims, which revealed they were between the ages of eighteen and twenty-five. They were in reasonably good health, considering their situation, although a little dehydrated. Their last meal consisted of chicken, pasta, and fruit. They all died from respiratory failure due to smoke inhalation. None of them had received any kind of regular dental care so the prospect of exploring dental records was a no-go. There were no useful DNA samples on their bodies we could use to trace an offender.

We all listened intently. So far there was nothing we weren't expecting.

'There were no signs of sexual assault.' Caroline glanced up.

'That's something good at least,' Koray muttered.

'Well, wait until you hear the rest. We'll look at Hayat first in more detail.' Caroline glanced down at her notes again. 'Although she had suffered some burns to her body, she was pretty well preserved. There was evidence of soot in her mouth, throat, and lungs, along with internal burns.' She looked up again. 'Here's where it gets bizarre. Apart from the smoke and fire damage, most of her internal organs were healthy. The important thing of note is that she had high levels of hormones associated with fertility drugs. She was also suffering from severe ovarian hyperstimulation syndrome, or OHSS. This is a condition usually associated with fertility treatment, where the fertility drugs overstimulate the development of eggs in the ovaries.'

I frowned, my mouth falling open. 'What?'

'Yes.' Caroline raised her eyebrows. 'These women were being subjected to fertility treatment. Hayat had recently had her eggs removed, and apparently OHSS can worsen after a hormone injection of hCG is given to trigger mature follicles to release their eggs. The condition is painful and can be deadly. As a result, at the time of her death, she had a lot of fluid in her abdomen and fluid-filled cysts on her ovaries, electrolyte disturbances, a blood clot in her left leg, her kidney function was impaired, and she was retaining water. Her symptoms most likely would've included a lot of pain, possibly breathing problems, hallucinations, nausea and sickness, and extreme thirst.' She looked at us each in turn. 'Although victims two and three were not suffering from OHSS, they were also both subjected to fertility drugs and were at different stages of egg maturity.'

I clenched my fist, turning over what that meant. 'So you're saying these girls were kept as egg-making machines?'

'That's exactly what I'm saying.'

'That's twisted,' Jack said.

Liz and Katrina glanced at each other with a look of horror.

'Why, though?' Koray asked.

'Apparently, the UK has a massive shortage of egg donors, especially those from ethnic minority groups,' Caroline said. 'We're all aware of the trafficking of body parts – kidneys, corneas, hearts, even skin. The waiting lists are huge and some people are prepared to risk or pay anything when it's a matter of life or death. This is exactly the same thing. It's a black-market commodity, created through supply and demand, and in today's market a healthy human egg can be worth more than gold.'

I shook my head with despair.

'The benchtop incubator and the cryogenic chest freezer at Brampton Hospital would've been used for fertilising and storing eggs, possibly to keep donors' frozen sperm, too,' Caroline said. 'Some of the needles found there were probably used in administering hormone injections. They were doing all the treatment of IVF cycles on site. Most likely the recipients of these fertilised eggs were also visiting Brampton Hospital to have them implanted there.'

We sat in stunned silence for a moment. Even though I was quiet, my mind worked overtime.

'I've had no luck tracing any suspicious purchases of that type of equipment,' Liz said. 'It's likely they either paid a wholesaler in cash or they're second-hand.'

'So . . . who were the fertilised eggs going to?' Katrina asked.

'People who desperately want to be parents,' Caroline said. 'People who were prepared to pay to get the treatment done quickly.'

'I'm wondering if they knew what was going on,' I said. 'If they knew those girls were being held there.'

Caroline shrugged. 'Who knows at this stage?'

Koray scrubbed his hands over his face. 'It's unreal.'

'This whole process would take specialised medical knowledge, which means a doctor is involved in it,' Caroline said. 'I know someone who might be able to help us. Professor Pullman is a leading UK fertility expert. He's got a private clinic in London. Can you talk to him and see if you can get some information that might help us?' She looked at me.

I nodded. 'Leave it with me.'

'DC Potter at Brampton Hospital is standing down now and he's got nothing else to report about anyone trying to get close to the place. After that bloody bad luck with a reporter driving past the scene it was always going to be unlikely the people responsible didn't get to hear about it.' She paused for a sip of coffee. 'Right. Let's leave it there for the night while we're waiting for paperwork records to come through. Go home. Get some rest. See you back here bright and early.'

As Liz, Jack, Katrina, and Koray gathered their things to leave, I headed back to my desk and logged on to my computer terminal with my new access code. I found the website address for the Pullman Clinic and looked up a contact number. I wasn't going home yet.

Unfortunately, Professor Pullman wasn't available when I rang as he was seeing patients. I left a message for him to contact me urgently and then turned my attention to the Constabulary's personnel records.

Colin Etheridge had joined the police seven years before, aged twenty-five, on the Accelerated Detective Constable Programme, which was a fast-track scheme where successful candidates completed a year of intensive training and obtained their detective qualification. Judging from his previous work history as a Customs and Excise officer, it was thought he had the essential skills suited to a detective's role. He'd been based at Letchworth CID until my retirement and Becky's promotion, and had then been seconded to Stevenage CID as a DC. He'd never been disciplined for any matters. Had no complaints against him. He was single, no dependents, and his next of kin was listed as his mother.

Jamal Faris had joined the police at twenty-three after an initial career as a plumber. Following his two-year probation, he became a patrol officer for three years, then passed his detective exam and became one of Letchworth CID's detective constables. Similarly, he had no complaints against him or disciplinary offences. He was married to Asima, a housewife, who was listed as next of kin. No dependents.

Susan Munroe was thirty-nine years old. She'd been fast-tracked through the ranks on an accelerated promotion course and had been the youngest ever officer to make Detective Chief Inspector within Hertfordshire Constabulary, at the age of thirty-three. She'd been commended for demonstrating the very highest standards of detective work four times during previous murder investigations and commended for bravery for acting in an outstandingly courageous and resourceful manner during another previous murder case. She was married to Paul, a prosecution barrister. Again, no dependents.

They were all squeaky clean without a hint of any improprieties in their past, but that didn't mean one of them wasn't involved. I'd expect a dirty cop to be better at knowing exactly how to hide things than the average criminal. It just meant I had to work harder.

I was still staring at the screen when my mobile phone rang. It was Professor Pullman.

'Thank you for getting back to me,' I said. 'I know you'll be busy so I'll get to the point. I'm really after some technical information regarding IVF and egg donors for a case I'm working on. And since you're an expert on the subject, I wondered if you'd mind answering a few of my questions. Chief Superintendent Caroline Barker suggested I speak with you.'

'Well, flattery always works well.' There was a hint of humour interjected in his voice. 'How is Caroline?'

I glanced through the glass partition into Caroline's office. She stared intently at something on her desk, swivelling in her chair, looking deep in thought. 'She's very well.'

'I'd be happy to help give any advice if I can. In fact, I'm intrigued as to why the police are involved in something involving fertility treatment. Has there been an allegation of misconduct or negligence somewhere?'

'No.' *Not yet anyway.* 'I'm conducting a sensitive murder investigation so I'm afraid I'm limited at the moment as to what I can tell you. But we have several female victims who were being subjected to fertility treatment against their will. It's very likely they were trafficked into the country for the purposes of egg-harvesting.'

A sharp intake of breath. Then, 'How *awful.*' A pause. 'Are you saying you don't know who was treating them?'

'That's correct.'

'Well, of course I'll help in any way.'

'Thank you. Can you tell me how easy it is to get the kind of fertility drugs used in fertility treatments?'

'As a patient in the UK you'd need either an NHS or private prescription that you could take to a pharmacy or give to a company supplying them by mail order. Hospitals and clinics would also have their own supplies. You could also obtain them from the internet abroad quite easily without a prescription. And there are many countries where anyone could visit a pharmacy and buy them over the counter. There's also probably some kind of black market for them as well, the same as any drug.'

I wrote down *anywhere in the world* and underlined it. Not what I wanted to hear.

'What about the actual treatment. Can you explain what a cycle using an egg donor specifically involves?'

'The donor would need to take daily medication that suppressed her natural cycle. Then they'd need injections that stimulated her ovaries to encourage multiple eggs to mature for retrieval. They'd be monitored throughout using blood tests and ultrasounds.'

'Could this be done in a non-clinic type of environment?'

'I take it you mean in secret?'

'Yes.'

'It could. A portable ultrasound machine could be used. There are hormone-testing kits used for blood tests, which could be used privately.'

I wrote that down.

'The recipient of the eggs, meanwhile, would be taking hormones to prepare her body for implantation. When the donor eggs are sufficiently developed, a trigger injection of hCG hormone would be given. Two days after that, her eggs would be retrieved under sedation, using an aspiration needle, guided by ultrasound to transvaginally remove the eggs. The eggs would then be fertilised with a partner's or donor's sperm and are then incubated and evaluated. Between three and five days, if there are any top-quality embryos, then they will be implanted into the recipient. In the UK, regulations mandate a maximum of two embryos are transferred per cycle.'

It made me cross my legs as he was talking. 'I understand there's a shortage of egg donors in the UK. Is that right?'

'Most definitely. Infertility is on the rise in general for many reasons, in both males and females. One in six couples will have trouble conceiving. And now we have same-sex partners wanting to be parents and seeking treatment also. In fact, recent studies are now calling it a crisis, so there is more demand for donor eggs than ever before and a significant decrease in donors. In part, because a change in the law in the UK in 2005 removed anonymity from sperm donors and egg donors, which means now that any donor-conceived child can have access to their donor's information when they reach eighteen. Coupled with that is the problem that selling eggs in the UK for profit is illegal. For an invasive medical procedure that spans up to fifty hours for egg-harvesting, and can carry many risks for the donor, the most a donor can receive is £250 remuneration.'

'So there's no incentive for people to donate eggs now.'

'Exactly. Which means that the waiting lists for donor eggs can sometimes be four years or more. Especially when recipients are of an ethnic minority group, where the available donors are far fewer. Often the choice is for people from the UK to go abroad, where there aren't as many restrictions on donor eggs. In other countries – the US, Europe, Russia, for example – donors can be paid a lot of money for their eggs, making it worthwhile for them and for the recipients. The cost of treatment is cheaper there and there are no waiting lists. UK fertility clinics can import embryos from other countries that have been fertilised using donor eggs, but they have to obtain a special licence from the Human Fertilisation and Embryology Authority.'

Which obviously wasn't happening in this case. Why pay for donor eggs from another country when you get them for free from trafficked slaves?

'You could contact the HFEA and see if there have been complaints or misconduct allegations about anyone. Let me give you a name and contact number.' He rattled off some details and I wrote them down.

'OK, thanks.'

'The strict British regulations could be helping to create an unsavoury market in human eggs. But even if foreign clinics can assure their egg donors are not being exploited, how can we be certain? I've read many reports of egg donors abroad being paid very low amounts, having their ovaries overstimulated, and basically being treated as a milking cow. They're often young women from poorer countries who are hungry and desperate for money. For some, this is their main source of income, going through the process up to five times a year. This is the seedier underside of the global market in baby-making.'

I tapped my pen on my pad. Supply and demand. The old story of commerce going back to the beginning of time. These young women's eggs were obviously a commodity in high demand and someone in the UK had wanted a piece of that market. Every time I thought I'd seen the worst of what people could do to each other, I was sickeningly proved wrong.

'How much would a cycle of IVF cost?'

'It will vary depending on specific treatment and the clinic, but let's say on average around £10,000.'

'How much would someone pay for a donor egg?' I asked, but I already knew it was a stupid question.

'How long is a piece of string? I've known couples remortgage their homes or take out huge loans to have treatment, not just once, but time and time again.'

Beg. Borrow. Steal. I rubbed at my forehead.

'It's a highly emotional issue, where people are *desperate* to conceive. Desperate with hope. Some couples will do anything to have a baby,' he said.

Anything, including using black-market eggs.

I asked a few more questions and hung up, shaking my head. Then I rang the mobile number of the contact at the HFEA Professor Pullman had given me. She said she was on her way home but since it was so important she'd head back to the office and check their system.

I glanced through to Caroline's office. She looked over and beckoned me in. Everyone else had left and it was quiet, apart from the Professor's words still ringing in my ear.

I leaned on the door-frame and tried to smile.

'Mad first day, huh?' She smiled back. It lit up her face. Her eyes sparkled. They were a unique colour of blue. Cornflower blue.

Cornflower blue? Where the hell did that come from?

I dragged my attention away from her eyes and coughed. 'You could say that.'

'Do you want a drink?' She opened her bottom drawer. 'I've got a good single malt.' Reaching inside she pulled out a bottle of whisky.

I glanced longingly at it. After what I'd heard and seen I could do with the whole bottle. 'I'd love to, but I haven't finished yet.' I sat down in the chair in front of her.

She studied the bottle for a moment then put it back in the drawer. 'Don't let me stop you.'

She shook her head. 'I hate drinking alone. So what did Professor Pullman say?'

I told her.

'I'm not surprised. When I had IVF, it was a lot easier. Egg donors weren't a problem then – there was plenty of choice. I had premature ovarian failure, and I was never going to conceive naturally, so my husband and I had IVF using donor eggs.'

'He treated you?'

'Yes.' She picked up a photo in a black frame on her desk and turned it around to show me. It was of Caroline with a girl of about fourteen. They looked so incredibly alike, even though they weren't technically related. Both blonde and tall. Both had those blue eyes. Both incredibly pretty. She turned the photo back around, smiled affectionately at it, and placed it back on her desk. 'Kira's eighteen now. She's backpacking round Australia with some friends. Unbelievable how time goes by so fast. It only seems like yesterday she was born.' The smile turned wistful then. 'The thing is, I know how desperate people can get to have a baby. Private adoptions from abroad can cost a fortune. Although IVF treatment costs less in some countries, if someone's offering the same treatment here, they're tapping into a massive market. It's perfectly feasible that prospective parents in the UK would pay a lot of money for a donor egg. £15,000, £20,000, even more, most probably.' She shrugged. 'Who knows how much? You can't put a price on it when you feel that strongly about being a parent.'

'So victim two alone, who had ten eggs when she died, could've been worth £200,000 plus.'

'That's per *cycle*. These were young, healthy women. They could be put through multiple cycles of IVF before being deemed useless and . . .' She trailed off.

'And killed?'

'Or sent somewhere else.'

I knew what she meant. It was possible that when those girls had stopped being breeding machines they were destined for the sex-slave industry.

I took a deep breath. Stood up. I had to keep going. This case wasn't going to solve itself. I paused at her doorway. 'Would you have done it, if someone had offered you that option?'

'Absolutely not. But faced with the prospect of years on a waiting list? I'm sure plenty of other people would.'

'So the recipients were complicit in what was going on?'

'Not necessarily.'

'But they would've been receiving treatment at Brampton Hospital. In secret. Whoever treated them was either acting alone or with a very skeleton staff because the fewer people who knew about it the better. That doctor must've told them it was all illegal. Didn't they question the ethics of that?'

'They could've been told the eggs came from willing donors abroad, or some other such bullshit.'

'Maybe. But I'm finding it hard to accept they weren't just as culpable.'

'If someone offers you a lifeline when you're desperate, you're going to take it and believe whatever they tell you because you want to.'

I shook my head.

'I'm sorry about your wife,' she said out of the blue.

My gaze met hers. 'Thank you.'

'I know how you feel. I lost my husband three years ago.'

'I'm sorry. I didn't know.'

'Why would you?' She opened her mouth as if to say something else, then shook her head. 'So what are you up to now then?'

'I'm going on a stake-out.'

She raised her eyebrows. 'Do you need a hand?'

My turn for raised eyebrows. I wasn't used to a boss who not only was on the same wavelength as me but actually wanted to get out in the field and do some legwork.

'Yeah, I'm delaying going home, too.' Her gaze drifted back to her daughter. 'Not much fun going back to an empty house.'

And in those few words it was like she knew me too well, even though she didn't know me at all.

DETECTIVE BECKY HARRIS
Chapter 22

For the second time that day Becky parked in the Lister Hospital car park. She'd been mulling everything over on the drive back from David Bennington's and she wanted to follow up on a few questions.

The PC guarding the door to Gillian's room had now gone, on DCI Munroe's authorisation. Munroe could see no reason for the killer to come back and try again when Gillian hadn't even seen his face. But Becky wasn't completely convinced. She was still concerned about why Gillian had been chased instead of the offender running from the scene when he'd had the chance.

Gillian sat up in bed, pillows plumped behind her, her eyes swollen and red from crying. On the trolley positioned over the bed was a tray of unappetising-looking food that Gillian stared at as if she was hardly seeing it.

'Hi,' Becky said when she entered the room. 'How are you feeling?'

'Pretty awful.' Her voice croaked as she spoke.

'Yeah. I'm not surprised.' Becky sat down on the same chair she'd been in earlier. 'God, what is that?' She peered at the tray of food. Actually, the word unappetising would be too polite. She couldn't tell if it was supposed to be mashed potato or blancmange. 'Shall I get you something from one of the shops downstairs?'

Gillian flopped her head back on the pillows and cradled the arm that was in plaster. 'No. I'm not hungry anyway. But would you mind taking it outside? The smell's making me feel sick.'

'No, course not.' Becky took the tray to a small kitchenette down the corridor and left it there. When she went back inside, Gillian wiped at the tears falling again.

'Dean came to see me.' Gillian sniffed. 'He told me he recognised that woman. Hannah . . . something. She's a journalist. *Was* a journalist.'

'That's right. I wanted to ask you about that. Your husband met Hannah Ryan at the camp in Jordan. She was doing a story on the refugees. I think it was purely a working relationship. He was helping her with information.'

'So he wasn't . . . he wasn't having an affair with her?'

'I don't think so, no. I've spoken to Hannah's mother and Neal's boss, David Bennington. None of them have said Hannah knew Neal in a personal capacity.'

'You're sure you're not just saying that to try and make me feel better?'

'I honestly don't think he was having an affair, Gillian.'

'But . . . if it was all innocent, why didn't Neal tell me about her, then? And why was she at the house at that time of night?'

'I don't know. They could've lost track of time while working on Hannah's story.'

Gillian stared at Becky with scepticism, obviously not convinced. 'We had what I *thought* was a good relationship. We didn't keep secrets. At least, I didn't think so until now. But he never mentioned any journalist. I don't understand why not if there was nothing going on.'

Neither did Becky. Yet. If it was all above board, why not tell his wife? Unless he was trying to protect her from something. 'Have you ever met David Bennington?'

'No.'

Becky paused. 'We didn't find Neal's laptop at the house. Or his mobile phone. Were they there when you left for Bali?'

'Yes. I saw his laptop in the study. And I called him on his mobile phone. Are you saying it was taken by whoever . . .'

'I think so.'

'Why?'

'I don't know yet. Maybe as a souvenir.' But Becky wasn't buying the official line from DCI Munroe. Collectively, with Hannah's missing items, it was a hell of a lot of trophies to take. One thing all the items had in common was that they were designed to hold data. It seemed more as if the killer wanted something that was on those devices. 'Did he keep his data backed up anywhere? A cloud or storage device?'

'He had several portable hard drives that he used to back up his work. He didn't trust clouds. He knew how vulnerable information was to hackers, so he used to keep things on external hard drives.'

'Where did he keep them?'

'They were in his office desk drawer.'

Becky wrote that down. She'd need to check with SOCO to see if the hard drives had been found. 'Can you give me any email addresses that Neal used?'

'Um . . . yes. He only had one.' She gave Becky the same Gmail address that Technical Services had discovered for Neal when going through Gillian's laptop.

'Do you know his password for it?'

'Yes.' Gillian gave her the password, which Becky scribbled down.

'That's really helpful, thanks. It would be good if you could accompany me to the house when you're discharged to see if anything else is missing.'

'They're letting me out tomorrow.' Gillian looked through the window, seeming lost. 'I can't be where it . . . where it all happened. And I bet the press will be hounding me on my doorstep.'

'I'll be with you. You'll be perfectly safe. Our forensic team is still in the house so it will be a while before you can move back in, if you want to. Can you stay with a friend or relative in the meantime?'

'Dean said I can stay with him. I'll sell the house. I'm not moving back in there.' She looked over at Becky, blinking back more tears. 'We've got a little cottage in Devon. It was left to me by my parents. Maybe when I'm feeling stronger, I'll go down there. Get away from everything.'

It was gone eight when Becky got back to the CID office. Box files sat in a neat row all along the back wall, the previous case files for the Wilsons' murder investigation. Ronnie pored over financial records belonging to Neal and Gillian Lane and Hannah Ryan. A ton of Post-it notes decorated his laptop screen, and pieces of paper were strewn everywhere. Jamal was going through phone records. Colin typed away at his laptop.

When Becky poked her head around Munroe's doorway she caught her staring at her laptop, mouth wide open, forehead bunched up in a frown.

'Sorry, it took longer than I thought. I just had a few follow-up questions for Gillian Lane. And this lot needs going through.' Becky held up the bags containing the paperwork she'd brought back from Hannah's house, but Munroe didn't appear to have heard her. She was too engrossed in her screen, her cheeks an angry shade of red.

'The sodding press are on to it now! That arsehole hack John Hinckley from the *Daily World* has got it splashed all over the tabloid's webpage, and he's the worst possible person to get hold of it. He never misses an opportunity to criticise and slag off the police! He's calling him the "Cupid Killer" and they've bloody well printed the words written on the wall! Listen to this . . . "Earlier this morning a brutal murder occurred at a home in Oak Drive, Stevenage. Neal Lane and Hannah

Ryan were enjoying a quiet night at the house, until the unknown killer entered through an unlocked rear door before stabbing them multiple times in a frenzied attack, and then strangling them. The words *DIE PIGGY DIE* had been scrawled on a wall in a macabre message. Neal's wife, Gillian Lane, disturbed the killer on her return home, and after fleeing the scene, was hit by a vehicle. She's currently in hospital with minor injuries. Sources close to the investigation say the murders have been linked to a previous case in December last year, where Jim and Donna Wilson were murdered in their home in Willian in identical circumstances, but police failed to shed any light on potential suspects. The investigation into the Wilsons' deaths has remained stalled ever since. The Cupid Killer is Hertfordshire's first serial killer since the sixties. He is at large and a serious danger to the public.

"'Crucial questions must be raised as to the ability of the Senior Investigating Officer, Detective Chief Inspector Munroe, to effectively do her job and apprehend this man before he strikes again.'" Munroe finished reading, jumped out of her chair and marched past Becky out into the CID office. 'Right, listen up, guys. The press has just got hold of the story and linked the deaths of Hannah Ryan and Neal Lane to the Wilsons. Not only that, they've got wind of the words written on the walls in both locations.' She glared at everyone. 'Does anyone want to tell me anything about how that got out?'

Becky glanced around. Ronnie's usual ruddy cheeks blushed redder. Colin's mouth formed a surprised O shape. Jamal scratched his head and shrugged.

'If I find out there's been a leak from this department, the guilty party won't just be demoted to walking the beat again. They'll be out of a job!' Munroe snapped.

Ronnie put his hand up.

'Yes? Have you got something to say on the matter?' Munroe narrowed her eyes at him.

'It might not . . . not be anyone here,' Ronnie said, flustered. 'There were other people who attended both murders.'

'Oh, why didn't I think of that?' Her nostrils flared. 'Of course there were. But that information was kept quiet and undisclosed for the last year while we worked on the Wilsons' murders and now, as soon as *this* team gets involved, it's exposed.' More glaring round the room before settling on Ronnie again. 'DC Pickering?'

'What, ma'am?' The red flush crept up his neck.

'Anything else to say on the matter?'

'It wasn't me.' He shook his head vehemently.

'Jamal?'

'I don't have a clue how it got out, ma'am.'

'Becky?'

'Definitely not me, guv.'

'Colin?'

'Absolutely not!'

'Well, this just upped the pressure. I've got to go and do another press conference in a minute, appealing for calm. But we're going to be crucified in public if we don't catch this guy quickly. I don't have time to take this further right now, but rest assured, once this is over, I *will* find the leak, and they will be dealt with severely.' She hardly paused for breath before saying, 'Before I go . . . Becky, what have you found?'

'I don't believe Hannah Ryan was having an affair with Neal Lane. She was a journalist who was writing a story on refugees, and Neal was helping her with it.' She gave them the rundown of conversations with Hannah's mother, Neal's brother, and David Bennington. 'I'll be speaking to more of Hannah's friends later. The missing laptop and mobile belonging to Neal, and the camera, laptop bag, laptop, mobile, and car keys belonging to Hannah Ryan are odd, though. Plus, Neal Lane always backed up his work on external hard drives and they weren't found at the scene, either. I spoke to SOCO at the house and they looked for me. He kept them in his desk drawer, which meant the killer was most likely rummaging around the house for items, so why didn't he take Neal's wallet when it was in plain sight, like they did before? Hannah backed up her work with flashdrives, which also seem to be missing, along with photos she must've taken for previous stories.'

'I disagree. It's not odd.' Munroe flicked a dismissive hand. 'As I've already explained, there were trophy items missing from the Wilson household, too.'

'Item,' Becky corrected. 'I think it's possible Hannah and Neal were stabbed repeatedly to torture them into giving up information about where these items were.'

Munroe shook her head. 'You're getting sidetracked on inconsequential issues. The stab wounds exactly match the wounds the Wilsons suffered.'

Becky blew out a breath, frustration building as a tight ball in her chest. 'I also think someone's been in Hannah's house. Why take her car keys if it wasn't to gain entry to her house?'

'Is there evidence of a break-in?' Colin asked.

'No. It's just a feeling,' Becky admitted reluctantly.

'We don't work on feelings. We work on evidence,' Jamal said haughtily.

Except Becky thought he was way wrong on that one. Gut instinct, feelings, intuition, call it what you like. It was an important tool to a detective. It came first, evidence came later. And it had served her well in the high-profile case she'd solved that had earned her the commendation.

'I think you're mistaken.' Munroe's tone was clipped as she glanced at her watch. 'Hannah and Neal, drinking wine together, at that time of night when his wife is supposed to be away? Not telling Gillian anything about her?' She raised her eyebrows. 'I believe they *were* having an affair, and Hannah just had the bad luck to be in the wrong place at the wrong time. This killer targets couples, and he must've mistaken Hannah for Gillian, so I'm certain whatever story she was writing has nothing to do with this investigation, and we're not wasting valuable time and resources on that line of inquiry.'

'But what's the motive for targeting couples?' Becky asked. 'What conclusion did you come to with the Wilsons?'

'There could be many reasons.' Munroe sighed with impatience. 'The killer hated their parents who had a happy marriage and neglected them. They've had bad relationships and they're jealous of other couples having what they don't have. I could go on, but I don't have time right now.'

'Yes but—'

'But *nothing*, DS Harris. That's the end of the discussion. I don't want to hear it again. What else do you have for me?'

It took every ounce of willpower for Becky to bite back a response telling Munroe that she was wrong about the affair. Instead she said, 'When I broke the news to Neal's boss, David Bennington, he didn't ask about Gillian once, even though he knew Neal was married to her. And he didn't ask me anything about Hannah's murder, either, even though he'd met her. It struck me as strange. As if he knew something already.'

'Maybe he was in shock after the news.' Jamal shrugged.

'I doubt that means anything at all,' Munroe said. 'You should know by now people behave in all sorts of strange ways after hearing shocking news like that. Did he know of any connection between the victims?'

'Only that Neal Lane had met Hannah Ryan at the Salama refugee camp when she went out there to do the story.'

'Which we're already aware of. So let's not waste time on Bennington then. Anything else?'

'Just that I've passed on Neal's email password to Technical Services,' Becky said.

Munroe nodded briskly then pointed at Ronnie.

Ronnie blushed again. 'Yes, ma'am?'

'Have you found anything from financial records?'

'I'm going through paperwork retrieved from the Lanes' house, checking for some kind of link between them and the Wilsons. I've put them into an analysis spreadsheet, which took a lot of time, but so far there's no link and no suspicious financial activity.'

'I've been going through the phone records of Hannah Ryan, Neal Lane, and Gillian Lane,' Jamal said. 'So far I've only established that Hannah and Neal were in contact in the last four months.'

'That's when they met at the Salama Camp in Jordan,' Becky added.

'And most likely when their affair started,' Munroe said.

Becky muttered to herself.

'Have you got something to add, DS Harris?' Munroe stared at her, eyebrows raised.

'No, ma'am.' Becky jigged her leg up and down, chewing on her lip.

'I'm still going through them all,' Jamal said. 'I need to cross-reference everything with the Wilsons' records, see if we can find a match to them or anyone in common.'

'And I've spoken to the list of friends Gillian Lane gave us, but none of them knew the Wilsons,' Colin said.

'I've got a list of colleagues Neal worked with in Jordan,' Becky said. 'I'll contact them, too.'

'Well, make sure you keep your enquiries to whether Neal knew the Wilsons and leave it at that,' Munroe said. 'Other possible avenues for enquiry are that Neal Lane's house was only four miles away from the Wilsons' house. They might've frequented the same places. They may have shopped somewhere in common or used the same tradesman for something. These murders required planning and knowledge of the victims' movements by watching them. We find the link between the Wilsons and Hannah Ryan and Neal Lane and we find the killer.' She ran a hand through her immaculate hair. 'Last point: SOCO have confirmed there's nothing of forensic interest found in Hannah's car and no handbag found there. Retrievable fingerprints found inside only match Hannah Ryan's. Is there anything else before I meet with the Chief Constable prior to this sodding press conference?'

Becky's mobile phone pinged at the same time as Munroe's. They both glanced down at their screens, swiped, opened an email.

'It's from fingerprints,' Becky said, reading it with disappointment. 'The glove print found at Neal Lane's house isn't in the database.'

Munroe looked up from her screen. 'We're still waiting on DNA results from the saliva found on Hannah's forehead. Fingers crossed it tells us something.'

'I've been doing CCTV enquiries for the time frame when the offender ran away, and there's no trace of them on camera,' Colin said. 'They must've run through the woods and to the fields beyond and there are no cameras anywhere nearby.'

'OK, that's it then,' Munroe said. 'It's getting late. You lot go home and come back refreshed first thing in the morning. I'm off to get annihilated in the press.' She collected her bag from her office and disappeared.

Becky gathered her things together with an exaggerated huff and looked at Colin and Jamal. 'Is she always like that?'

'Like what?' Jamal said.

'Blinkered on one line of inquiry. Totally dismissive of her team's input.'

'*Your* input, sarge,' Jamal raised his eyebrows with a sarcastic air. 'You're the only one who disagrees with her. The murders are identical in every way.'

'She's under a lot of pressure now it's hit the press,' Colin said. 'She'll have calmed down by the morning.'

'Don't forget, we know the previous case better than you,' Jamal said. 'DCI Munroe's the best SIO you could want. The Wilsons' murder is the *only* one she hasn't solved so she's bound to be uptight about getting a result now we've got new leads.'

Becky had a moment's doubt. Was she wrong about this? Jamal was right about one thing, even if he was annoyingly jumped up. DCI Munroe was an experienced, respected officer with hundreds of cases behind her. Becky was a newly promoted DS who'd solved a handful of crimes and only one big one.

She said her goodbyes and drove home, unable to switch off. It was too much of a coincidence not to think there was something on the missing equipment, something Hannah and Neal had been working on that someone didn't want found. Something, she suspected, that was linked to the story Hannah was writing. But what?

She couldn't deny that the manner in which they'd been killed matched the Wilsons' murder completely. But she wasn't convinced it was the same killer. Not convinced at all. Becky might be wrong, but there was only one way to find out, and that was to keep digging – with or without Munroe's approval.

HAYAT

Chapter 23

I follow Mr Gavin inside the Portakabin. Mr David is there, too, sitting at one of the desks. He looks up from his computer screen. Smiles. I have seen him many times, going through the camp. He stops and talks to the refugees in Arabic. He seems nice. Kind. He must be. He wouldn't do this job if he wasn't.

I hear the door lock behind me, and I turn around.

Mr Gavin sits down at a chair next to Mr David. 'This lady says she wants to get out of here.'

Mr David gives me what looks like an amused look. 'You know that's not advisable. You have no papers. You will struggle to survive out of the camp. The Jordanian government is stepping up their own security and deporting refugees back to Syria.'

I chew on my lip. Wonder if my friend was mistaken. But she couldn't have been. She left. Disappeared one night. I haven't seen her for months. 'I know you can help me.' My voice is desperate, my eyes imploring. '*Please.*'

Mr Gavin looks at Mr David.

Mr David looks me up and down. 'Who are you?'

'My name is Hayat Hasani. I have no family left. I want to go to another country, get a job. I speak good English, no?'

'No family here?' Mr David asks. 'You're sure?'

'It is true.'

He scrutinises me carefully. 'And are you healthy? Do you have any medical problems? It's a huge risk to transport people who are sick.'

'I am very healthy. I have not seen the doctor here since I arrived. You can check. I am fit and will be a hard worker.'

Mr David tears his gaze away from me and nods at Mr Gavin, who gets up and leaves. Mr David locks the door behind him.

He stands in front of me. Close, so I can smell his deodorant, something fresh and clean. Not like the rest of us. His jeans look new. His shirt is pressed. His hands are not covered in dust. I see a lot in that short space of time because I am used to watching. It is all I do these days.

He reaches out and touches my face. I want to flinch, but I do not. I am strong. I can do this. Whatever it takes. I am the only thing I have to trade.

'I can arrange for you to travel by lorry. We can get you to the UK. We can find you work, a place to live.'

I nod. And nod, and nod, and nod. Yes, yes, yes. I heave a sigh of gratitude. 'Thank you.' If I can get to the United Kingdom, I will be OK. I know I will.

'What do you need in return? I told you I am healthy. I can give a kidney.'

He laughs a little. 'My dear, we do not need your kidney You will earn your passage another way.' He strokes my face again, tucks my hair behind my ear. Runs his fingertips down my shoulder, across to my waist.

He unbuttons my blouse, staring at my body.

I close my eyes, hiding the fear and the revulsion.

I am a virgin. In my culture I will be ruined. Something cracks inside, too big to be an ironic scream, because my culture, my home, doesn't exist any more.

He presses his lips to my neck, pulls me closer.

This is not sex. It is my passage fare. It is freedom.

DETECTIVE WARREN CARTER
Chapter 24

Eeny meeny miny mo. Or rather, just eeny meeny miny. I had three houses to stake out and there was only one of me, so Caroline decided to check out DCI Susan Munroe's while I took Colin Etheridge's and Jamal Faris's. We'd hang around a while and see if anything suspicious jumped out at us before calling it a night.

I stopped off at a coffee shop and ordered a caffeine hit with a fancy-sized name that just meant huge. One slab of millionaire's shortbread later and I had a romantic meal for one with my job car.

I kept getting a whiff of smoke every now and then. I needed a shower and a good night's sleep. The shower would be easy to fix when I eventually got home, but I knew I'd see the faces of those women every time I closed my eyes, and that sleep would be elusive yet again.

Rain fell and then turned to sleet as I drove to Colin's flat, the wet road kicking up a haze of dirty spray. I switched on the wipers and the radio. Becky's serial-killer case was just breaking.

I'd missed the first part of the press conference by DCI Munroe but caught her delivering the tail-end with clipped precision. 'We believe the killer is male, of average height and large build. We do not know at this time how he's selecting his victims, but the investigation is extensive and is making good progress. All available resources are at our disposal and catching him is our number-one priority. Unfortunately, we can't give details of significant evidence we've uncovered so far. But we would like to assure the public that we're doing everything possible to identify and apprehend the killer. If anyone has any information relating to who this man is, then please call our hotline. The number will be given at the end of the briefing. We urge you to remain calm, but while this person is at large, the public should remain vigilant. Please take care with your safety when inside your property. We would advise you to keep all doors and windows locked. Use alarms where possible. Thank you for your time.'

There was a burst of shouted questions from the press:

'Detective Chief Inspector! Why did you allow this dangerous killer to strike again?'

'What are you doing to apprehend him?'

'Shouldn't you be removed from the case?'

'How could you have failed to identity him after the Wilsons were brutally murdered?'

'Are you the best person to head the investigation when you let him slip through the net before?'

'How can Hertfordshire Constabulary give any credible assurances to the public after the previous corruption exposed at Bloodbath Farm and this latest incompetence?'

I turned the radio off and phoned Becky on the hands-free.

'Blimey, you can't get enough of me today,' she said by way of greeting. 'Don't tell Ian. He'll think we're having an affair on top of everything else.' She tried to keep up the usual Becky scale of cheeriness but it fell flat.

'On top of what else? You mean your case?' I asked.

'No, the case I can handle. It's my personal life that's a pile of shite.' She sighed down the line. 'He's pissing me off, that's all.'

'Oh. Anything you want to talk about?'

'No. I need something to take my mind off him, so fire away with whatever you're calling for.'

'Well, you know where I am if you need me.'

'Thanks.'

'I take it you're not in the office.'

'Nah. On my way home. With some paperwork and my laptop, which Ian's going to be even more pissed off about. Why? Is this about the leak? That'll be looked at by PSD, won't it?'

'What leak?'

'Someone leaked the serial-killer angle to the press so Munroe's just had to do a press conference about it.'

'Yeah, I just heard the end of it on the radio.'

'Munroe thinks it was one of us.'

'And what do you think?'

'Well, I know it wasn't me. And I know Ronnie wouldn't do that. But it could've been anyone. Munroe's probably going to be speaking to PSD about it to investigate the source.'

I mulled that over for a moment. Then asked her what her impressions were about Jamal Faris and Susan Munroe.

'I only just met them today. All I can say right now is Jamal's having an even worse bad-hair day than me and seems a bit arrogant. And Munroe seems . . . I don't know . . . when I first met her, I was really pleased she was going to be SIO. I thought she was going to be great. But she's rigid, not open to suggestions, blinkered, seems a bit of a control freak, and she hasn't got much of a sense of humour. Like pretty much all my other bosses have been, actually. Apart from you and Ellie Nash. DI Thornton was bad enough to work for. I know she's under pressure to solve the cases, but I'm not convinced they're even related.'

'Why not?'

'On the surface they appear to be, but . . . look, I don't have anything concrete yet. Maybe I'm wrong, maybe it's a little thing that won't pan out anyway. She just doesn't want me to follow a particular line of inquiry that I think raises a lot of questions. But that's happened to us both before with our other bosses, as you well know.'

'OK, noted. But often it's the little things, the little pieces that don't quite fit, that snowball into cracking a case. So, what are you going to do about it?'

She laughed. 'I'm going to do exactly what you used to do when being told no by the guv'nor. Dig harder! Anyway, why are you asking about them?'

I paused. I wanted to tell her what was going on with my case, but I couldn't.

'Is this to do with the missing warrant card?' she asked.

I didn't say anything. Which was all the answer she needed.

'I'm not a detective for nothing, you know. It's to do with Colin's lost warrant card and the restricted log I saw this morning, isn't it?'

'I can't confirm or deny that.'

'Ha!'

'Can you let me know if you come across anything . . . suspicious, about Munroe, Etheridge, or Faris? Or if Munroe's resistance to your theories becomes more concerning.'

'You want me to *spy* on them?' she asked incredulously.

'Yeah.'

'Hmmm.' A silence while she thought about that.

'Six women died today,' I said. 'That's all I can tell you. And that can't go any further.'

'Fucking hell.'

I pictured her closing her eyes briefly with sadness. Then the anger kicking in. She was so like me she could've been my daughter. If I'd had one.

'What do you want me to do? Hopefully not bug them?'

'No. Just observe. Let me know anything else that doesn't seem right.'

'OK. But what are you going to do for me in return?' The playful edge crept back into her voice.

'What do you want?'

'Ooh, a trip to Vegas would be nice.'

'Are you trying to blackmail an anti-corruption officer?'

She chuckled. 'All right, I'll do it. Look, I'm at home now. I'd better get in before I get a bollocking off Ian for being late again.'

We hung up and a short while later I arrived at Colin Etheridge's building – a block of about twenty-five apartments with a communal car park. He lived at number three, which I deduced meant it would be on the ground floor. I didn't get to be an Acting Detective Inspector for nothing. The only problem was, if it was at the back of the building I wouldn't be able to see it from my parking spot in a surreptitious corner of the car park. I had good vision of six downstairs windows, two with curtains closed. A light shone in the third and fourth ones, through which I could see a woman on a ladder painting a wall. The rest were in darkness.

I sipped my coffee and munched on the shortbread, trying and failing not to get crumbs all over me. I calculated in my head how much the flat was worth. Around £180,000, I reckoned. I'd been looking at property myself lately. A few months back I'd finally decided to sell the home I'd lived in with Denise for almost twenty years. It was time to let go of all the memories that were trapped inside the place. I needed to downsize and had been contemplating a two-bed flat or house. I'd found a buyer quite quickly, but the sale had fallen through. Now I didn't know if it was an omen – Denise's ghost telling me not to leave her – so I hadn't put it back on the market, but I'd still been looking through property adverts in the local papers. Colin wasn't living in a palace, and he drove a seven-year-old Vauxhall Astra. The only reason I could see a copper being involved in trafficking women would be for money. Then again, if he was a halfway decent copper, he would know how to hide it and wouldn't be flashy about spending large amounts of cash.

My phone rang then. It was the contact at the HFEA getting back to me to report that they'd only had very minor complaints about three clinics in the last couple of years, which related to pricing, lost medical notes, and making what the patient considered false promises on success rates. Nothing involving any particular doctor or allegations of using black-market donor eggs. She said she'd keep alerted to any information that came through to them and would get back to me if she discovered more. She also suggested I contact the General Medical Council in case any doctors involved in the fertility industry were subject to ongoing complaints or disciplinary procedures.

I put the phone down and sat up a little straighter as Colin's Astra pulled up and parked in the opposite corner to me. He carried his briefcase to the communal doors, unlocked them, and a little while later two of the darkened windows lit up. Then he appeared in front of them, pulling the curtains closed.

Bugger. I wasn't going to get much from that.

I shifted in my seat, wondering how Caroline was getting on. About half an hour later, I pinched my legs together, cursing the coffee I'd drunk and busting for a wee. Stake-outs were not a good idea when you had a middle-aged bladder.

At that moment Colin appeared through the front door to the block, trailing a scruffy dog that looked as old as I felt right then. He walked down the pathway and turned left at the end of the street, the dog sniffing away every few minutes. I watched until Colin disappeared and then decided to make a move. I wasn't going to discover anything useful.

Next stop, Jamal Faris's house. A three-bed terraced place on a purpose-built development that was about twenty years old, where everything looked the same and the houses were shoehorned together so they didn't have driveways. Estimated property price over £250,000.

Again, not really cause for concern. They'd bought it fifteen years ago for £87,000. I wondered how big their mortgage was.

I found a parking spot in the communal car park that gave me a good view of the front of the house and waited. More curtains, more lights behind them. But the blind was up in Jamal's kitchen window, revealing a woman with her head down, probably washing up, who must've been his wife, Asima. She had long dark hair, a dark complexion.

A miniature fibre-optic Christmas tree on their window ledge changed colours every few seconds. I hadn't bothered to put up a Christmas tree again this year. I hadn't even put up any Christmas cards because there were still people who addressed them to both Denise and me. I didn't want to celebrate it without her, it seemed wrong. She'd always loved the festive period and had been like an excited kid, decorating the tree at the beginning of December. Wrapping gifts elaborately. Preparing the whole feast of Christmas Day. The—

Jamal entered the kitchen, knocking me out of my reverie. He got something from the fridge that I couldn't see and turned around and walked back out. Five minutes later the front door opened and Jamal and Asima came out dressed in coats.

They walked to their five-year-old Toyota Yaris, the value of which was probably between £5,000 and £10,000, depending on the model. Yes, I'd been looking at cars, too.

There was nothing interesting about that, except for the fact that Asima was pregnant.

DETECTIVE BECKY HARRIS
Chapter 25

Becky's house was in darkness when she arrived home. She entered the hallway and called out for Ian. No reply.

He'd obviously got the hump and gone out with one of his mates. And the thing was, her first thought was *good*. She couldn't be bothered to deal with another row. She was knackered, but her brain wouldn't stop turning over the case in her head.

She switched on the lights, kicked off her shoes, and carried the paperwork and laptop she'd brought home into the kitchen. She dumped everything on the kitchen table, then undid the scrunchy in her hair that was supposed to be holding her messy waves into a neat ponytail but always failed to contain them.

Running her fingers through her hair, she stepped towards the fridge, wondering what concoction she could whip up for dinner. That's when she saw the note on the worktop.

If you can't be bothered to come home on time for our anniversary, what does that say about us?

Then she noticed a bouquet of red roses, dumped head first into the bin, along with a card in a lilac envelope.

'Shit. Bollocks. Arse,' she said to the empty room. It was their wedding anniversary and she'd completely forgotten about it.

She blew out a sigh. Then reached into the fridge for a half-empty bottle of pinot grigio. She poured herself a large glass and took a hefty gulp, mentally preparing for the grovelling phone call she'd have to make.

She took another gulp with her mobile pressed to her ear, listening to it ring out and Ian's voicemail kick in. 'Look, I'm really sorry. I . . . it's a big case. You know how it is. I can't just leave early. We can celebrate another time. I'm . . .' She didn't know what else to say that she hadn't said a hundred times before, so she hung up instead.

Wearily, she rustled up a cheese sandwich and popped it in the sandwich maker to toast. While it was heating up she picked absentmindedly at a half-empty bag of jelly babies she'd left on the table and went through the paperwork from Hannah Ryan's house, flicking through receipts for household items. Reading some more of the articles Hannah had written.

It was an hour later, when her stomach rumbled loudly, that she realised she'd turned the sandwich maker off ages ago after it started sizzling and smoking, but she'd been so distracted by what she was reading that she'd forgotten to actually eat the toastie.

She scraped off the congealed blob of cremated sandwich, wolfed it down, then called the editor of *Life Style*, the friend Hannah's neighbour had told her about.

She introduced herself and told Katherine Meadows the sad news about Hannah.

'Oh, my God,' Katherine said. 'I only spoke to her a few days ago. I can't . . . I can't believe it.'

'I'm sorry for being insensitive at a time like this, but I really need to ask you some questions.'

'Um . . . yes. Of course. I want to do what I can to help you catch whoever did this.'

'Did Hannah ever mention knowing a couple called Jim or Donna Wilson?'

'Um . . . no.'

OK, now that question was out of the way, she'd follow her own line of inquiry. She picked up the copy of an article Hannah had written for *Life Style* earlier in the year about female genital mutilation. 'Hannah wrote a piece for you back in May.'

'She's written several. She was fantastic at what she did.'

'And you were friends, too?'

'Yes. We both worked at one of the London dailies years ago. Before she went freelance and I started as a features writer for *Life Style*. We've been friends ever since. She was always interested in the gritty stuff. Big exposés, corruption, social injustice, that sort of thing. She wanted to work on projects that meant something important.'

'Did she mention to you the story she was working on about refugees?'

'Yes, it was for the magazine. She said . . . oh . . . why? Do you think it had something to do with why she was killed?'

It was a theory that was growing in Becky's head. The serial-killer angle wasn't making sense to her when you figured in all the missing items. 'It's possible, yes.'

'Oh, God.' Katherine took a sharp intake of breath. 'Hannah said she'd discovered something going on at the camp in Jordan, and she said she'd found a whistleblower who was prepared to go on record about it.'

Becky gripped the phone tighter. A whistleblower? Neal Lane? 'But she didn't tell you exactly what was going on?'

'No. She liked to keep things close to her chest until a story was submitted. In this industry other journos will steal your scoop in a heartbeat. I got the impression it was to do with misappropriation of funds, but I could be wrong. World Food Corps, who run the camp, are an international NGO charity. And she could hardly go round making claims about them siphoning off cash meant for refugees without any proof.'

Becky wrote down *fraud/embezzling?* and underlined it.

'This is just between me and you,' Katherine said. 'I have no proof of that, but it's just what I thought, reading between the lines.'

'Did she mention Neal Lane to you as being the whistleblower?'

'No. She never revealed sources if they wanted to remain anonymous.'

'Did she ever say she was worried about her safety?'

'No. Hannah was pretty careful, though. She'd done some exposés before that were explosive. Ruffled a few nasty feathers. She'd had threats in the past, but they never amounted to anything.'

'But nothing lately? She didn't mention anyone following her? Watching her?'

'She didn't tell me anything like that. Four days ago I rang her to check up on when she thought the story would be ready for submission. As you can imagine, we work on content months in advance. She said she was still working on some angles. She wasn't sure exactly when it would be finished.'

'Do you know if Hannah used any other email address apart from the one listed on her website?'

'Um . . . not that I'm aware of, no.'

Becky asked a few more questions and hung up. She tapped her mobile against her chin as she reached for the wine, her mind racing. She thought about David Bennington not asking her any questions about how Gillian was. Was that because he already knew what had happened to her? In her head she kept seeing the bodies of Neal and Hannah, strangled and stabbed in the kitchen. The words *DIE PIGGY DIE* written on the wall. The dashcam footage of the man in the balaclava who'd chased Gillian down the road.

If their murders were all to do with keeping Hannah and Neal quiet because of misappropriation of funds from World Food Corps, then David Bennington would be a prime suspect.

DETECTIVE WARREN CARTER
Chapter 26

'Asima Faris is pregnant,' I told Caroline down the phone. 'I'm not good on bump sizes but she's big.'

'Really?' There was a pause. 'Well, that's interesting. And both of them are of Iranian descent. If the women were of Middle Eastern ethnicity, they could be a close egg-donor match to the women in the house. Let's get hold of their medical records tomorrow. Find out if they used donor eggs. But I've been thinking. If it's Ukrainians trafficking these women here, maybe they're using a foreign doctor from Ukraine as well. Bringing them all over to the UK to cash in on the egg-donor market.'

'It's possible. Is there anything interesting going on at Munroe's house?'

'She's only just arrived home. Nice house, too. A four-bed detached in Little Wymondley. Worth a few quid, but then her husband's a barrister. He'd be earning a fortune. And I can't see her being involved in the trafficking of women.'

'Why not? Because she's a woman?' Maybe it was an old-fashioned view but women were traditionally nurturers. Somehow it always seemed worse if a woman was involved in atrocities.

'Yes. Maybe that's partly it. But . . . I don't know. Just a feeling.'

'I've been a copper for more than thirty years so I can believe anything. And one thing I've learned is that people are never just one thing.'

'But why would she? She's a respected DCI with an impeccable record. She and her husband don't appear short of money so why would she do it?'

'Maybe they've got some expensive habits or vices. Maybe they're just greedy. Or maybe they're in debt up to their eyeballs. DS Harris just told me that sensitive information regarding Munroe's serial-killer case was leaked to the press earlier. If one of them might've done that, what else are they prepared to do? We need to dig deeper through the personal lives of Etheridge, Munroe, and Faris.'

'Yes, I think we should.'

Caroline told me there was nothing more to be gained by her stake-out and that she was going home to a leftover lasagne and her cat.

I agreed with her decision. Not about the lasagne, I didn't have any. And I'd been put off for the foreseeable future after what I'd seen at the HQ canteen earlier. I didn't have a cat, either, but as I left Jamal's house I was seriously thinking about getting a pet. Maybe all I needed was a bit of furry company to lessen the loneliness.

There was one more thing I wanted to do before I went back to my empty house, so I drove to a quiet country lane and parked up. I reached inside the glovebox and pulled out the anonymous pay-as-you-go phone and dialled.

I knew the number off by heart. Not because I'd called it frequently. In fact, I'd only ever called it once before. But I'd memorised it in case I ever needed it again. I didn't know the name of the man who answered on the seventh ring. I only ever knew him by the nickname I'd given him – the Vigilante. But I knew without a shadow of a doubt that he was ex-special forces. And he was one of two other people who knew what really happened at Bloodbath Farm the night I'd killed someone.

'Hi. It's me,' I said. 'I don't want to be one of those boring people who only ring when they want help but . . .'

He snorted with humour. It wasn't as if we were friends. We weren't anything, except killers in kind. And the thing was . . . I didn't even think what we'd done was wrong. I'd killed to save his life and the life of an innocent victim who was about to be tortured and murdered in the most horrific way. But it wasn't the act of killing that kept me awake at night, it was all those victims I *hadn't* saved that preyed desperately on my mind. I often wondered what that made me. The good guy or the bad guy? A hypocrite? A criminal or an enforcer of the law? The truth was there had been no choice. It had been kill or be killed. It had been about protecting good people. And even though I tried not to think about what else the Vigilante might've done, I knew without a shadow of a doubt he was one of the good guys.

'Can we meet?' I asked.

A pause. Then, 'Yes. Where are you?'

'Stevenage.'

'OK. Take the A1M to the South Mimms exit. Follow the signs for Potters Bar.' Then he named a quiet recreation park to meet at in forty-five minutes' time.

The park was dark when I arrived five minutes early and no one was around. The sleety rain that had started falling as I drove there was keeping everyone snuggled up at home.

The large car park and several football pitches in front of it were empty. I parked in the furthest corner and positioned my vehicle so I could see the road entrance. Exactly on time, a pick-up truck drove in and parked next to me.

I looked through my window at the Vigilante. He nodded in acknowledgement. Got out of his truck and into my passenger seat.

He shook my hand and said, 'How are you, detective? And what can I do for you?'

I explained about the job offer and gave him a rundown of the case I was working on.

'Trafficking women? Fucking bastards.' His voice hardened. 'What do you need from me?'

'I'm trying to find out who Odesa Investments are and we're drawing a blank. Since they're offshore and their bank is, too, I think we're going to struggle to get any info for them through normal police channels, if they even cough it up at all.' Whoever the Vigilante was, I knew he could gather intelligence that I could only dream of, in ways I couldn't even begin to guess. And he wasn't bound by rules and bureaucracy and laws. 'Any emails for Powell Acton and Acton Associates or background would be helpful, too. If we have to rely on the email providers we could be waiting months.'

'It might take a little while. Ukraine's banks are considered an up-and-coming offshore opportunity for criminal activities as they're typically run by the mafia, so money-laundering is rife, and privacy of clients is ultra-protected. I'll get on to my guy, though.'

I pictured his mate in my head as another shaven-headed, powerfully built, tattooed guy like the Vigilante.

'Is there anything else I can do to help?'

'I'm going to be digging into three coppers who might be involved. I can get hold of their standard phone and financial records, but I need to know if any of them have links to secret offshore banks or companies. Or any links to Powell Acton and his firm. I'm going to get whoever's involved if it bloody kills me.'

'But you know as well as I do, it doesn't always happen like that in real life.'

'Exactly.' Which was why I was willing to break the law to solve a case. I didn't feel guilty about that because I'd witnessed time and time again that the law, the judicial system, was often broken and failed repeatedly to protect the very people it was supposed to look after. If we hadn't done what we had at Bloodbath Farm, then I was certain that vicious, evil people would've got away with it all to do it again. Just because the law was 'legal' didn't mean it was right or fair or justice. This wasn't about me, it was about finding the killer of six young women and letting their voices be heard. The only thing that did worry me was that one day I might get caught.

We said our goodbyes. I was still hungry so I picked up a balti with pilau rice and a naan bread on the way back and drove home to my empty, lonely house.

I wondered what Caroline was doing. Then I quickly chastised myself for thinking about her again and felt the guilt kicking in. I shouldn't be thinking about another woman when my wife was dead. It was . . . well, I didn't know what it was, because it was something I hadn't experienced before. In all the years I'd been with Denise I'd never really thought about another woman. I'd looked, of course. I was still a normal guy, not a saint. But never once had I been properly attracted to someone other than my wife or tempted to stray. Apart from the fact Caroline was my superior officer, it was wrong.

Wrong, wrong, wrong, I told myself.

DETECTIVE BECKY HARRIS
Chapter 27

Becky dialled DCI Munroe's number and stood pacing until she picked up. 'Ma'am, I think Gillian Lane could be in danger. I've now spoken to the list of Hannah's friends I got from her mum. One of them is Katherine Meadows, an editor at *Life Style* magazine. She knew about the story Hannah was writing on the refugees, that Neal Lane was helping Hannah with. I think he was blowing the whistle on some financial irregularities at World Food Corps. It's a motive for their murder.' She gabbled on without pausing for breath, laying out her theory. 'Maybe the killer went after Gillian to try and kill her too because he suspected she knew something. Otherwise there was no reason to chase her out of that house instead of making his escape. That's why the laptops, phones, camera, photos, hard drives, and flashdrives aren't anywhere to be found. The killer wanted to get rid of any evidence. I don't think their murders are related to the Wilsons' murders at all. And I think he could try to get to Gillian again. We need to put someone guarding her door and get her into protective custody when she gets out of the hospital tomorrow.'

There was silence on the other end of the line.

'Ma'am, are you still there?'

'Yes, I was just making sure you'd completely finished,' Munroe said calmly. 'Do you have any evidence to prove this *theory*?'

'No. But—'

'Exactly. And how would you explain the words the killer wrote on the wall? Or the identical MO of the crime scene – the knife wounds and exact same cause of death as Donna and Jim Wilson?'

'It's a copycat.' Becky thought back to the conversation she'd had with Warren Carter. Although the words on the wall had never been released to the public prior to the death of Hannah Ryan and Neal Lane, there were plenty of people who knew about them. Everyone involved in the previous investigation, for starters, which included the very people Warren wanted her to spy on, which in turn included the DCI she was talking to right now. But it was a big leap for Becky to assume her own kind would be involved in killing Neal Lane and Hannah Ryan. A leap she wasn't comfortable with at all. What possible reason would there be? Police officers gossiped to each other all the time. DI Thornton had recognised those words at the scene straight away, as had Becky, but she couldn't remember where she'd heard it from. SOCO officers would've known, too. Any one of them may have told someone else who'd told someone else. 'But what if I'm right and the killer tries again? Surely we should look into David Bennington and World Food Corps more closely.'

'I think you're going off on a tangent that's totally off the mark. There's no way I can authorise the budget for protective custody when I don't believe she's in any danger,' Munroe said. 'The killer knows Gillian can't ID him so he's not going to try again. As far as I'm concerned, it's got to be the same killer as the Wilsons.' Her voice softened a notch. 'Well done for thinking outside the box, but this is way outside what the evidence is telling us. Any story Hannah was allegedly writing is purely coincidence.'

'Yes, but—'

'Look, I think you're a good copper, Becky. You didn't get a commendation for nothing. I want to see you get a DI promotion, and if we crack this case, you *will* be put forward for it. God knows, we need more females in top spots. And I, more than anyone, know how hard it is to get on in this job. We're on the same side here. But if you want to succeed in the force, and I think you do, you need to prove you can follow orders. There's a hierarchy and a chain of command for a reason.' She said it pleasantly enough but there was a warning in it, too. 'As I said in the briefing, we need to look for something that links the victims and we'll find the killer. Are we clear?'

'But the *only* thing we've found linking the cases is the *way* they were killed. None of the rest of it fits. The two sets of victims had no mutual friends. No crossover into each other's lives. I really think it's a copycat and—'

'And the way they were killed is *exactly* the same. I said, are we clear?' There was a brittle edge to her voice.

Becky hesitated, thinking about the promotion carrot dangled in front of her. Then she said, 'Yes, ma'am.'

'Good. Have a nice evening, and I'll see you at seven thirty tomorrow.'

Becky hung up and stared at the phone. She picked up a jelly baby and bit the head off it with a growl. Yes, she *was* ambitious. Of course she wanted promotion. But Susan Munroe didn't know her that well. And Becky hated carrots, dangled or otherwise.

She'd look for links, all right. But she'd be looking for a different kind of link entirely. She wouldn't get authorisation to look into David Bennington's comms, computer, and financial data from Munroe – she'd need help on that from somewhere else – but so what? That wasn't going to stop her. It wouldn't be the first time she'd gone against orders. And there might be a way to prove the Wilsons' killer wasn't the same as the one responsible for Hannah's and Neal's murders.

She opened her laptop, pulled up the digital photos of the crime scene at Oak Drive, stared at the *DIE PIGGY DIE* words on the wall written in block capital letters with black marker pen, most likely a standard one that could be picked up at a million different places. She still couldn't work out the significance of that phrase to the killer in relation to the victims, unless it was indeed meant to be a taunt to the police. She minimised the photo and found a photo from the Wilsons' house with the same words written on their wall. Minimised that one so the two were side by side. Stared at them for a while. They looked pretty damn similar but they would be easy enough to copy.

She scrolled through her phone, found a number of someone she thought might be able to help her prove it one way or another, then dialled.

HAYAT

Chapter 28

I stumble out of the cabin, clutching my arm around my waist. My legs wobble as I slip down the steps and land in a crumpled heap on my knees in the dirty, dusty soil.

I close my eyes for a brief moment. Blink back tears. Guilt and disgrace mushroom inside my chest.

Laughter sounds from somewhere far away. Two men. I wonder what they have to laugh about.

I walk slowly and with effort back towards my Portakabin, down a dusty path, past tents with families outside. The walk of shame with a painful throbbing sensation between my legs. Hope pushes the guilt away. Ten minutes of my life ruined but I will be free, Mr David has said so. He will tell me when the time is right, and I will finally be able to leave.

As I walk past one tent I hear my name being called from behind. I ignore it for as long as I can. I am not in the mood to talk.

But she catches up with me, the reporter. She rushes up beside me and comes around, standing in front of me, blocking my way.

'Hi.' She smiles.

'Hi,' I say softly.

'Is everything OK?'

I look down at the floor so I don't have to meet her gaze in case she knows what I have done.

'I saw you coming out of the admin cabin.'

My head snaps upwards. 'Were you following me?' I narrow my eyes at her. I cannot have her spying and ruining everything.

'Of course not. I was worried about you so I came to find you. I've been looking for you.'

I sidestep around her. Start walking. I need a shower. I need to get rid of him. 'I am going to bed.'

But she will not give up. She walks with me.

'I wanted to give you this.' She pulls something out of her trouser pocket and hands it to me. It is a small package, wrapped in pretty paper.

I stop walking. Stare at it.

'Go on, it's for you. I got it from the market. Happy birthday, Hayat. I'm sorry it's a late present.'

Tears prickle beneath my lids, but I can't let them out because if I do they will never stop. There will be a river of tears, enough to wash away this whole camp. Enough to carry me back home. But even though Syria is so close across the border, there is nothing left for me there but ghosts.

'Open it.' She looks so happy to be giving me a gift, and I do not want to be rude so I take it.

I unwrap it with trembling fingers. It is a bracelet made of beads. I choke back tears. 'Thank you. It is lovely.' And it is. But it is useless to me.

She stands there awkwardly for a moment. Then says, 'What's going on, Hayat?'

'Nothing,' I say too quickly.

'You started to tell me something before. About the trafficking. Who is involved in it?'

I shake my head, my hand clasped around the bracelet. 'I cannot tell you. If I tell you it will not happen.'

She grabs my arm to stop me leaving.

I let out a cry and shake her off. 'What? You cannot ruin my only chance. Stop asking me questions. I do not want to tell you,' I urge her quietly, my gaze dancing around at the tents on either side of us, people watching the exchange as if it is the most entertainment they have had in years. And the sad thing is, it probably is.

'Are they involved in something?' She jerks her head back towards the admin cabin.

I shake my head. Bite my lip.

She just looks at me. It is a look that seems to see right through me, to my bones, my heart, my head.

'If anyone tells you they can get you safe passage from here, they're lying,' she says. 'They will want something in return.'

'My friend left and she is fine.' I turn away and start walking.

But she doesn't give up. She is there again beside me, so close our elbows are touching. 'What friend? Where did she go? Have you heard from her?'

And now I have had enough. I feel bad already, and I do not want her spoiling things for me. So I tell her, just to get rid of her. Just to make her leave me alone. I stop suddenly and face her. 'Her name is Larisa Hamed. She left two months ago. She went to England.' I lift my chin in the air and stare at her.

'How do you know she is OK? Has she been granted asylum?'

'I know because word got around camp. Mr Gavin told a friend who told me. She has papers now. She is accepted by British government. She is free.'

The reporter blows out a breath and shakes her head as if she doesn't believe me. 'Yes, but how do you *know* that's true? How do you know she's not in one of those other camps I told you about? Or worse.'

I let out an angry noise. '*Arrrrughhhh*! Leave me alone. I cannot talk to you any more.' I run away from her, as fast as my wobbling legs will allow.

I get in the shower and wash and wash and wash. I will not listen to her. I know Mr David speaks the truth.

DETECTIVE WARREN CARTER
Chapter 29

I had five hours of uninterrupted sleep, which was an unheard-of improvement. The first night I could remember sleeping five solid hours in over eighteen months. They said you needed less sleep the older you got, but it had been getting ridiculous with the insomnia that had plagued me since Denise's illness, and I'd tried everything I could think of. Alcohol, some weird herbal concoctions that stank of cow-pats, hot baths before bed, even lavender oil on my pillow, yet nothing seemed to work. But for once I actually felt properly rested and energised, humming away with a bounce in my step as the kettle boiled, the dream I'd had last night suddenly coming to the forefront of my mind.

Shit. I froze for a moment. I'd only bloody well gone and dreamed of Caroline. Walking along a deserted beach. Hand in hand with me. In a bikini! Her, not me. What the hell was wrong with me?

I shook my head to try and rid it of the images of Caroline's blue bikini matching the colour of her eyes. I whistled extra loudly to put myself off thinking about her. Stirred the coffee vigorously.

After a couple of slices of toast with Marmite I was ready to stomach the new day, where corrupt coppers helped steal women and forced them to become baby-making slaves. And it had to be a copper involved. I didn't believe there could be an innocent explanation for the warrant card being found at Brampton Hospital. I was convinced someone had dropped it there. Whether Colin's story about losing it in the police station was a lie and he'd in fact lost it at the crime scene, or whether someone else had picked it up after he'd genuinely lost it and taken it with them for some unknown reason, remained to be seen.

The sun wasn't even a hint on the horizon when I got to the office, but I wasn't the first one in. Caroline was already there. I thought about the dream again. Tried *not* to think about it, which made me think about it even more, and took my jacket off, hanging it up on a coat stand in the corner. Yes, PSD even had one of those. All mod cons in this office.

'Morning, ma'am.' I hovered in her doorway, putting my professional head on and hoping I wasn't blushing.

'Morning.' She gave me a wide smile. 'Guess who called me last night? DCI Munroe. She wanted to report the leak of information to the press on her case. Wanted PSD to investigate it.'

I raised an eyebrow. 'What did you say?'

She grinned. 'I said we'd look into it, of course. But she put forward the names of DC Ronnie Pickering or DS Becky Harris as the possible source of the leak.'

I snorted. 'Really? There's no *way* Becky or Ronnie leaked anything. Do you think Munroe's just passing the buck, trying to get the heat away from her? She's not stupid – she knew we were asking about Colin's warrant card for a far more serious reason than him simply losing it. If she was involved, she could've realised she'd left it at Brampton Hospital and is trying to cover up her mistake.'

'It's possible. Or maybe she really is the exemplary officer she seems to be and she's just doing her job.'

'Maybe, although I spoke to Becky last night and she's having issues with Munroe's lines of inquiry on the serial-killer case.'

Caroline raised an eyebrow. 'That's interesting but it doesn't mean Munroe's not doing her job properly or that something sinister is going on. Superior officers often make decisions their team don't like. You seemed to have had that problem a lot with your SIOs.' The corners of her lips quirked up in a grin.

'Yes. But that's one of the reasons you wanted me here. Because I didn't ignore my instincts. Becky's the same. She's going to let me know if anything more comes of it.'

'OK. The historical phone and financial records I requested last night have come through for DCs Colin Etheridge and Jamal Faris. I've emailed them over to you. Still waiting on the others for Munroe. Info on all their known email addresses are going to take a lot longer. But I don't think we're ready to seize their work computers or phones just yet. Not until we have more to go on. I don't want them to know we're actively looking at them. I've also requested historical triangulation data for all their phones to see if it puts any of them at Brampton Hospital, but that's going to take a while to come through. And I've requested Jamal and Asima Faris's medical records.'

I nodded and went back to my desk, booted up my computer, and opened the attached files from Caroline. I started with Colin's calls from his personal phone for the last twelve months, perusing the list slowly. Calls to and from a care home in Hitchin. His sister who lived in Wales. His bank. Netflix helpline. Dentist. Doctor. Vet. All mundane and boring. And he could quite easily have had an unregistered, pay-as-you-go phone stashed away somewhere.

The numbers and names were swimming before my eyes by the time the rest of my team came in. I delegated all the records for Jamal Faris, and Colin's financial records, out to the others. Cross-referencing their police-issued mobile phones would be tedious and slow, trying to discount cases the officers had worked on with witnesses or colleagues they'd spoken to. But the hours of boring grunt work were what solved cases.

I'd just settled in for another bout of number overload when I spotted something interesting. Yesterday, Colin had made a call from his personal mobile phone to a John Hinckley, which was a name I recognised. I logged on to my own emails and found the one I was looking for from a John Hinckley who worked at the shitty tabloid the *Daily World* whose tag line was 'news, sport, celebrity, and gossip!' Although it was more focused on gossip than actual news. He'd emailed me after the Bloodbath Farm case, wanting me to call him and do a tell-all, but I'd refused flatly to talk to any journalists about it. He'd said he wanted to write a book about the case, although I seriously doubted he could even write a truthful shopping list.

I sat back, staring at the screen. Yep, it was the same number Hinckley had emailed me.

I couldn't see any good reason for Colin to be speaking to a smarmy, lying member of the tabloids unless he was leaking information. It didn't take a genius to work out what he was telling them, either. The media was going mad about the case Becky was working on. A new serial killer in town. The Cupid Killer. Colin had made the call to him and just over an hour later John Hinckley had broken the story.

'Naughty boy, Colin.' I tutted and shook my head.

Now we had two choices. We could question Colin, get him suspended while we gathered evidence, and then if proven he'd be sacked and most likely prosecuted for misconduct in public office. But that would let him know he was under investigation, and if he was leaking information, what else was he doing? Six dead women were way more serious than passing on confidential info to the press. Was Colin the one involved in trafficking and imprisoning those poor girls at Brampton Hospital? Option two was to keep him under surveillance through various methods and let him stay in post until we gathered more evidence.

I knocked on Caroline's door and told her what I'd found.

She sat back and swivelled in her chair as she thought, weighing up the risk assessment of leaving him in the job, unaware of an investigation, or arresting and suspending him. 'I don't want to tip him off. It had to be his warrant card we found at the scene, which is way more serious than being a press informant.'

'I agree. But it's still possible that he genuinely lost the warrant card in the bar or car park and another member of staff picked it up, maybe intending to give it back, but then lost it themselves at the hospital.'

'Yes, it could be anyone. We can arrange for some covert surveillance to be put in place on Colin and see what it brings to light.'

'Jack's going through his financial records now. And if Colin's stupid enough to use his personal mobile to call the press, then he may just be stupid enough to pay some dirty money from trafficking those women into his bank accounts.'

'We still need to keep looking at Munroe and Faris, though, just to be thorough.' She stood up and reached for her uniform jacket. 'Good work.' She buttoned it up. 'I'm heading to the second round of post-mortems now. Professor Hanley's starting early to get through the other three today.' She gave me a grimace.

I pictured the last three women on the cold, metal tables. The Y incision. The organs being removed and weighed. Their skulls being sliced open with a bone saw. The indignity, the finality. All that remained of them being reduced to nothing more than meat on a slab.

I clenched my fists and got back to work.

DETECTIVE BECKY HARRIS
Chapter 30

Becky had fallen asleep on her bed with the folders of paperwork from Hannah Ryan's house scattered around her. At the sound of the alarm she jerked upright, knocking them onto the floor.

'Shit.' She rubbed her eyes and looked at the space on the bed where Ian would usually be. He hadn't come home last night.

She swung her legs off the bed and picked up her mobile. No missed calls from him. He was punishing her. Maybe she deserved it, but she wouldn't be the first person in the world to forget an anniversary. And in the scheme of things, she didn't even think it was that important. They could celebrate any time, if they wanted, although she wasn't sure she wanted to right now. But a killer wouldn't be caught unless she cut through the layers of lies and found the truth. *That* was what was important.

She picked up the files then quickly showered and dressed. She was convinced that David Bennington was involved in the murders of Hannah Ryan and Neal Lane because Bennington had somehow found out he or World Food Corps were about to be exposed for fraud or embezzlement of charity funds. And if that was true, what better way to cover it up than to make it look like the work of the same killer who'd murdered the Wilsons? A copycat killing that would point everyone in the wrong direction. A serial killer would stir up a frenzy and direct attention away from the real offender. And the more she thought about it, the more she was sure someone close to the original investigation had to be involved to be able to duplicate the MO so completely.

It was slightly crazy. Definitely outside the box Munroe wanted her to think inside. Well, sod the box! Becky was certain she was on to something.

Her phone rang as she stuffed down a bowl of Rice Krispies.

It was the handwriting expert she'd called the night before, asking him to analyse the *DIE PIGGY DIE* words on the walls at both murder scenes, and it was bad news. There was little he could do without an imprint being on paper. And the usual handwriting analysis didn't apply to block capital letters, therefore he couldn't confirm or deny the possibility it was the same person's writing. All he could say was that there were similarities between the two samples.

Damn. Still, it wouldn't stop her. As she drove towards the station, her mind turned over which police officers could be involved in the passing on of information about the Wilson crime scene to David Bennington or whoever had killed Neal and Hannah. Well, Becky didn't believe in coincidences. Warren had asked her to spy on DCI Munroe, DC Etheridge, and DC Faris. All of whom had worked on the Wilsons' murders and knew all the details. Warren had been asking her about a lost warrant card belonging to Colin. And he'd mentioned a PSD case involving six dead women. So obviously a warrant card had been found at Warren's murder scene, but if it had been identifiable as Colin's he would've been arrested straight away.

Six dead women. Six dead women. She tapped the steering wheel, driving on autopilot.

Warren hadn't gone into more details but what if those dead women were witnesses to something, too? What if they knew something about Bennington and he wanted them silenced?

She dialled Warren Carter on the hands-free and tapped the steering wheel as she waited for him to pick up.

'Those six dead women you mentioned,' she said after he'd said hello. 'Did they have any connection to World Food Corps or David Bennington?'

'Who are they?'

'Bennington is the CEO and owner of World Food Corps – an international NGO charity who provide aid to refugees. They run a refugee camp in Jordan.' She gave him a brief rundown of her case.

A pause. And then: 'Oh, shit.'

'What?'

'We need to meet up. Right now. I think it's possible our cases might be related. Where are you?'

'Just heading to the nick. There's a briefing at half seven.'

'All right. I'll meet you in the car park outside McDonald's on the Roaring Meg Retail Park.'

Becky hung up and chewed on her lip as she sped to the RV point, pleased that her gut instinct seemed to be right, but sickened by the possibility that someone she worked with could be bent.

DETECTIVE WARREN CARTER
Chapter 31

Becky got into my car. For once, we didn't waste time on banter. I asked her to outline her investigation.

After she'd rushed through it all she said, 'DCI Munroe doesn't want me investigating the angle of Hannah's story and Neal being the whistleblower. She's adamant it's a serial killer and won't entertain other lines of inquiry.'

Was she adamant because she genuinely believed it was the same killer? Or was Munroe trying to cover up her tracks if she was involved, misdirecting the investigation from the start? Was Colin involved? Especially since he was feeding confidential info to the press so they'd detract away from Hannah Ryan and Neal Lane with outlandish stories of a serial killer that would cause wide-scale panic. Or were Faris and his wife involved because they had used black-market egg donors?

I rubbed at my forehead. 'What I'm going to tell you stays between us, OK?'

'Of course.' She twisted around in the seat, all ears.

I filled her in on everything I knew about the case. 'If Hannah's story was about the refugee camp in Jordan then it's likely it wasn't about anything to do with funds from World Food Corps. It's more likely to have been about exposing a ring of traffickers who've been taking female refugees from the camp and bringing them to the UK to become egg donors.'

'Bloody hell!'

'Colin's been leaking information to the press about your case,' I said.

She gasped. 'Sneaky bastard! Do you think he's the one involved in the trafficking ring, then?'

'I don't know for certain yet.' I shrugged. 'But I'm sure a copper is involved because of Colin's warrant card. Now your case seems to be connected to mine, it's got to be Munroe, Jamal, or Colin. Yes, someone else could've picked Colin's card up in the bar or car park but that's looking extremely unlikely now. I got a call from my office while I was waiting for you. Faris and his wife put themselves into debt with five cycles of IVF. They're both of Middle Eastern origin and his wife's pregnant. Those girls would've been a good match as egg donors.'

Becky shook her head. 'It's sick. But I'm suspicious of Munroe. I had a viable line of inquiry into Hannah and Neal and she shut me down. I'm certain their murder is a copycat, and Munroe could've been the one to organise it. Or at least pass info on to someone else to make it look like a serial killer.'

'We're going to be looking at all of them a lot closer now. And needless to say, I don't want any of them tipped off. I'll start looking into David Bennington, too. See if there's anything connecting him to the others.'

'Good, because Munroe won't give me authorisation to look into him. And what about Gillian? She's coming out of hospital today. If the killer thinks she knows something that her husband knew, he's likely to try and get to her again.'

I thought about that for a moment. 'You said all of the officers are aware that Gillian didn't know anything about her husband being a whistleblower, or that he was helping Hannah with her story, after you spoke to her?'

Becky nodded. 'Munroe even said that at the start of the press conference yesterday.'

'So if they know Gillian has no information that could compromise Bennington and whoever else is involved, then there's no reason to go after her again, is there?'

Becky drew in a deep breath, nodded slowly. 'I suppose not, no.'

'OK. You keep digging from your end.'

'One more thing. I got a list of colleagues Neal Lane worked with in Jordan from David Bennington. If there was something going on out there, then they might be able to shed some light on it.' She flipped through her notebook, took a photo of the relevant page and then emailed it to my phone. 'If that list came from Bennington, and he's involved, then it's doubtful he would've given the names of anyone who might help us, but it's worth a try.'

'Thanks.'

She looked at her watch. 'I've got just enough time to get to the briefing without being late.' She grabbed the door handle to get out of the car.

I put a hand on her arm. 'Thanks for this.'

'No problem. I just hope we can find something that sticks.'

'Make sure you watch your back, OK?'

She got into her own car while I called Jack, giving him an update on what I'd learned and passing on David Bennington's details to carry out the usual checks. Yet more paperwork to go through. All my team were going to be flat out data-mining through reams of it.

My mobile phone rang a few minutes later. It was Liz, who I'd assigned to the job of contacting the General Medical Council regarding any possible complaints or disciplinary action involving fertility doctors. She'd had a negative result. There were none on file or pending. She'd gone one step further and checked with the NHS to see if they had anything suspicious on file for any member of medical staff experienced in fertility treatments, but the result was the same.

I thanked her and blew out a frustrated breath as I opened the glovebox, turned on the pay-as-you-go phone, and sent a text to the Vigilante, asking if he could also find out anything about David Bennington, specifically if he had any involvement in Odesa Investments. I knew I was playing with fire, getting information that way. But the Ukrainian government and Privatnyy Bank still wouldn't play ball with us, and the image of those six women wouldn't go away. I could still smell the smoke like it was ingrained in my nose, my head. It was a risk I was willing to take to get answers I might never find using standard police methods.

With the burner phone replaced, I started the engine and drove off, turning the windscreen wipers on as sleet began to fall.

My phone rang then. It was Lyndsey Downs, the senior SOCO who was working the scene at Brampton Hospital.

'Please tell me you've found a proliferation of DNA and evidence,' I said.

'I'd love to, but unfortunately not. You knew how difficult it was going to be in that state.'

I sighed. 'Yeah. I can always live in hope.'

'But we have found one very interesting thing, though.'

DETECTIVE BECKY HARRIS
Chapter 32

By the time Becky rushed up the stairs to the CID office she was sweating and red-faced. She burst into the room to find the briefing had already started.

'Nice of you to join us,' DCI Munroe said.

'Sorry, ma'am. Traffic was a nightmare.' She hurried to her desk, dumped her handbag on the floor and picked up a pen, ready to take notes.

'As I was saying . . .' She eyed Becky again before carrying on. 'In response to the press's sensationalism, we've had a plethora of the usual nutters calling the hotline, along with panicked people ringing constantly, reporting numerous names as the killer. One crazy old woman even said her cat was responsible. So far we've had over four hundred calls, and however irrelevant they seem, every one of them has to be checked out, which is a bloody nightmare, and exactly what I wanted to avoid. I've managed to get some uniforms on that, but Jamal, you'll be liaising with them on anything that looks promising.'

Jamal nodded, looking unimpressed.

'Technical Services have said there's nothing helpful in Neal Lane's email account,' Munroe said. 'We're still waiting for the details of Hannah's to come through. Anyone got anything else to report?'

Yeah, plenty, Becky thought. But you won't want to hear it.

There were noes from Ronnie, Jamal, and Colin. Ronnie's pile of paperwork and Post-it notes had grown to mammoth proportions on his desk and he looked eager to get back to it.

Becky watched Munroe carefully with fresh eyes as she tapped at her phone screen. Was she involved and, if so, why? Becky glanced at Jamal dialling a phone number, at Colin typing. A ball of disgust ricocheted around her stomach at the thought of one of them doing something so heinous.

'Becky, Gillian Lane is going to be discharged soon,' Munroe said. 'You're on taxi duty. Pick her up and take her back to the marital home so she can collect some items and then deposit her at Dean Lane's house.'

Becky swallowed and pulled herself together. She had to act normal. 'Yes, ma'am.' She picked up her bag.

'A word, though, before you go.' Munroe jerked her head towards her office door.

Becky followed her in.

'Close the door, please.'

Becky obliged.

'I don't appreciate tardiness on my team.' Munroe crossed her arms and scrutinised Becky's face.

Well, I don't appreciate a bent copper, either, Becky thought as a muscle ticked away in her clenched jaw.

'I meant what I said last night. This is a high-profile case. When we catch the offender, I'll make sure you're in line for promotion if you prove to me you've earned it. But you have to decide what side you're on. You have to follow specified lines of inquiries laid down by me, and seriously tone down your aggressive and opinionated attitude around your superior officers. Do you understand?'

Becky got the message loud and clear. *Do as I say and I'll look after you. Don't question my judgement.* Becky smiled. Nodded. Yes, ma'am'd a few times. Because calling Munroe condescending and possibly corrupt to boot probably wasn't the best career choice she could make. But if Munroe was involved, Becky was going to help make damn sure she was exposed.

Becky drove the CID car out of the station and tried Ian again on the in-car Bluetooth system. No reply. She blew out a deep breath, thought about leaving a message on his voicemail, then decided against it.

By the time she arrived at Lister Hospital, Gillian was sitting on the bed, staring at the lino. She wore jogging bottoms and a jumper, and wrapped around her shoulders over the sling was a thick coat that her brother-in-law must have brought in.

'Morning,' Becky said. 'How are you feeling?' Which she knew was a stupid question, but she could hardly not ask it.

Gillian looked tiny and fragile, sitting there hunched up into herself, her face a rainbow of bruises. She shook her head as if there were no words to describe how she felt, which Becky understood completely.

'Are you ready to go?'

Gillian nodded.

There was a set of keys on the bedside locker. The ones Gillian had put into her coat pocket after she'd entered her house, although the coat and her clothing had since been taken for examination by SOCO. Gillian picked the keys up, clutched them in her good hand, and they walked out of the door, Gillian limping slightly.

'Have they finished . . . at the house?' Gillian asked after Becky had got her seated in the car.

'Almost. Your bedroom has been processed so we can get some clothes for you, though.'

Gillian stared out of the window as the world passed her by.

Becky glanced at Gillian's profile, fighting with herself about whether to tell Gillian what she suspected. There was a fine balance between being honest and seeming to toe the official line. But if the official line was bent, if Munroe was involved, then of course she was going to lead it off in a direction that wouldn't explore the theory Becky and Warren had formed. Would it make it easier on Gillian to hear that Neal must've kept Hannah a secret from her because he was trying to protect her? It might put Gillian's mind at rest about her husband's faithfulness, but it might only panic her further. No, she wouldn't say anything. Not yet. Not until she knew anything for certain. Becky bit her lip and carried on driving, the sound of Gillian's sniffs punctuating the silence.

Becky spotted the press vans and camera crews on the main road before she'd even turned into Oak Drive. More press were crammed down the lane, parked up before the new police cordon that had been erected in front of the house. Some reporters were doing pieces in front of the camera for their studio audience. That arsehole John Hinckley was in the thick of things, talking with another guy and laughing loudly.

Becky almost mowed him down, just for the fun of it. Hinckley had to jump out of the way suddenly, nearly hitting the deck.

Becky allowed herself a smug smile. Bloody hyenas.

She pulled up in front of the police cordon and showed her ID to a uniformed officer, who let her through. She parked the car outside Gillian's house and ushered Gillian towards it, a protective arm around her shoulder. Gillian trembled beneath her as reporters strained behind the cordon like a frenzy of great white sharks with a whiff of fish bait, shouting out questions.

'Was your husband having an affair?'

'Do you hold the police responsible for not catching the Wilsons' killer earlier?'

'How do you feel, knowing your husband was murdered by the Cupid Killer?'

Honestly, how did they think she felt? What did they expect Gillian to say? Insensitive bastards. Becky wanted to tell the lot of them to fuck right off. Instead, she bit back an outburst of profanity and whispered to Gillian, 'Just ignore them,' as she steered her up the driveway to the closed front door.

Becky rang the bell.

'I've got my keys.' Gillian held them up. She had fresh tears in her eyes and looked as if she was using all her strength to keep her composure.

'It's OK. Someone from SOCO will let us in.'

The door swung open and Emma Bolton stood there, white-suited with a mask on, just the peak of her red hair showing beneath the hood. She nodded sombrely at Becky and Gillian. 'I'm very sorry for your loss, Mrs Lane.'

Gillian didn't seem as if she'd heard her. She stood in the hallway, looking around vaguely at the surfaces covered in fingerprint powder, as if she'd never seen the place before.

'We've almost finished,' Emma said. 'Just doing the rear garden now,' she said, more to Becky than Gillian.

'Shall we go and get your things?' Becky lightly touched Gillian's good elbow and guided her up the stairs.

Twenty-five minutes later, Gillian had a suitcase packed and had confirmed, after a search around the house, that nothing else was missing. Becky and Gillian retraced their journey outside to a flash of cameras and more ridiculous questions.

After getting Gillian settled in the passenger seat, Becky's mobile rang. It was Dean Lane, telling her that the press were also now camped outside his house.

She fought the urge to swear, rolled her eyes, and asked him to hold on while she told Gillian.

Gillian wiped away the tears on her cheeks. 'Oh, God! I can't stand it. I can't stand them hounding us. How can I stay at his place now when they're going to be camped out on the doorstep, asking their nasty questions? Printing stories about Neal having an affair? I need to get away.'

'And go where?'

'To the cottage. In Devon. I want to go there. Can you . . . can you ask Dean if he could take me there?'

'Would you like to speak to him yourself?'

Gillian nodded and Becky passed over the phone.

After a quick conversation, arrangements were made for Dean to pack a bag and meet them at a supermarket car park so he could drive Gillian to the cottage and stay with her while she recuperated.

Half an hour later, Becky had helped a tearful Gillian into Dean's car and watched them drive away. She was just heading back to the nick when her phone rang.

A breathless DCI Munroe said, 'Where are you? You've been bloody ages.'

Becky fought back the urge to say it was *she* who had put Becky on taxi duties instead of being in the thick of things, when a uniformed officer could've done exactly the same thing. Or did Munroe just want her out of the way, not asking too many questions? Instead, she told her about the change of plan due to the press harassing Gillian.

'Where is Gillian now, then?' Munroe asked.

'Dean's driving her to their cottage in Devon.'

'Right. Well, I want you back at the nick immediately. We've got a suspect.'

DETECTIVE WARREN CARTER
Chapter 33

I stood in the briefing room at PSD. Caroline was still at the morgue, but I'd already given her an update by phone. Now it was time to tell my team what SOCO had told me.

'I'll give you the bad news first,' I said. 'SOCO haven't been able to find any footprints, useful fibres, fingerprints, or DNA in the chaos of the crime scene. We're still waiting for DNA search results of the national database to come back from the samples belonging to the victims. *But* they have found a glove print, which was on one of the metal brackets attached to the chains that Hayat was bound with. Found on the underside of the bracket where it was secured into the wall. Not as good as a fingerprint, but it's distinctive enough to be matched to other crime scenes, if it's been worn before. A database search is being conducted as we speak for any matches.' Next, I told them about Becky's case and our working theory.

'A copycat killing?' Koray said. 'It's a bit far-fetched, isn't it, guv?'

'Doesn't mean it isn't true,' I said. 'I trust Becky's judgement on this, and I agree with her that this is connected. Someone has gone to great lengths to silence Neal Lane and Hannah Ryan and remove any evidence they might've discovered. I don't know if there were any financial irregularities involved in World Food Corps, but I suspect the story Hannah was writing about was on trafficking refugees, not fraud or theft.'

'And what better way to cover it up than make it look like someone else did it?' Katrina said. 'Someone who'd killed before and left no forensic evidence at the scene.'

'The perfect patsy,' I said.

'Someone who also had expert knowledge of the previous case when the Wilsons were killed to make it look like the same offender,' Jack said. 'Someone who left a warrant card at Brampton Hospital.'

'So who is involved?' I looked around. 'DCI Munroe, DC Faris, or DC Etheridge? Anyone found anything useful in the paperwork trail?'

'Nothing untoward so far with DCI Munroe,' Jack said. 'Her house is worth in the region of a million quid, and they paid off what was left of their mortgage after an inheritance from her husband's parents. She and her husband have ISA savings accounts of £20,000 each. They own two vehicles worth around £50,000. Plus precious metals and bonds worth about £300,000 in total. So most of their assets are tied up in long-term investments. They're not particularly frivolous spenders. And they make the usual kinds of payments we all do – food, petrol, online shopping, Munroe's mother's care-home bills. No big amounts of cash going in or out of their accounts. They pay for most things using debit or credit cards. Their cashpoint withdrawals for spending money are between £100 and £250 per month throughout the last year. No debts. Munroe and her husband are legitimately well off. Can't see them being involved in a trafficking ring for money.'

I rubbed my jaw between my thumb and forefinger as I took that in.

'There's so much to go through,' Koray said. 'But the only thing of note I've found on Jamal Faris is what I told you earlier about the £20,000 debt he'd put himself in because of the IVF. They were desperate to have kids.'

'Desperate enough to use a trafficked donor, though?' I raised an eyebrow. 'The warrant's just come through for the Faris's medical records so I'll go and see their GP first. I want to know if Asima Faris got pregnant naturally or resorted to a black market in donor eggs.'

'I'm still digging into Colin Etheridge's stuff,' Jack said.

'And I have bad news from Interpol,' Liz said. 'They have no knowledge of the six women. And no intel on Odesa Investments.'

'After my fifth attempt to request info from Privatnyy Bank and the government in Ukraine, they're flat out refusing to answer any questions now, spouting about client confidentiality,' Jack said.

Which I'd always thought would be the case. I just hoped the Vigilante could get hold of something I couldn't. 'We knew it was going to be like pulling teeth. How are you getting on with Powell Acton's personal details?'

'Still waiting for them to come through from the bank. But his business account information has now arrived. I've just started going through it all, along with communications info. Powell Acton hasn't been in contact with Faris, Munroe, or Etheridge that we can see. But that obviously doesn't rule out unregistered, pay-as-you-go phones or other methods.'

'And I've got more paperwork to add to the pile, I'm afraid,' I told them. 'David Bennington, CEO of World Food Corps. I want everything on him and his company – phone records, financial details, his inside leg measurement.'

We wrapped up there, and I sat at my desk and pulled out my phone, bringing up the list I'd got from Becky of people Neal Lane had worked with at Salama Camp in Jordan. The first mobile number was unobtainable. The second number I tried was for someone called Doug Cooper. It was answered on the fifth ring.

I introduced myself and told him I was investigating a serious crime in the UK.

'Is this about Neal Lane? I heard about it yesterday on the news. We're all shocked out here. He was a great guy to work with.' Doug had an Australian twang.

'Can I ask what you do at the Salama Camp?'

'I'm the logistics manager. Which is basically a posh name that includes anything and everything.'

'Did you know Neal well?' I asked.

'Erm . . . reasonably well, I guess. He worked out here for about six months. He seemed very dedicated to the project. He was really easy to get along with.'

'Did he mention any problems he was having at Salama?'

'No. Not to me, anyway.'

'Did you ever meet a journalist called Hannah Ryan out there?'

'Yeah. She came out to do a story on the refugees. She spent a lot of time with Neal so I assume she was interested in what work he was doing out here. I heard she got murdered, too, but I didn't know they were having a thing, if that's what you want to know.'

'What kind of questions was she asking?'

'The usual, I guess. She spoke to a lot of the refugees, asking about their stories. She spoke to me and some of the other staff about what we did out here. She spoke to David Bennington about the running of the camp, funding, et cetera.'

'And does David Bennington get out there a lot?'

'Every few months or so he comes out for a few days at a time. Unless there's a major problem that needs his attention.'

I tapped my biro on the desk. 'Do you keep any records of the refugees in the camp? I'm assuming they have to register somehow when they arrive?'

'They have to register to get food cards and an ID card. When they arrive, they must give their names and date of birth and details of where they've come from.'

'Do you take photos of them?'

'We do now, since we took over the camp two years ago, but when the first wave of refugees came, it was just a makeshift camp being run by the Jordanian government, and they didn't have the infrastructure or funds to set things up properly or cope with the huge influx. Maybe half the people here still haven't been photographed and put on our official database.'

'So if I was trying to identify someone who'd turned up in the UK, and I suspected they were a refugee from Salama, could I trace them back to there?'

'Do you know their names?'

'No. Although I have a possible first name for one of them.'

There was a pause. 'Do you know how many people are here?'

'I dread to think.'

'Over 150,000. That's official, registered refugees inside the camp. Outside there are makeshift camps with thousands more who've never registered their details. Jordan currently hosts more than 650,000 refugees. It's mayhem. And over half a million people have passed through the camp at one time or another.'

'I have a possible first name for one girl and an estimated age. Could you find out if there are any matches, or if any of them are missing from the camp?'

'People go missing all the time. We can't keep track of all of them. If you can send some photos over I can see if we can go through the ones we do have on our database, but that's going to take a long time and, as I said, photos might not even be on there.'

'Actually, we'll need you to send over all the photos to us so we can go through them ourselves.'

'Um . . . OK. I can get that organised. But it will take a while. There are thousands.'

'Thank you, I really appreciate it. The sooner you can do it the better,' I said, but I was thinking that if the women in Brampton Hospital were from Salama, of course no one would want identifiable photos or details that would to be able to trace them, so whoever was involved could've easily deleted their records, but I had to try. 'There's one girl. We think her name was Hayat. She's late teens, early twenties. Can you check your database now to see if you have anyone who could match?'

'I can try. Hold on a second.' I heard typing and then a long wait. 'Sorry, our system's pretty slow. A lot of the time there are power failures out here and the generators knacker the computers up. Another long pause. Then, 'We've got one woman called Hayat, but she's in her sixties. And . . . let me just see the date of births here . . . OK, there's a baby of thirteen months old and a girl aged seven. Sorry.'

'OK, if you can send me over those photos as soon as possible, that would be great.'

'All right. If I get anything else, I'll come back to you.'

'Thanks. Oh, before you go, do you know what happened to Neal's work on the ID programme when he left? He must've collected quite a lot of data.'

'The laptop with all the data and software Neal was working on belonged to World Food Corps, and it was handed back to the security manager for the site. I was in the office at the time of the handover.'

But that didn't mean Neal Lane hadn't taken copies of it. Copies that had to have been on his personal laptop or hard drives. Copies, I suspected, that had been stolen by the killer to keep them hidden.

I hung up and called the last four numbers on the list, but they had nothing more helpful to add.

I put my head in my hands. A fire burned in my guts, a mixture of anger, helplessness, and sadness. Salama Camp was the perfect place to cover up a trafficking ring, where no one would notice and probably not even care. But someone did notice. Somehow Neal Lane and Hannah Ryan started asking the right questions. But possibly to the wrong people.

HAYAT

Chapter 34

It happens at night. Mr Gavin came to me yesterday and said to meet him at the supply depot at midnight tonight.

All day I am nervous. A bubbling fear rumbles in my belly. I feel sick. I do not want to eat but know I must, because I do not know how long the journey will take. Do not know when I will next have food.

I take nothing except what I am wearing, because I have nothing, apart from a few changes of clothes and a food card. I leave the card under my mattress. Maybe one of the other women in my Portakabin will find it and use it. I hope so.

I walk past the sleeping figures of my friends and sneak into the night. There are a few people outside but not many. Most are under cover of their tents or dormitories. The ones who are not are the bad men who have a black heart and belong in the darkness. I keep my head down, ears alert.

The gates to the storage depot are open, and a lorry is waiting with *World Food Corps* written on the side. Mr Gavin leans against it, smoking. There is one more person there, sitting in the driver's seat, looking at his mobile phone.

Mr Gavin sees me. Throws the cigarette on the ground and hurries towards me. 'Come on. In the back.' He takes my arm and pulls me round to the rear doors.

Before I can step up he tells me how it will be. I will not make any noise. There is food and water inside. I will do as he tells me, when he tells me. When he finishes his instructions, he says, 'Do you understand?'

'Yes.'

He helps me up, and I step inside. It is dark, but I can make out another few human shapes, piles of blankets, cardboard boxes with bottles of water and some food.

The doors close, plunging me into blackness. I outstretch my hand and walk towards the back of the lorry, towards the shapes. I almost fall when my foot hits something bulky and soft.

An *oof* noise comes from it. The voice is high. Another woman.

I get to my knees and scramble further, hands touching the blankets, until I feel the back wall of the lorry. I sit down, leaning against it, knees to my chest. I wrap my arms around myself and feel the engine begin to vibrate.

DETECTIVE BECKY HARRIS
Chapter 35

Steve Moore. Aged 35. Plumber. Previous criminal record included possession of cannabis ten years ago. Owned a white transit van.

Becky listened as DCI Munroe outlined the suspect's details. Moore lived in a rented one-bedroom property a few miles from the Lanes' house.

'That's it?' Becky asked. 'That's all we've got linking him? That he lives near the Lanes' house?'

'No, that's not it,' Munroe said. 'This morning, the incident line received an anonymous tip-off that his van was seen outside the Lanes' house a week before Neal Lane and Hannah Ryan were murdered. If you'd thoroughly gone through the previous case files, then you'd know that Moore did some plumbing work for Donna and Jim Wilson a few weeks before they were murdered. He was spoken to at the time, during the course of our enquiries, and eliminated.'

Jamal gave Becky a *told-you-so* look.

Yeah, and when did I have time to do that, Becky thought. She'd been working flat out on new leads for the latest murder. It was something Munroe should've mentioned, but she hadn't said anything specific about any previous potential suspects or witnesses they'd questioned, eliminated or not. Just like she hadn't mentioned Jim's missing wallet. Again, it was pertinent information she should've shared with her team. And Becky was even more concerned about Munroe's actions than ever. 'Was there any paperwork at the Lanes' house to show Moore had ever done any work for them?'

'No,' Munroe said. 'But that doesn't mean he didn't.'

'Well, I doubt he did any work for Hannah Ryan,' Becky said. 'She lived sixty-odd miles away in a different county.' Becky frowned, feeling completely uneasy. 'What exactly did this anonymous tip-off say about Moore, then? How did this caller identify the van? Has it got Moore's name on it or the name of his plumbing firm?'

Jamal looked down at his notes. 'It's got the name "Steve Moore Plumbing Contractor" on it, apparently.'

'So the anonymous caller was most likely a neighbour, then?' Becky said. 'Although no one I spoke to in the street remembered seeing anything like that.'

'They might've only just remembered it,' Munroe said.

'Then why ring up as an anonymous caller?' Becky asked. 'Why not give their details, if they were a neighbour?'

'The caller could quite easily have been someone walking past the Lanes' house as they went into the woods,' Munroe said, an impatient undertone to her voice. 'Could've been a dog walker.'

'Yeah, but how many dog walkers would notice a plumbing van in a street they don't live in and remember the name on it? How did they know it was going to be significant later on?'

Jamal shrugged. 'I didn't take the call. It was the hotline who passed it on to me. Caller refused to give his name or contact details, and it came from a pay-as-you-go phone.'

'Yes, but—'

Munroe cut off Becky by saying, 'So, Becky and Jamal, you're coming with me to go and nick Moore and bring him in for questioning.'

'But ma'am, shouldn't we do some more background into Moore first?' Becky asked. She wasn't just uneasy now, she was suspicious. It was all too convenient that they'd received an anonymous tip-off. What Becky still couldn't work out, as she observed the impatient set of Munroe's features, was whether Munroe was over-keen to arrest someone for the murders because of the pressure she must've been feeling from above to get the killer in custody asap and put a stop to the slagging-off she and the police were getting in the press. Or whether she was the one involved and was purposefully misdirecting the inquiry to cover her own arse.

'I'm not sitting around debating this,' Munroe said. 'Let's go. Right now.'

There was a flurry of activity as Becky, Jamal, and Munroe grabbed stab vests, ASP batons, and PAVA spray. Then they rushed downstairs, flinging open the backdoors and spilling out into the car park.

'Jamal, you take one car. Becky and I will take the other.' Munroe tossed Becky the keys.

As Becky drove, Munroe flicked through her phone. Becky watched her out of the corner of her eye, trying to see what she was looking at. 'So Moore was never a suspect in the previous investigation, even though he'd done some work for the Wilsons?' Becky asked.

Munroe looked over at Becky. 'No. He was ruled out and there was no need to look into him further.'

'Was he questioned about an alibi for the time Donna and Jim Wilson were murdered?'

'No. He gave a plausible account of the nature of the work he did for them two weeks prior to their death. Obviously, now there's been another killing, that's when connections between the previous victims have come to light. Are you questioning my judgement on these cases, DS Harris?'

Becky swallowed her annoyance and gave Munroe a sideways glance. 'No, ma'am.'

'Good.' Munroe looked out of the window.

Becky drove on, her lips pursed in a tense line.

Half an hour later, they drove into Moore's street, Munroe and Becky watching out for his house number to come into view.

'There it is. Park over there.' Munroe pointed to a gap in the on-street parking that would accommodate two cars.

Becky got to the end of the road and did a three-point turn. Then she pulled in so they were facing Moore's front door and cut the engine. Jamal stopped behind them.

Munroe and Becky stared at the shabby red front door of the target address – a narrow terraced house in a long row of identical houses. It had paint peeling off the door, and a leaky downpipe coming from a bathroom on the top floor, with a dirty, limescale mark trailing all the way along the wall. Moore's plumbing work obviously didn't extend to sorting out his own place.

'His van's not outside,' Becky said. 'He's probably at work at this time of day.'

Munroe phoned Jamal. 'The house backs onto a path. You go round to the rear. I don't want him legging it if he's in there.'

Jamal walked to the end of the street and swung a right. Munroe and Becky approached the front door. All the curtains were closed.

Munroe knocked on the door. Becky glanced up and down the street. All was quiet.

Munroe knocked again.

Becky pressed her ear to the door. 'Can't hear anything in there.' She crouched down and looked inside the letter box. 'No sign of anyone.'

'We'll wait.' Munroe dialled Jamal and told him to head back to the car.

Becky slid into the driver's seat again next to the DCI, itching to text Warren and give him an update but knowing that would be impossible with beady-eyed Munroe next to her.

DETECTIVE WARREN CARTER
Chapter 36

Asima and Jamal Faris's GP had coughed up their medical records after I'd presented them with the warrant, and I read through the pages he'd printed off for me in his office.

'I really don't see why this is a police matter,' the GP said, who was no advert for health himself with his bloodshot eyes, sallow complexion, sagging jowls, and the extra four stone he was carrying. Maybe he should go and see one of his colleagues before he started dishing out advice.

I ignored him and carried on reading until I got to the good parts. Jamal and Asima had used three fertility clinics in the past ten years. First, they'd had two free rounds of IVF on the NHS. Then they'd paid privately for IVF at Guy's and St Thomas' Hospital in London and had another two rounds. The last note from them had been that the treatment had failed because Asima's eggs had been of poor quality. They'd then gone to another private clinic and had a go with donor eggs. The notes were scant, but the clinic had informed the GP that one egg had been implanted. It later transpired that this failed to sustain a pregnancy. Then Asima had seen her GP five months ago suspecting she was pregnant. According to the notes, she said she'd conceived naturally.

'This says the quality of Asima Faris's eggs were the problem for the infertility.' I looked up at him.

'Apparently so.'

'But she then conceived naturally. Is that possible?'

'I'm not a fertility expert, but all it takes is one healthy egg.'

'And you think it's viable she did have one healthy egg, even though her notes say it's very unlikely she would ever conceive naturally.'

'As I said, I'm not a fertility expert. I'm a GP. You'd need to speak to the last clinic they attended for more accurate information.'

I looked down at the notes. The last clinic was Assisted Fertility UK in Harpenden. 'What can you tell me about the clinic?'

'Not much, I'm afraid.'

I glanced up from the notes. 'It says they requested to be referred to that particular clinic. Do they have a good reputation?'

'I'm not really sure. I did the referral to Mr Oliver Hammond as I was asked by Mr and Mrs Faris. They were paying privately, and as such it's their choice to use which clinic they prefer.' He looked pointedly at his watch. 'I don't know what else I can tell you. And if you don't mind, I've got patients coming out of my ears.'

I left him to it. Back in the car, I typed the address of the clinic into the satnav. Maybe this was a long shot, but they were the last people to treat Asima, and I wanted to know if it really was possible she could've conceived naturally or if there was something untoward going on.

Forty minutes later, I rolled up a long expanse of gravel driveway to find a building that looked as if it had once been a large family estate home.

The car park was three-quarters full. A spot with a sign saying 'Reserved for Mr Oliver Hammond' housed a gleaming charcoal-grey Porsche Panamera. Business in the infertility industry was obviously booming and—

I did a double-take of the car, thinking about what DC Potter had said when he was stationed at the gates of Brampton Hospital. He'd seen a similar-coloured sports car driving slowly outside. Coincidence? I didn't think so.

Hayat's face flashed before my eyes. I took a deep breath and tempered it down as I stepped into a reception area that looked more like an upmarket hotel than a medical clinic. Luxury sofas, antique coffee tables, plush interior decor. Five couples were waiting and two lone females. Their ages ranged from late twenties to early forties. Three of the women were pregnant so Oliver Hammond must've been doing something right.

The receptionist treated me to a wide smile and asked if she could help.

I showed her my warrant card. 'I need to speak to Oliver Hammond, please.'

'Oh!' She looked surprised. 'Mr Hammond is seeing some patients at the moment. If you'd like to wait, I'll let him know you're here. Can I tell him what it's about?' She tilted her head in a question.

'I can't divulge that, I'm afraid.'

'OK. Well, have a seat, please.' She tottered off on high heels and disappeared down a corridor.

I sat next to a man busy biting his nails. His wife clutched his hand so hard I could see fingernail marks in the skin, as if they were hopefully and desperately awaiting the results of their treatment.

I picked up a magazine from a pile on the coffee table in front of me before realising it was *Gynaecology Monthly*. I grimaced and set it back down again, hoping no one had noticed.

Instead, I picked up a promotional brochure for the clinic with a smiling photo of a couple holding a baby. I flicked through to the first page and read a load of bumf about Oliver Hammond, owner and chief fertility consultant. I was expecting a grey-haired, half-moon bespectacled man, wearing corduroy trousers and a tweed jacket. But his photo showed someone who looked early forties with curly brown hair, piercing blue eyes, and model good looks. I started reading his bio.

Oliver Hammond is the lead consultant gynaecologist and specialist in reproductive medicine at Assisted Fertility UK.

After qualifying in Obstetrics & Gynaecology, he undertook specialist training in fertility at the Assisted Conception Unit at Barts Hospital, working as a Fertility Unit Consultant after his fellowship.

After seven years in the NHS as a consultant, he went on to found the private Assisted Fertility UK clinic, where his mission statement is to bring patients a different approach of assisted conception: a safe, innovative, and patient-friendly package that focuses on quality and patient care.

I heard my name being called, so I put the brochure down and walked towards a young nurse waiting for me.

'If you can come this way, please. Mr Hammond will squeeze you in for a few moments before his next procedure.' She set off at a brisk pace along a corridor and stopped outside a door with a brass plaque bearing Hammond's name. She knocked, then swept her palm towards the door with a smile on her face, before speed-walking back down the corridor.

Hammond looked up from the laptop he'd been typing on as I stepped inside. He smiled, showing dimples on his cheeks. 'Detective? I'm intrigued. What can I do to help you?' He gave me a suitably intrigued look as he stood and leaned over the desk, hand out, ready to shake.

I hoped he'd worn gloves for his last procedure as I shook it.

'As far as I know I don't have any outstanding parking tickets.' He gave me a charming smile.

'I have a warrant for the medical records of your patients, Asima and Jamal Faris.'

He quirked one perfectly groomed eyebrow up. 'Really? Can I ask why?'

'I'm not at liberty to say, I'm afraid.' I handed him the warrant, which he took and read. 'I understand they had fertility treatment here.'

'I can't recall the treatment offhand. I have a lot of clients. Bear with me a minute.' He picked up the phone and requested whoever was on the other end of the line to pull out their paper file. Then he turned to his computer and entered some details. He studied the screen intently. Tapped some more keys. Studied some more. 'I don't know how much detail you want me to go into, but Mr and Mrs Faris came to see me for the first time . . . four years ago. They'd had four IVF treatments before that at previous clinics, which were carried out using Asima Faris's eggs, but it became apparent they were of poor quality. She then had a treatment here involving donor eggs and Jamal Faris's sperm, but unfortunately that was also unsuccessful.'

'When did you last see them?'

He looked at the screen. 'Just after the treatment failed they had a follow-up appointment, which was eleven months ago. We discussed doing another round with donor eggs in the future, and I put them down on our waiting list again.'

'Where did the donor eggs come from that the Farises used in their treatment here?'

He looked confused for a moment, then said, 'Well, we have an egg bank at this clinic. Our donors are either women who need IVF themselves and are donating through egg-sharing, or those who altruistically just want to help someone to have a family. All of our egg donors are healthy, fertile women between the ages of eighteen and thirty-five.'

'Egg-sharing?'

'Yes. Egg-sharing reduces the cost of IVF treatment for the patient. Those women who have more viable eggs than they need are given the option to donate some in return for reduced costs.'

'I thought there was a donor-egg shortage in the UK.'

'There most certainly is. Particularly among certain ethnic groups. Donors are matched to recipients using the recipient's ideal characteristics – things like eye and hair colour, ethnic group, et cetera. In most cases, patients want physical characteristics that match their own. Donors can also provide further information – a personal statement, if you like – that is more about their personality, which helps patients to choose if they think the donor would be a good match.' He steepled his fingers together. 'There's a very long waiting list for donor eggs at the moment, hence the delay in their initial appointment and their treatment.'

'How long is the waiting list in this clinic?'

'Three to four years.'

'And who did they use as a donor?'

He glanced down at the warrant. 'That's confidential information. I don't believe your authorisation covers that.'

Which was true. I'd need to get a new warrant for that information, but I wasn't sure I had enough cause. So far everything seemed legitimate and above board, apart from the niggling thought of the car sitting outside. 'So what *can* you tell me about the donor Mr and Mrs Faris used?'

'Nothing, I'm afraid.'

'But *you* know who the donors are?'

'Yes.'

'Who else would know, apart from you?'

'My staff members who have access to the database.'

'And Mr and Mrs Faris didn't know?'

'No. The only details they're made aware of when choosing a donor are the characteristics I previously mentioned. Although, any donor-conceived child would have access to the donor's personal details once they reached eighteen.'

'The egg donation and implantation in Asima Faris was carried out here in the clinic?'

'Yes, of course.'

'Is there any way someone can bypass the donor list?'

'I don't know exactly what you mean.'

'I mean, if someone was looking for donor eggs, could they find them on the black market, and if so, how?'

He sat back in his chair and tilted his head. 'You mean a donor selling their eggs illegally.'

'Something like that,' I said, not wanting to give too much away.

'I suppose anything's possible to get hold of on a black market, but it would need a fertility doctor to carry out the donor-egg retrieval and embryo implantation.'

'Yes,' I said, studying him carefully. 'Have you ever heard of that happening?'

He paused for a moment. 'There have been cases of donors selling their eggs privately, which is illegal in the UK. In those circumstances, donors advertised their eggs for sale and came to a private arrangement with the recipients. At the time of treatment at a fertility centre, both parties covered themselves by saying the donor was a friend of the recipients and was willingly donating for no fee. I assume that's what you mean?'

Obviously it wasn't. 'You can't think of any other way someone could obtain donor eggs?'

He shook his head. 'In the UK we're carefully monitored by the HFEA, the governing authority. I can't see a way around using any kind of donors in a fertility clinic here. But fertility tourism is also popular now. Patients can travel to other countries where the rules covering IVF are less stringent, and where egg donors are offered more incentives.'

'Offered money in exchange for their eggs, you mean?'

'Yes. Particularly in poorer countries.'

'If I told you Asima Faris had become pregnant naturally would you say that was possible?'

He glanced at the screen again, to his notes. Back to me. 'It would be unlikely but, as I'm sure you're aware, the body is unpredictable. It's not impossible. All it would take is one good-quality egg.' He glanced at his watch. 'And now I have another appointment, I'm afraid. If you stop by reception on your way out you can collect copies of Mr and Mrs Faris's records.' He picked up a business card in a silver holder on his desk. 'But if you have any more questions I'd be happy to answer them.'

I headed back to my car, thinking. It was possible that Jamal and Asima had travelled to a private clinic abroad for a donor egg and not told their GP. Or that she had really become pregnant naturally. But what if, after all attempts had failed, they were offered an alternative? A way to bypass the long waiting list.

I glanced over at the Porsche again. Had Jamal Faris found Colin's warrant card in the booth at the police bar, intending to give it back to him? Maybe he'd put it in his pocket for safekeeping, but before he could return it he'd taken his wife to Brampton Hospital for treatment and he'd lost it there. And was Oliver Hammond the doctor involved in it all? He'd been cool and collected, giving the perception of helpfulness, but he needed looking at more closely, too.

I rang Jack and told him to start digging into the doctor's life. I asked him if Powell Acton's personal bank account details had arrived yet, but he was having trouble getting them from his bank and had chased them up yet again.

I hung up, then pulled the burner phone out and sent a text to the Vigilante, asking if he could also look into Hammond. By the time I'd finished, my job phone rang.

'Hi Warren, it's Amy, in fingerprints.'

I knew Amy well, having hassled her on many occasions when trying to get my searches expedited. 'Hi, how's it going?'

'Well, I never thought I'd see your name on a case again. Couldn't keep away, eh?' She chuckled.

'Turns out retirement isn't all it's cracked up to be. I couldn't take one more crappy daytime TV programme. Have you found something on that glove print?'

'Yep. I'm going to email you the details but I wanted to give you a heads-up first. It's a match to another recent case.'

My heart sped up. 'Which one?'

'Double-murder scene at Oak Drive in Stevenage. Neal Lane and—'

'Hannah Ryan,' I finished off for her.

'Yeah. How did you—'

'Sorry, Amy. Got to go.' I hung up and dialled Caroline. It went to voicemail so I left a message telling her we now had solid proof the two cases were related, and I didn't want DCI Munroe, DC Faris, or DC Etheridge dealing with the murders of Hannah Ryan and Neal Lane unsupervised. One of them had to be involved in it. I needed some advice on PSD procedures – either we served them with a regulation notice, setting out details of our investigation into them, and brought them in for interview, which would then tip them off. Or we worked with them on the murder of Neal Lane and Hannah Ryan to ensure nothing was covered up. Or PSD took over the investigation in full without disclosing our investigation into the three officers. I left a message and told Caroline to call me back as soon as possible. Then I called Becky and sped out of the car park as I waited for her to pick up.

DETECTIVE BECKY HARRIS
Chapter 37

By the time Moore's van pulled up in his street, Becky had a numb arse and pins and needles in her right leg. Munroe wasn't talking, and Becky obviously wasn't her favourite person after constantly questioning the line of the investigation. But that was fine with Becky. She didn't feel like talking to her, either.

Munroe called Jamal on the police radio. 'You seen him?'

'Yes,' came the reply.

Becky watched the van park up in a space further down. Moore got out.

'As soon as he gets in the house, go round the back,' Munroe told Jamal.

Becky's phone rang. She looked at the screen. It was Warren Carter.

'Turn that thing off,' Munroe snapped.

Becky's thumb hesitated over the answer button for a moment before sending it to voicemail. She looked up again as Moore entered his house.

Jamal headed down the street that led to the path behind Moore's place.

A few minutes later, Jamal called and told them he was in position.

'Go, go, go.' Munroe reached for the door handle.

Becky stuffed her phone in her pocket, and they hurried to the front door.

Munroe knocked.

Steve Moore opened the door, dressed in navy overalls, half a banana in his hand.

'Steve Moore? DCI Munroe. DS Harris.' She held up her warrant card. 'I'm arresting you on suspicion of the murder of Neal Lane, Hannah Ryan, Donna Wilson, and Jim Wilson. You do not have to say—'

But she didn't get any further in cautioning him. His eyes widened, he dropped the banana, and legged it along the hallway towards the back of the house.

'He's coming your way!' Munroe yelled down the radio to Jamal as she and Becky followed suit.

By the time they'd got to the kitchen at the back, the patio door stood wide open and Moore was wriggling over the garden fence.

Munroe and Becky hurried to the fence. Becky made a grab for his legs but they slithered upwards and then disappeared over the fence.

'I'm going round the other way.' Munroe left through the house while Becky reached for the top of the fence and hefted herself up and over in time to see Faris launch himself at Moore, rugby-tackling him to the ground very nimbly for a guy who looked as if he'd break out in a sweat just walking to the coffee machine.

By the time Munroe appeared from the street that led to the path, Faris was cuffing Moore's hands behind his back.

'As I was saying,' Munroe said, strolling along casually. 'You do not have to say anything, but it may harm your—'

'My nose!' Moore yelled as Faris dragged him to his feet. 'You broke my nose! Police brutality! Police brutality!'

His nose was a mess. It looked like it had splattered on the concrete when Faris had launched himself on top of Moore.

Munroe finished cautioning him and said, 'That's what you get for resisting arrest. Take him back to the nick and book him in,' she directed at Faris. 'Becky and I will have a look around here until the search team arrives.'

'I'm going to sue!' Moore screamed in a bunged-up voice.

'Good work, Faris,' Munroe said as he pulled a struggling Moore up the road.

Munroe and Becky followed behind them, Munroe smiling with elation. But Becky didn't feel like celebrating, unable to shake the uneasy feeling she had about all this.

Becky watched Moore being loaded into Jamal's vehicle, still swearing his head off, and she and Munroe returned to their own vehicle to grab some latex gloves and evidence bags from the boot.

Munroe rubbed at her waist absentmindedly.

'You all right, ma'am?' she asked.

'Just a stitch from chasing him.' She winced.

Are you having a laugh, Becky thought. She hadn't done a thing to help them apprehend Moore. Becky was out of breath, but Munroe's breathing was completely normal, not even a sheen of sweat on her forehead.

'You have a look in his van.' Munroe nodded to the rusty white Ford transit further along. 'The keys will probably be in the house.' She marched off and disappeared through Moore's front door.

Becky followed her inside. 'Shouldn't we wait for the search team to get here?' If her suspicions about Munroe were right, she didn't want to leave her alone in the house with the opportunity to plant evidence.

'No, we're just having a look around.' Munroe walked further down the hallway.

'But, ma'am, why don't we—'

Munroe stopped walking. Swung around. 'Are you questioning a direct order?'

Becky did an inner growl and said through gritted teeth, 'No, ma'am.'

'Well, go and look in the van, then.' Munroe disappeared into the kitchen.

Becky spotted some keys on a key hook just inside the hallway with an old leather Ford fob. As she stomped back to the van, she phoned Warren back.

He answered on the second ring. 'Is this Becky or a pervy heavy breather who's stolen her phone?'

'Pervy heavy breather.' She tucked the phone under her chin as she pulled some latex gloves from her pocket and slid them on.

'Oh, good.'

'I haven't got time to talk dirty, though. Been too busy chasing a suspect for the murder of Hannah Ryan and Neal Lane.'

'What? You've nicked someone? Who?'

'I wanted to call you earlier and let you know, but I couldn't get away from Munroe.' Becky stopped in front of the van and peered in the driver's side door. It was a mess inside. Fast-food wrappers on the passenger seat and in the centre console. An oil-encrusted white T-shirt heaped on the foot mat. Half-crushed, empty cans of Coke in the passenger footwell. 'Steve Moore.' She told him about the plumbing connection and the anonymous tip-off.

'And what do you think?'

'I think it's pretty convenient.' She filled him in on her further suspicions about Munroe's actions as she opened the door with the key because the central locking didn't work. 'But Moore did do a runner when we turned up so something's not right. And Munroe is in the house now, which means if she is dodgy she could be planting evidence in there. I've been banished out to Moore's van.'

'Make a note of that in your pocket book. If she does *find* something, I'll be scrutinising it carefully.'

'Will do.'

'The glove print from your scene matches one found at the hospital.'

Becky froze as she was opening the door. 'Bloody hell, really? I haven't seen an email from fingerprints.'

'You won't. Our investigation is marked confidential. The results were for PSD eyes only. I want to take over your investigation, but I'm trying to get hold of my guv'nor to authorise it.'

'Hmmm. Munroe isn't going to like that. Especially not if she's involved in the murders.' She leaned inside the van and picked up the T-shirt, looking beneath it to where there were more dirty food wrappers.

'I'm going to head to the nick now. I don't want Munroe interviewing Moore.'

'OK. We're waiting for a search team to—' She stopped, mid-flow. Then she picked up a pair of well-used black leather gloves. Leather gloves that had distinctive pattern marks on the fingers.

'You still there?'

'I think I might've just found the gloves.'

DETECTIVE WARREN CARTER

Chapter 38

I was bombing along the A1M when Jack called. I gave him a quick rundown and asked if Caroline was back in the office yet. She wasn't.

'What are you thinking, guv?'

'Like Becky said, it's a bit convenient, isn't it? No one was in the frame for the Wilsons' murders and suddenly, the day after Neal Lane and Hannah Ryan are killed, Munroe's arrested a suspect, and we've possibly got the gloves in question found in Moore's van on the basis of an anonymous tip-off.'

'You think it's a set-up?'

'Don't know yet. Just very suspicious. How are you guys getting on?'

'We've just got all the files through from your contact at Salama Camp with the photos of women. I've forwarded them on to Tech Services to run through their facial-recognition software.'

'Good.'

'Powell Acton's personal financials came in so I'm just starting to wade through them now. His business records showed a lot of offshore companies purchasing UK properties. He could be money-laundering for them, especially if he's not carrying out the required regulatory background and anti-money laundering checks. Do you want me to look into that angle?'

'Not yet. That's going to be another investigation entirely.'

'I did find evidence that Odesa Investments had paid money into his business account for the purchase of Brampton Hospital nine months ago, so they were his client.'

'OK, good. Have you got anything else?'

'Someone from Acton Associates' office telephone number has been in contact with someone from Assisted Fertility UK's office telephone numbers over the years. And Acton Associates also acted as Oliver Hammond's lawyer when Hammond set up his company and to purchase the clinic's building.'

'So they have a solid connection, then. Have you found any calls on Powell Acton's personal phone records to Oliver Hammond?'

'No. Just the business numbers. Also, Colin Etheridge made several calls to John Hinckley over the last six months, and after every one, a story breaks in the media about the case he's attached to. I'm sure he's not doing it out of the goodness of his heart, but there's no trace of any payments going into his accounts, so Hinckley must be bunging him money in cash. So far we can't find anything dodgy with Munroe. And we're still going through Faris's financials and waiting for the historical cell phone triangulation data for them all to come in to see if they were ever in the vicinity of Brampton Hospital.'

'All right. Thanks.'

'We're still trudging through lots of data, and we're digging more into Oliver Hammond now. Wait a sec, guv. Koray's just waving at me.' There was a muffled conversation in the background and then Jack came back on the line. 'I think you can scrap the Faris possibility. Koray's found payments from Jamal Faris to a fertility clinic in Cyprus six months ago. He's checked with the UK Border Agency and they did leave the country for Cyprus at that time. Asima stayed for four weeks and Jamal stayed two weeks. She was having treatment there but failed to tell her doctor the truth. Koray's spoken to the clinic in question and confirmed that her pregnancy was definitely a result of that treatment.'

'Really? That's great work.' My phone beeped, signalling another caller was on the line. 'Got to go, Jack. Someone's trying to get through.' I hung up and answered the call.

'Warren, you were trying to get hold of me?' Caroline said.

At the sound of her voice the temperature in the car suddenly cranked up a few degrees. I opened the window and gave her the rundown of what had been happening.

She was silent for a moment, as if thinking. 'So it looks like Faris is out of the line of inquiry.'

'Yes, but we could bring him in for interview and ask him about Oliver Hammond. See if he ever offered Faris eggs on the black market in the past.'

'If the last time the Farises saw Hammond was eleven months ago for a legitimate treatment through his clinic, and Odesa Investments didn't purchase Brampton Hospital until nine months ago, it's likely Hammond wasn't doing illegal egg donations when they had their treatment. It looks like Faris isn't corrupt so if Hammond *had* offered them black-market eggs, I think he would've reported it. And I don't want Faris to have any chance to tip off Munroe about our investigation. We haven't got enough on either her or Etheridge to arrest them. If they don't think we're watching them then they might make a mistake. I'm going to speak to the Chief Constable. I want PSD taking over the Hannah Ryan–Neal Lane case so they can't potentially tamper with evidence or leads. The glove print at both scenes is a perfect reason to get it linked to our investigation, but I don't want to reveal that to Munroe or her team.'

'So how are we going to get them off the case without using that?'

'She came to us with a complaint about a leak in her department. We use that as the reason. We can't have someone from her team passing on sensitive, confidential information to the press. The Chief

Constable and the Constabulary in general is getting a kicking in the media over this. And they're already calling for Munroe's removal from the investigation. The Chief will probably welcome the idea of us taking over. We can just throw her complaint right back at her as ammunition.'

I grinned. My kind of thinking.

'I don't want Steve Moore interviewed without you being there. I'll get back to you as soon as I've got hold of the Chief.'

She hung up, and I exited the A1M at the Stevenage junction and drove through the back-up of annoying commuter traffic, trying not to get road rage.

When I finally screeched into the police station car park there were no available spaces so I dumped the car behind a SOCO van and left the keys in it. I entered through the rear door and headed for the 'custody suite', which was the Constabulary's idea of a joke. There was no turn-down service or pre-bedtime chocolate mints on the pillow, and I was pretty sure the arrestees wouldn't call it such. Still, whoever said police didn't have a sense of humour had no idea.

I knew the custody sergeant on duty well. PS Matheson raised his eyebrows at me and gave me a warm smile.

'What are you doing back here? If I was retired I'd be on the golf course now.'

'I'm not retired any more.'

'Seriously? Are you nuts? You back in CID?'

'PSD.'

His eyes widened. 'The complaints? Christ. You must be pretty quiet if you're getting here that quick.'

'Sorry?'

'Steve Moore. Complaining about police assault. I take it that's why you're here?'

'Yes and no. Where is he?'

'In with the force doctor, getting his nose checked. He had a run-in with the pavement.'

'Where's DCI Munroe?'

'In her office until Moore's cleared for interview and his brief turns up.'

'Great, thanks.' I headed off up the corridor and bounded up the stairs to the CID office.

Ronnie was bent over his desk, squinting at a pile of paperwork, about a million Post-it notes everywhere. DC Faris was nowhere to be seen. DC Etheridge was staring at his screen, but when he spotted me he sat upright in his seat and a flicker of worry flitted across his face.

I watched him squirm and said nothing as I knocked on Munroe's door, feeling Colin's eyes on my back. Becky was in with Munroe, holding a bag with a pair of black gloves and looking decidedly unsatisfied.

Munroe beckoned me in. She didn't look pleased to see me. She stood up, reaching for her jacket on the back of her chair. 'I take it you're here about the leak, but I haven't got time to speak to you about it now. I've got a suspect to interview in the serial-killer case.'

'Actually, no one from CID is going to be interviewing Steve Moore.'

'I beg your pardon? This is my case. What the hell has it got to do with you?'

'The leak of confidential information that you reported to us will seriously compromise the Constabulary's enquiries. The case is being transferred to PSD.'

'On whose authority? Who the hell do you think you are?' A red flush crept up her neck as her lips morphed into an angry, narrow line.

'As of this moment, Chief Superintendent Barker's given her authority. And we're waiting for the Chief Constable to confirm it.'

Becky looked from me to Munroe, a grin on her face that said she was enjoying the show.

'We'll see about that,' Munroe barked out. 'You're not interviewing *my* suspect without me.' She reached for her desk phone, dialled a number and said to us, 'Get out of my office. Both of you.'

I was polite. I even smiled on the way out. And I shut the door for her.

Sweat had broken out on DC Etheridge's forehead by the time Becky and I emerged. His eyes had a deer-in-the-headlights look, but what exactly was he worried about? That PSD had made the connection between his tip-offs to John Hinckley or that he was involved in trafficking women who'd horrifically died and a double murder? I watched him carefully as he put his head down and typed away frantically, looking very much like he wanted to avoid my gaze.

'Sarge, what's going on?' Ronnie asked.

Becky and I huddled around Ronnie's desk, treating Colin to a view of our backs. I tapped my nose at Ronnie and watched Munroe turning a weird puce colour as she yelled down the phone and gestured wildly with her hands.

'Are we getting back together again?' Ronnie asked in a hopeful whisper, leaning forward. 'The old team, like before?' Bless him, Ronnie didn't do well with change. 'Only I don't like Jamal. He keeps stealing my Post-it notes. And I had to fill in God knows how many pieces of paperwork for stationery before they'd give them to me in the first place.' He pointed at Faris's empty desk with a stack of unopened Post-it notes on it.

I glanced at Colin, staring at his screen and looking as if he was straining his ears to hear us over the shouting coming from Munroe's office that drowned out our hushed conversation.

Then Munroe's door swung open and she stormed out past us and along the corridor, swearing under her breath.

My phone rang and Caroline told me we were good to go. Munroe wouldn't be interviewing Moore. I would.

I walked out into the empty corridor and carried on listening to Caroline saying, 'Etheridge, Faris, and Munroe are off the case and are all being sent back to Letchworth police station. Orders are filtering through as we speak. You're going to take over the Neal Lane–Hannah Ryan murders. If it's connected to the Wilsons then you'll be involved in that, too.'

'I don't think they are connected,' I said. 'I think it's a copycat killing to make us think they are. And it's likely Moore's being set up.'

'I think you're right. But hopefully taking them off the case will make them panic and do something stupid. I've got authorisation for covert surveillance on Etheridge and Munroe. Phones, emails, all of their communications data will be monitored in real time as soon as we get it set up. Maybe this is exactly what we need to flush something out.'

Shake the tree. See what falls out. Or give Etheridge or Munroe enough rope to hang themselves with. A wicked grin spread across my face.

'This investigation has grown exponentially, and we're struggling to deal with all the data we've got,' Caroline said. 'We need a few more pairs of hands. I know you trust Becky Harris but who else do you trust in CID from your old team?'

'DC Ronnie Pickering, which is handy since they'll be the only two left in here.'

'You sure they're solid?'

'One hundred per cent.'

'Good. Take Becky in the interview with you.' She gave me a few more instructions and I headed back into the CID office.

Becky was just finishing a call on her own mobile.

She walked towards me and pulled me out into the corridor, away from Colin's hearing. 'That was the search team at Moore's house. They've found some marijuana hidden in Moore's bedroom.'

I quirked up an eyebrow. 'A perfectly good reason for him running away from you, then. Have they found anything else? The computers, phones, camera, hard drive, flashdrives?'

'Nothing yet. And I don't think they'll find anything, either.'

HAYAT

Chapter 39

The lorry rumbles on endlessly for I do not know how many hours. I am not the first one to speak.

It is a woman called Safa who says a shy hello in the darkness in Arabic. There is another woman called Leila. Slowly, we start to tell each other our stories. Our dreams. Our hopes. We only talk when the noise of the vehicle speeding along the roads safely masks our whispered voices. When the lorry stops, when we hear what we think are border guards, we are silent and frozen.

We drink water and eat fruit, chunks of bread, cheese, and cucumbers. It tastes like the best meal I have had in a long time. We wrap ourselves in the blankets until a sliver of sunlight filters through the gaps around the door and it becomes too hot. Then we sweat, lying on top of the blankets for comfort.

We sleep. We wake. Talk. Eat. Hold hands. Sometimes we stop so Mr Gavin can take over from the driver. Sometimes they take breaks and we stay locked inside the lorry.

After what feels like days, the nerves and fear turn into excitement. Into hope. I start to dream of my new life and smile. For the first time in five years I know what it is like to feel happiness.

It is three days until the lorry stops for good.

We are silent. We listen carefully, our ears straining. One of the cab doors opens. The other one opens. Footsteps come around the back. We each bury under the blankets to hide in case we have been stopped by officials.

The rear door is wrenched open. I freeze, trying not to even breathe.

'It's OK. You can come out,' Mr Gavin says.

I translate to the other women who don't speak English, and push the blanket away, my muscles stiff from hours of sitting and lying. I lean on the wall of the lorry to help me to my feet. And as I walk towards the doors I see it is night-time yet again. Mr Gavin holds out his hand. I take it and he helps me down onto the ground.

'Are we here? In England?' I ask, shivering in the cold.

'Yes.'

I look up at the dark night. The stars twinkle above me. I am under the same sky but in another world. A wide smile stretches my face as I look around, wanting to take in everything about the first glimpse of my new homeland. We are in another depot with fencing around it. On the outside of a big warehouse in front of us is a sign for World Food Corps. It is all in darkness. Two plain white vans are parked next to the lorry.

'Come on, there's still some way to go,' Mr Gavin says to us and walks towards one of the white vans.

The lorry driver beckons to the other two girls to get out. They hesitate and look at me.

For the first time I feel a twitch of worry that something is not right, but I push it away. They have looked after us so far. They did not make me give a kidney for my passage fare. I have to believe what Mr David told me was true. That I will go to be a maid with a nice family. That I will have a lovely home to live in. A roof over my head. Plenty of food. Wages.

'Quickly!' the driver says, tugging on my arm before helping down the others.

It will be all right, I repeat over and over again to myself as we get inside and the doors close.

DETECTIVE WARREN CARTER
Chapter 40

I hadn't missed the aroma of interview rooms in my two months off. The tangy odour – of rancid kebabs mixed with cheesy feet – hit me as Becky and I entered the room. The radiator only had one setting – subtropical. I took my jacket off, put it on the plastic chair in front of Steve Moore and the duty solicitor and sat down, rolling up my sleeves, taking my time. On the desk between us and the suspect, Becky placed a buff-coloured folder. Then she fiddled with the recording equipment.

'I really must insist on my client going to the hospital,' Moore's lawyer, Mark Clark, said.

I'd come across him before many times. He was balding, bland, and often looked as if he was asleep half the time during an interview. Like many of his clients, he was a sweater, and there was already a damp stain under the armpits of his pale blue shirt. I didn't want to think what it would be like after a few hours in there.

'Mr Moore has been cleared by the force doctor as being fit for interview,' I said.

'He's got a broken nose! Sustained while your colleagues threw him on the floor.'

'He was resisting arrest,' Becky said, turning her attention to the video recorder.

'He was not. He was running from who he thought were people breaking into his property. He was scared for his life.'

Becky snorted. 'He was running from police officers who identified themselves as such on the doorstep.'

'He's in a great deal of pain. He can hardly breathe. Don't think we won't be suing you for this.'

'Yeah,' I said. 'Good luck with that. Shall we get to it, then?'

Becky sat down and started the recording equipment, stating the preliminaries, who was present, the time and date, and so on.

'Why did you run from the police, Steve?' I asked.

He pointed to his lawyer. 'Like he said, I thought you were burglars.'

'Burglars don't usually identify themselves as police officers and tell you you're under arrest. Try again.'

Moore swallowed, beads of sweat pricking his forehead.

'Was it because you had something in the house you didn't want us to find?'

He shook his head vehemently.

I pointed to the recording equipment. 'I need an audible response.'

'Nah. I haven't got any drugs in there.'

Clark gasped, leaned closer and whispered to Moore.

Moore slapped a hand over his mouth.

My eyebrows did a little sarcastic rise. 'Interesting. Who said anything about drugs?' I looked at Becky. 'Did you?'

She grinned. 'No.'

'Although, now you mention it . . . did you mean a bag of marijuana, by any chance?' I asked. 'The *big* bag of it we found stashed in your bedroom under the mattress?'

More whispering from Clark to Moore. Moore's forehead was covered in sweat now as he whispered back.

'All right. My client admits to having a very small amount of marijuana for personal use, purely for medicinal purposes. He has a bad back. He's not a dealer. I'm sure we can clear this . . . this misunderstanding up quickly with just a caution.'

I studied Moore. He was tall, on the skinny side, which gave me an idea to explore later. 'There were ten ounces in the bag. That's about ten times more than could be considered for personal use. Unless you're an elephant. And there's a bit more to it than the drugs, I'm afraid. You were arrested for four murders.'

'Murders?' Clark looked surprised. Maybe he *had* been asleep during the part where he'd been told what his client had been nicked for.

Moore shook his head madly. 'It's a mistake. I didn't kill no one.' He chewed on his thumbnail, watching me expectantly.

'Do you recognise these gloves?' I reached inside the folder on the desk, took out a photograph of the black leather gloves and held it up.

He peered at it. 'No.'

'I found them in your van,' Becky said.

He shrugged. 'I've never seen them before.'

'What do those have to do with anything?' Clark asked.

'Neal Lane and Hannah Ryan were murdered yesterday in Mr Lane's house in Oak Drive, Stevenage. A distinctive glove print was found at the scene.' I put the photograph down on the desk. 'A few miles away, on the same evening, there was a fire in a disused hospital where six women who'd been held captive there died. An identical glove print was found at that scene, too. I reckon the lab will match those prints to these gloves.' I tapped the photo.

'What!' Moore's mouth fell open. He looked at the photo. Looked at his lawyer. Looked at me. Eyes wide and terrified. 'They're not *mine!* I've never seen them before.'

'How did they get in your van?'

'I don't know. I don't . . .' His head shook manically.

'A year ago, you did some plumbing work for Jim and Donna Wilson, didn't you? Two weeks before they were brutally murdered.' I opened the folder and slapped two photos down on the desk of Donna and Jim Wilson, dead in their kitchen.

Moore visibly recoiled. He scrambled up out of his chair and lurched backwards until he hit the wall behind him. 'I didn't . . . you can't think . . .'

'Sit down, Steve,' I said.

He shook his head, looking at the floor.

'Did you do this to them?' Becky tapped the photo of Donna Wilson.

He shook his head again, thumb in his mouth now, biting hard on the nail.

'For the benefit of the recording the suspect is shaking his head,' I said. 'Sit down, Steve.'

He stumbled back to the chair, sat down.

'Police officers found a receipt in the Wilsons' house for the work you did for them shortly before they were killed,' Becky said.

'All I did was fit a new ballcock on their toilet, not murder them!' His eyes glistened with tears. 'It's crazy. The police spoke to me at the time. They knew I didn't do anything.'

I watched him carefully as he chewed on his thumbnail again. 'But that's how you choose your victims, isn't it? Scoping them out when you do work for them? You're the Cupid Killer, aren't you?'

His eyes grew to the size of saucers. He looked at his lawyer, mouth agape. 'It's not me.'

'My client has already said that he didn't have anything to do with their murder. And doing plumbing work isn't a crime.'

'Oh, I don't know . . . some of the plumbing work I've had done has been shocking.' I slapped two more photos on the desk from the crime scene at Neal Lane's house. 'But how about this, then . . . Hannah Ryan and Neal Lane were brutally murdered in a very similar fashion.

It's been reported that your van was seen outside Neal Lane's house a week before his death.'

'No.' Moore gasped and squeezed his eyes shut. 'I didn't do that. I just went to give him a quote!'

'A quote,' Becky said. 'For what?'

'For a new boiler! When I got there . . . when I got there he said he'd never called me. Didn't know anything about it.'

'Right,' I said. 'So it was a man who called you?'

His eyes snapped open. 'Yes.'

'And what exactly did he say?'

'He . . . um . . . just that his name was Neal, and he wanted me to give him a quote for a new boiler. He said his was playing up. He gave me the address, and I swear . . . I just went to give him a quote.'

'And what happened when you got to the address?' I asked.

'Um . . . we stood on the doorstep. I said I was there about the quote, and he said he didn't know what I was talking about. He said he'd never called me. There must've been some kind of . . . a mistake . . . he was surprised. I just left after that. I didn't even go inside.' He looked at the floor, still avoiding the photographs.

'But you did go into the Wilsons' house and do some work for them,' Becky said.

'Y . . . yes. Like I said! But I didn't kill them.'

'These questions are pointless,' Clark interjected. 'My client has told you he had a legitimate reason for visiting the Wilsons. He's told you about the mix-up with Neal Lane. You're just desperate for leads and trying to pin the murders on my client because you're being crucified in the press and need an arrest quickly.'

'Did you try calling the number back?' I asked.

'What number?' Steve frowned.

'The number you say called you, pretending to be Neal Lane.'

'No. I just thought it was a wind-up. You know, like those people who ring up and order takeaways and taxis to your house but you've never ordered them. Kids most likely.'

'Is there anyone who likes winding you up, then?' Becky asked.

His gaze darted around the room, not settling on anything for long.

'Someone allegedly makes a crank call with a fake job and you didn't call them back to find out who? Seems a bit hard to believe.' I folded my arms and waited.

Moore leaned over to Clark, whispered something. Clark whispered back. Then Steve looked at me. 'I thought it could be my dealer, OK? Getting one of his mates to ring me up to annoy me because I owed him some money. But I haven't killed anyone! I honestly swear on my mum's life. I don't know how those gloves got in my van but sometimes I forget to lock it. Someone could've put them in there when I wasn't looking.'

'What do the words "Die Piggy Die" mean?' I changed tack suddenly to ruffle him.

He looked at me like I'd just spoken Chinese. 'I don't know.' His confused frown sought out his lawyer for a moment. 'What do they mean? Um . . . someone who doesn't like pigs?'

'Where were you on the night of thirteenth of December last year?' I asked. Moore had never been considered a suspect in the Wilsons' murders so he'd never been asked at the time.

'That was a year ago, Inspector. How is my client supposed to remember that?'

'Well?' I prompted him.

'I . . . I . . . dunno.'

'OK, how about yesterday? Between the hours of 1.30 a.m. and 2.30 a.m.?'

Moore stared down at the ground, his lips bunched up with concentration. 'I was working till six at a house in Baldock, installing a new radiator. And then . . .' He glanced up at me, his face white.

'What?' Becky asked.

'I was . . . oh, shit.' He leaned back towards Clark again. More whispering. Clark sighed and nodded. 'I went to see my dealer. My *personal use* dealer. I went to pay him back the money I owed him and was at his house all night. We had a few smokes and drinks, and I fell asleep on his sofa. Left there about six in the morning. But he's never going to admit that, is he?' he shrieked, eyes wide.

'My client has been more than helpful in this matter,' Clark said. 'It's obvious he's not involved in any murders.'

Moore glanced down at the photos of the four victims, his gaze flicking away immediately as if his eyeballs had been burned by the sun. 'I didn't do it. I didn't! I admitted the drugs. Can I go now?'

'No, Mr Moore. You can't. I'm terminating the interview now and you'll be taken back to the cells.'

Becky went through the closing procedures and we left the room.

I'd interviewed thousands of suspects in my time. Some of them cold-blooded killers. But I was certain Moore wasn't one of them. He was too stupid for one thing. He wouldn't be highly organised enough to leave no DNA at the scene of the Wilsons' murders, incapacitate his victims, and then murder them violently. And why hide a bag of drugs but not the gloves, which were the only link to the crimes? Plus, either he was a better actor than Morgan Freeman or those photos had genuinely upset and repulsed him.

'You thinking what I'm thinking?' Becky asked as we walked along the corridor.

'Yep. Moore's identification as a prime suspect was too neat and quick and easy. But they made two mistakes there. Someone wanted to make it look like he'd killed the Wilsons, Hannah Ryan, and Neal Lane, but he's too much of an idiot to kill anyone, let alone be involved in an organised trafficking ring. And they didn't know the glove print had been found at the hospital, which ties everything to my case and the warrant card and only incriminates them more.'

'I can't believe—' Becky broke off when a uniformed PC came into view along the corridor. He greeted us and then disappeared.

I stopped and leaned against the wall.

'I can't believe it's one of our own.' Becky curled her top lip up. 'Who's your money on? Colin or Munroe?'

'My bet's on Colin. My team's wading through reams of data, trying to find something solid.'

'Mine's on Munroe. I think she purposely directed me to look in his van so *I'd* find them, and it wouldn't seem as if she had anything to do with it.'

I pursed my lips together, thinking. 'You said there was dashcam footage of the man who chased Gillian Lane?'

'Yeah.'

'I want it analysed for height and build comparison to prove it wasn't Moore. I also want that phone number checked out to see who called him with the bogus boiler job at Neal Lane's house. Someone wanted him seen at the Lanes' house to stitch him up. And I want the dealer spoken to as well, although it's highly doubtful he's going to give Moore an alibi for smoking and buying drugs in his flat. Still, if we can prove it's not Moore on that dashcam, we'll just do him for possession and dealing and let him go.'

'What are you going to do?'

My phone beeped then with an email alert. I pulled it out of my pocket and read the few lines of text.

Special delivery package has arrived.

I grinned. 'I'm going to do a spot of research.'

GILLIAN

Chapter 41

Gillian unlocked the door to the cottage and stepped inside the cold hallway. The place had been shut up since the summer because she and Neal had both been too busy with work to come down. Gillian had suggested they visit for a short weekend break after the contract with World Food Corps had been terminated, but Neal had refused.

Tears sprang to her eyes as she walked into the kitchen-diner and put the keys back in the pocket of her coat. She clutched the edge of the table as her knees threatened to buckle at the thought of her husband, dead.

'We need to get the heating on.' Dean put her suitcase on the floor and rubbed his hands together. He glanced at her. Caught her desolate look. Sprang towards her and wrapped her in his arms. 'I'm so sorry.'

She clung onto him, letting the tears that she'd been trying so hard to hold at bay fall. 'That woman he was with . . .'

Dean held her gently so as not to squeeze her bad arm against him.

'Do you think Neal was having an affair?'

'Of course he wasn't,' Dean replied. 'He was helping Hannah Ryan with a story about the refugees. She was obviously at the house because of that.'

'I don't understand why he didn't *tell* me then!' she wailed.

'Shush.' Dean stroked her hair, trying to soothe her. He pulled back, hands on her shoulders. 'Let's get the heating on and have a cup of tea.'

She nodded and slumped onto a dining-room chair with her coat on, staring out of the window into the box garden that overlooked some fields running along the edge of Dartmoor National Park. Memories flitted into her head of all the times she and Neal had spent down here. Them sitting outside in the summer, indulging in sundowners, drinking icy-cold gin and tonics while watching the birds of prey soaring in the sky. Wandering around the postcard-worthy villages and eating Devonshire cream teas with thick cream and salty butter. Walking hand in hand through Dartmoor, exploring parts of the vast moorland with its craggy landscape, forests, waterfalls, and wetlands. Following trails through valleys with Neolithic tombs and Bronze Age stone circles, seeing the wild ponies roaming.

She rested her good elbow on the table and dropped her head into her hand.

How was she ever going to get over this? She'd lost her daughter and now her husband, too.

Dean came back from fiddling with the boiler. The radiators began clicking away as they heated up.

'Tea or coffee?' He looked at her over his shoulder as he filled the kettle, his own sorrow mirroring hers.

'There should be some whisky in the cupboard. I need some of that.'

'Is that OK to drink with your painkillers?'

'I really don't give a stuff about that. In fact, if I've got any hope of sleeping tonight then I need to drink the whole bottle.'

He nodded. Got two glasses from the cupboard, along with a half-empty bottle of Scotch, and poured them both a generous slug.

Gillian swallowed a large gulp. Felt the fire sliding down her throat. And wished she could see her husband once more.

DETECTIVE WARREN CARTER
Chapter 42

The press was camped outside the front door of the police station, clamouring for details on who we'd arrested as the Cupid Killer. No doubt they'd been given a tip-off from Colin Etheridge before he'd left the building. I swore under my breath as I went out the back way, hurrying to my car. I wanted to nail the bugger but that would have to wait until I knew just how bent Colin was.

I phoned Jack for an update on the way back to my house. He told me that since the departure of the Letchworth Three, Munroe had called her husband's mobile. And Colin, not unexpectedly, had called his mate John Hinckley at the *Daily World*. That didn't mean either of them hadn't used a pay-as-you-go phone or stopped at a call box to tip off their accomplices as to what was happening. The only spot of good news was the elimination of Jamal Faris so that we were down to two prime suspects.

'And Colin Etheridge wasn't being paid directly by John Hinckley for his info to him,' Jack said. 'Colin's mum is in a care home in Hitchin. Hinckley was paying her fees straight to the home. Apparently, there was a scandal at the previous home she was in – staff abusing some of the residents. Colin moved her to this new top-notch place but it's pricey, and he was obviously having trouble paying the bills.'

I groaned. That wasn't what I was expecting to hear. I could understand why he wanted to keep his mum safe in a reputable home. But was that all it was?

'Yeah. Doesn't make it right but it puts things into perspective,' Jack said.

'Is that all he's involved in, though? Just how corrupt is Colin?'

'We're still digging.'

I ended the call and parked on my drive. When I opened my front door and stood in the hallway, I had a weird sense of déjà vu. The last time I'd asked the Vigilante for help, he'd delivered a package that had tied a nice little bow on top of the investigation into a police officer's involvement in major crime. This time the bow came in the form of a flashdrive left on the kitchen worktop next to the kettle. Beneath it was a note.

Nothing interesting in World Food Corps' financial records. Either they're legit or they have another set of accounts somewhere. David Bennington's UK bank accounts are equally benign. But he has an offshore bank account with Privatnyy Bank in Ukraine under the name of Oxford Holdings, which is a shell company owned by him. Privatnyy Bank is mafia-owned by Ivan Tereshchenko, a well-known mob boss turned so-called legitimate 'businessman'.

Powell Acton's personal UK accounts include many cash deposits for around £5,000 a time, clearly under the threshold of legal reporting for suspicious activity. He then makes regular transfers from this account to the account of Odesa Investments in Privatnyy Bank. Odesa Investments is a shell company owned by Powell Acton, and he's listed as the beneficial owner. Once the money reaches Odesa Investments, Acton then transfers money from this account to Oxford Holdings on a regular basis. Most likely Bennington's cut for the trafficking ring. Acton Associates are also the lawyer for World Food Corps, plus some very dodgy oligarchs and mafia types from Ukraine.

I can't find anything on Oliver Hammond. His business and personal records look clean. No sign of any offshore companies or bank accounts. But Acton Associates also represent Assisted Fertility UK as their legal adviser. And I've included something interesting that I dug up.

No sign of any offshore accounts for Susan Munroe anywhere, but she does use another UK bank account. She has power of attorney for her mother, Belinda Cook, who's suffering from Alzheimer's and is in a residential care home. In the last three months she's withdrawn £25,000 from Mrs Cook's account.

Colin Etheridge and Jamal Faris are in financial difficulties, but again, no sign of offshore accounts or suspicious financial activity, although Etheridge is talking to reporter John Hinckley on a regular basis.

There were no traces of any emails between any of the parties. But calls between Assisted Fertility UK and Acton Associates, and World Food Corps and Acton Associates, have been made many times over the years, although they could argue, since Acton Associates is their corporate lawyer, that these were legitimate communications.

I asked myself whether I trusted the Vigilante's judgement in stating what was benign or suspicious, and was certain that even if I didn't know his name, he was a seeker of justice, too, and he knew as well as me exactly what was what. I didn't have a clue where he'd managed to get all his info from, but one thing was sure, if he'd found something that tied any of the records to the deaths of six trafficked women, he would've included it. And I would never have gained access to the offshore corporation and bank account details through legal channels. I booted up my laptop, sat down at the kitchen table, and plugged the flashdrive in.

There were hundreds of pages of bank statements to go through, although Faris's could now be ignored. I clicked on a copy of a passport photo for David Bennington, stamped with the name of Privatnyy Bank, which had been used to open the account in the name of Oxford Holdings. The account was sitting in the black at just over six million dollars. Some entries had been highlighted for me that came from Odesa Investments. Another passport photo ID had been used by Powell Acton to open the Odesa Investments bank account, the same account he was using to pay for utilities at Brampton Hospital. His account had just over three million in it.

I sat back, scrubbed a hand over my face, stared at the chaos of numbers, putting together in my head the trail of money.

So . . . from the entries, someone had been giving Powell Acton a cut of the money from the trafficking ring, which he'd regularly paid into his personal UK bank account over the last nine months at £5,000 a time, making sure it was beneath the €10,000 or equivalent mandatory-reporting threshold so no one started looking at it as suspicious. He then made regular payments to David Bennington at the Oxford Holdings Ukraine bank account via his own company account of Odesa Investments in payments of £2,500 a time. I suspected, too, that this was Bennington's cut from the trafficking ring and Acton was taking his half out of it before he passed it on. Bennington was being paid for his supply of women trafficked from Salama Camp in Jordan. Most likely smuggling them out with World Food Corp vehicles. If international aid vehicles were stopped, how likely is it they would be searched? And if they were, a few bribes here or there would do the trick. Neal Lane was working on a biometrics ID system. He must've discovered women going missing from the camp. He must've found some kind of evidence about it. Hannah Ryan went to Salama to research a story on refugees. They got talking. Trusted each other. He wanted to blow the whistle on what was going on. And they must've had evidence to prove it. Neal's and Hannah's missing laptops, camera, photos, hard drives, and flashdrives, stolen by the killer to stop this being blown out of the water.

Next player: Powell Acton, who owned an empty hospital via his own company Odesa Investments. I now had a rock-solid connection between the two men. But who was the third person in the chain – the one without whom nothing would work – the fertility doctor? Was it Oliver Hammond? So far he seemed clean, but it had to be him.

I tapped my foot, my mind turning everything over, thinking, thinking, thinking.

Powell Acton was Bennington's lawyer, but a so-called humanitarian CEO wouldn't suddenly approach his lawyer, telling him he has an endless supply of untraceable women and does he have any mates who know what to do with them. Similarly, a fertility doctor wouldn't suddenly approach his lawyer and say he fancied trafficking women into the country to steal their eggs for profit. No. There had to be another connection between them all prior to this. They had to trust each other. They had to be friends.

I stood and filled a glass with water from the tap, trying to get rid of the bitterness in my mouth. It felt like I was being smothered with the same thick, cloying fumes from Brampton Hospital.

I sat down again and waded through the personal bank statements of Oliver Hammond and the accounts for his business, Assisted Fertility UK, along with records of his phone bills. I perused everything, looking for a suspicious data or paper trail that would tie him to the others but there was nothing, just like the Vigilante had said. Hammond had only been in contact with Acton Associates via phone, which proved nothing, and they would argue was because of legitimate business dealings. Maybe they'd been using burner phones or anonymous email addresses to contact each other. If Hammond had no offshore accounts, and he hadn't made any significant deposits or withdrawals into his regular bank accounts, then he must've been dealing purely in cash if he was involved in this.

I carried on reading through more documents. Bios, background info, numbers, until they swam before my eyes.

And there it was, on one of the final documents. The original connection. Found in a photocopy of a newspaper report dated seventeen years previously. This was the item of interest the Vigilante thought I should see.

Oxford students celebrate end-of-year exams in a traditional 'thrashing' good way!

Oxford students celebrated finishing their finals this week with the annual 'thrashing', a tradition that sees students waiting outside exam halls for their friends to emerge, before spraying each other with champagne, foam, confetti, and food.

University officials have previously tried to put a stop to the 'disgraceful' partying behaviour, but as in previous years, students could be seen indulging in a last blow-out. Covered in foam as they swigged bottle after bottle of bubbly, these Oxford students celebrated as they wandered through the city centre in true end-of-term boozy, hi-jinks style.

The tradition has a habit of descending into a food fight, and officials have warned students not to use flour, eggs, beans, ketchup, or rotting food. One University source said: 'It's disgraceful behaviour, not to mention the potential dangers. Last year a female student was fined for rubbing a chocolate gateau in a friend's face. She was told by university officials that she must pay up or she would not be allowed to graduate.'

Beneath the article was a photo captioned:

Party time: Four Oxford student friends chug champagne as they celebrate the end of their final-year exams.

It showed three men and one woman. All dressed in black and white. They were spattered from head to foot in string foam, cream, and confetti. The photo had been taken in the middle of an Oxford street that was also littered with the multicoloured detritus of food and mess. They all had their arms around each other, wild grins on their faces. The woman was Susan Munroe. She held up a bottle of champagne to the camera. The other three were David Bennington, Powell Acton, and Oliver Hammond. All much younger, but all easily recognisable.

The Vigilante had included graduation records for the four of them. Powell Acton, David Bennington, and Susan Munroe had studied law at Oxford University at the same time. Oliver Hammond had also been there then, studying medicine. He *was* the third guy in the trafficking ring. Had to be. And I'd cocked up when I'd checked Munroe's personnel record. I hadn't bothered going back to her graduate history, just when she'd started with Hertfordshire Constabulary. If I had, I would've made a definite connection with what Jack had told me about Powell Acton studying at Oxford.

So Colin Etheridge had nothing to do with the murders. It was Munroe. She must've been getting paid for her part in it but where was the trail of money for her? I started going through her regular bank records that we'd already got hold of, looking for something that Jack had missed when he'd been searching through them. There were the usual, everyday payments for utilities, food, shopping, and so on. Plus monthly fees to Mrs Cook's care home. No cash deposits at all. Nothing unusual. I then turned to the bank statements for Munroe's mum, Belinda Cook.

The Vigilante was right. Between September and the middle of November, Munroe had taken out £25,000 in cash from cashpoints, in sums of around £500 a time. And he'd even included photos captured from the cashpoint machines to prove it was her.

I stared at the photos, wondering what she was using the money for. Something for Belinda Cook?

I checked Munroe's assets again – the precious-metals purchases that were stored with a bullion company in London, and the various bonds she and her husband had purchased. None had been bought after the eleventh of July. Both her and her husband's vehicles had been bought some years before, so the money wasn't for that, either.

I frowned at the screen. She wasn't being paid like the others with money going into her regular accounts, and she was withdrawing a lot of cash from her mum's account instead. And if Hammond, or one of the others, was paying her in cash instead of using a bank trail, why the need to withdraw so much extra money? What was she using it for? Did she have a gambling problem or some other kind of addiction? It was something to look into. And at least I'd found the connection between them. But even though my team were busy going through all of their regular financial details, there was no way I could introduce the incriminating offshore banking and company information if I wanted to get a conviction because it had been unlawfully obtained. And I had to find a way to show Munroe's access to her mother's account without it looking suspicious. So how the hell did I prove it all?

GILLIAN

Chapter 43

Gillian didn't know how long she'd been sitting at the dining-room table, staring into space, lost in memories of her husband. The whisky hadn't helped numb her. It had just made things worse. She was overwhelmed with sadness, exhausted, and in pain. Dean had wanted to sit with her, talk about Neal, but she'd just wanted to be left alone, so he'd disappeared upstairs to the spare room out of her way.

Darkness crept in outside and she could no longer make out shadows of the trees and the expanse of the national park through the kitchen door that led to the garden. Everything was black, just like she felt inside. Even though the heating blasted out now, she still felt chilled to the bone and put her good hand in the pocket of her coat to warm her fingers.

Her fingertips skimmed the keys inside. Neal's keys that she'd taken to the airport when her car wouldn't start and then rowed about with him. Her heart twisted at the thought that the last contact she'd had with him had been a fight, instead of kind and loving words.

She pulled the keys out of her pocket and put them on the dining-room table. A big bunch with a ceramic fob that had the words *Drive Safe Because I Love You!* written on it. She'd bought it for Neal in a shop near here that sold souvenirs and knick-knacks. She'd always grumbled if she'd borrowed his car and had to take his keys because there were so many on there and they were so heavy. The Mini's thick electronic key. Front- and back-door keys to the house in Oak Drive, the front- and back-door keys to this cottage, spare house key for Dean's place. She never knew why Neal insisted on keeping all of them together when he didn't need most of them on a daily basis. She stroked the words on the fob, as if they could comfort her somehow. And that's when she noticed something for the first time.

There was an extra key on there.

Frowning, she separated it from the others. It was small and slim with a number along the side, like a key for a locker. And she had no idea what it was for.

She was so busy staring at it that she didn't hear the knock on the front door at first. It was only Dean's footsteps thundering down the stairs that brought her out of her confusion.

She heard the front door opening. Heard Dean say, 'Oh, hello, officer.'

Gillian stepped into the doorway, looking down the hall towards the front door. Dean's back partially blocked a man standing on the step dressed in a police uniform. All she could see was the top of his head and half of his right side.

'Evening, Mr Lane. I'm PC Wallis from Devon and Cornwall Police. I'm just doing a patrol check on you and Mrs Lane, which was organised by Hertfordshire Constabulary.'

'Well, that's very kind of you, but we're both perfectly OK,' Dean replied.

'Are you sure? They were very insistent that I check on both of you. Can I speak to Gillian Lane, please?'

'Of course.' Dean stepped to the side a little.

The police officer peered around Dean and met Gillian's gaze.

He was thickset, with bad acne-scarred skin.

She tried to smile but something stopped her. A feeling. A chill rippling down her spine. A memory of being chased down the road by her husband's killer.

Dean turned around and looked in the same direction as the PC. 'Everything's fine, isn't it, Gillian?'

She couldn't speak.

'Are you all right, Mrs Lane?' the PC asked.

She didn't know what it was about him. She'd never seen the face of the man who'd chased her. But somehow she knew – with a strange kind of sixth sense – this was him.

She froze. Her heart slammed to a sudden stop. 'Yes, everything's fine,' she said, trying to sound as normal as possible while her brain tried to work out if Dean's mobile phone was in the kitchen. He'd had it when they'd arrived. But had he taken it upstairs with him? The landline had been disconnected years ago because they never used it.

'Thank you for checking up on us, but you can see everything's OK.' Dean turned back to the man. 'Sorry to drag you out here for nothing. I'll let you get back to work.' Dean tried to close the door.

The man's foot shot outwards, bringing the door to a sudden halt.

Gillian inched backwards, further into the kitchen area. Her wide eyes on the face of the uniformed man who'd stepped onto the doorstep now.

'Perhaps I should have a look around. Just to make sure you're safe.'

'No, really, we're fine. There's absolutely no need.' Dean stepped backwards a little as the man pushed the door open. Dean still hadn't worked out what was happening, his voice still pleasant and unsuspicious.

'I insist,' the PC said, smiling at Dean as he slid his hand into his blue fleece and pulled out an extendable baton in his right hand.

He swung it at Dean's head.

Dean slumped to the floor.

The man looked at Gillian, his eyes dark, like bottomless pools of black.

Gillian screamed.

HAYAT

Chapter 44

When the van stops I press myself upwards from the curled position I've been lying in, waiting for Mr Gavin to open the doors.

He leans in and holds out his hand to me, again helping me out. 'Come on.'

As I step out, a big building looms ahead in the shadows. The only light comes from a tiny slice of moon cutting through the night.

The driver helps the other two women out and then takes a key from his pocket and walks towards the big door at the front of the house.

Wow, I think. The family who live here must be very rich. It is almost as big as the hotel I worked at. And if they are rich and they want us to be maids for them, they will treat us well. I know they will.

The driver opens the door. We step inside and there is a big open entrance hallway with a staircase in front of us. Next to the stairs is a wooden desk. There are closed doors that lead off the entrance.

'This way.' Mr Gavin grips my elbow. 'We'll take you to your rooms where you can sleep. You must be tired. In the morning someone will come and give you breakfast.'

We turn right towards a long corridor. The first room we come to has a wooden door. I notice there is no keyhole to lock it but one of the key-card mechanisms that our hotel had. Mr Gavin swipes a plastic card in front of it and the door opens. The driver takes the other two girls further down the corridor.

Mr Gavin steps back and lets me enter first.

I smile as I take in the room. There is a bed in the centre. A doorway with a small bathroom to my right. There are curtains at the window, which are closed.

And then . . . I am confused. There is a chain attached to the wall with a cuff on one end.

I turn to look at him, my eyes wide. 'What is—'

But I do not get to finish. He pushes me roughly forwards. I stumble and stagger until I fall face forward onto the bed. His weight is on top of me, and I think he will rape me.

I scream, but my voice is muffled between the mattress and sheets. I feel his body jerking. Then I feel something cold and hard wrapped around my wrist. When his weight lifts away I look at the cuff on my arm.

'What? No!' I cry.

But he is already backing out of the room.

'No!' I twist around on the bed and look at him, tears in my eyes, my stomach as cold as the winter desert winds. 'Please come back!'

DETECTIVE WARREN CARTER
Chapter 45

'It's DCI Munroe,' I said to Caroline as I walked into her office.

She looked up from the paperwork she was reading. 'Have you found something?'

I couldn't reveal everything I'd found yet, especially not the offshore companies and accounts, but I'd worry about that later. I handed her a copy of the newspaper article I'd printed off at home.

She read it, a frown pinching at the bridge of her nose. 'Where did you dig this up from?'

'An anonymous source.'

She looked up. 'The same anonymous source who gave you something on Bloodbath Farm?'

'I don't know. That's the whole purpose of anonymity.' I smiled.

She scrutinised my face carefully.

I shrugged. 'It's a matter of public record. Anyone could've got hold of it.'

She looked down at the article again. 'So Susan Munroe, Powell Acton, David Bennington, and Oliver Hammond have known each other for years. Why, though?' Caroline shook her head. 'I don't get how she could be involved in the trafficking of women and the murder of Hannah Ryan and Neal Lane. And so far there's absolutely no link we've found between Munroe and any of them. No private or personal emails between her and them. No suspicious phone calls. No money changing hands. If she'd been in regular contact with one of them over the years, why hasn't it shown up?'

'Because she's clever. She didn't get to be a DCI without learning how to avoid getting caught.' I handed her a document I'd requested before I headed back to the office. 'Which is why I was suspicious that Munroe might've had access to other bank accounts, so I made an enquiry with the Office of the Public Guardian. She's got financial power of attorney for her mum, Belinda Cook, who's in a care home.' At least hopefully that would cover my arse for finding the link that the Vigilante had given me.

Caroline studied the copy of the power of attorney that was registered with the OPG. Then looked up at me again with one eyebrow quirked up. 'That was a long leap to make.'

I gave her my best innocent face. 'I knew her mum was in a care home, and I knew there was nothing strange going on in Munroe's regular accounts so I dug elsewhere. It was just a hunch.'

'A hunch. Hmmm.' Her eyebrow remained up.

Before she could question me further, I said, 'I made an enquiry with the bank that holds the account of Belinda Cook, and got them to expedite me the last year's statements.' I handed over copies that the bank had just that minute emailed through. The Vigilante's copies were safely hidden at home.

Caroline read through them. 'So £25,000 has been taken out in the last three months.'

'Yes. And Belinda Cook didn't take it out, because she's got advanced Alzheimer's and is bedridden. I checked. Munroe's dad is dead, and Munroe is the only other person with access to this account. And the care home said Munroe hasn't bought her mum anything recently, either. I think maybe Munroe's got a gambling problem or other addiction. And I think one of them is paying her in cash.'

She sat back. 'Sounds feasible.'

'But she's not actually as clever as she thinks. The trouble is, when you start lying about something, you have to make the lie bigger and bigger to keep convincing people it's true. They already made a mistake planting the gloves, because they tied directly to Brampton Hospital. She might've made other mistakes that will prove her guilt. Whoever killed Neal and Hannah and tried to frame Steve Moore underestimated his stupidity. Becky's trying to prove his innocence now.'

Jack knocked on the door then with a folder of paperwork in his hand. 'Do you want the good news or the bad news?'

'I don't know if I can take any more bad news,' I said.

'Well, Technical Services just called and said they can't find a match between any of the six victims and the photos of recorded refugees that were sent over from Salama.'

'I'm not that surprised. Either their records were deleted or they never existed in the first place,' I said. 'What's the good news?'

Jack grinned. 'Got something on Powell Acton's personal financial records.' He went on to explain what I'd already found out from the paperwork the Vigilante had given me. That Powell Acton had deposited regular amounts of £5,000 cash payments into his personal UK account and then transferred it to Odesa Investments at Privatnyy Bank.

'That's great!' Caroline said.

'But the bank's owned by the Ukrainian mafia. They've already refused to give any info to us,' I said.

'Those payments still prove Powell Acton's involvement because they're going to the same company that owns Brampton Hospital,' Caroline said.

'And if Odesa Investments were just a client, why was he making payments through his personal account and not his business one?' I added. 'He's got to be the beneficial owner of Odesa Investments.'

'Agreed,' Caroline said. 'But we can't prove that if the Ukrainians won't give us any more info. We need to find more on Munroe before we bring her or Acton in. Are we still waiting for David Bennington's financial and phone data to come through?' she asked Jack.

'Yes. And Oliver Hammond's. And we're already up to our eyeballs in data,' he said.

I nodded with sympathy. 'Which is why I'd like to get Ronnie onto Hammond's and Bennington's stuff as soon as it comes in. He's a whizz with numbers and it will really help us out.'

'OK,' Caroline said. 'But make it clear that he reports only to you in the strictest confidence.'

'Absolutely.'

Jack left and headed back to his desk.

'I take it there's nothing back on the historical triangulation data from Munroe's phones yet?' I asked Caroline.

'Still waiting for it. I'll request the same for Hammond, Bennington, and Acton now, too. See if we can place any of them at Brampton Hospital. One more interesting thing is that the lab found DNA from skin cells on the inside cuff area of the gloves. It's being tested now.' Her mobile phone pinged then at the same time as mine. She reached for hers as I pulled mine out of my pocket and read an email.

Subject: Update on unknown female victims – Case 463481/18

DNA test samples taken from the six victims at Brampton Hospital show no matches on the National DNA Database.

I pinched the bridge of my nose with my forefinger and thumb and let out an almighty sigh, disappointment welling inside. I didn't want those women to be buried in an unnamed grave, with no family able to pay their last respects. They deserved more than that. Much more. 'Did the last three post-mortems flag up anything helpful?'

An intense, haunted look crossed her face as she looked up from her phone screen. 'Basically the same as the first three. All were being subjected to invasive fertility treatment. They were just a commodity to use.' She rubbed her hand over her face, looking exhausted. 'I've witnessed hundreds of post-mortems, seen so many dead bodies, but this . . . well, this is going to stick with me for a long, long time.'

'You and me both.'

She glanced out through the glass window at Jack, Katrina, Liz, and Koray, their heads bent over desks or staring at screens. They looked zombied-out with the amount of information they'd been analysing and it was now gone 7 p.m. 'I think they've had enough for one day. You'd better send them home. We need everyone fresh and wide awake if we're going to nail DCI Munroe.'

GILLIAN

Chapter 46

Gillian slammed the door to the dining room and turned the key that was inside it, locking the man in the hallway. The door was old pine, solid. But it wouldn't hold for long.

She ran to the back door, fumbled with Neal's keys, trying to find the right one for the lock. The man kicked at the door, and her hand shook violently as she finally slid the key in. Twisted it. Opened the door.

She ran across the garden, clutching the keys in her hand, and climbed awkwardly over the three-foot post-and-rail fence separating the house from the fields and the national park beyond.

For the second time in two days, she ran for her life.

Every footstep sent a painful jolt on her arm and ankle. She kept the plaster cast tight against her chest, trying to make it as easy as possible. Not daring to turn around, she lumbered across the field, heading towards the forest in the distance.

Breathe, breathe, breathe, she told herself, trying to take her mind off the pain and fear. *Just get to the trees. He won't find you then. You'll be camouflaged.*

She heard him behind her, panting. The crack of a twig.

An involuntary, terrified shriek escaped her mouth as she shoved the keys in her coat pocket and zipped it up for safekeeping.

Then she crashed through the perimeter of trees, the darkness swallowing her whole.

She ran as fast as her swollen ankle would allow. Crunching over the fallen winter leaves, crispy with frost, branches tearing at her hair, thorns scratching her face.

She banged her broken arm on a tree trunk. Gasped out loud as an agonising wave seared through her, an explosion of black and white stars appearing before her eyes.

Footsteps behind her now, gaining speed.

She hurtled onwards.

And realised too late that the flat ground had given way to an embankment.

Her legs went out from under her and she slithered down the steep hill on her back, the world crashing around her.

DETECTIVE WARREN CARTER
Chapter 47

'You still here?' Caroline asked me. She wore an elegant red trench coat over her uniform, briefcase in hand. 'You need to get some sleep, too, you know. You look like you're dead on your feet.'

I stood in the briefing room, hands in my pockets, staring at the photos of the six unknown women again. I glanced over at her. 'Nearly finished. You off?'

'No. I'm about to update the Chief Constable.'

My stomach let forth an embarrassingly loud rumble, and I realised I hadn't eaten anything since breakfast.

'Hungry?' She laughed.

'Starving, now you mention it.'

'Do you want to grab something to eat when I finish up? I could definitely do with a drink, too, after those PMs today.' Her expression changed, the colour of her eyes darkening with sadness.

My stomach gave a little twirl inside. Hunger again. It must've been. 'Um . . . yes. Sure. Beats a microwave meal or a takeaway.'

'OK. I'll call you as soon as I finish.'

'Great.' I smiled, a bizarre warm feeling rushing to my extremities, and watched her breeze out the door.

Oh, God.

It's just a drink with a work colleague. A meal. Sustenance after a busy day.

Denise's face popped into my head. Guilt turned the warm feeling icy.

I shook my head and concentrated on dialling Becky's number.

She answered on the fourth ring. 'I was just about to call you with an update.' She told me that Steve Moore's dealer had denied Moore was there smoking drugs in his flat on the night Hannah Ryan and Neal Lane were murdered. Surprise, surprise. But she did have some good news. She was in the Technical Services office and they'd just finished analysing the dashcam footage from the taxi with some all-singing, all-dancing software that could measure things like a subject's height and body proportions.

'It's not Steve Moore on the footage,' she said. 'The guy who chased Gillian is at least three inches shorter and a lot bulkier than Moore. What do you want me to do with him?'

'I could think of a few things but none of them would be polite. Charge his drug-dealing arse and then go home. If you can get back in bright and early tomorrow there's going to be a lot to do.' I brought her up to speed on Munroe's involvement and her link to the others. 'Your suspicions were right all along.'

'Yeah, but that doesn't make me feel better. I bloody *knew* Bennington was dodgy, but Munroe . . . not her, of all people. I was hoping to be wrong. Why would she do it?'

'I don't know yet. Money, most likely, but we're still looking for a trail. Is Ronnie still there?'

'He's been going through the email accounts of Hannah Ryan, which came in earlier, but he's found nothing significant. He's waiting for a call from the phone providers trying to trace where the number came from that called Steve Moore pretending to be Neal Lane. Not likely to get anything back tonight, though.'

'OK. Tell him to go home and get some rest. Tomorrow I want him on number-crunching duty.'

'Will do. Um . . . do you fancy going for a drink? Maybe get some grub?'

'Uh . . .' I thought about the drink and meal lined up with Caroline, and I wanted to go with her. I *really* wanted to. But there was something in Becky's voice. Wistful. Sad. 'Are you OK?'

'Not really. Ian's left. I don't know where he's gone and he's not answering my calls.'

'Ah.'

'I just don't fancy going back to a depressingly empty house tonight. But no worries if you're busy.' She tried to inject an upbeat tone but failed miserably.

'Um . . . No, I'm not busy. How about we meet at the Chequers pub?'

I hung up and texted Caroline.

Really sorry but something's come up. Will have to give the drink a miss tonight. Next time.

I hesitated over the *X* button. Should I sign off with a kiss? Too familiar? Yep, most definitely. Why was I even thinking it?

I pressed send instead.

GILLIAN

Chapter 48

Gillian landed with a hard thud in a dip at the bottom of the embankment.

She bit her lip to stop herself from screaming in agony as the jolt tore at her shoulder and ribs, then scrambled onto her side, looking upwards. Just enough light from the moon filtered through the trees to see the top of the embankment.

He would've heard the crashing sound, and any minute now she knew he'd find her.

Her gaze darted around frantically, looking for somewhere to hide. The area in front of her was an open plain of grassy moorland. The nearest sizeable tree she could hide behind was about eighty metres to her right. No way could she make it there in time without being spotted. To her left was a large rocky outcrop. She heard water, a steady stream of gushing, and remembered there were waterfalls somewhere nearby that Neal had told her about.

Quickly she got to her feet, heading for the jagged rocks and praying their shadows would hide her from view.

She heard a crunch of leaves above her. Pictured him standing at the top of the embankment, staring down.

She crept forwards, nearing the rocks.

No sound behind her of footsteps following. Maybe he hadn't seen her in the darkness. She jogged on, hugging the side of the rocks.

Eventually the outcrop ended in a pathway of fallen stone that climbed upwards. She studied it for a moment.

Go up? Or . . . she swivelled her head around to her right and the open moorland surrounding her. She'd be spotted in an instant if she made a break for it across there. Plus, she was tiring now. Her best bet was to try to stay hidden. She could never outrun him.

Her chest tightened as she climbed upwards, scrambling over the damp boulders that had been eroded smooth over the years, her feet slipping occasionally. The noise of the waterfall roared louder, masking any sound she made. Her breath came in pants, sweat broke out on her forehead, her thigh muscles burned. Every part of her ached.

The path meandered higher. She turned to look behind her and felt giddy for a moment, her knees threatening to buckle. She put a hand on the rocks to steady herself.

Fear squeezed at her insides. She could see him below. A big, muscular shape, moving lithely. How had he found her? Was he wearing night-vision equipment or something?

Oh, god, oh, god, oh, god!

She climbed as fast as she could, pure terror releasing a new burst of adrenaline.

At the top of the path she saw the falls gushing frothy water down from an escarpment looming vertically above her. There was no way she could climb all the way up the escarpment. The rocks were a flat pillar of an obstacle.

Water spray splashed on her face, tiny droplets like ice, stinging her skin as she frantically looked around. There was a ridge of rocks and boulders around a circular pool that the falls had channelled out over the years.

She heard a noise behind her.

No time to think.

Gingerly, she stepped onto the ridge, the rocks slippery beneath her feet as she tried hard to keep her balance, stepping carefully from one boulder to the other as a stepping stone, heading around the left-hand edge of the pool, her good arm outstretched for balance. Water splashed her trainers with foamy wetness that she barely noticed.

As she got closer to the falls, she saw a shadow behind it, what she thought was a chasm that had been eroded into the escarpment from the force of the water.

The spray was in full force here. The roar of the falls vibrating through her brain.

Pressing her back against the escarpment so she didn't slip into the pool, she inched sideways towards the falls. Freezing water gushed over her, flattening her hair to her body, getting in her eyes. Quickly she batted it away from her face and took baby steps.

The chasm came into view. A narrow ledge of rock that ended at the bottom of the escarpment before the pool began provided a foothold. She tucked herself in behind the waterfall, her back pressed into the cold rock, her good hand flat against it for support.

And she prayed he wouldn't see her.

DETECTIVE WARREN CARTER
Chapter 49

I pushed away the empty plate of fish pie. 'I'm stuffed.'

'Me too,' Becky said.

I took a swig of Corona. 'So . . . do you want to talk about Ian?'

'Ever since . . .' She stopped. Paused. 'How did you manage it? You and Denise for all those years. You worked long hours. You're obsessed with the job. And you two got along great. Why is it so wrong for me to be the same?'

I pursed my lips, thinking what to say. I wasn't exactly good at relationship advice. I'd been with Denise since we were fifteen years old. But she'd got me. Maybe because she'd been a nurse and we were both the kind of people who couldn't switch off from our jobs. I'd been lucky. Very lucky, I knew that. A match made in heaven, soulmates. Maybe it was a cliché but we'd had that nevertheless. I felt a jolt of grief again as my mind wandered to my wife. But it wasn't the shard of pain that usually ripped me in two. It was getting easier. A little. Day by day. Then I felt a fresh wave of guilt *because* it was getting easier. Like I was somehow betraying her.

'I don't want to be the clichéd copper whose relationship ends just because I want to do my job well,' Becky grumbled.

'Clichés flying around all over the place tonight,' I said wistfully, my mind still on Denise.

'Huh?'

'Nothing.'

'He wants a baby.'

'Oh.'

'He wants me to be a stay-at-home mum.'

'Oh.'

'Stop saying oh.' She broke a cold chip in half, smeared it in a pool of ketchup and popped it in her mouth.

'Oh-kay.'

She snorted.

'And you don't want to start a family?' Denise and I had never been able to. We'd tried but it wasn't meant to be. And I knew that what Professor Pullman had told me was true. At the time we would've done anything to have kids. It had been one of the biggest tests in our relationship.

'No. I don't think I'm ready. I'm finally getting to where I want to be in the job. I want to make Inspector in the next few years. I don't want to have a baby and never see it because I'm working long hours. I don't think that's fair. But this job . . . it makes me feel alive. I can't give it up.'

'It's going to be a big stumbling block then.'

Another sigh. 'I know. What would you do if you were me?'

'Well, last time I checked I couldn't have a baby so it's not an issue. And I've never fancied Ian so I wouldn't have married him.'

'Ha, ha. Remind me again why I'm asking relationship advice from you?'

'I don't know.' I threw my hand in the air. 'I'm no good at it.'

She stopped chewing and pointed another chip at me. 'That's the thing, you see. I want what you and Denise had. That ease of being together. The way you both just . . . I don't know . . . understood each other. When I sit and think about things, Ian and me . . . well, it's always been a bit fiery.'

I leaned forward, elbows on the table of the quiet booth in the corner of the pub. 'Do you love him? That's the bottom line, isn't it, surely?'

'That's just it. I don't bloody know any more. Maybe we rushed into things. Maybe we're just too different.'

'OK. Look, at the end of the day, you have to do what makes you happy. But if you love him, you should try to work something out.'

'Like what? Get a cat instead?'

It was my time for a snort. I took a thoughtful swig of beer, trying to offer her something that might help and not being able to.

'I just don't think I want to bring a kid into this world. Everything's just shit.' She scrunched up her face.

I couldn't agree more. I'd seen too much horror on the job. It was only getting worse, too. 'OK, so what about—'

I was cut off by my mobile ringing. I pulled it out of my pocket, saw Caroline's name and answered. She gave me a quick update about her meeting with the Chief Constable and told me they were stepping up the audio surveillance from just Munroe's personal and job mobile phones to now including her house and office at Letchworth police station.

Someone laughed at the table behind us and Caroline said, 'Well, I'll let you get back to your evening. See you tomorrow.' And I had a double dose of guilt again for cancelling our dinner that was *just* a working meal.

I ended the call and stared at the phone for a second. When I looked up, Becky was grinning madly at me. 'What?'

'You like her, don't you?' She waggled her eyebrows up and down.

'Well . . . yes. In a professional capacity. She seems like a good copper. And she lets me do my own thing. It's nice to be appreciated for a change instead of being bollocked all the time and hampered from doing my job.'

'Uh-huh. *Appreciated.*' She leaned back, folded her arms, a smirk on her face. 'I mean you *really* like her.'

I waved my hand through the air dismissively. 'I think she's principled, hard-working, intuitive, and contentious, and is a superior officer who actually cares about what matters rather than the political shit. She seems like she's going to be a great boss, and I haven't liked any of my bosses since DI Ellie Nash left.'

'Uh-huh. Right.' She nodded with a smirk, then her face turned serious. 'You know, it's been over fifteen months since she died. You are allowed to live again. Denise would want you to be happy.'

I held my hands up to cut the conversation off. 'Not going there. I thought tonight was about you. Don't be turning everything around on me.'

'Yeah.' She sighed again, picking up her mobile from the table and checking the time on it. 'I'm going to give Gillian Lane a quick call and see how she's doing. I feel really sorry for her.'

I nodded and went to the bar for a couple more beers as she dialled the number. A rowdy group of women stumbled inside on a hen party, the bride-to-be complete with the requisite veil and various cock apparels. By the time I got back to the table, Becky had the phone pressed to her ear and a worried expression on her face.

'Bugger.' She ended the call and looked up at me.

'What?'

'There's no answer. And her brother-in-law's not answering, either.'

'It's probably nothing. Maybe she's in the bath and he's asleep.'

'What if we were wrong and she *is* in danger? What if the killer thinks she does know something about what her husband knew?'

'But Munroe's involved in it, and she was perfectly aware that Gillian didn't know anything. She would've passed that info on to her accomplices.'

Becky stood up. 'But Munroe also knew exactly where Gillian was going, because I bloody had to tell her. I don't know. But I don't like it.' She tried calling Gillian and Dean again but the calls went to voicemail. Three more times she tried with the same results. 'If anything's happened it's my fault. I wanted to tell Gillian what was really going on. Maybe I should've done. Should've warned her.'

'I still think it's nothing, but I'll get the control room to put a call in to Devon and Cornwall Police. Get them to do a welfare check at the address.' I left the bottles of Corona on the table and hustled out to my car with my mobile pressed against my ear, Becky following close behind.

GILLIAN

Chapter 50

Gillian's heart pounded in her chest as the water hurtled down in front of her on the ledge.

This was it. She was going to die.

She glanced to the side but couldn't see him approaching along the same route she'd taken. Glanced to the other side. No sign of him. But he'd know she was there, somewhere.

She looked down at the ledge, searching for a weapon of some kind, her whole body shivering violently with cold and fear and pain, but there was nothing there that would help protect her.

And then she saw him. Through the small gap afforded by the chasm. A black shadow coming towards her, stepping over the boulders around the pool with a panther-like ease.

DETECTIVE WARREN CARTER
Chapter 51

I paced my old CID office at Stevenage police station. Twelve steps forward. Twelve steps back. Becky sat in her chair and jigged her leg up and down repeatedly, making the chair squeak like there was a demented mouse trapped inside. She chewed on the inside of her cheek, staring at the clock on the wall, her face bunched up tightly.

My mobile, clutched in my hand, rang. I stopped walking, answered and was greeted by an inspector in the control room at Devon and Cornwall Police.

'We sent a unit to the address. We've found Dean Lane there with head injuries. He was barely conscious when we arrived but became a bit more responsive while they were waiting for the ambulance. He said someone dressed as a police officer came to the door and attacked him. It looks like Gillian ran out the back of the property. The door was left wide open. There's no sign of her anywhere.'

'Either he managed to get her or she escaped, then.' I looked at Becky. She stared back questioningly with a look of horror.

'There was a vehicle parked further along the track. We think that's how he arrived because the cottage is out in the middle of nowhere. Vehicle comes back as a cloned plate.'

'Right. I need to get the vehicle impounded and gone over by SOCO. I think whoever drove it was the same suspect involved in multiple murders up here. I'll email over an official request in a minute.'

'Understood. The problem in trying to find them is that the property is on the edge of the national park. There's a lot of ground to cover.'

I glanced out of the window. It was gone 10 p.m. now. It would be pitch black out there.

'Can you get a helicopter out? Dogs? A search-and-rescue team? If he finds her, I have no doubt he'll kill her.'

'Dogs and a helicopter are being arranged now. I'll keep you updated.'

I hung up and slammed my hand on the desk. 'Fuck! Fuck, fuck, fuck.' I told Becky what was going on.

She slumped forward, head in her hands. 'It's all my fault. I should've insisted she stay up here, get a panic alarm fitted.'

'It's my fault. I never thought he'd come back for her. Why *did* he come back for her?' I frowned. 'Munroe was well aware Gillian didn't know anything about the whistleblowing.'

'That always bugged me about the original crime scene.' Becky looked up, dragging her hands down her face before resting them on her cheeks. 'Why did he chase her?'

I started pacing again, thinking. 'I don't get it,' I kept repeating, muttering to myself under my breath. What had we missed? 'Unless Gillian lied to us.' I stopped pacing, swung around. 'Maybe Neal *did* tell Gillian he and Hannah Ryan were about to expose a trafficking ring.'

Becky sat upright. 'No.' She shook her head. 'I'm telling you she definitely didn't know anything.'

'But they must think she does. Why?'

Becky shrugged helplessly.

283

HAYAT

Chapter 52

The man says he is a doctor. He says I need medical treatment. That they will not allow me to live in England until I have been treated for the disease I have.

But I do not know if he tells the truth. He has given me tablets, but now I have a daily injection. He is quite nice to me. He is gentle. But I do not want to be chained up. I want to start my new life. I do not understand what illness I have.

In the bedroom there is nothing apart from the bed and some books. No radio. No TV. Nothing to pass the time except reading. There is nothing to look at, either, because there is nothing behind the curtains. The window is boarded from the inside with some kind of thick wood. I cannot even see the country I came to. I know every inch of the room. I have studied it for hours and hours and hours. How much longer will I have to be here?

Sometimes I hear Safa and Leila, and maybe others, screaming or banging on the doors or walls. I have tried that but it does not work so I have given up. Do they have the same illness as me? This is a hospital, I know that now, but I wasn't sick before I left Jordan.

I get off the bed and walk around it. There is enough length in the chain to go to the bathroom and to all four corners of the room. I can even reach the door, but there is no handle on the inside. It will not open. I have tried.

I hear the beep of the door from the electronic lock and sit upright on the bed, on high alert. The door swings open and the driver is there again. He is the one who brings us food when Mr Gavin or the doctor does not. He goes through the same process as before, unlocking the chain, clamping a hand tightly around my arm, pulling me towards the big hallway.

I try to ask him questions again. How long will I be here? How sick am I? Will I get better? But he doesn't answer.

We enter the treatment room that I have been in many times before. At one side there is an examination couch. There is some equipment on a table. A machine and some other medical items. A curtained screen on wheels.

'Please undress from the waist down and hop up onto the bed,' the doctor says.

Cold hard fear slams into me. He has examined me before in this room. Examined me *down there*. But he still doesn't tell me what is wrong with me.

I look behind me, at the driver in front of the door. I do not want to get undressed in front of him.

The doctor pulls the screen around the bed so the man won't be able to see me. 'It's all right. You'll have privacy behind it.'

I look between the doctor and the screen. I shake my head. 'Please. When can I go? What is *wrong* with me?'

He smiles. 'We need to treat you. We need to make you better before you can leave and start your new life. That *is* what you want, isn't it? Or do you want to go back?' He tilts his head and looks as if I have said something funny. I think he is laughing at me inside.

I take a deep breath and walk behind the screen. I take off my trousers and knickers and fold them up on a chair next to the wall. Just like the other times, a clean sheet has been left on top of the examination couch that I use to cover myself with. There are leg rests at the end of the couch, and I lift my legs up into them, waiting nervously.

The doctor comes around the screen and pulls the machine towards him. It has a wand on the end.

He opens a packet containing a plastic thing. He puts some jelly on it then says, 'Breathe in.'

I take a deep breath, wincing as he slides it inside me, feeling it stretching me. Then he picks up the wand, puts a condom on it and more jelly. Pushes it inside as well.

I look away, at the black and white screen he is watching that shows blobs and swirls and strange shapes. He clicks a mouse. Moves the wand. Clicks. Moves.

'Very good,' he says. 'Things are working nicely.' He removes the wand. Removes the plastic thing. 'Just one more injection. Then we can move on to stage two of your treatment.'

'And after that? Will I be leaving? I will be healthy to start a new job?'

He doesn't answer. He just disappears behind the screen.

I look around, once again searching for some means of escape, as I do every time I come into this room. But there is nothing but walls and—

And then I see it. A plastic card. White, with a strip of brown going through it. I think of the electronic lock on my room. The card they use to open the door. This has to be the same. It is poking out from beneath a metal trolley next to the plastic chair that I put my clothes on. Carefully, I ease off the bed. I know I won't have long before he prepares the injection.

The paper crackles a little. I bite my lip and press my bare feet to the cold floor. Two steps across. I bend down and pick it up. Hide it inside my bra.

The doctor rounds the curtain, syringe in hand. 'What are you doing?'

I point to my clothes, as if I am going to get dressed.

'I said I have another injection to give you. Back onto the couch.'

I nod meekly, hop up onto the couch. Inside I quiver with excitement as the huge needle slides into my stomach. I clench my eyes shut as I do every time.

He pats my hand. 'All done. Nothing to worry about.'

But that is all right for him to say.

'You can get dressed now.' He hands me some paper towels to wipe myself with as he turns his back on me and does something with the equipment.

The driver takes me back to my room. Chains me up again.

But when he leaves, this time I do not cry as I have all the other times. I press my ear against the door and listen to his footsteps retreating further up the hallway. He will go and take another girl to see the doctor now. I press my back against the door and slide down it until I am sitting cross-legged on the floor.

I listen and wait until all the noises have disappeared again.

Hours later, I am stiff from sitting. Slowly I unfurl myself, reach into my bra and pull out the card. It is now I notice that there is a photograph on the other side. A young man who I have not seen yet. There is writing, too.

Hertfordshire Constabulary.

I do not know what that means.

Detective Constable Colin Etheridge.

I understand the word detective. Police. Do the police have a master key, like we had at the hotel? Have they already been here, looking for us? Do they know what is going on? But why haven't they saved us if that is so?

I press the key-card to the door where the electronic lock is positioned on the other side, praying it will work from this side. I do not know how I will unchain myself yet but that is one thing I will worry about when I know the key works. Maybe I could use the metal spoon they give us at mealtimes to gouge around the bracket attached to the wall and somehow pull it off.

Nothing happens. No beep. No click.

I pull the card away. Press it back against the lock again.

Nothing.

I turn the card around and use the other side.

Nothing.

No. No, no, no. It must work. It must.

I do not know how long I keep trying. Hours. But nothing happens. The key-card doesn't work. I am still trapped here.

I slide back down to the floor, defeated. I put my head in my hands. And I cry.

GILLIAN

Chapter 53

Gillian suppressed a scream and shuffled along the chasm away from him.

He moved towards her.

She took another step, slipped on the wet rocks, her right foot sliding into the deep, dark pool.

She cried out as she lost her balance and tumbled in, submerging in the frigid water that took her breath away. She kicked her legs and swam for the surface with her good arm, spluttering for air as she grasped onto the ledge.

Her broken right arm was useless to try to pull herself out. She grappled with her left hand on the edge, attempting to push upwards, but she didn't have the strength to lift her whole body weight with just one arm.

And then he loomed above her, a twisted grin on his face.

He reached out to grab her.

She let go of the ledge and the force of the water from the falls above pushed her under the surface.

She kicked away from the wall of the escarpment beneath the water, sending her further into the centre of the pool.

Her heart almost stopped from the shock of the icy cold, but she had to keep moving. She bucked her legs frantically, and used her good arm. Headed towards the other side of the ridge of rocks, where the boulders were staggered to provide more leverage to get out.

He appeared in her peripheral vision, running over the boulders to her left-hand side, jumping from one to the other.

She kicked out madly. If only she could reach the edge before he did. She couldn't stay in here much longer without tiring and drowning or getting hypothermia.

And then he jumped from one big boulder down to the next. And slipped.

He toppled sideways into the pool behind her.

A wave of water gushed over her head, sending it into her mouth. She coughed, choking, flapping her arm, kicking as hard as she could.

She was nearly at the edge but fading rapidly.

She reached out to a boulder jutting into the water, half of it submerged, her fingertips skimming it, gripping it, grabbing on.

A tug on her left leg and a hand clamped around her swollen ankle.

Her fingers slipped away from the rock as he pulled her backwards. She sunk below the water.

She couldn't die. Not here. Not like this.

She kicked out with all her strength, her trainer connecting with something.

He let go.

She grabbed for the edge of the boulder again. If she could just pull herself up there onto her knees, she could climb up and out and then . . .

He grabbed her leg again.

There was a loose rock on top of the boulder, about the size of a fist. She strained to reach for it as he pulled her back towards him again. The wave of the rippling water worked in her favour and dashed her back against the boulder.

She grabbed the rock. Then twisted around, trying to tread water with the free leg he didn't have hold of.

With a tremendous effort she swung her good arm at the side of his head.

A *crack* as the rock hit his temple.

He let go of her leg and drifted downwards, beneath the surface.

The rock fell from her grasp.

She scrabbled up onto the boulder on her knees, panting hard, her chest heaving, her whole body shaking.

She pressed her hand onto the next boulder up, brought herself to standing as she clutched it to steady herself. Looked behind her.

He was somewhere down there in the inky black pool below.

Teeth chattering, she called on her final reserves of adrenaline and stepped from one boulder to the next until she'd found the path that had carried her up there.

DETECTIVE WARREN CARTER
Chapter 54

'You should go home and get some sleep,' I said to Becky.

She yawned. 'I'm not going anywhere until Gillian's safe. Anyway, it's not like I've got anything to go back for.' She stood up. 'Want a coffee?'

'Yeah, thanks.'

She headed towards the door.

'You're not going to the machine, are you? It's gross.' I nodded at the kettle that Ronnie was so overprotective about on top of the fridge in the corner. It had to be lined up at a perfect forty-five-degree angle against the wall or he'd freak out.

'Kettle won't work. Ronnie takes the base home at night now so no one will steal it.' She rolled her eyes, but in an amused Ronnie-will-be-Ronnie kind of way.

As she disappeared, I wondered what was going on in Devon. Wondered again why the killer was still after Gillian. Wondered why the hell Munroe had done all this when it was obvious she didn't need the money. Just how long had she been corrupt and what else had she done and got away with? By the time Becky came back I'd worked myself up into another angry stupor.

She handed me a plastic cup with some bizarre greeny-brown liquid in it that had lumps floating on the top.

I curled up my top lip. 'What's this supposed to be?'

'I pressed cappuccino. But I think it churned out half coffee, half vegetable soup.'

I pulled a face at it. Sniffed it. 'That is disgusting.'

'Just like old times.' Becky grinned at me.

I put the soupy coffee on the desk and glared at it. Sat down at my old chair and put my feet up on the desk, hoping for some good news.

GILLIAN

Chapter 55

She couldn't go on.

That was what Gillian thought as she held onto the rocks with her good hand and slowly, with insurmountable effort, put one foot in front of the other and made her way back down the uneven stone path.

Wracked with shivers, she wanted to collapse at the bottom of the rocky outcrop. She wanted to lie down and succumb to blissful sleep, maybe resting her head against a rock and falling into oblivion.

She couldn't feel her fingers or toes. The rest of her was going numb, her soaked clothing stuck to her body and dripped onto the ground, weighing her down. She wanted to give in now. It was all too much effort.

Slowly she sank to her knees. She would die after all. She'd escaped that man, but hypothermia would get her in the end.

She curled into a ball, too tired to even cry as her eyelids fluttered closed.

DETECTIVE WARREN CARTER
Chapter 56

I was sat in the police station canteen, which had long since closed but it had comfy sofas and my back was killing me from sitting in an office chair for so long. A sleeping Becky sprawled out beside me, her head resting on my shoulder as she snored loudly. She'd slept right through a conversation I'd just had with the Devon and Cornwall inspector giving me an update that the dogs and helicopters were now out and searching for Gillian.

I felt useless sitting there, but there was nothing I could do. The official, *lawfully* obtained financial records for David Bennington and Oliver Hammond wouldn't arrive until the morning at the earliest. When I'd spoken to Caroline a little while earlier to update her, she told me Munroe's work office had now been bugged. Ditto her car, which was surreptitiously done while it was parked on her driveway. Her home address couldn't be done until she and her husband were out. Her work and personal mobile phones had been remotely connected to a spy app that would not only relay audio surveillance back to us but would also give real-time access to her GPS location, texts, emails, photos, and videos. If she did or said anything incriminating hopefully we would get it – unless, of course, she was using a burner phone or another way of communicating with Hammond, Bennington, or Acton.

I yawned again, rested my head back on the soft cushion of the sofa and closed my eyes. I was exhausted but my mind was too busy to sleep, as usual.

My eyelids snapped open at the sound of a pinging alert on Becky's phone.

Becky grunt-snored in response and groaned sleepily. She opened her eyes, lifted her head off my shoulder and said, 'Oh, sorry for crashing out on you.'

'I haven't slept with another woman in years and that wasn't exactly what I had in mind. Especially with you drooling all over my jacket and snoring like a rhino with a cold.'

She pulled a face at me and picked up her phone from the arm of the sofa. 'Ooh, it's an email from Vodafone. This'll be about the phone number that called Steve Moore pretending to be Neal Lane.'

I leaned towards her, peering over her shoulder. Or rather, squinting at the small screen. I was going to need reading glasses soon. I angled my head back a bit. Nope, still no good.

Becky looked over at me. 'Why are you pulling that weird face?'

'I'm trying to see your screen. I bet I can guess that the bad news is it's an unregistered pay-as-you-go and was paid for with cash. Or it fell off the back of a lorry and was acquired unlawfully.'

'Yup. But the good news is the location from where the call to Moore was made. They reverse-traced it, which showed that the phone number used connected to a network in Aylesford. It's a village in Kent.'

'That's where David Bennington lives.'

'That's right. The towers there are too spread out to specify an exact location, but it's been pinned down to within fifty metres of his house. It's him.' She grinned and did a fist pump in the air.

'And the nasty bastard probably believed you could never trace an anonymous pay-as-you-go phone. This more than makes up for the crap coffee.' I winked at her and leaped to my feet, the familiar excitement of the chase kicking in. 'Let's go and nick him.'

GILLIAN

Chapter 57

Gillian was in a swimming pool in Bali. Neal sat at the bar, smiling at her, which was strange because she could've sworn he'd said he wasn't coming with her.

He waved a coconut at her. No, not a coconut, a cocktail *in* a coconut. As she swam closer to him, she saw there was an umbrella inside it and a fancy straw.

The sun warmed her shivering body. She lifted her chin up towards it, letting the rays sink into her bones. A smile drifted onto her face. This was what it felt like to be happy.

She kept swimming, but Neal seemed to be getting further away. And then she started panicking. She was going to drown. Neal waved the cocktail at her and pointed to the bar, a silent question asking if she wanted one. So nothing could be wrong, could it? She'd get to him eventually.

And then the sun disappeared behind the clouds. The world turned dark. She was the only one in the pool and Neal had vanished. Someone banged something. No, not banging. A whirring noise. Or a . . . something. Whitter, tator, ro . . . what was the word?

Footsteps. She was out of the pool now, running, her wet feet sliding on the slippery tiles next to the sunbeds. Someone was chasing her but she didn't know who.

Footsteps.

She heard wet, slapping footsteps.

With tremendous effort she opened her eyes. Swam up through the layers of fog in her brain and back to reality.

The man was coming after her again. Running down the path on the outcrop. A big monster flying through the darkness.

She pushed herself to her feet with every ounce of effort she possessed.

And started dragging herself across the grassy moorland in front of her.

DETECTIVE WARREN CARTER
Chapter 58

Lights shone in the downstairs window of David Bennington's house. Becky scooted round to the back of the property in case he decided to make a run for it.

I rang the doorbell.

Bennington opened the door, a bottle of Peroni in his hand. My stomach clenched with anger. How dare he be out here in the big wide world, drinking beer, putting his feet up, while the six women and God only knew how many others were dead.

He frowned when he saw me. 'Can I help you?'

'DI Warren Carter.' I smiled coldly, held up my warrant card. 'David Bennington, I'm arresting you on suspicion of the murders of Hannah Ryan, Neal Lane, six unidentified female victims, people-smuggling, human-trafficking, and perverting the course of justice.' And being an evil bastard, I wanted to add.

He laughed with disbelief. 'I don't have a clue what you're talking about. Don't you know who I am?' It wasn't just the presumptuous, entitled words he spouted that did it for me. It was the arrogant sneer when he said it. As if nothing could touch him.

While he was busy thinking he was above the law, I grabbed him by the front of his jumper, flipped him around and mashed his face up against the paintwork of his hallway.

I worked my cuffs out of my jacket pocket and secured his hands. Then I yanked him round again and marched him towards the front door, steering him into the door-frame as we passed.

His head boinked off the oak surround.

'Oops. Sorry, I'm so clumsy.'

'Hey! My head! You fucking did that on purpose. You bastard.'

Becky ran around from the back. She opened the rear doors of the pool car.

I shoved Bennington inside and looked at Becky, who had a very satisfied grin on her face. But we couldn't relax yet. We may have got him in custody but there was a long way to go before we nailed him.

GILLIAN

Chapter 59

Gillian got to her feet and stumbled forwards, willing her legs to move.

Just one more step. One more step. Just keep going.

It was open here. Exposed. She fixed her gaze on the area of forest in the distance behind the moorland. If she could just . . .

She pushed herself harder than she ever had in her life. Her laboured breathing came out in ragged puffs of steam, her heartbeat raged in her ears, pain pulsing through every part of her.

The ground was uneven, slippery, pools of partially frozen water settled on top of the muddy grass from the recent rain and sleet. The further she went, the more it turned into a boggy quagmire, her trainers cracking ice on the surface and collecting lumps of mud that weighed her down.

The effort of wading through it was too much. She slipped. Jolted her bad arm. Cried out. Kept trying to move, but her legs were like molten lava. Red-hot, liquid, even though she'd never been as cold in her life.

A helicopter whirred from somewhere in the distance. Dogs barked in the darkness.

And then her left foot sank into the ground, and she couldn't move. Frantically, she attempted to pull it out, but it was being tugged in further. Thick, sticky mud slid up to her knee and sucked her downwards.

She struggled, falling to the ground, her free right leg twisting beneath her. She pulled at her left leg with her good arm, but it was no use.

Then there was a whoosh of air from behind and he was upon her.

He straddled her chest, pinning her arms at her sides with his knees. 'Where is it?' he yelled. 'Where's the key?'

She looked into his cold, dark eyes, sure he was the man who'd killed her husband. Fear tightened her chest. She struggled to breathe.

'Where the fuck is it? I know you've got it. He told me you had it.' He slapped her round the face.

Her head jerked sideways with the force, her cheek hitting wet ground. Mud seeped into her mouth. She coughed, trying to spit it out.

The dogs. Barking. Louder. The moon lit up the sky suddenly. Except it wasn't the moon. It was a spotlight, trained on them.

His hands slid around her throat. He squeezed as he stared into her eyes. 'Where is it?'

She tried to wriggle her head but it didn't work. The mud held her fast and she had no energy left to fight.

His grip released. He glanced up to the sky at the helicopter circling. Back to her. 'Tell me where it is or I'll fucking kill you!'

But she knew he'd kill her anyway. Her gaze drifted upwards. She was sure the helicopter was getting closer to the ground. Or was she imagining it?

His hands around her neck again. This time squeezing harder.

She felt herself sinking, her eyes rolling up into their sockets. Was it the mud pulling her down or her own brain being starved of oxygen? She could see Neal again behind her eyelids, in Bali. Smiling. Waving that cocktail.

DETECTIVE WARREN CARTER
Chapter 60

Stevenage police station. 1.35 a.m. I'd overseen David Bennington being booked into custody and having his DNA, photo, and fingerprints taken. He kept looking over at me as he was processed and giving me a smug smile. I wanted to smash it off his face.

While we waited for his lawyer to arrive, I paced the interview room Becky and I were in. I wafted a hand over my face, trying to get rid of the smell of BO left from the previous prisoner.

My phone rang. It was the inspector from Devon and Cornwall Police.

'We've found her,' he said.

I breathed out a sigh of relief and stared up at the ceiling. 'Thank God for that.'

'She's been taken to the same hospital as her brother-in-law. She's suffering from second-stage hypothermia.'

'Can you put a police guard with her? I can't risk them trying again.'

'I've got someone already there. And we nicked the guy who was trying to kill her, but he's refusing to give his details or say anything. I take it you want him back in Hertfordshire?'

'Yes. Can you arrange for prisoner-escort and custody services to transport him to Stevenage police station?'

'Will do. The only thing on him was a mobile phone and a key to the vehicle I told you about. I'll send the phone down with him. And there's something else, too. Gillian Lane was mumbling about a locker key she'd found on her husband's set of keys. She said the man who tried to kill her was after it. We've taken a bunch of keys found on her person and I can send them down with the prisoner service,' the inspector said.

'Locker key,' I repeated, picturing the crime scene. Gillian Lane driving home from the airport, putting Neal's keys in the front door then putting them in her pocket. The murderer hearing her, chasing her because . . . because . . . maybe the killer *hadn't* taken Neal's hard drives and Hannah's flashdrives where they always backed up their work. Maybe the items hadn't been in the house because they were worried they could be stolen. Maybe they'd been secured in a locker somewhere for safekeeping. Neal Lane had put the key on *his* key ring, but Gillian had taken his car to the airport unexpectedly at the last minute. That's why he'd rowed with her about it. The stab wounds Hannah and Neal had suffered were most likely intended as torture to get them to talk, as Becky had thought. I suspected the killer had taken their laptops and phones from the scene because they were immediately to hand, taken photos and the camera from Hannah's house when they'd searched it, but the killer had wanted to know if there were copies anywhere else. They must've been after Gillian so she could tell them where the back-up evidence was, but she hadn't even known what she had in her possession until now.

'Great. Thanks a lot for all your help.' I hung up and relayed my thoughts to Becky.

She stared at me, wide-eyed. 'I knew there had to be a reason for him going after her and not legging it straight away.'

There was a knock on the door then and the custody sergeant brought in David Bennington. Trailing behind him was his lawyer, dressed in an unrumpled Armani suit, even though it was the early hours of the morning. He reeked of aftershave, something cloying that tickled my throat. Still, I'd take that over the overripe armpit smells any day.

They sat opposite us, and Becky set up the audio and video recording equipment. I stated the preliminaries and then dived straight in.

'07583612511. Does that phone number seem familiar to you?'

Bennington didn't answer as he folded his arms and leaned back, the smug smile never fading. The plastic chair made a farting sound, which kind of ruined the whole arrogance of the pose.

'Well, it should do,' I said. 'It was used to call Steve Moore on the seventh of December.'

'Who is Steve Moore and how on earth does he relate to my client?' the lawyer, whose name was Rupert Grant, said.

'He's a plumber,' I said. 'The caller was a male and pretended to be Neal Lane – your ex-employee – and stated that he had a problem with his boiler. But when Steve Moore turned up at the address the next day Neal Lane didn't have a clue what he was talking about. The call was made so it would seem like Steve Moore had a prior connection with Neal Lane. The caller wanted Moore's vehicle to be spotted at Neal Lane's house. When none of the neighbours reported seeing it, someone called us with an anonymous tip-off. That call was made so Moore could be fitted up for the murder of Neal Lane, Hannah Ryan, and Jim and Donna Wilson.'

Bennington took a breath. Sighed as if this was the most boring conversation in the world. 'I have no clue what I'm doing here. Yes, I employed Neal Lane but, unfortunately, we had to cancel the project he was working on, as I already explained to you.' He glared at Becky. 'I have no idea what on earth you're talking about in regards to any phone conversation with this Moss person.'

'Moore,' I emphasised, even though I knew damn well he was perfectly aware of Steve's name. 'The phone call, David. You know where it gets really good? Because that call was made from your house.' I grinned. OK, so that was a slight fib. The triangulation data could only pinpoint it to within fifty metres of his house but that was good enough for me.

The smug look faltered slightly.

'Do you live alone?' Becky asked.

Bennington didn't answer.

'It's not a hard question,' I said.

Grant whispered something to Bennington, who scratched his nose, trying to appear casual.

'Well, there's no one else listed at your address, so let's just assume for now that you do,' I carried on. 'And that was a big mistake, David, that call. You assumed it couldn't be traced because it was an unregistered, pay-as-you-go phone.'

'My client knows nothing about any call. Are you seriously wasting our time on a crank call?'

'No, Rupert. This is about multiple murders and human-trafficking.' I narrowed my eyes.

'What on earth do you have to support the claim my client is involved in anything like that? Don't you know who he is and what exemplary humanitarian work he does?' Rupert Grant asked.

'Oh, I know exactly who he is.' I flipped open the folder in front of me. Slapped the photos of Hayat and the other five victims on the desk, one next to the other. 'Do you recognise these women?'

Bennington flicked his gaze downwards. 'No.'

'I must object to you showing my clients such graphic images,' Grant snapped.

Well, you can shove your objection up your arse, I thought. 'We're certain these women came from Salama Camp in Jordan. The camp run by your company. Neal Lane and Hannah Ryan discovered a human-trafficking ring that started there and ended with these women being imprisoned in a disused building called Brampton Hospital.' I added the photos of Hannah and Neal next to the others and glared at Bennington, but he stared at a spot on the wall above my head. 'Those women were being held captive so someone could harvest their eggs.'

'How preposterous!' Grant bumbled. 'My client is a very well-respected man. He's received numerous awards and accolades for his work. You must be insane if you think he could be involved in something like this.'

Again, Bennington said nothing.

'There was a fire at the hospital. The women died. That makes you culpable in their death,' I went on. 'Which brings me to Oliver Hammond. Your friend. The one you went to Oxford University with. It was him you were supplying these women to, wasn't it?'

No reply.

'How was he paying you for the women?' I asked. 'Cash? Was there a middleman involved? Powell Acton, perhaps?' I couldn't mention the offshore accounts, not yet, not until I had some way to introduce in a lawful way the evidence found by the Vigilante.

No reply.

'My client doesn't know anything about this.'

I pulled out the newspaper article the Vigilante had found and put it on the desk. There was a flash of something in Bennington's eyes as he spotted the photograph of him as a young student.

I leaned forward. 'This is what I think happened . . . Oliver Hammond was studying medicine at Oxford. Powell Acton, Susan Munroe, and you were all studying law. You became friends. And together, years later, you cooked up a plan to traffic vulnerable women from Salama, a place where no one would notice them missing, so Hammond could use them as black-market egg donors. But then you had a problem. Neal Lane and Hannah Ryan found out what you were doing. They were going to expose it, so you got your old mate, Susan Munroe, to feed you information about a previous case so you could make it look like Neal's and Hannah's murders were carried out by a serial killer.'

He didn't look so smug now.

'Shall I carry on?'

'You're joking. What on earth does this have to do with anything?' Mr Pompous-Arse Lawyer said again. 'This picture was taken nearly twenty years ago! It's not proof of anything at all.'

'This is not a joke! Eight people are dead!' I slapped my hand down on the table. 'And this establishes the initial connection. Whose idea was it to make Neal Lane's and Hannah Ryan's murders look like the same person who'd murdered Donna and Jim Wilson a year ago? Was it yours?'

No reply.

'Was it DCI Munroe's idea?'

'Why did Munroe help cover it up for you?' Becky asked. 'What was she getting out of it?'

Bennington's gaze darted to me, then back again to the wall.

'Is this why Professional Standards are involved?' Grant asked. 'Because you've got another corrupt police officer who went to the same university almost two decades ago and you're trying to pin something on my client? It's outrageous!'

I ignored the question. 'Whoever killed Hannah Ryan and Neal Lane took laptops and a camera and photos belonging to them, didn't they? They searched Hannah's house. Hannah and Neal were both tortured with stab wounds before they were killed, because the killer was trying to get them to talk. To tell them where their back-up information was stored. Information that you and your cronies didn't want anyone to see. You didn't want anyone to find any evidence that they'd discovered your trafficking ring. Who killed them? You?'

Bennington's head shot up. His evil gaze locked onto mine, a reptilian smile quirking up the corners of his mouth. 'When were they killed?'

'Yesterday morning,' I said. 'Between the hours of 1.30 and 2.30 a.m.'

'Ah, well, you see, I couldn't possibly have killed them. I was on a flight back from Jordan at that time. I didn't arrive in the UK until gone 5 a.m.' The smile got bigger. 'There must be hundreds of witnesses.'

'There, you see? My client hasn't done anything wrong. This whole thing is a ridiculous waste of time.'

'Yeah, you said that already,' I said to Grant, then turned to Bennington. 'We'll definitely be checking that out. But if it wasn't you, then it was one of your mates – Hammond, Acton, or Munroe. Or another accomplice.'

'I don't have a clue what you're talking about,' Bennington snapped.

'Why did you do it?' Becky asked. 'Money? Or do you just like preying on vulnerable, desperate women? Can't get it up normally, is that it? Turns you on to see them scared? Turns you on to abuse people?'

David Bennington looked down at his manicured nails. I wanted to yank him out of his chair and kick him in the bollocks – see how *he* liked having his intimate parts abused.

'My client has given you a definitive alibi that proves he couldn't possibly be involved, and I'm recommending that he makes no further comment. Do you have any evidence to support this wild theory that my client is involved in any of this?' Grant asked.

I knew he'd ask that. And the problem was, we didn't. Yet. I was itching to question him about his offshore Oxford Holdings' bank account, but I had to bite it down. All I had to counter Grant's question were theories and a phone call. 'We have the phone call,' I said. 'We're analysing the data of that phone number right now. What's it going to tell us, David?' I glared at him.

He carried on admiring his manicure.

'Who else were you in contact with on that burner phone?'

'No comment,' Bennington said in a bored tone.

'Since you haven't got any substantial evidence to support such outlandish accusations,' Grant said, 'I demand that you release my client right now.'

'That's not going to happen,' I said. 'There was a glove print found at Neal Lane's house. The same print was found at Brampton Hospital, on the chains used to keep one of the women captive.' I watched Bennington carefully. His eyes widened a fraction – that was obviously news to him. He recovered quickly, though, and went back to arrogant nonchalance. 'But then you must've known the gloves had been used by the same person. Whose idea was it to plant the gloves in Steve Moore's van to make it look like he'd killed Hannah Ryan and Neal Lane?'

No response.

'Was it DCI Munroe's or yours?'

'This is a ludicrous fishing expedition!' Grant huffed.

'Inside the glove we found DNA from skin cells. Will they come back to you, I wonder? Or are you too high and mighty to get your hands dirty?'

'My client has already given an airtight alibi so please desist from that line of questioning.'

'Maybe he has an alibi for the time Hannah Ryan and Neal Lane were killed, but your *client* could quite easily have been at Brampton Hospital.'

Bennington gave me a look of contempt.

'Or will the DNA match your sidekick?' I asked. 'The one who was trying to murder Gillian Lane in Devon? Is he the same man who killed Hannah Ryan and Neal Lane on your orders so they'd be silenced? Well, he's in custody now.' I grinned.

A flash of something like shock flitted across Bennington's face, but it was gone just as quickly, replaced by the smug arrogance again.

'My client denies any knowledge of this.'

'What's he going to tell us, David?' I raised an eyebrow. 'Don't think he won't point the finger at you if it could lighten his sentence.'

David uncrossed his legs and recrossed them. Didn't say a word.

'There is nothing tying my client to any of these crimes,' Grant said. 'And I demand you release him.'

I rolled my eyes at the lawyer. Looked at Bennington. 'Have you got anything else to say?'

'Yes,' Bennington said. 'No. Comment.'

'All right. Have it your way. Interview suspended.' I stood up and left the room, waiting for Becky while she stopped the recordings. 'Arrogant wanker!' I seethed when she emerged.

'The bastard's not going to admit anything,' she said as we stomped down the corridor together. 'All we've got on him is the phone call made from *near* his house. A bloody barrister will throw that out of court easily.'

'We'll take him back to the cells and see what SOCO and the search team find at his house. We're going to get something else on him, I'm sure of it. He made a big mistake with the call. Now we just have to find any more he's made.' I thought about the flashdrive in my possession from the Vigilante. I had to wait a little while longer for an opportunity to unleash the information on it incriminating Bennington. This had to be done right, and that required patience. But one thing I'd never been good at was waiting.

HAYAT

Chapter 61

It is two days since I was sedated and the doctor did something to me. It is hazy because I was in and out of consciousness. There were the stirrups, the plastic thing, then something else. A long needle inside me. Or did I imagine that?

I curl up on the bed, sweating. The pain and sickness started last night. I managed to crawl to the toilet in the bathroom and vomited. I drank water from the tap but it didn't help to quell the nausea and thirst and the cramping pains in my belly.

I am sweating. The pillow is soaked. And whatever position I am in I cannot get comfortable. Cannot ease the cramps.

I am thirsty again, but I do not have the strength to pull myself up to the tap any more.

'You are not well, but I am here,' my mother says to me.

'Mama,' I groan.

She kneels beside me. 'You will get better, my child. Everything will be all right.' She strokes my hair, like she used to do when I was a child.

I nestle my head into her lap, feel the warmth of her against my cheek. 'I miss you.'

'But I am always here. Your father is, too. Be strong.'

I reach for her hand and hold it. Her hand is also warm. I smile. 'Can you help me get out of here?'

'I want to. But it is all inside *you*. The answers, the strength. You will find a way.'

'Where will they take me after this?'

'I do not know, my child.'

I drift away then, into a dream. We are walking through the market, Mama and I, chattering away. It is very busy, and my interests are caught by the stalls with bright-coloured fruit so I do not notice I am drifting further away from her. And suddenly I am in the middle of a mass of people, crowding around me, jostling. The smell of sweet, ripe figs and fresh lemons fills the air. I look around and cannot see Mama. I cry out but she does not come.

'Mama!' I yell over and over again while the whole crowd ignores me. They cannot see me. I am not really there. A ghost, maybe? A man barges into me and knocks me flying into a stall selling spices. I land in the open buckets of brown and red and golden. Turmeric, cinnamon, and paprika cover my dress, my skin.

I scream and start to cry but still no one hears me. I run and run and run. But I never get anywhere. My feet are stuck to the dusty floor with honey.

Someone says, 'I am going to die, aren't I?' A mumble that sounds like me.

Mama appears, pushing her way through the crowds. She runs towards me. 'Hayat, are you OK?'

I look down at myself. Red, yellow, brown. Red, yellow, brown. Colours swirling in front of my face. Red. Blood. The colour of fear of death. Of love.

'I love you, my sweet,' Mama says.

'I love you, too, Mama.'

Maybe it is not a dream. Maybe it is real. Maybe I have finally gone mad.

DETECTIVE WARREN CARTER
Chapter 62

I sat at my old desk in the CID office and slapped my face to wake myself up. I was knackered, but there was still so much to do if I was going to prove everything.

Becky slumped down in the chair next to mine, yawning loudly.

'You should go home. Get some kip. The prisoner from Devon won't be here for a good few hours yet.'

She nodded, fighting another yawn. 'You should go home, too. You look like you haven't slept in a week.'

'I'm used to it. I'll see you back here at 7 a.m.'

'OK.' She grabbed her bag and left.

My eyes felt dry and gritty, like someone had sandblasted them. I yawned then, too. But I knew exactly what would happen. By the time I got home and got into bed I'd be wide a-bloody-wake again and turning over everything in my head.

I settled for resting my head on the desk and closing my eyes. Which was exactly the same position I was roused from sleep in when my mobile rang at 5.45 a.m.

'Morning, sir. It's Sergeant Jones in custody. Your prisoner's arrived and he's refusing to give his name.'

I sat up. Stretched my neck from side to side. 'Right. Thanks. Be down in a minute.' I went into the men's room and splashed water on my face. Looked at myself in the mirror. Bloodshot eyes, a day's worth of stubble. Wrinkled shirt. I sniffed my armpits. Slightly ripe but not too offensive.

I needed a coffee but couldn't face the crap from the machine. My stomach rumbled. I ignored it and headed to the custody suite.

The prisoner was about mid-thirties, brown hair, stocky, average height, blue eyes, skin one mass of old acne scars. He stood in front of the custody desk, hands cuffed, a prisoner-escort service officer next to him from a private contractor used throughout the UK police and court services. I strode over. The prisoner gave me a dirty look.

'What's your name?' I asked.

The man didn't respond.

PS Jones rolled his eyes. It wasn't the first time a prisoner had refused to give their name and it wouldn't be the last. He turned to me. 'What name shall I book him in under?'

I shrugged. 'Don Duck?'

PS Jones quirked up one eyebrow and read aloud as he typed the name into the custody log. 'Don Duck. Catchy that. What charges?'

I gave him the details – murder of Hannah Ryan and Neal Lane, attempted murder of Gillian Lane and Dean Lane, murder of the six unknown women, human-trafficking, perverting the course of justice. And I threw in a withholding-information and obstruction offence in there, too.

The prisoner-escort officer handed PS Jones a clear plastic bag containing a phone that belonged to Don Duck and had been switched off. PS Jones booked it into custody, and after the prisoner was fingerprinted, photographed, and had DNA collected, he was carted off down the corridor.

While PS Jones unlocked one of the cells to deposit the little shit in, Don Duck looked over at me. I gave him a girly little wave and a grin.

I was betting it was only a matter of time before his DNA would be matched to that found inside the gloves planted in Steve Moore's van. I was sure the saliva found on Hannah's forehead would come back to him, too, whoever he was.

The prisoner-escort officer handed me another package, which I signed for. After leaving Mr Duck to his new abode, I strode up the stairs to my office, tearing the Jiffy bag open. Inside was the bunch of keys from Gillian Lane, which had been placed in a clear evidence bag and numbered, dated, and initialled.

I put them on my desk and fanned out the keys. A car key, a ceramic fob, what looked like various door keys, and a slim key with a number on the side of it that could indeed be for a locker or safety-deposit box.

I logged on to the computer at the desk next to Ronnie's, rested one elbow on a pile of paperwork and put my chin in my hand as I searched the databases for anything I could find to identify where the key came from.

I was still looking when Ronnie strolled in. 'Morning, sir.' He put his man bag on his desk, unzipped it and pulled out three individual paper bags that he lined up on the edge of the desk in a perfect row.

'Morning,' I said, stretching my back and rubbing my eyes.

Ronnie also removed the base of the kettle from his bag and plugged it in. 'Do you want a cup of coffee?'

'I could murder one.'

He disappeared to get some water. Then came back and switched the kettle on. 'You look like you've been here all night, guv.'

'I have. Have you got any deodorant in your bag?' The prospect of working another twelve hours or so wasn't going to do my armpits much good, but I wasn't going to waste time going home now. I knew Ronnie kept a plethora of every supply you could possibly need. Headache tablets, antihistamine cream, deodorant, Alka-Seltzer, plasters, antibacterial gel. Once a boy scout, always a boy scout.

'Yes, I have. I've got a travel shower gel in my bag, too.' He peered in his bag. 'Or a packet of wet wipes, some dry shampoo, and hand sanitiser?' He peered over at me expectantly.

I took the wet wipes and deodorant off to the toilet. Wiped my face and armpits, sprayed liberally, and was back in the office smothered in the aroma of 'lemon-fresh burst' just in time for Ronnie to deposit a steaming cup of wake-up juice on the desk.

'You got anything to eat in there, too?' I looked at Ronnie's bag.

He picked up one of the paper bags. 'Um . . . I've got a selection of raw almonds.' He picked up the next two. 'Sunflower seeds. Or parsnip chips.'

'Yes, but have you got any proper food?'

'These are good for your digestion. Since I've been eating them instead of cereal, my irritable bowel's been so much better. I used to go six times a day but now I'm on thi—'

Luckily, Becky waltzed in then and saved me from hearing any more about Ronnie's bowel movements.

She stopped when she saw me. 'I knew you wouldn't go home.' She sat on the edge of the desk. 'What happened after I left?'

I brought them both up to speed as I sipped the caffeine-induced hit. Then said, 'Ronnie, we're still waiting for David Bennington's and Oliver Hammond's financial records to come in. In the meantime, try and find out where this key came from.' I held up the key in its plastic bag, took another slug of coffee then asked Becky, 'Did Gillian mention Neal having a safety-deposit box, storage unit, or locker somewhere?'

'No.'

'Damn. I—' I was interrupted by one of the search-team members who'd been at David Bennington's house.

He entered the office, carrying an armful of paperwork in clear plastic evidence bags. 'Morning all.'

'Morning,' I said. 'How did you get on?'

He dumped everything on the desk in front of me. 'OK, we found one laptop, one iPhone, and two cheap Nokia phones. The SIM in one of the Nokias matched the number used to ring Steve Moore. They've all gone to Technical Services for analysis but there were a lot of calls on them.' He waved his hand at the paperwork. 'Apart from that, this is pretty much all we found of interest.'

'OK, thanks for that.' I signed for everything.

He yawned, which made me yawn in response, then left.

'So we've got Bennington now on the phone call,' Becky said. 'But ringing Steve Moore isn't the same as proof of murder and trafficking. We need more.'

I piled the paperwork on Ronnie's desk. 'Can you make a start on that lot, please? It's only a matter of time before we find a solid trail between our suspects somewhere.'

'What about the key?' Ronnie asked.

'I'll get back to it later,' I said. 'Becky, I want you to get back in with David Bennington to interview him again. Tell him we've found the phone he used now and see if that will persuade him to talk.'

I went into the empty DI's office and phoned Caroline to update her on what had happened. Then said, 'I'm going to interview the man who tried to kill Gillian Lane soon, but if he won't give his name, I doubt he'll give me anything else.'

'OK, good work. Financials are now in for Oliver Hammond and David Bennington. I'll get them sent over so Ronnie can make a start on them. There's tons of stuff here to go through.'

'I take it there's nothing on Munroe from the surveillance?' I asked.

'Not so far. We've got someone monitoring her in real time. I'll let you know as soon as anything happens.'

DETECTIVE WARREN CARTER
Chapter 63

Interview with Don Duck. Stevenage police station. 7.15 a.m. Lingering aroma of second-hand vomit and bleach.

Don Duck sat in the chair opposite me, knees splayed out in a classically arrogant my-cock's-bigger-than-yours pose, sneering at me as I ran through the preliminaries. Hatred burned in my throat. I swallowed it down when all I really wanted to do was pummel his face into the desk, and replaced it with a cold smile.

'Do you understand that you're currently under caution and haven't requested legal representation?'

No response.

'Do you speak English?'

Nothing.

'What's your name?'

Don Duck's expression didn't change.

'You think you're being clever?' I snorted. 'This isn't going to help you, you know. Your DNA is currently being processed, and I know what it's going to tell us. You murdered Hannah Ryan and Neal Lane, didn't you?' I opened the folder in front of me and slapped the crime-scene photos of the two victims on the desk. He didn't blink or look at them, so I held them up in front of his face instead. 'That was your work, wasn't it?'

A smirk appeared on his face.

'You think this is funny?' I slapped the photos down. 'Think you're clever? Well, it could be time for a reality check. If you were that clever you wouldn't be sitting here.' I opened my arms wide, taking in the room. 'I trust the mini bar in your cell is satisfactory?' I tilted my head. 'You're going to have to get used to being locked up because you're looking at multiple life sentences. You'll never get out of prison. If you think you're the hard man now, just wait until you get banged up.' I looked him up and down. 'You've got that come-hither look on your face that I'm sure the boys inside will love.'

No response.

I was sick of him already. 'I've got a funny little hunch that the evidence is going to tell us that the gloves you used in Neal Lane's house contain your skin cells. Saliva found on Hannah Ryan is going to match yours, isn't it?' My time for a smirk. 'So, is there anything you want to tell me now?'

He crossed his arms and stared back at me.

'You tried to murder Gillian Lane to get hold of the key on her husband's key ring, didn't you? That's what Neal Lane told you about when you tortured him, isn't it? That he'd hidden evidence somewhere safe?'

No response.

'What does the key open? Where's the locker?'

Don Duck laughed. The evil bastard actually fucking laughed about the slaughter of innocent victims. A hot flame ignited inside me but I had to ignore it, let it go. I'd been in the same situation many times with hostile, evil prisoners. I wasn't going to pussyfoot around him with interview techniques, trying to draw the truth out, because it was obvious he wasn't going to tell me anything. I didn't have time for that.

This was purely an exercise in ticking procedural boxes. He wanted to wind me up, taunt me. But I was going to have the last laugh.

'Those same glove prints found at the murder scene of Hannah Ryan and Neal Lane were also found at Brampton Hospital, behind a metal plate that chained a woman to the wall. Five other women were found there, all held captive. You did that to them, didn't you?'

Mr Duck smiled.

'They all died a gruesome death in a fire. When the flames and smoke engulfed the building, they couldn't escape because you'd chained them up. Those women were being used as unwilling egg donors. You're responsible for their deaths.' I pointed at him.

He didn't say a word.

I shrugged. 'It doesn't matter if you don't tell me anything. You'll be prosecuted for eight counts of murder, the attempted murder of Gillian Lane and Dean Lane, plus a whole host of other offences.'

Don Duck crossed his arms and splayed his knees out even wider, going for the casual psycho look.

'Unless you want to cooperate? The judge and jury would look favourably on you assisting us with our enquiries.' I leaned forward. 'Maybe I could even get you a deal in exchange for telling us about your accomplices. I mean, you're just the hired thug, aren't you? The brainless muscle. You're not clever enough to be the top dog behind all this. And you know what they'll do? They're going to blame you for everything unless you start talking first. Do you really want to take the fall for all of them?' I waited. Ten seconds. Twenty. I stretched it to half a minute, staring into his cold, dark eyes. 'No? Can't tempt you?' I waited another moment. 'Last chance.' I cocked my head. 'OK, a bit of male bonding in the shower blocks it is, then. Word of advice, though, I wouldn't go round sitting like that in there if I was you.' I nodded to his wide-open legs and blew him a kiss. 'Interview terminated at 7.45 a.m.'

DETECTIVE WARREN CARTER
Chapter 64

'Bloody bastard. Bastarding bastard,' I mumbled under my breath, along with many multiple variations of swear words. All the way back up to the CID office, I reeled off a load of expletives.

Ronnie sat hunched over the desk when I walked in. He sprang to attention, back upright. 'You all right, sir?'

'No.' I picked up the nearest thing to hand, a stapler on the edge of the desk, and threw it at the wall.

Ronnie gasped, looking at me in horror. 'Do you know how much paperwork I'll have to fill in to get a new stapler?' He stared at the remnants on the floor, the top and bottom of the stapler hanging loosely open where the hinge should've been.

I took a deep breath. Counted to ten. 'Sorry, Ronnie.' I rubbed a hand over my forehead and told myself to calm down. I was no good to the investigation if I lost my shit. I sat for a moment, put my head in my hands.

'Are you OK?'

I looked up at him. 'I am now. How are you getting on?'

Ronnie told me he'd been through all the paperwork recovered at Bennington's house but there was nothing of interest. So far he'd found nothing in Bennington's or Hammond's personal bank accounts that would help us. Although one interesting thing he'd found was that Hammond had put himself in huge debt to set up his clinic three years previously, which had maybe spurred him on in turning to crime. Ronnie would carry on ploughing through everything else in Assisted Fertility UK's records before turning his attention to World Food Corps. 'But there are reams of the business stuff. It's going to take me a while.'

Due to what the Vigilante had given me, I already knew we wouldn't find anything there, but I had to make it look like we were going through the motions. What I needed was a way to introduce the offshore accounts into the investigation, and the only way to do that was to find whatever lock the key fitted. I was convinced it held the evidence Hannah Ryan and Neal Lane had discovered.

I went back to my search through various databases, trying to find a match for the key. But there was no name of the manufacturer. I had no clue who had even produced it.

An hour later, I tugged at my hair, no further forward. I'd fired off thirty emails to the most commonly used key manufacturers in the UK to see if they could identify it. And I'd called most of the UK banks to see if it could be a safety-deposit key, even though there was no record of either Hannah Ryan or the Lanes ever renting one, but I'd had no joy.

My phone rang then. It was a civilian in our Technical Services team.

'We're still going through the laptop for David Bennington. Can't find anything of interest in his email accounts. There's quite a lot of documents on there to go through, but nothing of note so far.'

I groaned. More of nothing.

'I think the search team updated you that one of the Nokias found at Bennington's house was the one used to phone Steve Moore.'

'Yeah.'

'Well, the other one was used to call a number repeatedly over the last nine months. It's another unregistered pay-as-you-go.'

I rubbed a hand over my face. 'Great.'

'But . . . the phone that received the call was only just switched off last night, and the service provider has come back with a last-known location for it. A police station in Devon.'

'Fantastic! I know who it belongs to then. We've got a guy in custody who's refusing to give his name. His phone would've been switched off by the custody sergeant in Devon when he was booked in there. Great stuff. Thanks for that.'

'We'll keep digging and I'll let you know if we get anything else.'

I hung up and rushed to the custody suite. After examining the phone that had been found on Don Duck's person when he'd been arrested by Devon and Cornwall Police, I confirmed it was the same number. We were getting closer but not close enough.

I headed down to interview room two, where Becky was interrogating Bennington. I knocked on the door, poked my head round, called her out. She suspended the interview.

'Anything?' I asked.

'No. Jumped-up little fuck.'

I relayed the info I'd just received. 'We can prove more of a connection than him simply calling Steve Moore with a fake job. Bennington's second pay-as-you-go phone was in constant contact with Don Duck. I'm sure Bennington was the one who gave the orders to kill Hannah Ryan and Neal Lane. Use it to put pressure on him.'

'Will do, guv.' She turned and went back in.

I grabbed a bottle of water from the drinks machine because surely I couldn't go wrong with that. I unscrewed it, took a long guzzle, then headed back to the CID office.

My phone rang just as I sat down. I didn't recognise the number before I answered.

'Oh, hi. My name's Kelly from DBS Limited.' One of the key manufacturers I'd emailed. 'I'm calling in response to your enquiry earlier.'

'Thanks for getting back to me. Is it one of yours?'

'Yes, it is. I checked our databases, and it belongs to a safety-deposit box installed at Secure Safe Deposits. Do you want their details?'

'Yes, please.' I grabbed a pen and my pocket book and took down the details. They were based in Barnet. I thanked her, hung up, then dialled their number to let them know I would be attending their address.

I rang Caroline on the hands-free as I drove to Barnet. She was in the briefing room, getting an update from the team, and she put me on loud speaker.

'Neal Lane opened a safety-deposit box at a place in Barnet two weeks ago and paid cash,' I told them. 'I'm on my way there. Hopefully we'll find whatever it is he and Hannah Ryan had dug up.'

'Great news,' Caroline said. 'But we're no closer to getting any evidence on DCI Munroe or Oliver Hammond.'

I told them what had been happening at my end. 'Bennington ordered the hit on Hannah Ryan and Neal Lane, I'm sure of it. But right now I can't prove much of anything other than Don Duck's attempted murder of Gillian and Dean Lane in Devon, and neither Bennington nor Don Duck are talking at all.'

'We'll just have to hope whatever is in the safety-deposit box blows this thing wide open,' Caroline said.

I hung up. It was time to plant some evidence.

DETECTIVE WARREN CARTER
Chapter 65

I couldn't imagine a building any less suited to safety-deposit boxes than the one I found. I was expecting something that looked impenetrable, with high fencing topped with barbed wire, but it was a non-assuming brick affair, sandwiched between a row of narrow terraced houses and a Chinese supermarket, with a big sign up out front emblazoned with the company's name for all to see.

There were CCTV cameras all over the front of it, though. And the door was made of sturdy metal that I hoped was reinforced. I stared up at the camera above the door as I tried to push it open. It didn't budge. At least that was one concession to security. There was a keypad next to the door and an intercom system. I looked up at the camera as I pressed the button to speak to someone.

'Can I help you?' a female voice answered.

I held my warrant card up to the camera. 'Detective Inspector Carter. I spoke with Mr Rodgers on the phone. He's expecting me.'

'Please come in.'

The door buzzed. I pulled it open. Yep, it was heavy, all right.

I stepped into a narrow lobby. A smartly dressed woman behind the desk smiled and said, 'Mr Rodgers will be with you in a moment. Can I get you something to drink?'

'I'm fine, thanks.' I stared at a steel door to my right. It was black. Looked impenetrable. Which gave me a bit more confidence in their security.

An older guy with thick white hair came through from behind the steel door with a smile.

'Detective.' He held his hand out. I shook it. 'Can I just see your ID and search warrant, please?'

'Sure.' I handed over my warrant card and the paperwork.

Rodgers studied them for a moment then handed me my ID back. 'This way, please.'

He opened the steel door and led me down a corridor to another steel door at the end. He punched a set of numbers into a keypad. Then pressed his forefinger to a digital fingerprint reader. Then a camera scanned his retina. It seemed ironic to me that this kind of biometric data was exactly what Neal Lane had been working on at the Salama Camp to help refugees, and he was dead because of it.

The door slid open to reveal a large room, walls lined with steel safety-deposit boxes in varying sizes on either side. In the middle was a polished metal table with nothing on it.

He marched towards the far corner and pointed at a box. 'This is the one. Do you have the key?'

I'd removed it from the evidence bag back at the station and put it in my pocket. As I pulled it out, my fingertips skimmed the flashdrive I'd received from the Vigilante.

'If you can put it in the lock, please.'

I did as he asked, and he put his own master key into an identical lock next to it.

He turned both keys. Opened the box's door. Pulled out a metal container.

He handed it to me and said, 'You can use the table.' He tilted his head towards it, then hovered at my elbow.

I looked up at him. 'This is confidential.'

'Oh, yes. Yes, of course. I just hope it hasn't been used for some kind of illegal activity. We pride ourselves here at Secure Safe Deposits for being a legitimate depository facility.'

'I don't think you've got anything to worry about.' I eyed him until he turned around and walked towards the steel door.

'Just bang when you need to come out.'

I waited until he'd left before opening the lid of the box. Inside were a portable hard drive and two flashdrives. I bagged them up and added my own flashdrive from the Vigilante. I'd previously removed any documents from it that we didn't need any more because we'd already obtained them legally, leaving only the offshore corporation and banking information. I sealed it before initialling and dating it. Yes, it was ironic that an anti-corruption officer had just committed noble-cause corruption by planting evidence obtained unlawfully. But I didn't think of it as corruption at all. I was balancing the scales of justice. I was getting evil off the streets. We didn't have enough to convict Bennington yet. He'd get expensive counsel who could easily explain away that even if he had called Steve Moore and Don Duck, it wasn't to incite murder, and he had an alibi because he'd never got his own hands dirty. We had nothing on Munroe or Hammond yet. The only person we could probably nail was Powell Acton because of the payments from his personal UK bank account to Odesa Investments in the Ukraine, but again, a good barrister could twist a story in his favour that the jury might buy. I'd seen it happen too many times. Probably without the evidence of the offshore companies and bank accounts we never would have anything absolutely solid. So it had to be done. Because I wasn't going to risk the real chance of any of them getting away with the horrific acts they'd carried out and all the pain they'd inflicted.

The journey back seemed to take for ever, with tailbacks and queues everywhere. Snow began to fall, thick flakes hitting the windscreen, which exacerbated the snail's pace of the traffic. And a gritting lorry – a sight usually unseen until it was far too late to matter – hogged one lane and further slowed everyone down.

By the time I stepped inside the PSD office, I was sweating from the overheated car and the frustration of dodging mad Christmas shoppers on the roads.

Caroline strode out of her office as soon as she saw me approaching the desks, a wide smile lighting up her face. 'You're going to love this. Munroe just fucked up big time.'

DETECTIVE WARREN CARTER
Chapter 66

We all piled into the briefing room. Caroline put her laptop on the desk at the front and started the audio recording.

CALLER: It's me.

DCI MUNROE: Why the hell are you ringing me here?

CALLER: I'm in a call box. And I rang through your switchboard. Internal lines can't be traced. You told me that before. Who the fuck am I supposed to call? David's been arrested! I thought you were supposed to be controlling things at your end.

DCI MUNROE: I've been turfed off the case so I've got no control over the investigation any more. Bloody Professional Standards are involved. I've got to keep a low profile.

CALLER: I know. That detective came to see me. You'd better *do* something. If you hadn't dropped that warrant card we wouldn't be in this mess. Christ . . . this was supposed to be foolproof. This is *your* fault.

DCI MUNROE: Mine? Six of those women are dead because of you! Not to mention Neal Lane and Hannah Ryan. It's going to come out. All of it. How can you sleep at night?

CALLER: Well, we're not so different, are we, Susan? You should take a look in the mirror before you start pointing fingers. You'd better do something. Fast.

DCI MUNROE: I've done everything you asked. I can't do any more. Stop calling me.

The recording stopped.

Caroline looked at us all with an elated smile. 'Munroe's not so clever now, is she?'

'That was Powell Acton's voice,' I said, wanting to smile smugly back and let out a triumphant roar that we'd got something to use against both of them. But six women were dead. Hannah Ryan and Neal Lane were also lying on a cold slab. Dean Lane was in intensive care and Gillian Lane had almost been killed twice. I was too angry to be triumphant.

'I hope there's something on that lot that will prove Oliver Hammond was involved, too.' Caroline nodded to the evidence bag still in my hand.

'So do I.'

'Leave the flashdrives and hard drive with Koray to look through,' Caroline said. 'In the meantime—'

She was cut off by my phone ringing.

I glanced at the screen. 'Technical Services,' I told them before answering.

'We've found something else,' the same guy I'd spoken to earlier said.

'Go on.' I glanced up at Caroline, who watched me.

'That second burner phone found at David Bennington's that I spoke to you about earlier . . .'

'The one used to call the phone in custody belonging to Don Duck?'

'Yep. It was also used to make calls to two other numbers. Both pay-as-you-go phones. But we got the historical triangulation data for the numbers that the phone *dialled*. The first number's locations were at Powell Acton's home and work addresses. The second number's location was DCI Munroe's home address.'

'Brilliant. Anything else?'

'Not yet. But I thought you'd want the heads-up as soon as.'

I thanked him, hung up, and passed the information on to my team.

Caroline said, 'Right. Jack, I want you to nick Powell Acton. You might as well take him to Stevenage police station if they've got room in custody, since that's where everyone else is. Warren, you and I are going to arrest Munroe.'

DETECTIVE WARREN CARTER
Chapter 67

'Bennington's not talking,' Becky said grumpily down the phone as Caroline and I drove to Munroe's office at Letchworth police station. 'He's been taken back to the cells. But we have had an ID on Don Duck from the UK Border Agency.'

'Oh, yeah? And who is that delightful little bastard?'

'His name's Gavin Holmes. Made some enquiries this end, and Ronnie's discovered Holmes is on the payroll of World Food Corps, listed as a transport manager. He makes regular trips from Jordan to the UK, using World Food Corps vehicles to transport goods.'

'That's how they were getting the women out of Jordan and into the UK,' I said. 'Go back and give Holmes a grilling. I doubt he'll say anything but it's worth a try.' I gave her an update from my end and hung up.

Caroline's perfume filtered through the air as I drove. Something feminine and flowery that softened the sharp lines of her black and white uniform. I glanced over at her. She was still smiling.

'As soon as we get this case sorted out, we'll deal with Colin Etheridge,' she said. 'I understand why he did it, but we can't have officers abusing their position of trust and undermining ongoing investigations by passing on confidential information to unauthorised sources. He'll be sacked and prosecuted for misconduct in public office.'

I nodded.

She glanced over at me. 'How did you really get that old newspaper article that showed they were all friends at Oxford?'

'Anonymous tip-off,' I repeated.

'Uh-huh.' She quirked an eyebrow up. It made her look sexy. 'And what really made you think to check if Munroe had power of attorney for her mother?'

'Like I said, it was a hunch. I thought the reason you wanted me on the team was because I thought outside the box.'

She carried on staring at me with what looked like a half-amused face.

I swallowed, turned my attention back to the road. 'Did the team find anything about a possible addiction habit Munroe had?'

'Nothing yet, no.'

'I've been thinking about that. She withdrew £25,000 from her mum's account in small payments between September and November. It kept bugging me why she'd be involved in trafficking, and I didn't think it was for the money. Maybe they were blackmailing her to do what she did. She was paying *them* not the other way around.'

'Blackmailing her over what?'

'I don't know. But she was there, at Brampton Hospital, because Acton said on tape *she* dropped the warrant card there. Most likely she did pick it up when Colin left it in the bar, intending to give it back to him, but before that happened she somehow lost it herself at the hospital. But what was she doing there? Checking on the merchandise? She doesn't seem like the type of person to get her own hands dirty.'

She thought about that for a moment. 'I dread to think. I—'

We were interrupted by a text message on her phone.

Caroline read it, then said, 'Koray's found a space in custody at St Albans police station for Munroe.' Since Munroe had to be taken to a police station away from where she worked or was known, and booked in under an anonymous name, her holding location needed to be prepared in advance.

We were silent for the rest of the way, both of us lost in our own thoughts, the thrill of the chase that I'd missed during the last few months of retirement rushing through me.

When we entered the Letchworth CID office, where Munroe's team had been transferred back to, I spotted DC Jamal Faris on the phone with his back to us. DI Thornton had been relegated to a desk next to him, which he didn't look particularly pleased about. DC Colin Etheridge sat typing on his computer. His face went white when he saw us. Sneaky little bugger. His time would come soon.

We marched past the lot of them to DCI Munroe's office at the back. I watched her expression as she glanced up at us. She attempted a professional, calm smile but it didn't sit quite right. There was a slight panic in her eyes, which were swollen, as if she'd been crying. Who was she crying for, though, I wondered? Herself? Or those who'd died so brutally?

Caroline opened Munroe's office door. I stepped in behind her.

Munroe stood up. 'Have you finally discovered who the leak is so I can get back to the Lane–Ryan murder inquiry?'

Caroline looked at me, wanting me to have the satisfaction of doing the honours.

Don't mind if I do. 'Susan Munroe, I'm arresting you on suspicion of conspiracy to murder Hannah Ryan and Neal Lane, suspicion of conspiracy to murder six unidentified female victims, conspiracy to murder Gillian Lane and Dean Lane, perverting the course of justice . . .'

DETECTIVE WARREN CARTER
Chapter 68

St Albans police station. Interview room four.

Surprisingly, Munroe had waived her right to have a federation rep or lawyer present. If she thought it showed she had nothing to hide, and she could save her skin all by herself, she was going to be mistaken. Her face was flushed slightly but she otherwise looked poised and in control. Maybe she still thought she was cleverer than she was.

I sorted out the recording equipment and stated the preliminaries.

'Do you understand why you've been arrested?' Caroline asked her.

Munroe sat straight-backed, her expression neutral, like the one she'd been taught to show the public for press briefings. 'No. I have no idea why you think I could be involved in something as heinous as this. I was *investigating* the murders of Hannah Ryan and Neal Lane, not participating in them. And I have no knowledge of six female victims. Is this seriously what PSD do all day? Hindering good officers trying to do their jobs?'

'Can you confirm for the tape that you've waived your right to a lawyer or federation rep?' Caroline said.

'Yes, because I've done absolutely nothing wrong.' Munroe's expression didn't change, but a little twitch of a muscle in her jaw gave her away.

Caroline looked at me. 'OK, let's start, shall we?'

I settled back in my chair. 'Let me tell you a story. And feel free to jump in any time and add to it.'

Munroe crossed her legs. Pinched her lips together.

'Once upon a time, there was a man called David Bennington, who was the CEO of World Food Corps. In the eyes of the public he was a big humanitarian. Except he was hiding a dark side. With his aid work, he was able to prey on young, desperate women who wanted to escape the struggles of being in a refugee camp to go to the UK for a better life. At some point he must've discussed this with his mate Oliver Hammond, fertility expert extraordinaire, and they spoke about the endless supply of women he could get hold of. Women who were untraceable, had no identities, whom no one would miss if they disappeared. Hammond wanted egg donors for his clients. There was a huge shortage in the UK, particularly for donors of Middle Eastern ethnicity. A shortage that no doubt affected his business, and he'd already put himself into debt to set up his clinic. Feeding on his clients' desperation to have a baby, Hammond knew he could charge them a high premium for illegal donor eggs.

'So together they cooked up a plan. Bennington would traffic women into the UK using his sidekick Gavin Holmes and the protection of World Food Corps vehicles. Hammond would hold them captive and force them to undergo medical treatment to produce eggs. And lo and behold, he's making a big, fat profit. Enter Powell Acton, also a long-time friend of them both. He knew just the place where Hammond could stash his kidnapped victims – Brampton Hospital – where Hammond could arrange private donor transfers to wealthy clients who didn't care where they came from. We believe he owned the place. Maybe Acton bought the old hospital as an investment with potential for development, but it was sitting there empty while he waited for an upturn in the market and so he thought he'd put it to good use.'

'Anything you want to say yet?' Caroline asked.

Munroe swallowed. 'No. Like I said, I have nothing to do with any of this and absolutely no knowledge of what you're talking about.'

'Hannah Ryan and Neal Lane found out about the trafficking ring David Bennington and Gavin Holmes were running,' I carried on. 'They were going to expose it all. So Bennington got in touch with his mate Powell Acton to discuss what to do. They decided they needed to silence Hannah Ryan and Neal Lane, and make their murders look like something else entirely to throw the scent off them and the whistleblowing that Ryan and Lane were about to do. But they needed help for that, didn't they? And they got it from you. You were also old friends with Acton, Bennington, and Hammond. You knew each other from studying at Oxford Uni. Want to add anything yet?'

Munroe's face turned paler. 'This is ridiculous. I have no idea about any of this. I don't even recall having met those people at Oxford. In case you didn't know, it's a big place. And it was nearly two decades ago when I was there!'

'Really?' Caroline asked. 'You're sure you want to deny that?'

Munroe blinked a few times. 'Of course.'

'You *were* in touch with them,' I said. 'And you told Bennington about an unsolved murder case you'd had before, conveniently where the killer had left no DNA at the scene. You fed him information about it so they could use it to make it look like Hannah Ryan and Neal Lane had been killed by the same person. And then you covered it up.'

'No! It was either DC Pickering or DS Harris who were feeding information out from the department. I came to you and told you about my concerns and you took *me* off the case!' Munroe clenched her jaw for a moment. Then sat back in the chair and crossed her arms. 'I know exactly what this is.'

'Oh, and what's that?' Caroline raised an eyebrow.

'It's a campaign against me. Because we're getting criticised in the press over the Cupid Killer – me in particular – so I'm being used as a scapegoat. You're trying to pin the blame on me, and ruin my reputation, so the rest of the force doesn't look bad, just because I was the SIO in both cases.' She narrowed her eyes, looked at us with pure hatred. 'Instead of catching *real* criminals, you're trying to fabricate malicious evidence about one of your own.'

'Perhaps you should wait until you hear the rest.' Caroline looked at me to carry on.

'You were involved in controlling and manipulating the Ryan–Lane investigation, and you probably thought it would be easy to set up a serial-killer scenario. What you couldn't plan for – what none of you could plan for – was the electrical fire at Brampton Hospital that exposed the trafficking ring.'

Munroe's mouth snapped open as if she was going to say something.

'Yes, DCI Munroe? Do you have anything to add?' Caroline asked.

Munroe closed her mouth again. Shook her head.

'And you made mistakes,' I said. 'DS Becky Harris started questioning that not everything was as it seemed. She didn't believe the serial-killer angle and started digging into things further. Bennington already had the perfect patsy, thanks to you and the information you gave him about the previous murders of Donna and Jim Wilson.' I paused, waited for her to say something. She didn't. 'Before the murders, Bennington called Steve Moore, pretending to be Neal Lane, asking him to come and give him a quote to fix his boiler. And lo and behold, then an anonymous tip-off placed Moore at the scene. Evidence in the form of the gloves was conveniently planted in Moore's van to prove he was involved. Except you messed up there.' I watched her calm facade slipping bit by bit. She looked down at the floor. 'Moore couldn't have been the killer of Hannah Ryan and Neal Lane. The dashcam footage proved it, which again, you didn't bank on. You didn't cover everything as well as you thought you had. Want to say anything yet?' I asked.

'I have *never* planted evidence on anybody. I strenuously deny all these allegations.'

'So who did then? Someone put those gloves in Moore's van,' Caroline said.

'I have no idea. Maybe DS Harris, since she was the one who found them!'

'Ha!' I laughed. 'Nice try.'

'Look, as I said, I had nothing to do with any of this, other than as SIO, investigating, doing my job.'

'Deny all you want. I haven't finished yet,' I said. 'What you didn't realise was that those same gloves were also used at Brampton Hospital. A print from them was found on one of the chains binding an unknown female victim to the wall in a bedroom there. Instead of those gloves taking the heat away from you and your associates, it incriminated you all even more and provided irrefutable proof the cases were linked.'

'What evidence do you have to support my involvement in any of this?' Munroe said, a slight waver detectable beneath the calm way it was delivered. 'Nothing. Because there is none.'

'That's where you're very much mistaken.' Caroline opened the folder in front of her and listed the exhibit numbers as she laid out pieces of paper in front of her, with certain parts that had been highlighted. 'A pattern of calls using burner phones from David Bennington to *your* burner phone. Yes, we've got triangulation data of these calls putting the receiver at *your* home address. And just before we came into the interview, we received historical cell phone data from your work mobile phone, which puts you at the location of Brampton Hospital on the night of the fifteenth November. The same night, incidentally, that DC Colin Etheridge lost his warrant card, but we'll get back to that. Another mistake made there. You should've turned your phone off.'

Munroe looked at the paperwork. The twitch was back in her jaw.

'What were you talking about with Bennington on all those occasions?' Caroline tapped the call data pages.

Munroe didn't say a word.

'I'll tell you, shall I?' Caroline said. 'You were discussing how to set up the murders of Hannah Ryan and Neal Lane so it didn't come back on them. Why did you do it?'

Munroe blew out a breath but remained silent.

Caroline fiddled with some recording equipment. 'I'm going to play you an audio file recorded this morning.' She let the sound of Munroe and Acton's voices fill the air.

Munroe looked down at the desk, her eyes widening, realisation kicking in. When it stopped, Caroline said, 'Do you have anything to say now?'

Silence as Munroe stared at the floor.

'That's you and Powell Acton,' I said. 'Talking about your involvement in manipulating the murder investigation. Talking about you being at Brampton Hospital. So you see, we have clear, irrefutable, damning evidence of your involvement.'

Munroe licked her lips. Her hands trembled slightly in her lap.

I leaned forward. 'Did *you* kill Hannah Ryan and Neal Lane?'

'No!' Munroe said.

'You seriously expect us to believe that?' Caroline snapped. 'You were the one who knew everything about the Wilsons' murders, and you replicated it with Hannah Ryan and Neal Lane. Or at least you tried to, until you started making mistakes. You misdirected the inquiry from day one, and you planted evidence on Steve Moore and tried to frame him!'

'I strongly deny that! I didn't kill them!' Munroe shook her head.

'So who did?' I asked.

Munroe went silent again.

'You don't even have the *guts* to admit what you've done,' Caroline said.

Munroe swiped away the sweat beading at her forehead.

'OK. Let's get back to the warrant card,' I said. 'What happened? After DC Etheridge left it behind, you picked it up – maybe you intended to give it back to him. But you lost it at Brampton Hospital.' I pointed a finger at her. 'We know that from the tape.'

Munroe didn't answer. She dropped her gaze to her lap and wouldn't look at us.

'You were there, at Brampton Hospital, and you must've known those women were being held captive inside and you did *nothing* to help them,' Caroline said, her voice hard as steel as she opened the folder again and slapped photos of the six unknown victims on the desk in front of Munroe. 'This is what you did.'

Munroe looked away.

'Look at them!' Caroline barked out.

'I haven't done anything wrong,' Munroe said, but her voice held a lot less conviction now.

'You failed in your lawful duty as a police officer many, many times over,' Caroline said. 'You were complicit in multiple murders. You perverted the course of justice and obstructed inquiries. You're going to be rotting away behind bars for the rest of your life. What motivated you to do it? Help me out here because I'm trying to understand. Was it an addiction? Bribery? Blackmail? What? Please tell me it wasn't just for the money.'

Munroe closed her eyes, her lower lip trembling. She turned her face up to the ceiling. When she opened them again she swallowed hard, looking cowed. Nothing like the woman with the ball-breaker reputation that she'd earned over the years. She looked between me and Caroline. 'I can't go to prison. I *can't*. You know what they'd do to a police officer in there. And I'm . . .' She took a deep, shuddering breath. 'I want immunity from prosecution before I say anything.'

Caroline folded her arms and leaned back in her chair. 'I bet you do. Well, we need to determine how valuable your information is before we discuss the possibility of immunity with the CPS.' Caroline glared at Munroe. 'You and your accomplices have left a trail of eight dead, innocent victims in your wake. It could've been Gillian and Dean Lane, too, if you'd had your way. You're going to have to come up with something substantial if you expect us to entertain the possibility of any deal with you.'

Munroe's neck wobbled, as if she had a nervous tick. Tears streamed down her face. 'I can help you get them. I *never* wanted to get involved in this. But *please*, I can't go to prison.'

'What makes you so special that you think you don't have to pay for what you've done?' I asked.

'Because I'm pregnant!' she wailed.

HAYAT

Chapter 69

I am curled up on the bed. The pain is worse. I do not know what to do. I do not know when someone last came to feed us. I do not know the day or the month or the time.

I smell smoke, coming from somewhere. I smile. It is smoke from the clay oven in our courtyard garden. Mama is baking flatbread inside it. I can almost taste it in my mouth. Hot dough, soft on the inside, a little crispy on the outside. I will dip it in honey and yoghurt. Spread it with cherry jam.

I lick my fingertips, sweet jam sticking to them.

Smoke.

I cough and retch. I hear someone screaming. It is Mama, screaming for me to go somewhere.

'Come on, Hayat, wake up,' she says. 'Break the door.'

'What door?' I giggle. The giggle turns into a cough.

Smoke.

I lift my head from the bed. Or do I? I do not know what is real any more. The medicine has made me sick. Or is it the illness?

Wisps of smoke dance underneath the door, like octopus arms, tentacles reaching out. It is friendly. It wants to hold me, keep me safe.

'The octopus is coming,' I say to Mama. 'Did you send it to me?'

'You must get up now.'

I watch the octopus. It is trying to reach me. I cough again. Cough and cough and cough. Screaming. Smoke. Noise. Crackling. It is hot. I am so hot. Sweat plasters my hair to my face. Summertime in Syria.

'Come *on!*' Mama says. 'Do something!'

I try to get off the bed but fall to the floor. I crawl towards the door, coughing, spluttering. The crackling is louder now. I cannot hear Mama screaming any more.

The floor is melting beneath me. The octopus wants to swallow me whole.

I am tired again. Sleeping, sleep, sleepy.

Hot. Fiery. Heat.

Smoke . . .

Wake up!

I reach inside my bra. I will tell the octopus my name so it knows me. If it knows my name it will spit me out and keep me safe because I am a person. I am a human being. My life is worth something. And the octopus will not let me die.

I pull out the key-card that doesn't work and scratch into the plastic floor so the octopus can see I am real . . .

H . . . A . . . Y . . . A . . . T

'I . . . am . . . Hayat,' I gasp out to the octopus.

The octopus says nothing.

I try to tell the octopus something else about me, but its tentacles grip my throat, squeezing, squeezing. My lungs do not work.

I cannot breathe.

Please don't kill me . . .

DETECTIVE WARREN CARTER

Chapter 70

I exchanged a surprised glance with Caroline. Munroe announcing she was pregnant was the last thing I'd been expecting.

'You know I'd probably be killed in prison,' Munroe said. 'Even if I was segregated they'd find a way! They'd kill my baby. Do you want that on your hands? And it would be taken away from me. I can't let that happen.'

'Oh, that's bloody rich,' I snapped. 'Don't you dare turn this around onto someone else. You had a choice, and what you were involved in got eight people killed. You were supposed to be protecting innocent, vulnerable people like that!'

'I can help you . . . I know how it worked, who was involved. I know everything. I can give evidence against them in court. Please . . . *please*. I need immunity.'

Caroline hesitated, staring at Munroe with a look that would crack glass.

Munroe wiped at her tears with a shaky hand and put her other hand to her stomach.

Caroline looked at me. Before either of us could say more both our mobile phones started ringing. Caroline suspended the interview, and we stepped outside to answer our respective calls.

'Hi, Koray,' I said as I walked further down the corridor.

'I wanted to update you. I've found some interesting stuff on the evidence you retrieved from the deposit box.' He told me everything he'd gleaned from the Vigilante's flashdrive.

'Wow, really? That's fantastic.' I put on a suitably surprised voice.

'I also found details of some of our victim's biometric data taken by Neal Lane, and photos of the others taken by Hannah Ryan at Salama Camp, proving that's where they came from. There's tons more to go through but I thought you could use it when questioning Munroe.'

'You need to call Becky and tell her so she can put it to Bennington in the interview she's conducting. And also call Jack so he can put it to Powell Acton. Maybe that will encourage them to talk.' I hung up as Caroline walked towards me, off her own call now.

'What have you got?'

I told her.

'Brilliant news.' She held her phone up. 'That was the lab. The skin samples inside the wrist area of the gloves found in Steve Moore's van have been matched to DNA from Gavin Holmes.'

I leaned against the wall. 'So we can prove Gavin Holmes killed Hannah Ryan and Neal Lane, and that he was at Brampton Hospital. We can prove Bennington and Acton's involvement via the offshore money transactions and corporations. We can prove Munroe was in contact with Bennington and gave inside information and helped cover things up, and that she was at Brampton Hospital. But we're still missing one big piece. We've got nothing on Oliver Hammond.'

'We need Munroe to get to him. None of the others are talking so far,' Caroline said with a rigid set to her jaw.

'You're not seriously going to request that the CPS gives her immunity for her testimony, are you?'

'I don't like it any more than you.' She chewed on her lip for a moment. 'All we can prove with Hammond is that he used Acton Associates as a corporate lawyer. That, and their communications via work phones over the years is all we have connecting them. And Hammond's lawyer will easily argue they were just talking about normal business affairs. If we don't find anything else, and she doesn't testify, he'll walk.'

I shook my head, gritted my teeth. 'If she gets immunity she'll get away with it! I've seen some scumbags in my time but she's one of the most cold-hearted, calculating people I've ever met.' And what really turned my stomach was that she was one of our own.

'I know exactly how you feel, but I don't think there's much of a choice right now. We need to speak to the CPS. They'll have to weigh up what her testimony is worth and decide if they'll grant her immunity to get her to implicate the others in court, or prosecute her instead. It's not our decision to make.'

I paused for a moment as a thought slammed into my head. 'She's pregnant. Maybe she used Hammond to implant donor eggs and that's what the £25,000 coming out of her mum's account was used for. Maybe she was desperate for kids and didn't care where the eggs came from. And then she was in too deep. Bennington needed Hannah Ryan and Neal Lane killed. Hammond had leverage against Munroe if she'd used black-market eggs from trafficked girls, and got her on board to help them get rid of their problem. She wasn't checking the merchandise at Brampton Hospital. She was there to be implanted. It's the only thing that makes sense now.'

She chewed on her lip for a moment, turning that over in her head. 'Well, let's find out.' She jerked her head towards the door, indicating that we go back inside.

After restarting the tape, Caroline said, 'All right. We're listening.' And Munroe started talking.

DETECTIVE WARREN CARTER
Chapter 71

'I couldn't have children,' Munroe said. 'I had an infection in my early twenties that damaged my ovaries. I knew . . . I knew Oliver Hammond at Oxford Uni, you're right. He was David Bennington's best friend. I was going out with David at that time, and Powell Acton was also friends with us all.' She swallowed and wrapped her arms around herself. 'I'd had attempts at IVF at a private clinic using donor eggs in the past but they'd failed. So I decided to go and see Oliver for treatment because his success rate appeared to be better. Until then, I hadn't seen him for years. I hadn't seen or been in touch with any of them. Hammond told me there were no eggs available through legitimate channels, unless I wanted to wait at least three years, but he could get hold of good-quality eggs another way.' She paused, looked up at the ceiling.

Caroline glanced knowingly at me. It didn't give me any pleasure to know I'd just sussed that out.

'And where on earth did you think these eggs were coming from?' Caroline asked.

'He told me they were from egg-donation programmes in other clinics outside the EU. From Eastern Europe. I believed him. I had no reason not to. Although it wasn't strictly legal in the UK without an import licence, I didn't think there was anything wrong with that. He assured me that all the relevant checks had been done on the donors. That they were all above board. That in other countries donors were given financial incentives to donate. So I went to Brampton Hospital to have them implanted. I swear I didn't know at that time they were trafficking girls to use for the eggs.'

'So you didn't see any of the women there?' I asked.

'No.'

'You didn't think it was odd that clandestine medical procedures were being done at Brampton Hospital instead of a proper clinic?' Caroline asked.

'Of course, I knew they would be done in secret since Oliver Hammond was obtaining them without a licence. But that's *all* I thought. I never at that time thought any crime was being committed.' She sniffed. 'The night Colin lost his warrant card, I did pick it up after he'd left, intending to give it back. It must've fallen out of my bag when I went to Brampton Hospital later that night for the egg transfer. I realised the next day I didn't have it, but I didn't know where I'd lost it, so I just didn't say anything to Colin. I honestly didn't think I'd done anything wrong at that stage.'

'And what about your husband, Paul?' Caroline asked. 'I assume he went with you to Brampton Hospital for treatment? Provided his sperm? Did he know what was going on?'

Munroe took a deep breath. 'We used donor sperm that Oliver Hammond also provided. My husband also has fertility issues. He never attended the appointments with me, he was always too busy with work. He didn't have a clue about any of this.'

Caroline folded her arms, leaned back in her chair. 'So, what happened afterwards? What about Hannah Ryan and Neal Lane and *your* involvement in trying to cover up their murders?'

Munroe rested her hand on her stomach again. 'Can I have some water, please?'

Caroline glared at her as if she wanted to throttle her. She stopped the interview. Disappeared to get some water.

Munroe sobbed, her shoulders hunched in on themselves. I didn't feel any pity.

Caroline came back into the room and paused in front of Munroe, looking like she wanted to throw the bottle of water in her face. She handed it to Munroe, who gulped a quarter of it and placed it on the table.

Caroline settled back in her chair, crossed her arms. 'Carry on. Hannah Ryan and Neal Lane.'

'Oh, God,' Munroe wailed, dropping her head in her hands.

'If you want immunity, you need to tell us everything,' Caroline barked.

Munroe looked up at us. 'I never meant for this to happen.'

'Yeah, well, it's too late for that sentiment,' I said. 'Too late for all the victims whose lives you stole.'

Munroe took a deep breath again, steadying herself. 'By then I was in too deep. When they told me what they wanted me to do, I found out about the trafficked women. About their eggs I'd used. They needed someone on the inside, and they blackmailed me. I had to help them or I'd be exposed, too, and I had a baby to think of.' She wiped her eyes. 'Hannah Ryan and Neal Lane discovered that women were missing from the camp at Salama. Neal went to Bennington about it but David dismissed it. Said they must've escaped the camp, which was easy to do. The place is the size of a big city. People leave or disappear all the time and are never seen again.' She sniffed, blinked back more tears. 'Then Hannah Ryan went out to the camp to do a humanitarian piece on the refugees. She met Neal. He told her he suspected some of the people were being trafficked. She'd come to the same conclusion after speaking to a woman out there who had also disappeared suddenly.'

Munroe carried on, telling us how Bennington became suspicious of all the questions from Lane and Ryan. He sacked Lane, telling him the funding had run out. Hannah Ryan went back to the UK. But they were both still working on the story in secret, sharing evidence. Hannah was going to expose Neal's whistleblowing evidence contained in the hours of data he'd taken for the project. Hannah had photos of the missing interviewee of hers. They were trying to find out where the women were being trafficked to when they were killed.

'Apparently Bennington knew they were getting close to exposing his own involvement so he ordered Gavin Holmes to kill them and dress it up as a serial killing,' Munroe said.

'And you told Bennington about the Wilson murders so they could do a copycat crime scene.' I looked at her with pure disgust. 'Then you were in an ideal position to get yourself embedded in the investigation as SIO in Hannah Ryan's and Neal Lane's murders, and then plant evidence and cover up the identity of the real killer.'

'I . . . I didn't want to do it.' She blinked a few times, tears splashing down her cheeks. 'He made me.'

'Oh, don't give me that crap,' I said. 'You could've come forward with what you knew at that stage. You say Oliver Hammond lied to you about the origin of the donor eggs. You should've done your duty as a police officer but you didn't. If what you say is true, and you believed they were eggs from a legitimate source, from an overseas clinic, you should've reported it as soon as you found out and most likely nothing would've happened to you.'

'But you don't know that for certain. I could've been charged with assisting an offender. Or gross misconduct. Or perverting the course of justice, which carries a maximum life sentence! Even if I wasn't convicted of anything, I could've lost my job, my pension.'

'So, for purely selfish reasons, you wanted it covered up,' I said. 'I don't go round covering up murder for my friends,' I said. Which was a lie. I'd killed, and I'd covered up murders at Bloodbath Farm for someone I didn't even know. But that was different. I was protecting people. A good man doing a bad thing for a good reason. I didn't believe the same applied to Munroe.

'That's what I'm struggling with, too,' Caroline added. 'I find it incredibly hard to believe you didn't come forward as soon as you found out where the eggs had really come from. Instead, you dug yourself in deeper, and became involved in substantially more serious crimes by conspiring in the murders of Hannah Ryan and Neal Lane, and failing to report the six kidnapped women. Even if you'd come forward at the time of discovering exactly where the donor eggs came from, and you *had* lost your job and pension, you're not exactly living on the bread-line, are you? Your husband earns good money. You're financially sound. You would've been OK. But that selfishness got Hannah Ryan, Neal Lane, and those six women *killed*.'

'Not to mention conspiring in the attempted murders of Dean Lane and Gillian Lane,' I said.

'So why didn't you report it at the time?' Caroline asked.

'I already told you. I was scared I'd lose everything and end up in prison.'

I exchanged a look with Caroline. I was convinced there was more to it than that. From Caroline's expression it was obvious she thought the same.

'Is there something else you're not telling us?' Caroline asked her.

'No. I swear.'

'I don't believe you,' I said.

'I was blackmailed! I never meant for it to happen like this.' Then she broke down sobbing. 'I . . . I . . . never . . . meant . . .' she said, hiccupping in breaths. 'Oh, God. I was . . . he was . . . he blackmailed me.' She closed her eyes, her shoulder heaving.

'Yes, you said,' Caroline muttered. 'And that's no excuse. You failed in your duty not to reveal the fact that those trafficked women were locked in that hospital when you found out about it. You could've saved their lives. And instead they were abused terribly and died a horrific, agonising death. Are you absolutely sure that's the extent of your involvement or is there more you want to add?'

Munroe wiped her tears away. 'That's it. That's everything.'

Caroline stood up. 'Interview terminated.'

Munroe looked at Caroline, wide-eyed. 'So you're going to recommend the CPS gives me immunity? You need me, you know you do.'

Caroline strode towards the door. She stopped, looked over her shoulder with narrowed eyes. 'If it was up to me I'd throw the bloody book at you.'

DETECTIVE WARREN CARTER
Chapter 72

Two Weeks Later

It was the day before Christmas Eve. Snow fell in fat flakes around us in movie-worthy splendour. It really was going to be a white Christmas.

I wrapped my coat tighter around me as I stood beside Caroline and Becky in front of six freshly dug graves.

Six women. Gone but no longer nameless. And definitely not forgotten. I would see their faces as long as I lived.

I stared at the headstones of the 'paupers' graves'. Paid for by the council because they had no family here. No family anywhere. No one to mourn them, except us.

A simple inscription on each one showed their names, their dates of birth, and the date the fateful fire stole lives that had been stolen already.

Hayat Hasani
Haya Farzat
Safa Youssef
Larisa Hamed
Riffat Fakhri

Leila Nasry

All identified through a mixture of Neal Lane's biometric work and Hannah Ryan's investigative work, contained on the hard drive and flashdrives we'd found.

I blinked back tears as a shiver ran through me that had nothing to do with the cold, biting wind. Caroline and Becky sniffed back their own tears.

Oliver Hammond, David Bennington, Gavin Holmes, Powell Acton, and the driver working for Bennington, who Susan Munroe had named, had all been denied bail and were remanded in prison, awaiting trial for numerous offences. Hopefully their Christmas dinner would include a few broken lightbulbs in their mashed potatoes and gravy. I had no sympathy for them.

Caroline took one last sniff and laid a yellow rose on top of each grave. When she'd finished she stood back and said, 'Yellow roses were first discovered growing wild in the Middle East in the eighteenth century. They symbolise freedom. I thought it was appropriate.'

'A good choice,' I agreed.

She looked over at me and Becky. 'Come on. Let's go.'

We walked back across the graveyard towards the car park.

I stared at the ground as I walked, a rigid set to my jaw. 'Munroe's got away with everything.'

'Unfortunately, that's not our call,' Caroline said. 'Our job is to catch them. What happens next is up to the CPS.'

So yet again, justice hadn't prevailed. We'd dug and dug into Hammond, along with help from the Vigilante, and still found nothing on him. We'd torn apart his life, looked into his friends and family, his business. But we discovered no money trail, no patients he'd implanted the donor eggs into – apart from Munroe – no evidence he'd been involved at all. Hammond had been cleverer than all of the rest, and none of them were talking, all refusing to incriminate themselves.

Hammond had given a 'no comment' interview when arrested, as had Powell Acton.

'You know as well as I do that 40 per cent of jury trials end in a not-guilty verdict,' Caroline said. 'She's the CPS's only chance at bringing Hammond and the rest of them down. What else could they do?' Caroline said.

And it still tore me up that she was right. Without Munroe's testimony there was always the possibility a good defence barrister could get all of them off. Justice wasn't about the truth. It was about who told the better story.

I didn't believe Munroe innocently went to Hammond for fertility treatment. I think she knew full well what he was up to and knowingly participated in accepting black-market eggs from him using trafficked women. I thought Munroe was manipulative, a liar, selfish, narcissistic, and possibly a sociopath. The only good bit was that she'd lost her job, her police pension, and her reputation. Even her husband had left her after he'd found out exactly what she'd done. Four days ago she'd also lost her baby. I wasn't sure if that was from stress or a backlash of karma. One of the six women whose eggs Munroe had used taking back what was rightfully theirs from beyond the grave.

'You both did really well,' Caroline said. 'It's a positive result.'

I turned to look across at the headstones of the six victims. Took a deep breath. I looked back at her. 'Not good enough, though.'

'Give it time and you'll feel differently.'

'And to think I was ever inspired by her.' Becky tutted to herself.

'She fooled a lot of people,' Caroline said. 'But you were the one who spotted it first. Be your own inspiration. You're already an incredible detective and a huge asset to the force.'

Becky grinned widely. 'Thank you, ma'am.' Her mobile rang then. She pulled it out of her pocket. Looked at the screen. Looked at us. 'Sorry, I've got to take this. It's Ian.' She wandered off towards her car.

Caroline stopped walking. Turned to face me. Rested a hand on my shoulder. 'So are you staying? Or has this case completely put you off?'

'Sorry?'

'Do you want to make this a permanent thing with PSD? You could do your inspector's exam. You wouldn't just be an Acting DI then.'

I stared at their graves again, but I wasn't seeing their final resting place, their remains lying six feet under the dirt. Instead, I pictured Hayat and the others in my head as six living, breathing women. Their lives had been cruelly cut short, but in my head they'd carry on living. I felt responsible for them, which was irrational, I knew. I couldn't go back to mind-numbing retirement after this. I'd now uncovered two cases of serious police corruption in the last few months. If that wasn't supposed to be some kind of message, I didn't know what was. Maybe I'd found exactly where I was supposed to be. 'I'm staying.'

She grinned. 'Good. And I'm going to be recommending you for a commendation.' She started walking again.

'I don't deserve it,' I said, still thinking about Munroe. The one who'd got away.

She quirked up an eyebrow. 'You do. Trust me. You should've been commended many times over the years.'

'Thank you, ma'am. I don't know what to say.'

She shrugged. 'You fight for what's right and bugger the politics and consequences. That's what makes you ideal for PSD.'

I glanced over at her, our gazes meeting, and I saw in her exactly the qualities she'd just described about me. But what would she think of me if she really knew all the lines I'd crossed to get there?

'What are you doing for Christmas?' She changed the subject completely.

A montage of Christmases gone past flashed through my head: the first time Denise had ever cooked a turkey. We had been twenty and living in our first house, a poky little thing where you could hear everything the neighbours next door were saying. The turkey was burned on the outside and raw in the middle. We'd dumped it and had cheese on toast instead. Fifteen years later, and the ecstatic look on her face as she'd opened up her present from me, an itinerary for a once-in-a-lifetime holiday we'd always talked about, travelling around Sri Lanka for three weeks. It was the happy memories I thought of then, not the worst of times that I'd spent too much time dwelling on since she'd died, like the Christmas after she was diagnosed with cancer.

I smiled to myself wistfully as the pictures in my head lingered. I finally had to accept that Denise wasn't coming back. That I had to start trying to move on with my life without her.

I turned to Caroline. 'I'll probably have a Netflix binge with some turkey sandwiches. What about you?'

'Kira's celebrating on a beach in Australia, having a *barbie*,' she said in a terrible Australian accent. 'The Netflix binge sounds like a pretty good idea, but no turkey for me. I'm vegetarian.' She stopped walking and turned to face me. 'I don't suppose you want to come to me for dinner? I can make a mean nut roast with all the trimmings.' Her lips curled up in a smile.

I tilted my head, looking into her eyes. We worked together. She was my boss. And I *did* like her, as Becky had noticed. So it was probably a bad idea. But I also wanted some comfort. Something to ease the loneliness. Friendship. Closeness. A connection. Something that would take my mind off the fact I'd still failed the six victims by not getting Munroe put away.

Yes, maybe it was a bad idea. But it wouldn't be the first bad idea I'd ever had. And I knew it definitely wouldn't be the last.

EPILOGUE

DETECTIVE WARREN CARTER
Chapter 73

Seven Months Later

I walked into the PSD office and found my team already in the briefing room, eyes glued to the TV screen, mugs filled with celebratory prosecco. I stepped in behind them to their loud cheers as the news reporter gave a rundown of the verdict. I didn't need to hear it. I'd heard it first hand in the court room I'd just returned from, where I'd watched those bastards' faces when they had their lives stolen from them in return for the lives they'd taken.

Munroe had done her part. She'd testified, and the jury had come back with guilty verdicts for Oliver Hammond, Powell Acton, David Bennington, Gavin Holmes, and the driver of the vehicle Munroe had identified. They'd all be languishing behind bars for a long time. All except Munroe.

Caroline turned and saw me standing there, her eyes lighting up as she smiled. 'And here he is, the man of the moment. Grab a mug and I'll pour you a glass.'

I didn't feel like celebrating, but I needed a drink to take away the bitter taste of failure in my mouth, so I took a mug from the desk at the front of the room, held it out for Caroline to pour me some.

She held her own mug up and said, 'Well done, guys. Cheers to a fantastic result.'

Jack, Koray, Liz, Caroline, and Katrina chinked their mugs together with wide grins. I hesitated for a moment then followed suit, but my smile didn't sit quite right on my face.

Before I could take a sip, DC Potter from A Team poked his head through the door and told me there was a call for me. I put my mug down and left them to their celebrations. I sat at my desk, and DC Potter put the call through to my extension.

'DI Carter,' I answered.

'This is Rupert Grant.'

I frowned, wondering why Rupert Grant – Bennington's pompous, overpaid lawyer who'd been with him when I'd interviewed him – was calling me. In fact, he'd been the lawyer on record for all of the defendants. He'd been in court with the defendants' barrister every time I'd been there watching the trial. 'What can I do for you?'

'As you know, I was retained by Oliver Hammond.'

'Yes.'

'Mr Hammond would like to see you. He's just advised me that he has some information you'll want to hear.'

I frowned. 'It's too late to try and make a deal for an exchange of information. The trial's over. The jury has given its verdict.'

'I'm perfectly well aware of that. This is about Munroe.'

'What?' I wondered if he was winding me up, trying to get a dig in there because his client had been found guilty and she hadn't.

'Let's just say it will be beneficial for you to listen to him.'

And as I was about to find out, karma wasn't done with Munroe yet. And sometimes, karma came from the most unlikely sources.

DETECTIVE WARREN CARTER

Chapter 74

I sat in the visiting room at Belmarsh Prison, opposite Oliver Hammond. He wore the inmate uniform of grey jogging bottoms and grey sweatshirt. His face was grey, too, as a result of the lack of sunlight he'd suffered inside while on remand. He looked as if he'd aged ten years in the last seven months – a far cry from the polished man I'd seen in his office all those months ago.

'OK. You've got me here. What do you want to tell me?' I asked, trying hard to keep the contempt out of my voice and failing.

'I don't appreciate your tone.' Hammond glared at me. His arrogance still hadn't been knocked out of him yet. Give it time, though. The sentences he'd been given for various charges were a minimum of twenty-five years. Two and a half decades behind bars would definitely knock it out of him. 'I'm trying to do you a favour here.'

'Really?' I snorted. 'What kind of favour is that?'

He paused for a moment. Tapped his fingertips on the table between us. 'You want Munroe. I want to help you get her.'

I leaned forward. 'And how can you do that?'

'I've got something you need to see.'

'What?'

'A videotape. From years ago. It's got something on it that you can use to put her away.'

I paused for a moment, studying his face. 'What's on it?'

He folded his arms and leaned back in the chair. 'It's with my lawyer. I've given him instructions to pass it on to you.'

'And why would you help me?'

His eyes narrowed to angry slits. 'Revenge. Why else? If I'm not getting out of here for years then I don't see why she should be walking around free. It's payback time for her putting me away. You have no idea about her. No idea at all.'

'This video . . . where has it been? We didn't find it at your home or office. How do I know you're not trying to send me on some pointless wild goose chase?'

He stood up and tapped his nose. 'I had it well hidden. Like everything.' He walked towards the locked door and banged on it to be let out. Then looked back over his shoulder at me. 'Just watch it.'

DETECTIVE WARREN CARTER
Chapter 75

The package I collected from Hammond's lawyer was sealed in a Jiffy bag containing an old video cassette tape, the kind used in handheld camcorders from way back, along with a sworn affidavit by Hammond.

After a quick trip to Technical Services to borrow a camcorder so I could watch it, I took everything back to the office. It was late and everyone had gone to the pub to carry on celebrating, so I was the only one around as I sat in the briefing room. A chill inched its way up my spine as I read the statement. Then I hooked up the camcorder to the TV and started watching.

Susan Munroe had been a twenty-one-year-old student. David Bennington was her boyfriend at that time, as she'd said during the interview. They'd gone to a party at Powell Acton's flat on the night of their graduation, after a day spent drinking and celebrating. Munroe had driven her car there. They'd all got pissed out of their heads, along with Oliver Hammond. And when Munroe had driven back to her own flat – speeding, weaving down the road, having reckless regard for anyone else, with David Bennington in the passenger seat beside her and Oliver Hammond in the back – Hammond, who'd been given a camcorder as a graduation present, had been drunkenly filming the day's celebrations for posterity.

And then . . . *smack!* Her car had slammed straight into a ten-year-old child, cycling across the road. A little boy called Noah Priestly who none of them had seen until it was too late, because they were all blind drunk. In his statement, Hammond said he attended to Noah but he was already dead. Munroe had panicked. She didn't want a record for causing death by careless driving while under the influence of alcohol. She couldn't risk her impending career as a police officer. An ambition she already had mapped out in front of her with an accepted graduate-entry job. So they'd left Noah there, in the middle of the road, and driven off. Maybe it had been too late to save Noah when they fled the scene, but maybe not. Noah hadn't been discovered until five hours later, by someone out walking their dog.

The three of them had vowed never to talk about it again. Maybe Munroe made a promise to herself that she'd work hard to give something back after what she'd done, but look how that had turned out. Hammond had told her he'd destroyed the video tape, but he never did. He'd kept it in a safe place, one that we'd never found when we were digging into his life. A place where, I suspected, he'd also stashed all the cash he'd amassed from selling black-market donor eggs. And after Munroe had gone to him for her own treatment, Hammond had a double whammy of payback evidence against her.

Lies built on lies. Crimes built on crimes.

My eyes watered as I stared at the video on the screen. The sickening point of impact was clear, as was the aftermath of drunken yelling by Munroe and the others, the blood on the road, the broken body. Had he really been dead when they'd left him there alone or could they have done more to save him? I wondered if he'd died quickly. Or if he'd been in agonising pain. Had he cried out for his mother? A mother who'd never known what his last seconds had been like. A mother who would've been searching for the truth all these years.

It was enough to put Munroe away. Even though it had happened when she was twenty-one, there was no statute of limitations. And due to a new change in the law, causing death by careless driving while under the influence of drink or drugs now carried a life sentence.

A noise from behind startled me. I twisted around in my seat and saw Caroline standing there, dressed in her red trench coat, her cheeks flushed from alcohol. She looked beautiful.

'I thought you'd be here. What did Hammond say?' she asked.

I stood up. Turned to face her. I wanted to smile because I'd done it. I finally had something against Munroe. I could put some sort of closure on it all. There was relief, for sure. A certain amount of pride that I'd been able to balance the scales of justice for everyone who'd suffered and died. And yes, a feeling of elation that Munroe would be put behind bars, where she belonged. But I couldn't smile. The death of a child was nothing to smile about.

'What?' Caroline asked.

'We got her. We got Munroe.'

A NOTE FROM THE AUTHOR

Those of you who've kindly read some of my previous novels will know that I've written about trafficking in many different formats. This time Hayat's story was inspired by the tragedies of refugees all over the world. According to current figures from UNHCR (the UN Refugee Agency), a shocking 68.5 million people globally have been forcibly displaced from their homes. Of those, 25.4 million are refugees, over half of whom are under eighteen years old. This book is dedicated to every one of them.

Firstly, I'd like to say a huge thanks to my readers from the bottom of my heart for choosing my books! I really hope you enjoyed *Their Last Breath*. If you did, I would be so grateful if you could leave a review or recommend it to family and friends. I always love to hear from readers, so please keep your emails and Facebook messages coming (contact details are on my website: www.sibelhodge.com). They make my day! If you want to read more from Detective Carter, you can find him investigating other crimes in *Duplicity* and *Into the Darkness*. Detective Harris investigates her own case in *The Disappeared*.

As always, a massive thanks goes out to my husband, Brad, for supporting me, being my chief beta reader, fleshing out ideas with me, and putting up with me ignoring him when he's trying to talk and my brain's overloaded with plot noise.

Big, big thanks to the lovely author and police officer Lisa Cutts for all her help with PSD procedures (hopefully I wasn't too annoying!). If you haven't read her fabulously authentic police-procedural novels then you're definitely missing out!

A huge thank-you to Emily Ruston for all of her editing suggestions, and to Charlotte Atyeo for catching all the things I didn't.

Big thanks to Laura Deacon, along with Nicole, Sana, Hatty, and the rest of the Thomas & Mercer team. It's very much appreciated.

And finally, a loud shout-out and hugs to all the amazing book bloggers and book reviewers out there who enthusiastically support us authors with their passion for reading.

Sibel xx

ABOUT THE AUTHOR

Sibel Hodge is the author of number-one bestsellers *Look Behind You, Untouchable, Duplicity* and *Into the Darkness*. Her books have sold over one million copies and are international bestsellers in the UK, USA, Australia, France, Canada and Germany. She writes in an eclectic mix of genres, and is a passionate human- and animal-rights advocate.

Her work has been nominated and shortlisted for numerous prizes, including the Harry Bowling Prize, the Yeovil Literary Prize, the Chapter One Promotions Novel Competition, The Romance Reviews' Prize for Best Novel with Romantic Elements, and Indie Book Bargains' Best Indie Book of 2012 in two categories. She was the winner of Best Children's Book in the 2013 eFestival of Words; nominated for the 2015 BigAl's Books and Pals Young Adult Readers' Choice Award; winner of the Crime, Thrillers & Mystery Book from a Series Award in the SpaSpa Book Awards 2013; winner of the Readers' Favorite Young Adult (Coming of Age) Honorable Award in 2015; a

New Adult finalist in the Oklahoma Romance Writers of America's International Digital Awards 2015; 2017 International Thriller Writers Award finalist for Best E-book Original Novel; Honorable Mention Award Winner in the USA 2018 Readers' Choice Awards; and winner of the No.1 Best Thriller in the Top Shelf Magazine Indie Book Awards 2018. Her novella *Trafficked: The Diary of a Sex Slave* has been listed as one of the top forty books about human rights by Accredited Online Colleges.

For Sibel's latest book releases, giveaways and gossip, sign up to her newsletter at www.sibelhodge.com.

Printed in Great
Britain
by Amazon